DIVINITIES, ENTANGLED

∞

Also by Harambee K. Grey-Sun

The EVE OF LIGHT Series

The Novels
BloodLight: The Apocalypse of Robert Goldner (*Prequel*)
Broken Angels (*Book I*)
Divinities, Entangled (*Book II*)

The Short Stories
FoolKillers
The Lark
Heaven's Gun
Knotty & Ice
Rogue Beauty
Deviant-Hunter's Sabbath

By Harambee Grey-Sun

Poetry
Spring's Fall (Autumn Numbers • Book I)
Wine Songs, Vinegar Verses

DIVINITIES, ENTANGLED

Eve of Light ∞ Book II

Harambee K. Grey-Sun

DIVINITIES, ENTANGLED

ISBN: 978-1-64044-007-4

Cover design by The Cover Collection

Published by HyperVerse Books
http://www.hyperversebooks.com/
writing between and beyond the lines

Second Edition: March 2017

*Every solid in the universe is ready to become
fluid on the approach of the mind, and the power
to flux it is the measure of the mind.*

RALPH WALDO EMERSON, "FATE"

Chapter 1

Truth be told, Robert could've escaped at any time. Tricked out the monitors and disappeared, avoiding detection from authorities high and low for as long as necessary. But he'd waited until he heard the gunfire and screams outside his door.

He couldn't just plug his ears and sit still. Not in a cramped studio apartment. A bullet could easily come through the door and bite him. He instead waited until his instincts told him it was safe to stand a couple of feet behind it. He then shifted his vision down the electromagnetic spectrum, into the range of x-rays. The door shimmered until it was as translucent as onionskin. There was nothing on the other side. And his ears told him the ruckus had moved several feet down the hall. He was out of danger, but others weren't.

The police may've been on their way. It was always a coin toss in this neighborhood. But Robert knew a surefire way to get them there in a hurry, with a fed or two in tow.

He concentrated, bending the light around his body, making himself invisible to any normal man or woman. The shooter may've been down the hall, but he probably wouldn't mind firing a bullet or two in the direction of a nosy neighbor.

Robert opened his door, making a gap just wide enough to stick his head out. He didn't see anyone. He did see another open apartment door, two down on his left. Several objects were scattered on the floor outside it. An iron, a ripped peach-colored blouse, and three of its popped-off buttons. He adjusted his vision again and saw a few small spots of blood.

Robert knew the young woman who lived there. An attractive twenty-four-year-old Salvadorian who worked at the McDonald's inside the nearest Wal-Mart. He also knew the types of vermin she ran around with.

He pieced together what had probably happened based on the sounds he'd heard. Her non-English-speaking boyfriend had somehow gotten into the building, determined to confront her about her alleged affairs. They were always arguing, and she was often in the hall on her cell complaining to her friends about it, loudly. Robert wasn't fluent in the language, but from what he could tell, her boyfriend's anger wasn't based only on the fact she could speak some English but also on the fact she worked at a job that brought her into face-to-face contact with a wide variety of men, some with more than one type of hunger. The boyfriend couldn't watch her 24-7, so he just knew she had to be screwing around on him. Robert figured she probably was. He'd seen plenty of young bucks going in and out of her apartment at all hours of the night. Today she'd refused to let her nearest and dearest inside. She'd opened the door for him, though, and they'd engaged in their latest-and-greatest argument in the doorway. The boyfriend may've tried to force his way into the apartment. She'd threatened him with the iron, maybe even thrown it before trying to get past him. He'd grabbed her by the blouse and probably smacked her up a bit. She had somehow gotten free and run down the hall as he'd pulled his gun and fired. He'd missed but chased after her.

And she wasn't dead yet.

Robert could still hear the boyfriend yelling at her. Best guess: the girl must've taken refuge in a friend's apartment in one of the adjoining halls.

Robert locked his door behind him. It was the first time in almost two weeks he'd been outside his apartment. He was still under house arrest—or "monitored suspension" as the chairman had called it—and he was supposed to be for another few days. Now that he'd stepped over the threshold, the ankle bracelets, wrist monitors, and collar would send a signal that'd have the badges there in a flash. But someone could get shot in even less time.

Robert moved.

He didn't really know the woman, had only said "hello" in passing to her, and had no real desire to get to know her at all—but he definitely didn't want to see her killed. He also liked the neighbors with whom he bothered to make small talk. Most of them were young married couples with very young kids. If any of them were to get shot accidentally…

Robert turned a corner and saw the gunman. He was dressed as if he'd woken up naked in a ditch and had found his clothes lying in the middle of the Beltway after rush hour. He was holding a Glock. Model 19. A favorite among cops. And gangbangers. It was also one of many items envied and unowned by law-abiding citizens, who in this day and age constantly felt the urge and need to defend themselves and their families.

There was a small chance the asshole was affiliated with the MS-13, the vicious Salvadorian gang. Not that it mattered at the moment. Whether skilled in the art of killing or just a wannabe thug, the punk was alone today, yelling at a closed door. He'd already put a couple of bullet holes in it. Probably kicked it a few times, too. Robert could hear screaming and at least one child crying on the other side. He couldn't see exactly who was in danger. And the thug couldn't see the still-invisible Robert.

Robert took slow steps forward as he squinted at the hand holding the gun and concentrated. He'd had plenty of practice over the past couple of years, but it was still difficult using more than one parasite-given talent at once. He did his best to stay unseen as he directed a stream of infrared radiation at the guy's hand, trying to heat up the skin till it felt like it was on fire. Robert was hoping he'd drop the gun, at least long enough for him to run and make a tackle.

No such luck.

The punk-ass must've been used to pain. Must've been a gang-banger after all, one who'd survived some serious hazing to get in good with his boys. He just yelled as he was being burned, got more pissed off, and fired twice more at the door.

There was screaming and pleading and crying from inside the apartment and a heated, determined, and armed thug outside it. And Robert—invisible, unarmed, and nothing close to bulletproof.

Shit. It was time to see if he could dodge bullets.

Robert knew appearing out of thin air may or may not scare the guy, and it would definitely increase his chances of getting shot at. But, one way or the other, he was going to have to give the thug something to shoot at, something besides the frightened folks behind door number one.

He concentrated again, pulling all visible light from within a reasonable reach of his intuitional strength and willpower into a tighter radius around his body.

The thug's tone of voice shifted from anger to excited shock as the hallway got darker. The tone shifted again when he turned and saw where the light was gathering. He went silent as Robert translated himself from an invisible man into a faceless seven-foot-tall thing-on-fire. Bright-red and dark-blue fire. The flames weren't real, but Robert damn sure hoped they were intimidating.

The retracted light left darkness in its place, making the illusory fire engulfing Robert all the more prominent as he quickened his pace and shouted, "Drop it!"

He figured most people, whatever their backgrounds, would either obey the command or turn and run if they saw a living, shouting pillar of fire approaching them. But this thug was just as hardened as Robert had feared. He raised his gun and fired.

Thank fortune Robert's illusion-cloaked body appeared not only much taller than it really was but also much wider than his thirty-four-inch-waist frame. The three bullets went over and around him before the thug lost his nerve and turned to retreat. Robert broke into a sprint.

He leaped when close enough and tackled the shooter, shifting his weight and positioning his body so the thug would stay down and the arm with the gun remained flat and pointed forward.

The guy was muscular; he was also feeding off rage, which made him even stronger, harder to control. But three years of high school wrestling and three additional years of IAI training gave Robert the advantage. This bastard wasn't going anywhere.

Others, unfortunately, just wouldn't stay put.

Robert saw a door open on the right-hand side of the hall in front of them. Someone stepped halfway out.

"Get back inside—now!"

The old man wasn't sure whether he wanted to follow Robert's command. Maybe he didn't speak English. Or maybe he didn't see the gun. Or maybe he was just fascinated with the light show Robert was putting on as he wrestled with the guy under him.

The thug still had a firm grip on his Glock, and he could easily pull the trigger, accidentally or purposely hitting the old man. It could happen any second. Robert had to act.

He'd heard about a certain mind-to-mind trick from some of his fellow Watcher agents. He'd never thought to try it before, but now was as good a time as any.

He looked at the old man's eyes and concentrated, imagining a human skull. A skull that talked. A skull that warned the man if he didn't get back inside and away from the door, his soul might soon join the skull in Hell.

This was a much different way of manipulating light than Robert was used to. He rarely did anything with his eye but study objects or burn skin. He preferred to use his hands to cast images, but they were busy at the moment. And the parasites in his skin and blood were also in his eye; he didn't need his fingers to exercise his abilities. With enough concentration, he could look and cast the intended image, not in front of the old man's face but into one of his eyes, into his mind. Make it seem too real. The words were another matter. Without speaking them, Robert wasn't sure how to transmit them, how to make it seem as if they were truly coming from the image. His fellow agents had told him all he needed to do was recite the words in his head, like a chant, while maintaining the visual link with his target. Mind reading he'd heard of; this was more like mind speaking. Robert thought it was all pretty much bullshit. He'd read up on the false science and low art of Mentalism as part of his training. He'd always thought it a waste of precious time.

But it worked.

Or maybe the old man got scared by something else. Or maybe his phone was ringing. Whatever, he retreated back into his apartment, behind a locked door. A success was a success. Robert would take whatever he could get.

He then heard another door open behind him. The door that had been putting a damper on the sounds of screaming and crying. Now the sounds were louder. The previous targets of the threats and gunfire were making themselves accessible.

Dammit.

Since they were behind him, Robert couldn't try the same trick to coerce them back inside. He couldn't even see them. Were they just peeping out around the door frame, or were they coming out into the hall? And if someone was coming, then who? The girlfriend? Was she armed? Was she alone, or did she have a kid with her? Would she—or they—try to attack the boyfriend now that he was (sort of) subdued? Would they try to take out Robert to get to him?

There were too many noises for Robert to try to sort and form a coherent picture. And he didn't have time to mull possibilities and probabilities. He had time only to act, to make one big move to ensure his and everyone else's safety.

He scrambled and positioned his body so that his hips and the distribution of most of his weight were on the small of the punk's back. He jammed his left elbow into the guy's right ear, forcing his eyes away from the gun in his right hand, and grabbed his wrist with both hands. Robert could've easily broken it, but he instead applied pressure, cutting off the blood flow as he ran an electromagnetic current through the guy's skin, connecting with his ulnar nerve.

This was one trick he'd perfected long ago. In a matter of seconds, the punk would lose control of the hand. It would feel numb, then dead. There'd be no way for him to make a fist, let alone pull a trigger. There was a small chance of a spasm, but fortunately the trigger finger was outside the trigger guard. Robert was able to quickly get the hand off the gun and use the frozen limb to push it a few inches out of reach.

He thought about applying more pressure and breaking the wrist or maybe shifting his body and breaking the thug's neck with his elbow. But, no, that wouldn't help anyone.

Robert stopped the light show and appeared, not as a creature on fire, but mostly as himself: a twenty-year-old black guy in charcoal sneakers, blue jeans, and a black T-shirt. He continued to manipulate the light around his head in order to blur his facial features. No need for the people he heard behind him to recognize him as a neighbor.

He still couldn't see them, but they were close. Probably close enough to lunge for him if, for some godforsaken reason, they actually sided with the gangbanger and saw Robert as the real aggressor. In a hostile situation, never stay put.

Robert scrambled off the guy and grabbed the gun. He came up to his feet and spun around.

He saw the girlfriend and another girl. But they were of little concern to him.

Robert's attention immediately went to the two cops at the far end of the hall as they drew their weapons.

They didn't even bother to say "freeze."

Chapter 2

The cops did shout something at Robert, but through the overall cacophony he had no idea what it was.

He dropped the gun when he saw them and kicked it to his right. Away from himself and away from the gangbanger who might scramble for it.

He kept his eye on the thug as the cops advanced and shouted. There were now four of them. The increase in numbers seemed to make them even more belligerent.

They shouted at the two girls as one cop entered the apartment to shout at whoever was left inside. The girls were too frightened to obey orders, so they were given the same treatment as the real criminal. They cried about what had happened and the way they were being treated while the thug cried about his allegedly dead hand.

Robert knew the drill. Keeping quiet, he unblurred his face, dropped to the ground, and did as instructed with his hands as he kept a close eye on everyone. Cops or no cops, any one of these people could turn extra hysterical, go berserk, and get loose, becoming a violent danger to everyone. And, understaffed and overwhelmed, the cops in this area weren't known for staying within legal limits. With Fire Virus-carriers, it was usually shoot first, ask questions never.

He was all for obeying the law, but above all he was for surviving to see the next day. The manner of these men and women in blue and black wasn't giving him any confidence about tomorrow. Their manner changed, however, once they confirmed his identity.

One of the female cops pulled him to his feet and escorted him down the hall toward the lobby of the building. She said nothing coherent to him beyond "come on" before mumbling something that sounded like "buttered bullshit." It was time to get his ears examined—Robert couldn't have heard that right. And he almost couldn't believe what he saw waiting for them in the lobby.

Heartland Security agents, fine. They were the rank-and-file employees of the federal agency that had been keeping him under lock and key for the past ten days, monitoring his every movement; their temporary camera in his apartment recorded every time he got up to take a piss. But he didn't expect to see and be greeted by one of the Agency's top officials. And certainly not warmly.

"Mister Goldner," Cyrus Shahrooz said. "Welcome back to the land of the free and happy." The stout six-foot man in the porkpie hat spoke with a grin, looking at Robert as if he were his best pal, and as if Robert were a sixteen-year-old boy who'd just lost his virginity. A strange expression, and stranger words.

"Free, Mister Shahrooz? I'd think you'd be here to slap me with an even longer sentence."

Cyrus modified his expression to one more professional but no less friendly. "I'm not here to slap. Just to shake the free hand of a valuable man."

Robert discreetly rolled his eye at what was probably a bad pun on his surname as Cyrus motioned toward a subordinate agent. The subordinate produced keys and approached.

Tensions had lately been growing between some at the Heartland Security Agency and the Isaac-Abraham Institution. As a member of the latter, Robert had been expecting a smackdown and had readied himself for it. He stood motionless, uncomprehending, as the agent unlocked the collar around his neck. This was serious. He was being released early. He held up his wrists, allowing the agent to remove the bracelet monitors.

"I'm truly sorry you had to go through all this," Cyrus said.

"Through no fault of my own." Robert flexed his feet in every direction after his ankle bracelets were removed. He could now go wherever he wanted without being tracked.

"Oh no? Breaking and entering, armed assault…"

"It was a rescue operation, sir." He was careful to keep his tone respectful. "The kind I'd been trained for."

"It was a home invasion," Cyrus said. "Not that I'm not sympathetic, mind you, considering the targets. But we still have laws." He put two fingers on the brim of his porkpie, tipping it slightly. It seemed to Robert like a slightly less obvious wink. "I'm not knocking what you do, mind you, or even what you did in the halls back there. Pure heroics. All of it. But you have to remember, even when you think you're operating in secret, the public's eye has a way of seeing through veils. What you do reflects on your allies. All of them. You're aware we *can* and *will* shut down the IAI if we're left with little choice?"

"They—" Robert paused, making a conscious effort to stay respectful while he stuck up for himself. "Those *terrorists* kidnapped my partner, sir. I had to get him back. And I did. *Alive.* No one else could've gotten to him in time."

"Right. No one else. Except you weren't working alone that night."

Robert didn't respond. He only looked to his side, out through the glass double doors that served as the building's main entrance. He was dying for some fresh air. Cyrus seemed to take the hint.

"Walk with me, son."

Robert followed him and the two other agents, neither of whom had said a word since he'd laid his eye on them. On their way out, he nodded at the elderly lady standing behind the receptionist's desk. Eunice only stared back at him, her eyes almost the size of half-dollars. They'd exchanged hellos and small talk in the past, but Robert had never explained to her exactly what he did for a living. He'd only painted over his job description with phrases like "social work" and, with a coy smile, "a duty, sacred and secret." Eunice probably didn't want any elaboration after what had just taken place. Behind those wide eyes watching him exit the building, she was probably calculating schemes on how to get him kicked out of the complex for good. *Oh, well.* He could use a change of scenery.

The parking lot was certainly a sight for Robert's sore eye. It was in pretty bad shape, with its numerous potholes, faded parking-space lines, and the usual broken-glass remnants of dropped or thrown beer bottles. But it was a familiar sight, not seen in so long. Refreshing if nothing else.

Cyrus dismissed the junior agents and asked, "Might I offer you a ride to The Burrow?"

Robert looked over at his Mustang. Last time he'd seen it, the three-year-old vehicle had looked almost three times its age. The additional dings and dents it'd taken on over the past two weeks didn't make it appear any younger. The expected results of careless or malicious drivers parking too close and banging their doors against his. Nothing serious enough to trigger the car alarm but bad enough to leave visible marks. It wasn't pretty, but Robert was itching to get behind the Stang's wheel, rev up the V-8 engine, and roar it down Northern Virginia's highways and back roads.

But that was just an itch. He was practically aching to catch up on community affairs. He'd been out of the loop for far too long. A Watcher agent was duty-bound to stay up on the latest information on the gangs, cults, terrorists, and other types of plagues prevalent in the world, especially those too close to home.

"Sure. Thanks."

He followed Cyrus to the nondescript white van that appeared to have never been washed and to have defied every rainstorm since its first purchase. Hundreds of vans sharing its make and model were all over the Washington metro area. Most were cleaner. Few if any were driven by someone as vital to the nation's security as Cyrus. A good man to know. A dangerous man to piss off. Robert refrained from suggesting they make a detour to a Mr. Wash.

He settled himself in the front passenger's seat as Cyrus locked the doors and started the engine. After they pulled out of the lot, he heard Cyrus chuckling to himself.

"Miss 'em, huh?"

Robert said, "Sir?" When Cyrus chuckled again, Robert figured out what he was referencing before he even said it.

"Your watches."

Cyrus must've seen him rubbing his wrists, absentmindedly, like succumbing to a nervous tic. Robert couldn't help it. His wrists felt naked. He knew something was missing from his life, something that needed to be returned. And Cyrus was smart enough to see he wasn't feeling nostalgic for the monitor bracelets that had just been removed.

The watches he'd worn constantly before his detention told the correct date and time only as a secondary function. They were first and foremost communication devices: one exclusively used to communicate encrypted messages to his superiors at the Isaac-Abraham Institution, the other used to communicate directly with his unit partner. Watcher Agent Darryl Ridley. His partner for three years. The friend who was no longer his partner.

"How's Darryl doing, sir? They wouldn't even let me make a phone call to the hospital, you know. I wasn't allowed to call anybody. Not even Mister Smith." And the HSA medical specialist who'd stopped by Robert's apartment every two days to check on his health and medication supply wasn't much for chitchat. "How's he been making out?"

"He was out in three days," Cyrus said. "After the beating he'd taken, the condition he was in, the fact his body stitched itself back together so quickly—with minimal assistance from medical science—was nothing short of remarkable. Mister Ridley said his good-byes at the IAI and reported for work at the Agency the next day. I just love a man who's hurtin' to get down to business!"

"Yeah, well," Robert said with a shrug, "he'd been hurtin' to be a part of the HSA for a while now."

"Believe me, his enthusiasm was never a secret." Cyrus chuckled again, as if at a joke he wasn't willing to share.

"So what exactly is he doing?" Robert asked. "He fitting in okay?"

The man's face fell. His jaw hardened. Robert didn't need to shift his vision into the range of x-rays to see Cyrus was grinding his teeth.

The big man didn't say a word. He just sat in silence, waiting for the light to change, waiting patiently for the pedestrians to clear the crosswalk before he turned the van.

Robert knew not to push it. He instead looked out the window, not really focusing on anything but the feeling of freedom. That feeling grew tighter, however, at the sight of the men and women, middle-aged and older, wearing ragged pants and open shirts, carrying what was probably their entire world in duffel bags on their backs or pushing it before them in wobbly shopping carts. Others, more pressed and clean-shaven, walked quickly around them, careful to keep at least two arms' distance. This corner wasn't known for harboring the homeless, and certainly not a half dozen of them. Could the recession have gotten so much worse in the little time he'd been locked up?

Apparently. As Cyrus turned the corner, two shufflers exchanged blows and two others rushed in their direction to either break it up or join in. The situation was little better on the next street.

There were a lot more For Lease signs than Robert remembered seeing two weeks ago. At the stoplight, his stomach tightened when he saw his favorite sandwich shop had closed. He focused his vision, telescoping it to read the crooked sign taped to the door. Rather than coming into focus, the letters, the sign, even the door itself, danced out of his view; shuddering into its place was a landscape, not from Northern Virginia or even from this world. Trees, rocks, and unnameable structures plucked from some old Warner Bros. cartoon about Mars. Much like a cartoon character, Robert blinked and shook his head until the scene returned to normal. The stoplight turned green, and he looked straight ahead. To hell with what the sign said.

"When we hired Darryl, and a few others like him," Cyrus said finally, "my sources had told me the President was behind us. All the way. They told me that, in spite of the unfortunate state of our economy, our dear President was in support of doing whatever it took to secure the country from domestic threats, of every stripe and flavor. That information turned out to be false." He spoke in a tone noticeably different from the one Robert was accustomed to hearing him use; it was stripped of personality and ethnic accent. "Our dear Madam President wouldn't give the go-ahead. I still don't understand the damned problem. Congress needn't even be involved. And I…"

Cyrus shook his head and cleared his throat.

"Well, your former partner has been given a desk job for the time being." His voice had returned to normal. "Right now, he's in West Virginia, attending a seminar so excruciatingly boring I wouldn't wish it on my worst enemies. Assuming he can stay awake, I'm sure his thoughts are occupied with the unjustness of him having to return here to fill a position he didn't want and for which he and I both believe he is grossly overqualified. All I can tell you right now is that I'm damn well looking forward to that grand, glorious Tuesday in November. I'm rootin' hard for that Indian fellow. He knows how to play ball. Pleasant riddance, Madam Sagan."

It wasn't as if she had a choice to stay or go. The second of President Sagan's two terms was ending, and the election was in less than six weeks. Robert thought she'd been a pretty good President, even if the sagging economy had failed to support that opinion.

As they drove, Robert kept an eye out for other unnatural changes of scenery—a sign, he hoped, of his own fatigue. All the while he counted and compartmentalized the economy's victims: the druggies, the homeless, the packs of kids either searching for trouble or destined to have it find them. He did the same with the litter; there was more garbage and recyclables on the ground than in the overfull bins. No doubt about it—things looked seven times worse than they had just two weeks ago.

Manipulating his vision as he scanned the scenery again, he saw a pack of teenage boys harassing a couple of girls no older than twelve two blocks ahead. In low-hanging jeans, fluorescent-colored thongs, and glittering halter tops, the girls apparently weren't showing enough for the boys' tastes; two boys had already lowered their own jeans as their pals surrounded and snatched at the girls. Cyrus would see it all soon, stop the van, and put an end to the bullshit.

Robert had long ago wearied of dwelling on the root of modern problems; he wanted solutions. Society was deteriorating. The environment was suffering. If he were still religious, he'd pray for change. Spontaneous change.

That had been the theme of the decade after all. Spontaneous change, anytime and any place. Like last year's Fourth of July, when teenager riots spontaneously erupted all over the district. He and Darryl had happened to be in the city at the time, enjoying a production of the Shakespeare Theatre Company, when they'd gotten caught up in the biggest and most violent riot in the area. The duo had been instrumental in helping to restore normalcy. Cyrus, grateful and grinning, had personally thanked them. Since then, their paths had crossed on a seemingly random basis.

He'd never been shy around Robert. Although they were affiliated with different and sometimes head-butting organizations, Cyrus had more than once said he felt they were kindred spirits, blood warriors. But Robert's duties were much more limited than his. The Watcher agent was only tasked with locating and, when allowed, recovering missing children, the truest and most valuable of treasures. As the head of the HSA's Office of Operations Coordination and the guru of its massive surveillance program, Cyrus had broader responsibilities.

Too broad apparently to help the two little girls whose halter tops had been ripped off. He drove by without so much as turning his head.

Robert quickly looked into the side-view mirror, lined up the angles as easily as taking a breath, and concentrated. Shots of infrared radiation pelted each boy in his face, enough to hurt and disorient, giving the girls time to scamper away. Robert just hoped none of the punks decided to give chase. He then wondered about his driver's callousness.

Cyrus was mumbling something, but he couldn't make it out. For several reasons, Robert thought it best not to question him or his decision. Kindred spirits or not, you don't poke a bear. But the big man was already stoked. That was clear when he started grousing about the election again.

Whether it was Cyrus's official duty or not, Robert was sure he'd thoroughly vetted both major candidates, as well as the minor ones.

"You know," Robert said as they merged onto the highway, "there're a lot of questions out there about Senator Sinha's citizenship—"

"Imbeciles," Cyrus said. "Goddamned idiots."

Fantastic. Robert hadn't meant to get him riled up further. He was just uneasy with one-sided conversations. But he'd swerved this one down a path he really didn't want to travel.

"How can so many people believe something so *stupid*?" Cyrus said. "So evidently false? That someone could get elected to the Senate without a background check? That a presidential candidate could get this far in the process without actually being a citizen of the United States?"

Anything was possible in this day and age, but politics—the so-called art of the possible—wasn't one of Robert's favorite subjects. He decided to just agree with Cyrus, hopefully shutting him up before steering him back onto a topic of greater interest.

"Because they want to believe it," Robert said. "They've got a prejudice. Or an agenda. But rather than being up front about it, they wall it behind lies and illusions. Painted obstacles. We as a species improve, proceed through the gauntlet of evolution, dodge the metaphorical minotaurs, by training ourselves to see our way through to the end."

Cyrus raised an eyebrow and then grinned. "Well, well, well—some rather interesting turns of phrase. Has someone been making a special effort to improve his vocabulary these last two weeks?"

"Uh, well, no," Robert said. "Not intentionally. I just did a lot of reading. And thinking. And push-ups. Not much else I could do."

"Oh? Who did you read?"

"No particular authors. Just the usual. Some books on physics. Math. And poetry."

He regretted his last word even before Cyrus got the weird, sneering look on his face.

"You never exactly struck me as the artsy-craftsy type," he said.

"No—I'm not." Robert was more likely to frequent a natural history museum than the painting kind. And although he loved what some jazz vocalists did with words, he said, "I hate poetry."

"Then why were you reading it?"

Because it appeared the greatest terrorist threat in the history of humankind seemed to have an affinity for it. Over the past few years, he, Cyrus, and all the other good guys and gals had been fighting an idea—or rather the lack of one. Robert felt theories of the creative arts—poetry in particular—made up one small but vital piece to the puzzle of the enemy, and the enemy had to be understood fully in order to be stopped completely. "Just seemed to make the time pass quicker," he said. He didn't think it appropriate to share mere hunches with the man. They were on the same side and had some of the same enemies, but they dealt with them in different ways. "It induces sleep, you know."

"Well, don't think you're going to start sleeping any more soundly now that you're a free man on this morning," Cyrus said. "Not if you have the good sense I believe you do."

"Sir?"

The man sighed and shook his head. Robert hoped he wasn't about to launch into yet another longer rant about the election.

"I suppose I shouldn't tell you before your Institution's chairman does," Cyrus said, "but the IAI Board has decided to welcome

Stavan 'Ava' Darden as a trainee for its Watcher program. Not unanimously, I might add."

Robert wasn't sure he shared the man's dismay. He'd his own misgivings about her motivations, but Robert knew Ava cared deeply about missing kids and would probably make a decent agent. She'd also been placed under house arrest for accompanying him on the mission to recover his partner after Darryl had been taken hostage and tortured by a cult of Sprytes. She'd been confined to an apartment at The Burrow, the main office of the IAI, for two weeks, the same amount of time as Robert. Since she was parentless, homeless, and missing most of her memories of the previous eighteen months, Ava's options were limited. Robert guessed there was really nothing else they could do with Ava but keep her with the Institution after she'd served her time, even if she wasn't exactly like the other orphans there.

"Does she know?" Robert asked.

"I'm sure," Cyrus said. "She was released this morning. I'm sure whoever let her out of her cage told her the wondrous news."

"This morning?"

Cyrus sighed again. "All I will say is I pulled a string or two to get you released early because the decision was made to release her early—for saintly behavior. I have no say in your Institution's internal affairs, unfortunately. But you, Mister Goldner, you've formed some sort of relationship with this girl."

"Me?" He wasn't sure what Cyrus was insinuating, but he didn't like it. "Not really. Just because she was with me when—"

"Exactly what I mean. She was *with* you when you embarked on obviously illegal activity. She wasn't against you. She probably trusts you, or thinks you trust her. Whichever, more than anyone else, you've established a bond with her. It may be only tenuous now, but I'm asking you to maintain it. In fact, I'm asking you to strengthen it. I don't know how well your instincts work on her, but I don't trust the girl. Not one bit. Nor should you."

Of course he didn't. Not fully. Robert hadn't trusted her from day one—or, more precisely, day two. On day one, he and Darryl had found the battered girl and had her delivered to a private hospital for a long recovery. On day two, she'd escaped from the secure hospital, evading all detection, made her way to Robert's apartment, broke in, bypassed all his alarms, and took a near-complete inventory of his studio's contents before he'd arrived to be surprised by her presence. Even though his trust in her had increased as they'd worked together to find the kidnapped Darryl, Ava wasn't exactly on Robert's best friends list. He'd a few good excuses to be wary of her. But Cyrus?

"Any particular reason?" Robert asked.

Cyrus sighed even deeper this time. "Starting less than two weeks ago, the day after you and she were confined, the Agency began to detect patterns…"

He trailed off, cueing Robert to ask, "What kind of patterns?"

"Washington, DC, has always had a higher concentration of Virus-carriers than any other US city. But it has suddenly become a beacon. More are trekking this way. Anyone who's not imprisoned or secure in one of our hospitals or other facilities. The homeless, the orphans, and runaways of all ages."

"Why?" Robert asked.

"We don't know, but my best sources tell me it has to do with Miss Darden."

Robert couldn't see the connection, other than the fact Ava had lived in a homeless shelter before he and Darryl had found her.

"And, as you well know," Cyrus said, "if the average sick-and-tired carriers are working their way here, so are The Infinite Definite. Agents around the nation are monitoring, and fighting when necessary, but…"

Yes, *but*…With the types of extraordinary plagues and supernaturally gifted terrorists spreading across the face of the planet, the world could crack open at any second. The ID were waging a silent and, up until now, mostly invisible war for all Creation. Robert hoped Cyrus would give him some good or useful news before they made it to The Burrow.

"As I'm sure you've noticed," Cyrus said, "even without the contributions of Virus-carriers, the situation on the streets are worse than ever. Legitimate law enforcement is stretched thin. I need my most trusted allies targeted on my most mysterious enemies."

Robert had no response. And Cyrus apparently felt he'd said enough. He waved at the car opposite him, signaling the other driver should make the turn before he did, then turned on the radio. It was set on a classical music station playing Wagner's *Ride of the Valkyries*. Cyrus pressed the Tune button until he found another classical music station playing something unfamiliar to Robert, something much more dissonant, much more modern.

He remained silent until he pulled the van up alongside the parking garage. They'd arrived. He didn't shut off the engine, but he turned on the emergency lights to tell drivers coming from behind to go around.

"Open the glove compartment and take out what's on top."

Robert removed a black leather carrying case for a smartphone, with the phone inside. He handed it to Cyrus, guessing he wanted to call someone. Cyrus shook his head.

"It's yours," he said with an expression that was half sneer and half grin. "Consider it a welcome-back gift."

The fact he didn't own a cell was well-known and often ridiculed by his friends. Just another unnecessary object to carry. He was usually carrying plenty enough when he was out in the field. And having one at home or The Burrow would've just been redundant.

Before he could say "thanks but no thanks," Cyrus told him, "It's an Agency issue. Most secure phone on the planet. Best of all, that red button in the center there acts as a speed dial to my phone. In an emergency, even if you can't talk, push it and I'll locate you and respond with whatever assistance fits the situation. Keep it with you at all times. Never let it out of your sight."

It was generous, but…"Why, sir? Why are you giving this to me?"

"I like you," Cyrus said. "I have faith in you. I don't like seeing you in trouble. And I don't like the idea of Miss Darden."

No, of course not. Not if everything he'd hinted at was a possibility. Ava believed she'd transcended humanity, that she was divinely gifted. Most other carriers Robert had met faced the truth: that they'd in one way or another contracted the sexually transmitted White Fire Virus.

Almost all Virus-carriers were extremely sensitive to radiation falling within select ranges of the electromagnetic spectrum. Nothing spectacular in and of itself; a lot of sick people were highly sensitive to light, noise, and certain colors. But at least half of surviving Virus-carriers possessed the limited-range ability to manipulate some of the properties of electromagnetic radiation. By skillfully coordinating their semiconscious thoughts, reflexes, and voluntary actions, certain sections of the spectrum were available to them, notably visible light, infrared, ultraviolet, and x-rays. All at a price, though. Always at a price.

Robert and other Watcher agents used their training and abilities in service of the Institution's mission while trying to forget or push back the thought that the billions of microscopic parasites infecting each of their bodies, the very creatures that enabled their abilities, could at any moment violently consume their bodies, giving them an epileptic fit and leaving them lifeless husks. The thought of that never crossed the mind of blessed Ava.

In the little time he'd spent with her, Robert had surmised Ava had not only a fractured mind but also a fragile one. Her missing eighteen months' worth of memories was most likely not the result of an accident. Robert swore she'd been programmed for some nefarious purpose. There was no other way to explain how she didn't know she had a virus that had been in existence for eight years.

The Virus had claimed more than eight million lives in less than a decade. It was estimated that, at any given time, there were about 150,000 Virus-carriers on the planet, living in constant pain with the promise of even more torture to come in the moments before death. Most of them, apparently, were now headed his way.

"Your chairman was insistent about quite a lot of things," Cyrus said. "Much of which I disagree with. But he's connected to better men than me. Still, between you and me, he's not as *wise* as he is smart. Miss Darden may be the devil for your Institution, and—Heaven help us—the region."

Robert remembered he'd had the same fear about the girl, right after she'd broken into his apartment. He'd almost immediately informed the IAI's chairman, and in turn the chairman had insisted Robert bring her to The Burrow. The chairman had even gone further, insisting without good reason that everyone affiliated with the Institution continue to let Ava believe she truly was an angel; the Virus was not to be mentioned in her presence. Ava wasn't like an Infinite Definite terrorist, but Robert had suspected from the beginning that she probably had other affiliations.

"Remember your creed," Cyrus said. "And don't be afraid to reach out."

Cyrus unlocked the van's passenger's side door. A wordless way of saying, "We're done here. Get out."

"Thanks for the lift," Robert said as he stepped onto the sidewalk. "And for the phone. Hopefully you won't be hearing from me anytime soon."

Cyrus smiled and nodded at him, as if he knew they'd be in touch much sooner than Robert thought. "Take care, son."

The van pulled away from the curb. When it turned the corner, Robert walked toward the door to the nearest stairwell.

The parking garage was ostensibly for the convenience of the shopping center's customers; their numbers had been dwindling as more and more people lost their jobs and homes. But empty, half-packed, or full, very few who parked there knew the garage contained the primary entry point for the secret structure located deep underneath it.

The Burrow comprised three secure floors of apartments, conference rooms, offices, and workshops, all for the exclusive use of members of the Isaac-Abraham Institution, a not-for-profit organization whose members firmly believed in the strength of the human family, that it should be preserved and its treasures—its children—should be empowered, encouraged, and recovered when lost. Many of the adults affiliated with the IAI believed a childless family was a broken family. Robert believed, whether in their parents' sight or out of it, the thoughtless actions of some children broke the stability of entire communities.

Lost kids; kids, lost. Robert was tasked with finding the former, but too often found himself facing off against the latter. This morning, he'd tangled with a man in his mid-twenties, but more often over the past couple of years he'd faced off against hooligans and terrorists in their mid-teens. His life was a tangle of contradictions and complications. It had only taken a few years for him to see and learn far too much about the antisocial relationships comprising society, and compromising it. A model citizen in a society sicker than he was.

If he'd been a bright-side-of-life type of guy, Robert would've admitted a nice consequence of the White Fire Virus was that it seemed to spur or at least correspond with an artistic renaissance in the areas in which it was most prevalent. In spite of his reticence on the subject when speaking with Cyrus, he certainly had nothing against artistic expression, controlled or guerilla-style. But he still felt it hard to excuse the ubiquitous graffiti. The signatures of bored kids and aiming-low street artists, the tags of vagrants and gangbangers, and—worst of all—the red-flag-waving phrases and words like those confronting him as he topped the third flight of stairs.

alVa loVes Valentinus.

He wasn't sure what it meant. Maybe a boast. Maybe a threat. But Robert was focused more on three letters than three words.

V and *V* and *V.*

V.V. was the signature of the two angel-Sprytes who'd captured and tortured Darryl two weeks prior. Veronica Blake and Vanessa Blight. The two had been taken into custody, but there were more of their kind that hadn't been caught. Less than two weeks later, three Vs, painted close—*too* close—to the entrance of The Burrow…

Whatever it was, whatever it meant, it wasn't a good sign. Just once, he'd like to see a good sign.

He walked away from the graffiti, lost in his thoughts until he had good enough reason to refocus. The reason was someone in front of him, someone he might have recognized if they hadn't smacked him across the left cheek before he could get a good look.

On any other occasion, he would've recovered by swinging his fist first and looking at the fallen body afterward. But something—instinct maybe—told him to just take a step back and take no other action.

He followed instinct, and he saw one pissed off angel in front of him.

Ava was wearing the exact same clothes she'd been wearing the last time Robert had seen her. The black ballet flats, the black capri pants, and the cream-colored tank top were wearing out their welcome. The dime-size diamond pendant on her necklace, however, would always capture Robert's attention, at least until he could figure out how a prisoner of identity thieves had managed to keep it hidden and safe from the crooks. Ava's auburn hair had grown a little past her shoulders; it had been combed or brushed recently, but not with a lot of effort or attention. Robert also saw she still hadn't gotten her eyeglasses properly adjusted. She had to push them up on her nose—twice—before either of them spoke.

"You're welcome," Robert said.

She stared at him for a moment—her brow furrowed, her lips slightly parted—until she finally said, "What?"

"A nonsensical response to a nonsensical action. You could've just said hi. Or given me the finger."

"I should give you a fist."

"Want to tell me why?" he asked. "Or should we just go at it?"

"I want you to tell me why—*why* didn't you tell me you found Marie-Lydia?"

"What?"

"Marie-Lydia McGillis. Remember?"

Yeah, he remembered. She was the fifteen-year-old girl he and Darryl had been searching for when they'd found nineteen-year-old Ava instead. Days later, when Robert and Ava were searching for the missing Darryl, Robert had found Marie-Lydia; both Darryl and Ava were unconscious by that point. He hadn't had the opportunity to tell Ava the good news before he was outfitted in anklets, bracelets, and a collar.

"Are you kidding? I haven't even seen you awake since then. When the hell was I supposed to tell you?"

"Angels share a bond, Robert. When there's mutual trust and respect, we can communicate subconsciously."

Robert sighed. "What are you doing up here anyway?"

"Waiting for you. Partner."

"Uh-huh." That was some leap. He hadn't even been officially told the news of her joining yet, and here she was already part of his Watcher unit. Or at least she thought she was. "How long you been waiting?"

"About an hour, hour and a half."

"Just for me? I feel special."

"You shouldn't. It was my first taste of fresh air in two weeks. I wasn't just going to take three quick breaths, then hurry back into The Burrow. Plus, they're giving me Darryl's Miata. Zel promised to customize it for me in the next week or two, but I wanted to take a look at it now."

She hadn't even been free for a full day yet and they were already promising Ava his old partner's car? Things were moving just a little too fast. Robert had a bad taste in his mouth. He needed some water, he needed to speak to the Institution's chairman, and it was about time to take his Virus medication.

"Well, I hope you got a good enough look," he said, "because we need to go back down. I've got to speak to Adam, plus say a few other hellos."

Ava followed him toward the elevator bank. "You were missed. Both Zel and Vince were asking about you, said they had something to give you. And Sam—she was pretty upset they wouldn't allow her to visit you at your place."

He shouldn't have been surprised Sam and Ava had spoken. Out of all the IAI personnel, the Institution's chief medical specialist seemed to take the most interest in Ava—after the chairman of course. Robert could see Sam being miffed she wasn't allowed to check up on him, unhappy someone above her had decided it'd be best to send some impersonal HSA nurse instead. He would've loved to have been a spider on the wall, eavesdropping on the conversation between Sam and Ava, the doctor and the angel, watching the expressions on Sam's face as she danced around any mention of the Virus.

The first elevator that arrived for them was empty. *Perfect.* No need to wait for another one.

Ava held up a key and smiled as they stepped inside. Robert smiled back. "A key to the kingdom?" he said as he reached into his jeans pocket. "Congratulations. But if you don't mind, I'd like to try mine, just to be sure it still works. And to make sure I'm really welcome back."

He inserted his special key into one of the many slots near the buttons. Ava pushed the button for the top floor; the cab ascended. The keys wouldn't work if used on any level below six. An extra measure of security for The Burrow.

"I just told you people were asking about you," Ava said. "Why wouldn't you be welcome back?"

"Maybe they found out about some other things I've done," he said, only half joking. "Maybe they have some new punishments they want to dish out."

"Wasn't so bad being cooped up," Ava said. "I had a lot of time to think and plan."

"Oh yeah? Plotting against us?"

It just slipped out. An absentminded comment that under other circumstances would've been a little joke at best. But from Cyrus's intimations, through Robert's nagging thoughts, out of his mouth, and into Ava's ears, it couldn't have sounded that way.

"Don't start that junk again," Ava said. "Don't even start. After everything we went through together—"

"I know, I know—I'm sorry. Just a witless witticism."

Neither said anything more as the elevator reached the top floor, hummed, then rattled and shook as it turned around. After completing a 180-degree spin, the elevator doors slid open onto an opaque darkness. Robert adjusted his eyesight in order to see through a blackness no normal human's eyes could ever penetrate. He and Ava then stepped off the elevator and approached the one a few feet ahead of them.

"You can do the honors this time," he said, making a meager attempt to get them back on warm-and-friendly footing. No need to get smart-mouthed or accusatory till he had a good and hard reason to do so. Adam seemed to have placed full trust in her, and, for many reasons, Robert tended to fall in line with the IAI chairman over any HSA employee.

After giving him a look indicating she hadn't quite warmed back up to friendly yet, Ava took off her glasses. She inserted her key into the hole near the button and looked into the retina scanner. Robert heard the sound indicating it had worked. The elevator cab was approaching their level from far below.

"Zel or Vince explain how the watches work?" Robert asked.

"Zel did," Ava said. "I only saw Vince in passing. He just popped his head into Zel's workshop when I was there. He didn't seem like he wanted to discuss anything with me."

"Well, he's no chatterbox," Robert said. "More the philosophical type."

"It was more than that," Ava said. "He gave me a funny look when he saw me. Reminded me of a few of the looks you used to give me after we first met."

"Must just be in your head."

"Whether it is or not, I'll get to the bottom of it," Ava said. "He's got something I want. So he's going to have to talk to me sooner or later."

Before that, Robert thought, someone should have a talk with her about the IAI's hierarchy. Vince was a Board member. Ava was just a Watcher trainee. The folks in charge of the cleaning and maintenance of The Burrow had more authority than her.

"One thing at a time," he said. "First, you and I are going to respectfully request an audience with Adam, hear what the chairman has to tell us about our alleged partnership."

"I can tell you a few things—"

Ava stopped short when the elevator doors opened.

Neither of them made a motion to step inside the waiting cab. They only looked down. One of them gasped—Robert wasn't sure if it was him or Ava—but they both saw it, they both reacted, and they may or may not have been thinking the same thing.

Chairman Adam Smith would certainly grant them an immediate meeting. He'd want to discuss everything the two of them knew—or suspected—about the dead Watcher agent in the elevator.

Chapter 3

Ava saw the crumpled body. The boy was nearly naked, wearing nothing but his socks and underwear. The rest of his clothes had been tossed into the elevator cab's corners.

The run of his skin seemed to follow some kind of indecipherable pattern. It looked like a topographic map found in some old geography textbook. The skin pattern alternated between ghostly pale patches, normal Caucasian flesh-colored spots, and raspberry bruises. Almost every area was marked with ridged scars and varicolored sores, some of them open. A greenish pus flowed from thumbtack-size volcanoes on his back. Rivulets of dirty car oil—*blood*—still drying, crisscrossed his thighs and lower abdomen. And then there were the dark-pink mounds—everywhere—moist-looking, rubbery-looking. Tumors.

None of it grossed her out. Ava had seen much worse. From the torture-porno dramatization of Christ's passion to the even more graphic retelling of the Book of Job. Granted, those were just films—but, until that moment, Ava had considered them effective training for withstanding the repulsive.

It wasn't what was on the skin that caused her to turn away with her hands on her stomach. It was what she saw just underneath the surface.

She hadn't been wearing her glasses when the elevator door opened. Without the lenses Zel Bernard had designed for her, it took a little extra effort to control the range of her divine vision, especially after the shock-sudden appearance of the body. Her eyesight snap-flashed through many ranges before settling on a range that allowed her to see the microorganisms, the billions of tiny, tiny bugs—a cross between hairlike worms and spiders—just under the skin's surface, scrambling as if in a panic.

Her eyes didn't linger. Ava didn't know what the tiny creatures were or what they were doing. She tried to get a firm grasp over her emotions and her body's reactions while Robert shouted at her to use her right-wristwatch and contact someone down in The Burrow.

"Tell them it's Watcher Agent Canton! Unit X_8O!"

She did. Zel Bernard's instructions had been useful. Ava's faith in her divine intuition, and Zel's encouragement in the use of it, didn't fail her. Her fingertips pressing and playing on the face of her wristwatch somehow communicated the meaning and urgency of her thoughts to Adam Smith. She and Robert then stepped onto the elevator, careful not to touch anything, and took the slow ride down to The Burrow's top level. Both were careful about not only where they stood but also where they looked. Robert appeared as if he wanted to speak but didn't. Ava kept her questions to herself, turning them over and over inside her head.

The mystery of the dead angel…Though she knew well enough that even angels could die. Just like their Creator.

The angels of the modern world weren't the angels of her long-ago Sunday School lessons. Her kind had little in common with the angels portrayed in pop literature, Hollywood flicks, or even the lore of most religions. It was true the angels of the real world had a direct link to the Creator, but the Source of Creation gave angels few favors, and none at all it seemed to regular human beings. It was the angels—the wisest and most benevolent of them, anyway—who had taken up the duty to prepare and enable humankind to survive and thrive in the finished Creation, all while the Creator suffered and extinguished itself to finish the grand work in progress. And, until The End came, angels were well equipped to do their duty. They were blessed with gifts and abilities beyond mortals. But, like mortals, they too could die before achieving their life's big goal, or even a few modest ones.

The Isaac-Abraham Institution was rife with angels, and it as a whole focused on a few modest goals. During her benign imprisonment, she had learned the nonprofit, nongovernmental organization counted just a little fewer than one hundred as its DC-area members, a handful of whom were just normal human beings and all of whom were using whatever talents they possessed to locate missing children. The priority were Chairman Smith's "children," the one or ones he couldn't even remember ever existing, the one or ones whose names allegedly rhymed with the word *air*, or maybe just the sound of the letter *R*. A lot of time, money, and energy had been spent searching for children that may or may not have even been real—but the organization had done plenty of tangible good in the meantime, like recovering other missing or captive children and young adults.

Ava was one of their most recent finds, and she'd been found in a similar—if not quite as severe—amnesiac condition as Adam. She also shared another unsettling similarity with the chairman—the nagging subconscious desire to search for, find, and hold on to *something* that rhymed with *R* or *air*. If only she knew why. One thing she did know was that the answer could be found one of two ways: returning to her temple-palace in XynKroma or having a face-to-face and heart-to-heart with her former best friend, Marie Lydia McGillis. Both were priorities. But the mystery of this freshly dead body at her feet would have to take precedent.

"Adam's office." Medical specialist Sam Goines and two assistants greeted them with grim faces when the elevator's doors opened. "Now. He's waiting for you both. We'll take care of Agent Canton."

Ava was just one step behind Robert as they hustled down The Burrow's dim labyrinthine corridors and—with permission granted—entered an even dimmer office. They took the seats offered in front of the large oak desk.

Adam said very little before Ava began asking the questions on her long list.

"I thought I was pretty smart, but, thinking about it, I just can't figure it out. Who or what could've done that to him? He was so young, about my age, and…Well, what happened to him?"

"I do not know, Miss Darden," Adam said. "But going on what little I have, it is possible he was poisoned."

Ava stared at the faceless face of the chairman. The concave mirror that was the faceplate of his helmet had no holes, no slits, or any other kind of openings for his eyes, nose, or mouth. Ava had fruitlessly been trying to x-ray it from the first moment she'd met him. Someway and somehow Adam could breathe, see, and speak through this holeless helmet. His speech patterns were a little off, but Ava could always hear him clearly. At the moment, though, she didn't believe what she was hearing.

She wasn't from the area, but her upbringing in the southern half of Virginia had led her to believe most *somebodies* in the Washington, DC, area wore three-piece suits. Not Adam Smith. He wore a suit that made him appear almost like a medieval knight, ready for battle, his armor updated for the twenty-first century. The plate armor that covered every part of his body was more white than silver or gray, seemed far less cumbersome, tighter fitting, more flexible, and just overall more comfortable than the armor worn by the knights of times nearly forgotten. It also had several slits the length and width of needles; their purpose was presumably to allow the body underneath to breathe a little. What in the Good Word's name type of angel was he? She'd been wondering since day one. Now she began to worry less about his way of dressing and more about his way of thinking.

"The lights in the elevator were much brighter than usual," Robert said. "Much too bright for the comfort of anyone at the Institution. Anyone who's accustomed to the way things are around here."

"I understand, Mister Goldner," Adam said.

So did Ava. She wasn't as stupid as Robert seemed to think. He'd made a clumsy attempt to talk in code, insinuating a stranger had somehow amped up the lights in the elevator. Since only those who knew about the existence of The Burrow knew about the elevator, and since she was still essentially a stranger, she was undoubtedly on their list of suspects. But what the heck did *lights* have to do with that boy's death? Angels manipulated light, bent it to their will, as was their divine prerogative. But that boy…Ava could tell he'd been sick for a long time. The condition of his skin was proof of that. He should've been removed from the premises a long time before today. And Adam's facile guess of *poison*…The chairman wasn't stupid, but he and Robert seemed to be of the same mind about her.

"Poison, Mister Smith?" she said. "As in someone here at the Institution poisoned Agent Canton?"

"As in something was inside him that should not have been, Miss Darden," Adam said. "A foreign substance his body could not handle. It may have been an accident. He may have done it to himself. Whatever the case, it most likely just overwhelmed him, attacked his body—suddenly—while he was in the elevator. It is too early to be sure at this point, but that is what autopsies are for."

Yes, and Ava would be sure to ask Sam about the destination of Canton's body. She'd be sure to trace it and get a copy of that autopsy report.

"Will the police or medical examiners need to question us?" Ava asked. "Me and Robert?"

"No," Adam said. "I will tell anyone who asks everything you two know, which apparently is very little."

His tone wasn't expressive, but Ava picked up something there. Something accusatory. She wasn't about to sit still for that garbage.

"Mister Smith, if I'm to be a Watcher agent—"

"You are, Miss Darden. And I believe a very key one."

That was a little better.

"Mister Goldner, I am sure Miss Darden has already told you I am coupling you into a unit. X_3O."

"She told me the good news."

"I have more that may serve as a counterweight," Adam said. "The Infinite Definite are converging on Washington. Something is driving them here."

Agents of chaos, Ava thought, *coming to the capital of the world's only superpower*. It was only a matter of time. Up until now, the terrorists had seemed to operate at random, with no plan or goal, just wandering about committing random acts of violence, some big, some small. But randomness notwithstanding, they had one specific end: to unleash XynKroma, letting it wash over the planet, the solar system, and the entire universe in a flash flood, bathing all of what humans knew as a sane and ordered Reality in primal chaos, where neither the laws of common sense nor physics would be at play.

"Do we have any…" Robert hesitated as he glanced at Ava. "Any theories?"

"I have a couple of good ones," Adam said. "Both of you may as well know Marie-Lydia is still in custody, but she has been moved to an undisclosed location."

Ava said, "Can I arrange to visit—"

"An undisclosed location," Adam repeated.

Rude, but Ava understood. Marie-Lydia was a rogue angel, one who'd been impelled to try to slaughter their entire high school just eighteen months ago. Ava had stopped her—barely—and woken up more than a year and a half later with her memory of everything that had happened in between practically erased. Bits and pieces of the intervening months had come back to her over the past two weeks, but not enough. Marie-Lydia had come to the Northern Virginia area, drawn to it for some reason.

"I have had an opportunity over the past couple of weeks to look into her situation," Adam said. "We have before discussed her potential connection with The Infinite Definite. For years, the only thing that connected the amorphous Infinite Definite was an idea, that of spreading chaos. Now there is evidence the once autonomous affiliates are structuring themselves, organizing under a strong leadership. The two-person cells are no longer engaging in random acts of wanton violence. Some of them seem to have a mission in mind. Last week a Watcher unit—Agent Canton's unit, in fact—subdued a pair of Infinite Definite terrorists. After their arrest and subsequent medical examination, both were found to have chips attached to the backs of their eyelids."

"Chips?" Ava said.

"Like microchips or something?"

"Or something, Mister Goldner. The size and color of a detached fingernail, these chips were composed of a plastic-like substance, several razor-thin layers of it. An image of Marie-Lydia McGillis was imprinted on one of the inner layers, positioned as if on a holy card, portrayed like a saint."

"Okay…weird. But why?" Robert asked.

Ava took the pendant hanging from her necklace between her thumb and forefinger and focused on the symbol inside. The bottom half resembled an anchor; the top half was unmistakably a Christian cross. The symbol was encased inside the diamond pendant like a bug in amber.

"Devotion," she said. "Devotion to the divine."

"Behind the eyelids?" Robert said. "What—"

"So the blessed, the *marked*, always have her on their minds when their eyes close to the world, during a blink, a nap, or longer sleep," Ava said. "The Archangel told me that angels don't dream. But these fallen angels Mister Smith is talking about, they saw Marie-Lydia in the place of lost escapes."

As she spoke, still regarding her pendant, Ava remembered the time she'd taken Marie-Lydia to a pawnshop to buy a cheap crucifix. It had been shortly after the younger girl's baptism, the one that had washed away her subservience to her parents' ungodly rules, her fear of making friends, her lackadaisical Romanist faith; it had made her Born-Again. Of course, the ceremony and the new-life aftermath all had had to be kept secret from her parents. It had been like buying a cheap wedding ring, after eloping.

Marie-Lydia's life had just been starting to go right and then made a sharp left. Where, *when* had it all gone so wrong?

"So." Robert lowered his head, obviously considering different questions. "This is badness, bursting the worst." He almost seemed to be talking to himself.

"Yes. The situation has evolved. And thus has the mission for your Watcher unit. You are no longer to search for and help recover missing children, not anytime soon. The Heartland Security Agency and its affiliates are putting all angels under a microscope. They are reassessing our permissions."

Listening through the monotone, it was hard to pick up—and the tinny echo that accompanied Adam's voice didn't help—but Ava sensed passion on his part. Anger.

"I am asserting whatever authority I have," Adam said. "But for now…Well, you know the process, Mister Goldner."

Robert nodded as Ava asked, "Process?"

"Whether we're searching for missing kids, fighting The ID, or just going sightseeing, we can't just run out into the field like a couple of jackrabbits," Robert said. "If we're going to be partners, we've got to familiarize ourselves. Get to know each other. Bond."

"What?" Ava said. "We don't have time for all that—they're coming!"

"I know," Robert said. "But we've got to *know* each other first, or there is no 'we.'"

"That is the process." Adam's words cut off Ava's hot-but-too-slow response to her new partner. "Six days of bonding, establishing mutual trust. Physical training in The Burrow, observation only out in the field. On the seventh day, if all goes well, you may assume the full privileges of a Watcher unit."

"*Privileges?*" Ava said. "We're angels! What authority does a government agency have over the Creator's faithful? If we see a child getting hit by a bad parent, or—"

"Use your right-wristwatch and call it in," Adam said, "but do not interfere. Even if there were no reassessment by the Heartland Security Agency, the normal rules would be hardened for you two due to your previous actions. You are now free but still on probation. Consider me your probation officer. Any deviations, any unlawful interactions, will result in me having no choice but to turn you over to the Agency for further detention. That was our agreement with them, the reason why you two got such light sentences for a violent home invasion."

Ava couldn't believe this nonsense. Noninterventionist angels? Whether for six days or six minutes, it was an absurd idea. And the threat to turn them over to a government agency for incarceration, for saving children, abiding by their divine mission.

Submitting divine will to human demands—she wondered what kind of silly fool angels she'd allied herself with.

And this *bonding* foolishness. That sort of stuff was all well and good back at Bible Camp, during summers spent in human fellowship and Mother Nature's wilderness, back before the weirdness, before she was inverted by Heaven's Raven-Dove—the Archangel Artemisia—and Ava's humanity was enhanced until she'd been elevated to the order of an Arkangel.

"So what's first?" she asked. "Am I supposed to fall backwards, trusting Robert to catch me?"

Robert stifled a laugh. Despite what he'd said, she had a faint suspicion her partner might've found this six-day waiting period a bunch of garbage, too.

Adam said nothing. He only moved one of his armor-gloved hands under his desk. Ava adjusted her vision and, through the wood, saw Adam depressing a blue button.

Ava had seen plenty of TV shows where just those types of buttons, located in just those types of places, brought security guards running.

Fewer than thirty seconds after Adam pushed the button, Ava heard the recorded voice linked to the office door's retinal scanner announce, "Enter Mister Ceniza."

This wasn't security. Just another danger.

Vince Ceniza, the angel in the organization she trusted least. And it wasn't a short list. There was something about his eyes, those piercing turquoise eyes, the dark circles underneath them, and the way he always seemed to be squinting at her. If she was capable of being creeped out by anything on two legs, she would've been creeped out. Instead Ava was just uneasy in his presence, as if he might at any moment pull a knife on her—and she might have no choice but to twist his wrist and jam the blade into his eye sockets.

Vince passed by them and stood next to Adam's desk. He nodded a greeting at Robert, then shifted his eyes to gaze at Ava. She squinted back at him.

"To answer your question, Miss Darden," Adam said, "the first step in the process of trust and bonding is to share what we have in common in order to eliminate secrets."

She wanted to invite him to take off his helmet, eliminate the secret of his face and how he breathed. But she held her tongue.

"For instance," Adam said, "you and Mister Goldner are both orphans. You and I are both missing significant portions of our memories."

She waited for Adam to spill the beans on what she and Vince had in common, but Vince took over, jerking the conversation into an unexpected direction.

"We have videos of you, Ava."

Delightful. This strange angel had been watching her sleep or shower or something while she was under arrest. Ava said nothing as she glared at him, waiting for him to ask something like if she'd consider getting a tattoo on her thigh to match one of the ones on his hands and neck.

"We have videos of your knock-down, drag-out fight with Marie-Lydia McGillis," he continued. "Recorded at your high school."

"How? Who could've possibly—?" She shut up when she remembered.

She'd arrived at the school late, too long after Marie-Lydia had snapped and started attacking people. Ava had banged up a few cars before parking and sprinting like a madwoman to the nearest door, only to find it and all the others locked. But she'd gotten in. A talented and resilient angel always found a way. Her way had been through a second-story window of the school's auxiliary gymnasium. The gym had been empty, and all the doors leading outside, to the halls of the school and to the gym teacher's offices, had been locked—all except one. It was in that office that she'd found Sally. "Sally the Salamander," she used to call her. A phony friend and reluctant member of the Bible Study Club Ava and her boyfriend had co-led. A member, Ava believed, only because Luke, her "boyfriend" at the time—*no*. No time to dwell on that. That wasn't important. What had been and remained important was that, while every other child and adult in the school was in danger, Sally was safe. Suspicious Sally, who, after years of not giving a hang about Marie-Lydia, had suddenly noticed and befriended her, just two weeks before Marie-Lydia went berserk. Sly Sally, the aspiring filmmaker who, when not up to something devious, had been deep into her computer or out somewhere with her camcorder, recording and putting together short films, including the incredibly graphic one about Job that she'd screened during a Bible Study Club get-together at Luke's house. It had succeeded in catching Luke's eye; now Ava's eyes were open. Sally had something to do with this. She'd in some way been involved in getting video of her fight with Marie-Lydia on the web. It wasn't a straight line. Ava didn't see the direct connection yet. But angelic intuition sure did count for a heck of a lot.

"The films of your fight were plastered all over the net shortly after it happened," Robert said.

"Okay," she said, shaking her head. They surely weren't going to ask her how the films got there. There was another purpose to this. "So what?"

"We have others," Vince said. "Films of you recorded after that fight."

Something stuck in Ava's throat. She wanted to swallow—tried three times—but couldn't. She hadn't considered the possibility her memory loss might've been a good thing. There was something ominous in Vince's voice. She wasn't sure she wanted to know what she'd been missing.

Adam took hold of the iron cane leaning against his desk and used it to push himself to his feet.

"Come," he said as he moved toward the door leading to his inner office.

Even as most of her thoughts were elsewhere, Ava couldn't help but think how awkward Adam looked when walking, how he looked so much in pain when moving. What had he been through to end up in such a condition?

Adam pushed a green button next to the door, and it slid open. He walked in as Vince stepped aside to let Robert and Ava pass through first. Ava didn't look at him but was sure he gave her one of his funny looks as she passed by. Maybe he was right to.

The inner office looked like a television addict's heaven. Scores of monitors of various shapes and sizes were embedded in five of the hexagonal room's six walls. All of them showed scrambled images, snow, or bland screen savers.

Adam took his seat behind the oval-shaped glass desk. He didn't invite anyone else to sit down, so his three guests remained standing as he pressed a few keys on one of the desk's keyboards.

One by one, the monitors on the wall directly behind the desk showed footage of Ava. The scenes were unfamiliar, and she didn't remember doing what she saw herself doing. But as she watched, the actions she performed did invoke a good sense of familiarity and a great sense of pride.

They all watched in silence as, on multiple monitors, Ava took on a wide variety of people: men and women; alone, in pairs, or in groups; in parking lots, on putt-putt golf courses, and inside fast-food restaurants. A different movie on each screen. She sometimes fought by herself, sometimes with an unnameable partner, and at other times with a group of other unrecognized female angels at her side. They used their fists, their feet, their supranatural agility, and various tricks of light. No two videos were alike. Some were in color, some in black-and-white. Some were blurry; others were in high-definition. Some had sound; others were mute. Some had been recorded by stationary cameras, others by devices that followed the center of the action. No two recordings were alike, but they all had a common theme.

Save the Children. The thought crossed Ava's mind more than once as she watched, and patches of her memory came back to her.

At least one child was present in all the videos, if only as a cameo. The children were always crying or showing other obvious signs of fear. Ava knew she wasn't the source of their fright. It was the menaces Ava and her allies were confronting. Abusive adults. Parents who hit their kids in public. Parents who screamed profanity at their kids. And parents at the other end of the spectrum, those who turned a blind eye and deaf ear as their kids acted out in public settings. Little terrors—blameless—wrecking havoc. Those children all deserved better parents, a better life, a better world.

Time seemed to stop as the four of them watched. Ava had certainly lost herself in the images and the memories they evoked. But after the screens went back to snow, black, or scrambled, an unease crept over her. She was glad Adam finally invited them all to sit down.

Vince remained standing.

Ava had several questions, but she held her tongue, hoping someone would provide unprompted answers.

"You have been very busy over the past year and a half," Adam said.

"Saving the children," she said, louder than she'd meant to.

"Yes," Adam said. "But saving them where?"

Everyone looked at her. She couldn't meet their eyes. It was a good question, and, with those memories blacked out, the answer was a scary one. She didn't want anyone to see the fear in her eyes. It was easier, safer, to stare down at the translucent desktop, letting her vision blur instead of focusing.

"And for what purpose?" Vince asked, no doubt encouraging everyone to stare even harder at her.

Silence overtook the room for who knows how many moments until Robert—bless him—spoke up, drawing everyone's attention to him.

"Sir, I've looked into some of these videos, had a little time to do some digging before I was shut off from the world, and I found that a lot of them can be traced to one source: MC³ Productions. Whoever's behind it is responsible for putting this stuff out on the web. This stuff and other questionable videos involving…angels. Since Ava's memories are blocked, maybe someone can look deeper into this shady outfit, see what they're all about. We may be able to find some answer that way, quicker than waiting for Ava to have some kind of epiphany."

"MC³ Productions?" Didn't ring a bell with her, but Ava would definitely keep the name in mind.

"We may not have to wait so long," Vince said as he pulled something out of his back pocket. Ava glanced at a nervous-looking Robert as Vince unfolded the piece of paper on Adam's desk. Vince, too, must've noticed Robert's uneasiness. He said, "I'm sorry. I can't keep this a secret any longer. Now seems about the right time to show the results to someone else, particularly the someone who inspired it."

The "results" was an elaborate map of the sections of Northern Virginia that bordered Washington, DC. Only about half of the unfolded paper was an actual map; the rest was a key to the map—notes providing details for each of the map's marked spots, of which there were plenty.

"Ava." She looked at Vince as he addressed her, gritting her teeth in equal measure to his squinting eyes. "Full disclosure. A few weeks ago, when you, Robert, and Darryl met with Adam for your official introduction to the IAI, Darryl heard you whisper the words *Save the Children*. Darryl told me you appeared to be in a momentary trance when you said it. You may or may not know the phrase *Save the Children* happens to be a popular but unique graffiti tag here in Northern Virginia. Popular in that it's found in a lot of places, and unique in that it's one of the few apparently positive messages to be found written in spray paint. Darryl jotted notes on each place he could find the phrase written, and he came to me with a list of the locations, hoping I could piece them together in order to help solve the mystery of your whereabouts for the past year."

Of course he would go to Vince. Darryl, the self-absorbed romantic, third-rate philosopher, and bad-poetry lover. He would most certainly go to the IAI Board member Sam had described as a bruised poet turned psychological mapmaker. Vince Ceniza was an angel whose specialty was joining unlike ideas and dissimilar items in such a way that the results made sense. Good poets did that. Dream decipherers did that. Scientists did that. But Vince was no scientist. Angels didn't dream. And, according to Sam, Vince did not write or recite poetry. He worked with the mind, the Great Mind in which the minds of all living creatures were joined—*XynKroma*. Vince's role with the IAI was to map the chaotic realm, make some sense of it. Ava knew nothing of his work, but she was sure it was futile. He was neither an Archangel nor an Arkangel. And they were the only two orders of angels who knew how to bring order to chaos.

The map, however, intrigued her. It seemed Vince had made order out of one sort of chaos.

"Piecing together everything I know about these locations, and everything I know about you"—another piercing look—"I've been able to determine that you, Ava, were or are part of an organized contingent of angels whose primary directive has been to rescue children."

"And what's so horrible about that?" Ava said.

"Let me finish. Your definition of 'rescue' doesn't necessarily line up with mine. We at the IAI search for children that have been lost or kidnapped. You and your cohorts seemed to zero in on kids who were in some way or manner being mistreated by their parents or guardians. These children were taken from their legal guardians, who were beaten up, all by angels who sometimes shouted out a familiar slogan."

"Save the children," Robert said.

"Yes," Vince said. "But for what? And *where*? Wherever these children have gone, no one has ever seen them again. We at the IAI haven't recovered any of them. Neither have the FBI, the HSA, metro area police—no one."

So that was it. Vince suspected her of being some sort of demented kidnapper.

She ran her eyes over every section of the map, seeing if she could pick up a pattern, any hints that might lead toward a nice discovery. But no—all she saw on the map itself were numerous red, green, and blue dots, all together seeming to make up the vague outline of a beetle. All she saw in skimming the notes in the map's key were references to the names of parents and children and angels. Ava didn't recognize any of the names except her own.

"The map is yours," Vince said. "For you and Robert to study while you're in your bonding period. Study it, discuss it, and come to Adam or me with any…epiphanies."

"Will do." Robert began to refold the map. "We'll let you both know if there's any breakthrough."

"Mister Smith," Ava said, then, with a twist of frost, "Mister Ceniza. There is a way to cut to the chase in all of this. My memory loss, whatever secrets that map may be holding, The ID's purpose in coming here—there is one good, possibly perfect solution to all these questions."

"XynKroma." Robert said it before anyone could even ask what she was leading to. The bonding process was off to a good start. He could already read her mind.

"That's right. If Robert could accompany me to XynKroma, I'm sure I could—"

"I'm not going to Xyn." Robert put the map in his back pocket. "Not on your life. Or anyone else's."

One step forward in the process, two steps back.

"Ava," Vince said, "you know that I supervise all visits to Xyn-Kroma for IAI members. You don't need a partner to go. If you want to make an appointment to visit my office and—"

"No," Ava said. "Thank you. But I prefer to go with my partner." With someone she at least mostly trusted, and far away from the creepy eyes and despicable suspicions of Vince Ceniza.

"A visit to XynKroma is an excellent idea," Adam said. "And it was something I was going to insist you undertake within the next six days."

Ava saw the look on Robert's face. "Shocked" and "peeved" would be understatements. She suppressed her smirk. It was easier than usual; she shared some of Robert's surprise. Maybe Adam wasn't completely focused on nonsense after all.

"But first, Mister Goldner, you need to take Miss Darden shopping."

Chapter 4

Cyrus secured the van with the push of two buttons on his keychain. No need to push the third. There were no sensitive items inside. No need to give anyone who touched his property more than a debilitating shock.

He adjusted his porkpie and left the parking garage. A creature of dangerous habits, he thought nothing of looking for a crosswalk or of stepping into the street without checking for traffic. A man of his unique training and extraordinary experiences put more faith in his ears than his eyes, using them to measure the approximate distance of any potentially hostile object. He also had enough faith that the drivers who saw him would abide by the law, slow, and brake, giving the pedestrian the right of way. And if they didn't…well, his two-hundred-and-seventy-five-pound frame was more agile than it looked. And if his eyes weren't quick enough to get the plate numbers, at least one of the four street-level cameras would. Or maybe a drone, if one happened to be gliding by up above.

No matter how many arms he twisted, national budget restraints would permit only so many cameras, drones, and other surveillance devices. The national Rings of Light security system—his *baby*, his legacy to the nation—wasn't nearly as strong as it needed to be. Even historic Old Town Alexandria, at a stone's throw from the nation's capital, didn't have as many electronic eyes as it should. As he crossed the two-lane street, Cyrus was sure he heard at least one stabbing, a shot or two, and three different women screaming from three different street corners. All of them, whatever the situations, were minor. *Good.* He'd no time to deal with any of them. But soon, and very soon, there'd be a sentinel on every corner, all of them his eyes and ears and at his beck and call.

He made it across the street and to the door of the Torpedo Factory unharmed. It was 9:30 A.M. Half an hour before the Factory would open up to the public. Cyrus wasn't the public. He got inside the building and went about his business.

The Torpedo Factory Art Center comprised three floors of a few galleries and many more studios. It was no place for the reclusive genius. Visitors were allowed and encouraged to watch the various artists as they worked. Painters, photographers, sculptors, and other creative types occupied the eighty-two working studios. Cyrus was there to see just one of them. Edward T. Howard. A young man who wasn't shy about proclaiming himself a mad genius. Cyrus wanted to hear what the genius might have to say about some other types of mad artists, similar to but far more nefarious than the ones he now passed: self-mutilators on metal pedestals, image-shifters in cages hanging from the ceiling, and the tattooed and pierced body artists who crucified themselves on the walls for days at a time, allowing visitors to throw rotten fruit at them—all for a small donation, of course.

He walked into Edward's studio and looked around. His sensitive ears determined he and the artist were alone. His eyes, sharp as they were, might've never reached the same conclusion.

It was impossible for anyone who entered this particular studio to only glance at an artwork. Each was designed to capture even the most casual onlooker's attention and to enrapture the senses. The works had been created with the purpose of injecting visions of fantastic possibilities into the minds of those leading mundane lives. Some of the visions were more than mere possibilities.

Cyrus knew very well some of the fantasias and grotesqueries the artworks portrayed weren't just products of a troubled mind but true-view sections of another plane of existence, one believed by some of its visitors to be the Ultimate sphere accessible to sentient creatures: XynKroma, every possible version of fictional Heaven and Hell combined into one too-real and chaotic Reality. An unstable dimension poised—his sources told him—to shift its position and sift its contents into the familiar world of Earth and its well-ordered universe.

Fair and accurate compositions of such a place couldn't be limited to two dimensions, or even three. The artworks surrounding Cyrus seemed to extend into four or five or more. Colors, shapes, and even faint sounds leaped off the unusual canvases, flickered, curled, and sank back into them, like waves on a stormy ocean's surface, while the canvases themselves vibrated, undulated, and modified their shapes. Moon dances.

Edward didn't rely exclusively on paint and the usual substances for his creations. He also used electricity, alchemical powders, and bodily fluids. Urine, saliva, and oftentimes contaminated blood. Sometimes his own. All that in addition to many unnamed substances Cyrus didn't want to know anything about.

The big man made his way through the tumultuous works and approached their creator. The artist was so engrossed in his current masterpiece in the making, he didn't taken his eyes off it once, not even when Cyrus stopped to stand two feet behind him.

The vision Edward was reproducing appeared to be an eleven-limbed squid whose top half   above its five eyes—metamorphosed into a bright-blue tree with dozens of branches displaying silver-shingled leaves and bearing the ripe fruit of ruptured human organs. The bizarre creature hovered above an immense sandy landscape dotted with skulls, bones, and foreboding treasure chests decorated with a variety of dull jewels. No doubt once the work was finished, one or more of these chests would open in the eyes and mind of each viewer, rewarding them, scaring them, or scarring them with the contents.

The entire work so far appeared to be one of Edward's least interesting. But even in its incomplete state it had already managed to disturb Cyrus and to stir thoughts.

"Hieronymus Bosch," he said.

Edward didn't flinch at the big man's booming voice. He just kept on working through a few silent moments before saying, "Well what about him?"

"Your obvious inspiration. Him, Dalí, van Gogh—"

"None of them on my level," Edward said. "My thoughts dip deeper, taking a peep at those of the Supreme Being. Sure, those others had some interesting things to say, and to show. But my concern is the base of Creation."

"Really?" Cyrus said. "Destroying it, or preserving it?"

"Creation is destroying itself well enough without my assistance, thank you."

Edward dipped his right hand into a bucket filled with something having the appearance and odor of vomit. Cyrus scrunched his nose and took a step back as the artist used whatever it was to give his work's indefinite background more definition.

"Who'd want to preserve this fractured world anyway?" Edward said. "Though I suppose thirty years from now there'll be some middle-aged knot-heads saying these were the greatest times of all. These suffocating times, they're the times to remember, the times they'd like to come back to."

"Thirty years from now." Cyrus chuckled at the idea. "I don't think that way about the seventies."

"Then maybe you're not a knot-head." Edward sat down on his stool. "Maybe." He dipped his left hand into another bucket, this one filled with something that looked like strawberry yogurt. He picked up a tool resembling a laser pointer with his right hand. With it and the gunk on his left, the artist began to apply intricate details to the squid's limbs.

"I'm not so sure what a phrase like 'thirty years from now' might even mean," Cyrus said, "if our friends in The ID have their way."

"They're just zombies," Edward said. "Living-dead poets."

"Yes—after the hearts and brains of all the rest of us."

"They think they know but actually have no clue what they're doing. Just white-and-black background noise. They don't matter in the end."

"Maybe not," Cyrus said. "But they matter to me right now. And they damn well better to you."

"Meh." Edward shrugged his shoulders and went on with his work.

Cyrus wanted to put one of his beefy hands on one of those malnourished shoulders, apply some pressure, inflict a little pain, make the carefree artist give him his undivided attention. Instead he just moved to the side of Edward so he could see the artist's eyes, those bloodshot eyes that refused to divert from the unfinished work in front of them.

"Listen to me," he said. "I tried to meet with Ezra, but he's on travel. I'd requested a meeting with Ezekiel, but I've heard nothing back. So I am forced to make do with you. I'm asking you—nicely, for the moment—not to waste my time."

"I'm not," Edward said. "You haven't asked any questions yet. You're actually wasting my time."

Any other time, in any other place, during any other type of interrogation, Cyrus would've picked the smart-ass up by his neck and slammed his hard head against something harder. But Edward wasn't a street punk, a terrorist, or even a subordinate. He served as a ranking member of the Trinfecta, an off-the-books outfit affiliated with one of the private companies to which the HSA outsourced some of its operations. The private company itself was paid to hold and care for Virus-carriers who were a threat to society, making their dying days peaceful and pleasant while keeping them walled away from the populace—but the doctors, engineers, and creative types affiliated with the third-party Trinfecta went beyond this modest mission. They studied the Virus and its carriers, inside and out, as they considered possibilities, grand and creative possibilities that would work toward the betterment of society. Cyrus had become acquainted with the Trinfecta and some of their ideas years ago. With mutual understanding and a shared long-term goal, he had quietly entered into a business relationship with them after their first informal meeting. They'd proven to be a valuable asset. But time was running out; there were no more long-terms. And while Edward was a loyal member of the Trinfecta, he'd never seen eye to eye with Cyrus on the big man's scheme. Edward had made it clear, repeatedly, he wanted nothing to do with it. Cyrus didn't feel the need to play gentleman with him, but he would have to work extra hard in order to restrain his more aggressive tendencies.

"You know why I'm here," Cyrus said.

"Apparently to keep me from working," Edward said. "By the way, isn't that where you should be right about now? Shouldn't you be in an office or a conference room, staring at some TV screens or something?"

"I am working, damn you. And I want to know, I want someone in your organization to tell me straight, how those eight got out of The SeptiGuarden. Who let those rabid animals escape?"

"They're actually calling themselves 'flowers' now, you know. The FlowerShow. Guess your methods of reeducation had some positive effect after all. From fauna to flora—fantastic job."

Edward stood up and began to work on another section of the canvas. It looked like he was creating clouds. Looked like. As he added more detail, it turned out the "clouds" were composed of the disconnected body parts of various types of colorful birds—flamingos, peacocks, cardinals, and many others Cyrus didn't recognize. The guy worked at an amazing speed.

"And by the way," Edward said, "no one let them do anything. You were the one with the brilliant idea of letting Hernandez out of her cell."

Yes, way back in March. "Under strict monitoring. She'd been fully reformed and evaluated before being released. Besides, I—*we* needed a test case."

"Well, you've failed, sir. Hernandez dropped her measuring tape, made her way back to your prison, and broke the eight out."

Holly Hernandez. Real name: Yessina Hernandez. A onetime professional dentist and hobby horticulturist who'd had the misfortune of becoming infected with the White Fire Virus. Most died shortly after contracting it; some of the survivors coped better than others. The Virus-induced designs and voices in her head had seduced Hernandez, who began referring to herself as "The Hummingbird" and fell in with those violent sadists the HSA classified as "The Infinite Definite" or, with a nod to Freud, "The ID." She was eventually captured, but only after she'd committed or been involved in more than fifty grisly assaults and twenty unspeakable murders. Too vicious and crafty for any routine means of incarceration, she was squirreled away to The SeptiGuarden, involuntarily enlisted in an experiment dreamed up by Cyrus, and resocialized to help usher in the next world.

After her trial release, Hernandez had gone forth to pursue honest work as a day laborer. She'd been unique in that most day laborers in the area were males. But she had the strength and stamina and smarts to hold her own. Her pursuit had filled Cyrus with a little pride and a lot of joy. She'd seemed eager to go on a straight path rather than running off to pursue the path of a street-corner performer, a public parks singer, or a freelance club musician.

All associates of The ID had artistic inclinations; that was one way to tell they were associated with The ID. That and the facts they manipulated electromagnetism, committed random and gratuitous acts of violence, and operated in pairs. The artistic inclinations of The Hummingbird—who'd used her voice as well as a handheld drill when she killed—had been successfully suppressed. Those inclinations wouldn't remanifest unless and until Cyrus and his business partners said so.

Cyrus had been good about keeping Hernandez under tight surveillance during her six months of freedom. Whether sleeping, showering, or strolling down the street, she'd never wandered out of the sight of a surveillance camera or an undercover agent. To all appearances, she'd shown no signs of slipping back into her former ways. She'd often turned the other cheek when harassed on job sites. And even when forced to throttle an aggressive pig, she'd never used excessive force. Another good sign the reformatory methods used in The SeptiGuarden had been successful.

And now this. Cyrus had intended to give Hernandez six months of time alone before recalling her and introducing her to her true moral purpose. Her time had almost been up. Just another week to go. But about twelve hours ago, she went off the grid, broke into The SeptiGuarden, and freed eight of the most fearsome Infinite Definite associates there were, none of whom were anywhere near being reformed.

How had it been possible? Of all the captured ID terrorists, he'd given her the most attention. She'd shown the most progress.

And he should've been alerted first and foremost if anything seemed wrong. "But—"

"But she was under strict monitoring at all times, right?" Edward said. "Not strict enough apparently. I'm not on the R&D side of things at the Trin, but maybe I should be. I was under the impression the smarts who were had a little bit of sense. Whatever jokester had the bright idea to stick the allegedly fail-safe monitoring device inside one of her false teeth must've been yukking it up during the whole operation. Ha-ha—she used to be a dentist, so let's stick it there! Yeah, she used to be a dentist, and then she got the Virus, and then she went bad—remember? She had no compunction about ripping the tooth out, getting it knocked out, whatever. She probably strung it on a necklace and gave it to one of the illegals she was palling around with. Might as well have given her an earring and code-named her Vincess van Go."

An idea…pliers, a screwdriver, a hammer, a fountain pen—if any of them had been in hand at the moment, Cyrus would've tried to rip, knock, or dig something out of Edward. He was thankful nothing happened to be nearby. He needed more information out of this one. More important, he knew nothing about the ways and means of Diviners.

Edward was one of those scarce Virus-carriers whose abilities went far beyond most others. Cyrus didn't know the how or why of it, and unlike with other Virus-carriers, he didn't know how to counter or defend against the best and worst of what they could do. All Cyrus knew was this select group could manipulate the properties of electromagnetism so well the results were often too wondrous for words. Edward mostly channeled his knowledge and abilities into his art. But from what Cyrus had seen in the presence of others, from what he'd experienced, he very well knew a Diviner could put a man or woman through a fate worse than a thousand deaths in a matter of seconds. They were the closest things to real-life sorcerers in existence. Going beyond mere light manipulators, it seemed as if they might've had tiny suns in the place of their hearts. Yes, they were essentially just another class of sick human beings, humans infected with a variant strain of the White Fire Virus. And although they could do so much more with electromagnetic radiation, their abilities were limited to a much tighter range, a very tight radius. But Cyrus happened to be standing well within Edward's power-circle. At the moment, the canvas was taking the brunt of Edward's abilities. Ever conscious, the big man kept his tone stern but civil. Cyrus wanted to exert his authority, but he didn't want a lightning bolt shoved up his ass.

"So there are nine, total, on the loose?" Cyrus asked. "How is that even possible? How is it possible that many could escape from one of the most secure underground facilities in the area?"

"Uh, you're the only one I've ever heard claim The SeptiGuarden was Fort Knox secure," Edward said. "Maybe if you hadn't been so wise as to rely almost exclusively on cameras and electronic monitoring devices, no matter how state-of-the-art and deeply embedded…Whatever conditions their minds may be in, they—*all* of us—are masters at evading detection, you know. Hernandez could've neutralized your silly little device even if she hadn't lost her tooth.

"Now, maybe if you'd squeezed a few of your resources, or borrowed some cash from your other partners, used it to hire a few nativist rednecks who'd be only too happy to fire at any freakish thing that moves in front of them, then you wouldn't be in this mess."

"It's *our* mess."

"In fact," Edward said, "you probably wouldn't even need a loan. You could easily find a dozen or so good ol' boys whose farms probably went under this year, can't find work, have plenty of their own guns and ammunition, and would take at least half their pay in cheap beer and whiskey."

The artist chuckled. Not once during his word flow had he broken his flow of work. Not once had he even so much as glanced at Cyrus. The big man wouldn't take much more of this. Something would have to give.

"I'm glad you find this all so amusing," he said.

"I'm glad you're glad," Edward said.

"I'm also amused."

"So we're both glad and amused."

"I'm amused by the fact you think this is more a setback for me than for the Trinfecta. This is a tremendous loss for your organization. You're going to feel this. This isn't just a case of one or two of them getting loose in an arena, in a controlled environment. The Infinite Definite are amassing, and some of the worst of the worst have escaped our bonds. This could end up being—"

"You know, standing there and spitting on my ear isn't going to bring them back," Edward said. "And the Trinfecta isn't my organization—I'm just a volunteer. Go find Ezekiel and scream at him. Better yet, go round up your HSA Peacemakers, form a posse, and hunt the escaped convicts down. Isn't that what the Peacemaker agents are for?"

Cyrus sighed, wondering why he'd even come here. He wasn't going to get any useful information out of this one. All Edward was doing was heightening his anxiety. He needed to speak to Ezra or Ezekiel or someone else who was closer to The SeptiGuarden, someone who saw the escapees face-to-face on a day-to-day basis. They would know exactly how far the escapees had come down the path of reformation (Cyrus suspected not very far at all, based on the reports he'd seen). Better yet, they'd have a good idea of where they might go and the best way to neutralize them so they could be brought back to where they belonged. Brought back unharmed, before they'd caused any harm. Turned in time, to be used for the positive purpose he'd intended.

Cyrus could've rounded up a posse of Agency Peacemakers, told them only scant details, only what they needed to know, and sent them forth to fix the problem. But Peacemakers were essentially soldiers, not social workers. Calling the attention of the Peacemakers or any other law enforcement authority to this situation was out of the question. And although the shadowy Trinfecta had a few individuals, including three or four Diviners, who could've been employed as shock troopers, he couldn't trust a one of them not to cause irreparable damage to the subjects. Cyrus was the only one fully invested in the fate of the nine and the fate of the others in The SeptiGuarden. It seemed everyone affiliated with the Trinfecta was too quick to let a failed experiment go the way of ashes and dust. For all their brilliance, they were short on patience. For all their abilities, so many of them lacked the proper vision to capture the big picture. For all their rhetoric, few seemed truly interested in the Big Promise.

Cyrus had to find and entrust someone with a more immediate promise. Not an eventual reclamation of the world from uncertainty and insecurity, but a sooner-than-later reclamation of the nine rogue experiments. Quickly, quietly, bloodlessly—if the problem couldn't be solved by hitting all three of those marks…

Worried and weary, his lips loosened, and a thought meant to be kept private slipped out.

"Those nine were my responsibility. All mine, and mine alone."

"There, you see?" Edward said. "We've made a breakthrough. You've admitted all this was your fault. You can go away now."

"Yes." Cyrus regained his composure, took three steps backward. "It was my fault to allow too much control, to put too much faith into a group of freaks, fruits, and dice-rollers to help reeducate sadistic adolescent sociopaths."

"A path you seem to know well," Edward said through a grin. "If what Carmilla has told me is accurate, you were the one responsible for enlisting two of the most notorious Definite loony tunes for the purpose of turning those bright-eyed adolescents into sociopaths in the first place."

"That—" Cyrus shut up when he heard others entering the studio. It was a few minutes past ten o'clock. The Factory had officially opened to visitors, and it didn't take long for those in the studio to gasp in fearful admiration of what they saw. It was time for Cyrus to cut his own visit short. He'd a day job to get back to anyway.

First he lowered his voice and finished what he had to say.

"Those kids were already on a dark path, and following it to the end." How dare Carmilla say otherwise. How dare she say anything about Project Can&Will at all, especially to Edward. It was a classified project, privy only to the clear eyes and full knowledge of three. "I did what I did to rescue those bad seeds. Save them, redeem them, redirect them to a path where they could save and inspire others. And whatever she told you, that sunburnt bitch Carmilla was a hand-in-hand partner from the plan's inception."

"Then go ask your sunny partner what happened to them," Edward said. "Maybe they went to go thank her for her part in their liberation from a dark future. Or maybe they went someplace dark and are waiting to thank you."

Edward cracked a smile, then broke into a chuckle. *Goddamned ass-clown.* If only Edward wasn't what he was. If only Cyrus had some device offering assured protection from those abilities. If only there weren't so many other bystanders around them. Cyrus didn't like the attention, and he certainly didn't need it. Worse, now that their eyes had seen the artist, working his heart out, the studio visitors would definitely want to meet him, speak with him, observe his technique, question him about meanings and symbolism, learn his philosophy.

Cyrus already knew his philosophy; Edward might as well have been one of The ID. A waste of a human being, he composed pictures of the realm that might very well consume the world and redesign the universe. And so what? The pictures weren't meant as a warning. They didn't conceal codes, instructions, or magick spells that might help avoid or beat back the catastrophe. No—they were just taunts. Thin-lipped taunts from a wastefully gifted bully.

But at least the meeting hadn't been a total waste. As Cyrus left the studio, he began to consider what little he knew about the concept of *magick* as practiced by certain Virus-carriers. It was based on the fundamental force of electromagnetism, of course, but also an esoteric form of numerology and wordplay. What did it mean that Hernandez changed her first name to "Holly"? What did it mean that she broke out *eight*, those eight in particular, who, according to Edward, now considered themselves "flowers" (whatever that meant)?

Cyrus had a lot to consider. Unfortunately, there were very few he could talk to, less than a handful of people with whom he could play pitch-and-catch with his airy speculations.

The SeptiGuarden had been too good of a secret, though clearly it hadn't been too secure. No one at the HSA or any other government agency knew anything about it. Nor could they. It was far too soon. It hadn't borne any fruit. One day—hopefully very soon—it would feed the HSA project he'd been planning. It would provide him with a supernaturally talented team, anti-apocalyptic horsemen who would wipe out The ID and keep the chaos of Xyn-Kroma at bay, keeping the world secure from Armageddon. But this breakout was the latest and worst of so many recent setbacks.

Nine of the would-be horsemen were now out running free, their minds not yet corrected.

He hated to do it. He'd almost rather cut off his own arms. But Cyrus felt he had little choice but to request an audience with the witch.

Chapter 5

Robert would've almost preferred being thrown into the sun to the experience of shopping with a clothes-hungry girl armed with a $1,500 debit card. But it was his duty. As was pretending to be a fellow *angel*.

When the two left The Burrow, Robert had joked that Ava, as an angel, shouldn't require more than a few robes and maybe a pair of sandals for her wardrobe. She didn't find the lame joke funny. True, it lacked everything a good joke should, but he'd sensed Ava was still disturbed by the corpse they'd found in the elevator, not to mention the flicks she'd been forced to watch afterward. And the news. The news of The ID and Marie-Lydia McGillis.

Though the chairman had been making some odd decisions lately, Robert at least saw the logic in this particular directive. After they left his office and Robert was given his watches, the chairman sent him a private message. Adam was sure the Virus-carriers were making their way toward DC because of Marie-Lydia *and* Ava. That's why the chairman wanted her as part of a unit, partnered with an agent that somehow knew her. Adam had a strong suspicion some of Ava's old running buddies—those seen on the films—would be making contact with her soon. Coming to the mall was really a scouting mission. Robert was to keep an eye out and contact The Burrow upon spotting one; then the IAI could hopefully subdue and interrogate, getting to the bottom of the mysterious convergence, keeping the HSA blind all the while.

The mall was a great gathering place of all sordid types: gangs, dealers, Trixster rings, and all other sorts of crafty no-goodniks. This was as good a place as any for one of Ava's old crew to make contact, after her trigger was pulled.

Her memory loss, unlike Adam's, wasn't an accident or the result of a Virus-related seizure. She'd been programmed, and not in such an obvious way as pasting painted contacts onto the backs of her eyelids. She was unconsciously waiting for some kind of trigger. Something verbal or visual. And everyone at the Institution was intent on finding out just what that trigger was, especially Vince. But all of them wanted to bring her along slowly. They didn't want to set off a bomb. They preferred something more along the lines of a jill-in-the-box.

Nothing had been set off by watching the videos. Not a surprise. Robert had initially suspected the trigger would be an in-person exposure to a carrier consumed by the Virus. But then she'd seen Agent Canton…and nothing. It might not have helped that they'd spoken around the subject in the chairman's office, per Adam's prior instructions. As far as Robert could tell, Ava had completely swallowed the half-truth that Canton had been poisoned. He'd been waiting for Ava to broach the subject of "angel poisoning" during their drive to the mall; so far, though, Ava seemed preoccupied with her own illusions.

"I don't know what to call him," she said while taking a left turn at nearly forty miles an hour. "I've never run across his type before, as far as I know."

"I think 'Mister Smith' would suffice." Robert loosened the grip on his knees. "Or 'Adam' when he's out of earshot." The muscles in his arms and legs were tight and sore from all the reflexive tensing, but at least they got a break at stop signs. There was, however, little relief for his scalp.

The deal had been for her to drive while he gave directions. Then, once at their destination, she could take her time finding garments and accessories while he stood around and nodded approval at whatever she chose. He just wished she hadn't retracted the hard top before pulling the Miata out of the garage. It was tough to control the effects caused by a cloudless sky's sun.

Just as chlorophyll absorbed mainly red-and-blue wavelengths of light, the parasites living in Virus-carriers' skin and blood cells fed on wavelengths of light within and near the visible range; it was only those sections of the electromagnetic spectrum that made the parasites' host lose control when exposed to too much. However, the parasites' waste product was rearranged light from the entire electromagnetic spectrum, including the sections felt but never seen. Robert could hear the short, curly hairs on his head crackling, while the skin underneath felt like jelly coming to a boil. He exercised a mild level of control over the reaction, but it was tough to concentrate while she drove like a Duke of Hazzard. He wasn't about to ask her to stop and put the top back on, so he gritted and bore it as he humored her, yet again.

"You know what I'm talking about." Ava merged into the adjacent lane without looking. "What's Adam's rank?"

He finally exhaled after seeing they hadn't hit anyone or run them off the road. "He's the founder and chairman of the Isaac-Abraham Inst—"

"I mean his angelic classification, Robert. His rank in the divine order."

He sighed.

"I've been thinking about it for weeks," she said. "But there's really no one there I can discuss these things with, except the one I know best."

"Me?" Robert laughed. "What about Sam?"

"Yeah…" Ava removed her right hand from the steering wheel and ran her fingers through her hair. "I like her and all…"

"But?"

"You know, she's really great—but she's…I don't know. A little too motherly."

While she wasn't exactly an army sergeant, Sam had never been the least bit motherly to Robert, or to any of the other Watcher agents with whom he'd seen her interact. Courteous, friendly, professional—you name it—but "motherly" wouldn't fit anywhere in his description of the middle-aged doctor.

"Besides," Ava said, "she's not one of us."

That was true, at least. Sam was one of the tiny handful of people associated with the IAI who didn't have the Virus. But clearly the doctor wouldn't have just handed that information to Ava. She'd probably responded to an inevitable question from the girl, saying, "I'm not an angel" or "I'm just a human," playing along just as Adam had instructed everyone at the IAI to do shortly after Ava had first stepped foot in The Burrow.

"I know of Archangels," Ava said. "Arkangels, Sprytes, and—since meeting you and Darryl—Watchers. But Adam—"

"What the hell does it matter? Do you have a book contract to compile an encyclopedia of angels or something?" He'd blurted it out, mildly joking but mostly frustrated at having to tolerate her delusions. As soon as he'd said it, though, he wondered if her inquisitiveness was part of her subliminal mission. Maybe her programmers wanted her to catalogue the varieties of so-called angels for some odd reason—or for some nefarious one.

Ava did refer to herself as an "Arkangel," after all; the pronunciation differed from "Archangel" only in its added emphasis on the first syllable. She swore that the Flood of XynKroma was coming and couldn't be stopped. Whatever she was doing, whatever she was building, the rank and order of angels figured prominently in the plan. Had to. Ava was just a bit too preoccupied with the subject.

"That suit of Adam's," she said. "I know it's mostly ceremonial."

"No—" Robert stopped himself before saying more. The suit was somewhat ostentatious but wholly a necessity. Adam couldn't even live, let alone function, without it. The seizures that so often accompanied the initial effects of the Virus had been so ramped up in their intensity, Adam had been severely crippled shortly after contracting the disease. Physically and mentally. It was a wonder he was able to operate at the high level he did.

Adam wasn't just sensitive to visible light. He was also sensitive to a much broader section of the spectrum, and probably most sensitive to the light that couldn't be seen by humans—microwaves, radio waves, and so on. Without the suit, he'd be overwhelmed, pushed through an unimaginable tortuous circuit before ending up looking far worse than Agent Canton. He'd be able to do nothing to save himself. As he'd often lamented, Adam fell within the class of Virus-carriers who were only manipulated by light and could do nothing at all to bend it to their will.

Ava fell within an even more select group of Virus-carriers, which undoubtedly made her such a good candidate for programming. She could manipulate electromagnetic radiation like nobody's business. However, she was no more affected by it than a noninfected woman or man. The sun falling on her bare skin probably felt refreshing rather than like an acid bath. An adherence to a conservative dress code, several sessions of therapy, and frequent intakes of pill cocktails were what enabled most Virus-carriers to venture outdoors with some degree of comfort. Ava had no need of any Virus medication and apparently no knowledge of it. She probably thought Robert was purposely making his hair perform crispy, crackling light tricks, showing off to amuse himself.

"Listen," he said. "When you first met Adam, he told you all about our little underground community. All that you needed to know. Can't you just leave it at that? There are the orphans—us Watchers. There are the advisory committee members. And there are the Board members."

"Board members," Ava said huffily. "Whom Adam said were called 'Matchmakers.' Right?" Robert didn't even nod. He wanted her off the subject already. "Watchers, Matchmakers—Adam's in a much different category from them."

"He's the chairman," Robert said. "Turn left at the second light."

She made the turn going thirty—barely missing a cyclist in the opposite lane—and said nothing as she drove straight for two blocks. Her foot got heavier on the gas as the light ahead turned yellow. When it switched to red, she stomped on the brakes and shouted, "Mechangel!"

His seat belt was secure, but Robert reflexively put both hands on the dashboard at the sudden stop. "What?"

"That's the word I've been trying to pull up," Ava said. "When I first saw Adam, the word *Metatron* came to mind, and after I got a night's rest, I woke up with *Mechangel*. I'm sure the Archangel who guided my inversion told me of their kind. That must be it."

"Metatron?" It sounded like the character name for a toy robot.

"One of the highest angels," Ava said. "Referenced and named in some nonbiblical writings. A fictional angel."

Nice to hear she made some distinctions between facts and fiction.

"And, I hope you remember, just because I have signed on as an agent, I'm not truly a Watcher. I'm an *Arkangel*."

"Fine," Robert said. "Turn right, Arkangel." One day he'd slip and call her Sick-angel. Maybe on purpose, just to see what happened next. Someone had to keep a firm grip on reality.

There were plenty of open spaces in the mall's parking garage. Before they got out of the car, Robert made sure anything that might entice a potential thief was hidden out of sight. He needn't have worried too much—the security system Zel Bernard had designed for the Miata was far superior to most cars—but one could never be too cautious.

He'd stopped by to say hello to the IAI's chief engineer before they'd left The Burrow. Zel was a close friend. He'd also been holding on to a few items Robert wanted close at hand the next time he found himself in an unexpected scuffle. Even though Adam had instructed they not leave The Burrow armed with anything but their watches and debit cards, Zel had presented Robert with a special belt buckle, just as a welcome-back gift. An especially handy fashion accessory he hoped he wouldn't have to use at Pentagon City's Fashion Centre.

"I sure hope there's enough on my card," Ava said as they went through the glass doors. "Because I need a lot. Stuff for my hair, comfortable undergarments, shoes, at least two jackets, one light, one dark…But sensible shoes, especially. We'll have to save that for last, because that'll take a while."

Robert started to wish his house arrest had lasted a day longer than hers, just so someone else could've dealt with all this. A task necessary but unpleasant, in an atmosphere where one might meet his end in any number of ways.

The interior's bright lights were tolerable thanks only to his medication and an extra dose of willpower, but there was nothing he could do to shut out the assault of noise. It was the Tower of Babel, leveled into a four-story mall featuring more languages and people than one of even Robert's mathematical talents could probably count, all imposing on him, annexing his personal space as he tried to move forward to the main escalator.

Reflexively, his throat constricted; his jaw tightened. The experience seemed to have the opposite effect on his partner.

"Look at that…Look at those girls…Do you see? In the name of the Word…Lord help them…Help us all…I mean *look*. They can't be much older than eleven, twelve, and they look like—"

"Their parents should've spent years one through ten putting better sense in their heads," Robert said. "You want to talk about a flood? The fabric of society is already unraveling."

Ava may've come from tiny-town Virginia, but Robert thought she couldn't have been that shocked at the prevailing culture of tweendom girls dressing like ladies of the desperate night: padded bras, four-inch heels, shorts too short for even a one-hundred-yard dasher, and shorn or too-tight T-shirts bearing misogynist slogans and come-ons that the proverbial drunken sailor might even be too embarrassed to repeat out loud: "First Taste Is Free"… "You Squeeze It, You Bought It"…"Stop Staring and Stake Your Claim," a slogan helpfully accompanied by an arrow pointing to where such "claim" should be staked. These were the more tasteful of what he read.

The offending words were everywhere, as were the offenders, half of them texting or yapping on smartphones, mostly oblivious to those who stared, pinched, snuck a kiss, or did otherwise as the words on the girls' chests or bottoms instructed. Ava didn't cease expressing her disgust, often to the very faces of the victim girls or victimizing teenage boys, all of whom ignored her.

The land of the free—in thought, speech, and spirit. Even though Robert agreed with everything Ava was saying, there wasn't much either of them could do. No one was getting hurt—at least not that he could see. And no one was screaming she was being abused—at least not that he could hear. But his low-ranking Watcher abilities were limited, as was the number of shameless girls. They were surely numerous, but they didn't make up the majority of this suffering, suffocating crowd.

Everywhere were kids, teens, and young twentysomethings walking around in sunglasses and earphones, loudly "singing" or reciting snippets of lyrics. The current cool thing for folks his age and younger was to make a public nuisance of themselves while acting blind, deaf, and dumb but certainly not silent. Robert had never acted his age, and he never would. As two singing, fist-pumping kids bumped into him without pausing to say "excuse me" or even "fuck you," Robert shook his head, trying to figure exactly when "cool" had been redefined.

The sunglasses were at least in theory justifiable—the Watcher agent wished his vision of most of what he was seeing was obscured, too, as the eye patch wasn't enough—in practice, though, the problem was obvious. And the shout-singing while wearing earphones?

Ironically, there was a concert or presentation of some sort happening down in the food court area, at the bottom center of the mall, playing loudly and proudly to a packed audience that couldn't give a crap about it, whatever it was. Even two levels up, walking near the overlooking edge, Robert could neither by sight nor sound quite make it out. He could only hear incoherent words—and feedback—amplified through a microphone. He briefly amused himself considering it was a riot squad captain futilely trying to restore order amid the typhoon of degenerates, hooligans, and no-goodniks.

It seemed as if everyone in the area who'd been expelled from school had made their way to the mall. More recession-proof than the others in the area, Pentagon City was practically the only shopping center that still had half of its stores open for business. But most of those milling about clearly didn't have the desire or probably even the cash to shop. Those who did—mostly adults—were either ensconced in the stores or trying not to drown in the sea of young fools.

One two-year-old boy was doing his best to tread water, standing chest-deep in a fountain, splashing, showing off his rebellion, screaming, daring his mom to do something about it. Robert thought she could at least pretend to pay attention, wave at him or something, *anything* rather than stay focused on her smartphone, her back turned all the while.

He tapped Ava's elbow as he almost involuntarily said, "No wonder so many kids get snatched."

Ava looked, then shrugged. "Maybe some of them are better off."

Robert thought of his own mother as he muttered, "I don't know about that."

"Out of the Garden"—Ava's voice took on a slight edge—"without the Burden."

"What?"

"The Burden. Of creating and taking care of those creations. Without the Burden, life has no purpose. Life is all about sacrificing oneself in order to create, following the example of the Lord."

Robert ignored what he considered two-parts mumbo jumbo as his focus shifted to the packs of young thugs, everywhere he turned, pushing and weaving themselves through the throng. They were of every flavor and color, but in his view, far too many fell within the darker ranges of the skin-color spectrum. He didn't realize he'd spoken aloud his desire about what he'd like to do if not under strict orders from Adam, not until a somewhat horrified Ava turned to him.

"They're just *kids*, Robert."

It took a moment for him to consider what he'd said, but he wasn't about to apologize or backtrack.

"No such thing as 'just kids' anymore, Arkangel. Not in *this* world. Look around you."

"Sounds like you've become a proponent of The Flood."

He almost missed the thin layer of sarcasm at the bottom of her comment. "I just don't like anyone misrepresenting my kind. Or *our* kind. These days good names turn bad like unrefrigerated milk, and there's no turning back."

Almost on cue, directly across the square, a swarm of at least a dozen teens poured out of a store; bundles of clothes, most still on their hangers, filled the boys' and girls' arms, while their bodies bombarded the crowd like bowling balls against Nerf tenpins, bumping, pushing, trampling any in their way before darting and dispersing in multiple directions, leaving the two security guards chasing them with several hard choices about which way to go.

Mob-robbing. Shoplifting taken to a bold extreme. It had been common in the DC area for several years, with the number of incidents multiplying since the downturn. Few authorities had any good workable ideas on how to curb the practice.

"Would you like to smack them into oblivion, too?" Ava said. "Or just pummel them mercilessly?"

"Those punks will get what's coming to them," he said. "A facility like this has enough cameras to cover every corner, nook, and cranny. You come to Pentagon City, you enter one of the Rings of Light. The proper authorities will have them before too long."

Ava shook her head and mumbled something about "clothing the naked in spirit." Whatever it was, it made as little sense as what he witnessed. A bedlam of consumerists and down-and-outs keeping up appearances of not giving a shit about the toilet-flushed economy. The gray-and-lively masses—ashes to coins, dollars to dust. This was the now culture: show up to show off and act out. Hell, Robert thought maybe that was the forever culture. Certainly been that way ever since he'd been alive. But today it just seemed grotesque.

It seemed the entire generation of kids and teens were like consumerist zombies, devouring the most despicable garbage marketed to them while their parents looked away, looked on dumbly, or happily aided and abetted by stuffing their pockets with money or just outright buying the shit for them.

Robert recognized he was on the verge of becoming a bit too cynical, but he'd seen too much abuse, too much neglect. He was beyond sick of what society let happen to children, disgusted with how parents and even other kids were allowed to treat the most vulnerable. Victims of bullies, abusers, and authoritarians acting on no real authority. Gutter culture was a symptom, not the problem. The problem went back generations. Robert had no clue how to solve it. He felt powerless and wanted to lash out. Ava beat him to it.

He saw it the same time she did. A child, no older than four, being strangled by a much older, much bigger adult. Could just as well have been the boy's parent as a stranger. Either way, the crowd milling around the victim and victimizer didn't give them a second glance. Most didn't look at all. Robert and Ava were both appalled, but she was quicker on the draw.

She reached back and, using the bright artificial light, fashioned a very visible but intangible arm's-length yellow-and-orange spear sharpened with infrared radiation. Heads turned.

Before Robert could shout, "No—wait!" Ava had already hopped up, perched on the railing, and flung the spear of light. That drew even more attention.

As the hit woman shrieked and fell backward, her hands on her forehead, too many eyes were either on Ava or her target. Robert's mind moved much quicker than his body; experience had taught him Ava was just getting started. No doubt she was planning to run down a slope of air before giving the adult a taste of her own medicine. Robert felt they'd more than enough attention already. All in full view of the Rings of Light.

Ava took her first step off the ledge. Robert grabbed her arm.

"That's enough." His voice was as firm as his grip, but Ava had shifted from peeved shopping girl to thoroughly pissed off Arkangel of the Lord. She wasn't herself—or maybe she was too much herself.

"A child needs saving." Her voice was that of a stage play's king character. Robert was more shocked by the tonal shift than by the kick in the chest she used to wrench free.

She was certainly quicker when it came to throwing and kicking, but Robert was a master grappler, one of the best wrestlers on his state-ranked high school team. If there was one thing he knew, it was how to never give up wrist or ankle control of an opponent. Ava had her instincts; he had his.

Rather than letting the hard kick put him on his back, Robert shifted his hips and grabbed the ankle that was still on the ledge.

"Pervert!"

It wasn't Ava talking. Not anymore. And it wasn't her twisting around to jackhammer her fist on the top his head. She was in an altered state. At long last, her programming had kicked in. Robert realized now—it wasn't one trigger that would set her off but a combination. The first part of the combination was seeing a kid being abused by an adult. But this thoroughly modern consumerist jungle wasn't the place to let her go wild.

As the fist made rapid-fire contact with his now crackling, sparkling scalp, Robert managed to grab her wrist and shift his weight, using hers against her as he pulled her to the ground and got on top of her.

Some surrounding them egged them on—"Fight!" "Fuck her!"—eager for whatever was coming next. Robert decided the unwelcome audience had had enough of an illicit show.

He bent the light around himself and Ava, making both invisible. This didn't quiet the crowd, but Robert didn't care. His first priority was to keep them away from cameras, and the slowly-but-surely-coming Pentagon City rent-a-cops.

"Goddammit, Arkangel, stop struggling." He spoke in a low enough voice for only her to hear, but forcefully enough for her to also know he meant business.

"Let go of me! A *child* is in danger!"

"*We're* the ones in danger," he said. "If you don't do what I say, both of us will be in jail—a real one—before sundown."

"I don't care!" Robert was slipping; Ava seemed to be getting stronger as she struggled to get her words out. "That child must be saved from this world, for the next one!"

He couldn't stay on top of her. She pushed him off, but he kept a steel grip on her wrists.

"Ava, please, *look…*" Although invisible, Robert knew she could see him just fine. He nodded toward the ledge. Ava turned and saw that mall security was tending to the severely burned woman and the child. Mall security was also looking in their direction.

"The kid will be fine," he said, "but we've got to move."

He knew words wouldn't have much of an effect on the Arkangel, so he put pressure on Ava's wrist, massaged the pulse, slowing the heart, partially paralyzing her. Another trick from his wrestling days.

It was like dragging a bag of cement, but Robert managed to steer Ava into the nearest entrance to Nordstrom before the first security guard arrived on the scene.

∞ ∞ ∞

It was a chore shopping for clothes in disguise. The face part was easy. Both Robert and Ava were experts at using light to alter their facial features. But altering the colors and features of their clothes was much harder, particularly for Ava, who every so often had to remove them.

But it worked. A feint to ward off the attentions of normal folks; any of her old allies who wanted to make contact wouldn't be fooled. They continued shopping mostly unnoticed and wholly unmolested for more than three hours. Ava seemed to return to her relatively normal self, so much so that their shopping trip ended not with a fight over angelic clothes but with an argument over shoes.

"I still need another pair."

"The ones you got will last you through another day," Robert said. "We need to get out of here before we blow it and end up locked up before tomorrow."

He thought he saw her stick her tongue out at him after he turned to grab the majority of the shopping bags and head for the nearest parking garage entrance.

They said nothing as they made their way to the Miata, both focused on keeping an eye out for security—or real cops—thinking the badges might make their move away from the crowds. Robert also kept his eye out for any of Ava's allies. He thought he saw a honey-shaded glimmer near a column, but it was nothing.

"Pop the trunk," Robert said.

"Just put those in the backseat."

"Why? With the top down, some of this stuff will be flying all over the place."

"I don't want them in the trunk. They'll spill out and get dirty. Darryl didn't keep it very clean back there. There's leaves and dirt everywhere."

"So what? You don't wear new clothes without washing them first anyway."

"I want them in the backseat. I'm putting the top up, since the wind seemed to bother you so much on the way here."

Stupid argument. But if the top was going up, he would shut up, even though the backseat was far too small to comfortably hold all the bags. She asked him to hold a couple in his lap. Again, no argument. Extra cushioning, he figured, for when the air bags inevitably deployed after she hit a lamppost.

"Forget heading back to The Burrow," Robert said as they approached the garage's exit. "Let's go to my place."

"Trying to get fresh?"

"No, I want to get freshened up." He also wanted to get behind the wheel of his Mustang. "You can come in and do the same if you want. Your choice."

"I'd rather stay and keep an eye on my stuff. Might even try some of it on again, give your neighbors a show. Introduce some scandal to your area." Ava's sense of humor was making a comeback. Feebly but surely. Despite their tussle, shopping seemed to have lifted her spirits. Then again, spending someone else's money to get what you wanted would put a pep in anyone's step. "Off to your gray-walled studio we go."

Ava looked neither way as she pulled out of the garage and sped out into the street. Robert began to give her directions.

"I know where we are," she said. "I remember the way."

Her memory was certainly strong in some areas. Programmed, just like a robot. *Avatron.*

Robert considered it more than a little odd that, since it had ended, Ava hadn't even alluded to their confrontation. He thanked fortune she didn't argue when he told her to keep her appearance altered, even if she didn't remember the reason. Perhaps her crusades were on auto-delete. Once completed, she simply forgot them.

She certainly hadn't forgotten how to drive like a maniac. Ava tore up the streets as if she were trying to tame a radical new NASCAR track. Dangerous drivers weren't scarce in the area, but Ava seemed intent on outshining everyone else on the road. Thank fortune she respected stop signals. Too bad the red lights were few and far between.

"My building isn't going to grow legs and run away," Robert said. "You could slow up a bit."

"Couldn't you just wash up at The Burrow?" she asked. Her foot got a little lighter on the gas pedal. Good to know talking helped.

"I could. But I need clothes that're more appropriate for the place we're going next." Ava took a sharp turn, making him bump his elbow against the door. He rubbed it as he said, "In my car."

"What kind of place?"

"Outdoor cabaret."

"Seriously?"

"There's a plaza in Reston where they sometimes have performances," Robert said. "Too small for a serious concert. It's usually just a singer or two and a couple of musicians. I'm meeting some friends out there. They tell me there's a singer that I need to see."

While Ava had been doing whatever in one of the many dressing rooms into which she'd carried piles of garments, Robert had made his maiden call on his new cell. He'd asked an old friend if they could meet as soon as possible.

Two weeks back, right before the infamous home invasion, Robert had asked his two best friends to handle a little private research project. At the time, his laptop was recovering from injuries caused by being thrown across a room and stomped on. Even if he'd had a working laptop, he probably still would've asked for their help. He was good at computer research, but Kurtis and Anika were experts. If there was anything at all to be found out via computer about the shady MC³ Productions and its stars, Kurtis and Anika would find it.

"Meeting friends to see a singer," she said. "Is this really the best use of our time based on what Adam told us?"

"Trust me," he said. "We're not going to a beach party. This could be important."

"Well, I'd like to meet your friends anyway." Ava put on a curious smile. "As part of my training, I think it'd be most helpful to know as many of my partner's friends as possible. Maybe make them my friends, too."

"I'd love for you to meet them," he said. "Just so long as you promise to let me meet your friends one day."

"When I remember who they are," she said, "I'll let you know."

"Well, I've already met Marie-Lydia McGillis. I spoke to her—briefly—when I found her. Strange girl." He almost didn't want to go there. He didn't want to shove her, but it was past time he pushed Ava into spilling the beans on why the redhead was so dear to her. He wanted to solve the mystery of their relationship.

"Yeah," Ava said as she checked the mirrors and switched lanes. "Stranger angel. But she was a friend. A very good friend."

"Must've been, after all you've gone through so far to find her. After all you went through to take her down at your school."

"Yeah."

The pep and vigor had gone out of Ava's voice. He wasn't a master of deciphering women's emotions, but Robert could tell his steering of the conversation hadn't angered her. After all, the redhead was Ava's favorite topic of discussion. Her and XynK-roma. No, it was something else affecting Ava's mood. It was like the rusted gears in her mind were turning, trying to make a go of it, trying to make Avatron's memory machinery work.

"Marie-Lydia and I go way back." Her voice now had a dreamy quality; it conjured new images in his mind.

"So you were there to witness her first kiss or something?"

A chilled silence. Robert considered maybe his words had pushed her from pensive to pissed. But after driving a few more miles, she responded, "Something like that." Then more silence.

He'd tried. Now he'd just let her mental machinery do whatever it was trying to.

She turned on the car radio. For some reason, Darryl had had it tuned to a station playing big band numbers. Ava hit the Shuffle button and stopped it on a station playing Christian rock. After a minute, Robert began to long for the swing music.

Then Ava's lips moved. Robert concentrated on her voice. It was just above a whisper. Was music helping her recover memories? It took a moment, but he realized Ava wasn't telling herself stories about better days with Marie-Lydia. She was only singing along with the song's three female vocalists.

He'd sampled Christian rock before, following the enthusiastic endorsement of someone he'd never trust again. He found much of it to be a pale imitation of real rock music, which he also didn't much care for—but at least the real stuff had something, a spirit, that Christian rock seemed to be lacking. Maybe it was the devil's spirit. Sex, drugs, and the devil's soul.

He cracked a smile.

"Are you laughing at me?" Ava said.

"No, at—" He stopped, realizing it'd be best to keep the joke to himself. "I was just thinking how fictions energize other fictions." Ava's days as a fervent evangelical had clearly made her more susceptible to believing she was an angel rather than a Born-Again virgin who'd contracted an STD. "Art feeding art, as my dad used to say."

"Was he an artist?"

"No. Just a huge jazz fan."

"Oh. So you want me to change the station."

He didn't think it a question, so he didn't answer. All she'd probably heard was an orphan mentioning something his dad had loved. She probably thought she could read his mind. She reached for the tuning button, probably all set to find a jazz station. Robert caught her hand.

"No," he said, "this is your time. This car, your space. Listen to whatever you want. Besides, we'll be getting our fill of jazz soon enough."

Chapter 6

Ava didn't want to get out of the car.

The plaza Robert had spoken of was near a lake. Lake Anne.

Something about that name pricked at the back of her neck.

"C'mon." Robert opened the passenger's side door. "The show isn't going to spill out into the parking lot."

She took his hand and let him help her stand. She almost didn't want to let go. But a subtle tug from Robert made it clear he didn't want them to appear as boyfriend and girlfriend as they approached the plaza's entrance.

Lake Anne Plaza.

The water was the first thing she saw. Directly opposite, a short sprint away. It was in the shape of a rectangle, lined on either side with buildings, no more than three stories high on the left, four times that height on the right. The structures enabled the setting sun's rays to hit the little geometrical finger of water at strange angles, making her see bronze serpents, diving out and in, out and in.

She knew it was just a trick of the mind, her subconscious helping to quench any desire she might've had to adjust her divine vision and take in the full scope of the man-made lake's unnatural body. Forget it. Let the joyriders in their pontoon boats and those sitting on the benches at the water's edge try their eyes at it.

She wished the evening sun would just hurry up and set already, maybe making it easier for her to avoid unpleasant sights.

Her wish was in part granted as Robert guided her to the left, toward a grouping of twenty-five or so square and round tables, all set up outside a restaurant called Tavern on the Lake. There were only a few dozen patrons, eating and talking while watching the performers who'd set up between them and water: a young teenage singer and her three significantly older backup musicians. It wasn't the type of performance Ava had been expecting.

The singer wasn't singing, but she sure was running off at the mouth. She and an agitated band member spoke at and over each other a mile a second in some old-world foreign language while another band member looked on, bewildered at the spectacle, and the third just looked bored.

Robert waved at a young couple seated near the middle row. They waved back with a lot more enthusiasm.

"The hell've you been, man?" the male in the couple said when they reached the table. "The shit's almost over!"

Robert cleared his throat and made a side nod toward his partner.

"Kurtis, Anika, this is Ava Darden."

And they weren't angels, she could tell. The foul language wasn't the only tip-off. They seemed friendly, though. Especially Anika. She'd hopped up from her seat and thrust out her hand the moment Robert had spoken her name.

She was about a foot shorter than Ava but had a much fuller figure. Her sepia skin tone was almost a perfect match for Robert's. Anika smiled broadly and said how great it was to finally meet her face-to-face. Ava would have to remember to ask just what she meant by "finally."

Kurtis took his time getting up from his seat, but his smile was sincere. An African American whose small afro was so jet-black and curly it seemed to have been professionally styled. Pretty different from the too-short-to-comb, rust-color-flecked mess on Robert's head.

Ava shook hands firmly, confidently. A good handshake enabled an angel to tell so much about another. Fingertips bending electromagnetism, so close to an enemy's or friend's pulse…She maybe squeezed a bit too hard. Kurtis shook his hand by the side of his hip afterward, looking as if he was trying to get the blood flowing again.

"Sorry," Ava said as she sat down. She knew enough to decide Kurtis and his companion were no threats to her. It was sad to think it, but out of her three tablemates, the one she'd known longest was the one she was least sure about.

Robert may've been an angel, but he was clearly a reluctant one. Ava had wondered what his story was, had tried getting some information out of both Zel and Sam. So far she'd been unsuccessful. Maybe his good friends could offer some insight.

"So what's up?" Robert said. "Why did we have to meet here of all places?"

"For you, chief," Kurtis said. "We haven't seen you in two weeks and wanted to give you a nice-to-see-ya present."

"So you're paying for food and drinks, huh?" Robert said. "Live it up, Ava. We got two rich college students here. Be sure to order the crab cakes *and* the lobster cakes."

Ava smiled, intending to do no such thing. Seafood made her nauseous.

"Uh, no, that's not what I meant." Kurtis pointed at the singer. "She's the gift."

"Or rather," Anika said, "she *has* the gift."

The singer had apparently settled her tiff with her band; they'd started another number. Or maybe they were just tuning up.

It sounded as if they were trying to play something vaguely medieval, like something one would hear at one of the region's better renaissance fairs. But the music sounded too discordant, as if one of the musicians couldn't get his instrument to work properly. Made sense. Ava doubted electric guitars were suited for whatever they were trying to play. What didn't make sense was why even the flute player's instrument sounded so off.

Robert looked like he'd swallowed a tack.

"We thought you'd like this," Anika said to him. "It's Reina."

"It's painful," he said. "I've never heard of her, and I wish I wasn't hearing this."

"She's Sin Limite's fourteen-year-old niece," Kurtis said.

"So?"

"You haven't stopped loving *her* now, have you?"

"Funny," Robert said. "But love's got nothing to do with it. I don't like professional kid singers. The concept just bugs me."

"Sin Limite is Rob's favorite singer." Anika touched Ava's hand as she spoke to her. "She's pretty old."

"First of all," Robert said, "she's only thirty-six."

"Middle-aged."

"*Second* of all, experience comes with age. The woman is a brilliant singer."

"How so?" Ava asked.

"She has an astounding range. Within just a single song, one moment she'll sound like Sarah Vaughan, the next like Sarah Brightman. She can go from Ana Gabriel to Anne Murray to Kate Bush to Karen Carpenter and make it all sound perfect."

Ava had only heard of two of those singers, but she was taken by the fact that, when talking about them, Robert seemed livelier than she'd ever seen him. Looked like the one-eyed Watcher was capable of some happiness after all. He wasn't always in a sour, dull, sarcastic, or suspicious mood.

"Sin Limite can match any singer around, past or present."

"In other words," Anika said with a smile, "she's astounding at mimicry."

"Yeah," Robert said. "I guess that's a way to put it."

"Just like a crow," Anika said. "An old crow."

"That's not—"

Kurtis shushed them both as Reina lifted her cordless mic, finally gearing up to sing after two full minutes of quirky tunings. "Just listen to her. And watch."

> "Elementary learning experience:
> My sense of Presence, from where did it come?
> In the Spirit, mystifying sensations,
> presentations of God's Nature to one."

Ava had never heard of Reina, either, but after the first couple of lines she knew she liked what she heard. The girl had such an unusual voice. Maybe it was the old-world accent; maybe it was her age; or maybe it was something *inholy*.

As she sang on, Reina left her band and approached the drinkers and diners, weaving among the tables, touching a shoulder here, an empty glass or dirty utensil there, winking and smiling.

> "Your stature is irrelevant, audience—"

She carried something besides the mic as she moved: an increasingly visible aura. Pinkish green. The soy-milk-tinted skin on her arms, her calves, her neck—everything that was bare—shifted its pigmentation. Ava clearly saw its texture wasn't like most humans.

> "Love blew a kiss to one sun,
> the reaction spun—"

She danced back toward her band, whirling like a drowsy dervish, in veils of convoluted colors. Then every nonliving thing she'd touched exploded.

> "moist air, manifold halos, spiraling
> splendor of indigo, green, red bands…"

The empty glasses burst into miniature models of conical huts. Utensils writhed and bent into life as dancing silver stick figures. Fist-size peacocks appeared, perched, and flexed their plumage on the shoulders of the shocked and delighted—Reina had apparently had the good fortune not to touch anyone with a weak heart.

The increasing number of onlookers clapped and pointed at every new fantastical discovery while Reina danced and played with her ephemeral veils. The only table not cheering the spectacle was Ava's. She was too astonished to react to the singing and dancing angel who was manipulating a lot more than light. She also heard ugly noises from her tablemates, mostly from Robert.

The singer continued to sing. The music's intensity increased. And then came more changes.

> "Blue calm in my eye belies the process of maturation,
>   accelerated:
> Going deeper within, centering, to find Truth, the pressure
>   level is lowered low,
> pushing outward; your eyes are opened to a suffering society…"

Her clothes changed as her body became taller, fuller, and older.

> "But, once Love's found within, you release—"

And out of her mouth flowed visible musical notes, a visual accompaniment to her voice, black notes that flew and almost instantaneously metamorphosed into…Peppered moths? Varicolored fairies?

> "A bountiful array of yellow, violet spray:
> Frozen Love melted by holy fire.
> Visual lyrics dousing all surrounding,
> arousing passions for submission to the Beautiful."

The winged things were far more foreign to this world than any fairy would've been. They were spyders. Seven-legged insects with wings featuring multihued patterns and hieroglyphic markings and abdomens that flashed like slow-motion strobes. They numbered in the hundreds, flittering and fluttering among all the members of the audience, most of whom would probably be freaked out by flying spiders under normal circumstances. But these insectlike creatures from another dimension were somehow palatable. Perhaps it was their exotic nature. Maybe it was the music. Ava was even surprised that, when one of them landed on her nose, she wasn't as repulsed as she'd been when she'd first encountered the creatures in Xyn. Maybe it was because she was now more intrigued than anything. A spyder's stinging-but-pleasurable contact with her skin allowed her to confirm it wasn't a trick of light. It was as real as the glasses on her face.

Robert cursed and batted at the spyders flying too close as Kurtis tried to calm him down. Anika clapped along with the music, contributing her own sounds of delight. Ava let the spyder on her nose crawl onto her finger. As its dewdrop body moved, it released an electrically charged filament of its unique silk that seemed in appearance and substance equal parts honey, sunlight, and the thinnest tinsel—a combination more festive than frightening.

Reina's song was reaching its finale, signaled not only by the shift in music but by the shimmering-in appearance of a structure on the lake behind the performers. The structure took on greater shape and definition as Reina sang louder, over and through the gasps, oohs, and ahhs of the audience.

> "Usher in this new age of reason:
> A philosopher-poet will set the Multiverse
> with diverse seasons, rationing more than four—"

It was a pseudo-Egyptian temple, small but magnificent in its detail, dilapidated but stunning to observe. Floating atop the water, it took up an area no more than fifteen square feet. Like the spyders, this was no mere illusion; two pontoon boats actually bumped into it. There'd been a wide tear in the fabric of thin air.

> "The supreme charity is Love's clarity."

After this last lyric, the music and singing stopped. The peacocks and spyders took flight en masse toward the temple and disappeared inside its crumbling walls. The dancing utensils and blossomed glasses resumed their former shapes on the tables. And the temple itself shimmered back out of view.

The band took a bow, not toward the audience but toward the singer, who now appeared forty years old and was dressed like a cross between a fairy-tale princess and someone's idea of a New Age priestess.

Ava didn't clap. Neither did the men at her table. They were the only three.

Against the backdrop of a sadly mundane sunset, the four performers turned together to take a bow toward the audience. They said a few thank-yous and then huddled together, arms over shoulders, appearing as if they were sharing a secret or plotting their next move. Ava wondered just what they could possibly do for an encore.

The huddled four swayed. Were they singing to themselves, dancing to their own private song? If so, it must've been some song. The four swayed faster, in unison, as their clothes, their skin, their entire bodies bleached themselves in pieces and patches. They were fading out—not disappearing, but appearing more as bodies of thick steam. Unable to maintain the coherent shapes for long, the visible vapors wafted in every direction, thinning out into nothing until every trace of the performers was gone, everything except their instruments. Ava guessed they were rentals.

It was an odd way to end a performance, especially a well-received one, but Ava understood. The magick makers had come to put on one heck of a show, not to be mobbed by folks asking about their angelic secrets.

"Their big finish," Kurtis said. "Song called 'New Age of Reason.' That's what I wanted you to see. They're working on dramatizing yet another book of poetry written by the guy who wrote *Death's Heart.*"

Robert didn't say anything. He stared blankly at the abandoned instruments. Ava stared at him. He shook his head slowly as he took an orange plastic bottle out of his jacket's inner breast pocket and reached for Kurtis's untouched glass of water. Robert wet his tongue with a sip then meted out three multicolored capsules in his hand. He paused but didn't even look at the pills before popping them and swallowing them all in two gulps. They were undoubtedly a sedative of some sort. Ava had a feeling what he was thinking.

Or maybe he had a feeling what she was thinking. As if reacting to a telekinetic prompt, his brow furrowed as he turned his eye toward her.

"These folks think they just saw one hell of a show. Some David Blaine bullshit." He looked toward the lake, as if searching for any trace of the performers. "But we know what it really was, don't we?"

"Xyn," Ava said. "That girl—woman—brought XynKroma here. Willfully."

"Yeah," Robert said. "She not only caused a dimensional rift. She manipulated everything that came through."

"We figured," Kurtis said. "Which is why we'd thought this would be the perfect spot to tell you what we found out about—uh, well, that research project you asked us to help with. *Both* of them."

"Now?" Robert glanced at Ava, a little too quickly.

"Yes," Kurtis said. "Because they have a connection."

"MC³ Productions is more than just some shady outfit that puts out lurid videos of magickal beings beating the crap out of each other," Anika said. "If you dig deep enough, you can find some really interesting things online. Some really enlightening discussion forums. Some are all about angels and the Flood."

MC³ again. Ava had been thinking plenty about them since finding out she was an unwilling star of some of their shows. She'd also been thinking about why Robert had kept his knowledge of them a secret until today. And the nervous look he'd just given her…He was still hiding something. His friends were more direct, so she directed her question to them.

"You two have seen videos of me on the net, right? Specifically videos of me fighting a redheaded girl inside a high school?"

Kurtis raised an eyebrow and turned to Robert as Anika said, "Of course."

"MC³." Sally Ellin Chambers. "Were they behind that?"

"We can't say. It doesn't have their imprint. And we couldn't find any sign of them distributing it."

"Yeah," Robert said, "that one's a stretch."

"Then who—*how* was it possibly recorded?" Ava said.

"The HSA installed a security and surveillance system in your school," Robert said. "Shortly before the incident. Everyone at the Institution figured someone ripped off the HSA, got hold of the footage, and distributed it."

"Some security system," Ava said. "I remember the doors were locked. No one could get in or out. Everyone was trapped in the building."

"So we heard."

"What did the HSA have to say about it?" Ava asked.

"Malfunction. They said since they were only given limited time—a week—to set the system up, there were bound to be problems."

"Well, didn't they test it on other schools first? Weren't they aware of the kinks?"

"No," Robert said. "Yours was the first school."

"I wonder why?"

"So did we. Adam looked into it but didn't get anywhere."

"We looked into it, too," Anika said, "and got just as far."

"We'd never had any security problems at our school before," Ava said. "The first and only major one was that one time."

"Maybe someone at the HSA is psychic," Kurtis said.

"Or psychotic," Ava said. This went beyond Sally Ellin, and beyond anyone she'd known in Spencer. "A major assault on the school, and the brand-spanking-new security system works in its favor. And all of it ends up on the Internet. It's too coincidental." Dark angels had to have played a part.

"I don't believe in coincidence," Robert said. "Any more than I believe in wishing with coins."

"Me, neither," Ava said. Somehow, someway, she'd have to arrange to have a little one-on-one talk with the Institution's Agency contacts.

"It's not too far from the realm of possibility to think MC³ was involved in that, or maybe another competing outfit," Kurtis said. "We do know MC³ isn't just about making a profit from their films, though that's clearly a short-term goal. They're more about studying angels. Their behavior."

"Why?" Ava asked.

"You ever heard the term *Hollywood magic*?" Anika asked.

After her conversion to evangelical Christianity in middle school, Ava had gone out of her way to avoid anything having to do with Hollywood. Little attention paid to mainstream movies and certainly none paid to any news or gossip having to do with the morally bankrupt folks associated with them. She'd been more or less successful. She'd heard of the term, but it had never held any meaning for her.

"Teaching the world new ways to dream," Anika said. "That's one definition."

"MC³ is all about that."

"And then some."

"We couldn't find any names or faces behind the veils," Kurtis said to Robert. "But we did manage to discover they sponsor a lot of different types of artists. Your idol Sin Limite's multigenre troupe Phantasie's rEVEnge, Reina and her crew, the band Kill All the Poets, the Garbage Lovers, and quite a few others."

"And it's not just harmless entertainment, either. Their most recent films feature new stars. The Artzmen."

"Great," Robert said, "another cult of angels." He looked at Ava. "Another entry for your encyclopedia."

She furrowed her brow at him as Kurtis said, "Their leader is some angel calling himself Saint Valentinus. Near as we can tell, they're operating out of West Virginia."

"The scenario of most of the half-hour episodes is pretty basic," Anika said. "Child molesters are pranked, tricked, and lured to some place where they think they're going to hook up with some unsupervised children. They meet the children, alone, and are allowed to go just far enough to show they really are molesters. One or more Artzmen ambush them before things go too far, and, after the children are hurried away from the scene, the Artzmen proceed to gouge out the eyes and rip the skin off the molesters, as artfully and magick skillfully as possible. It's like a candid-camera show segueing into child porn before abruptly switching into sci-fi torture porn. All of it's disgustingly popular."

"I don't doubt it," Robert said.

"There's no video of it," Anika said, "but there're blogs saying some towns have literally been turned into ghost towns."

"We couldn't figure the connection between MC^3 and all of its film subjects," Kurtis said, "but the pieces are art, angels, and magick. Real magick."

"Yeah," Robert said. "Like what we all just saw. Dirty Light Magick, or some other kind."

"I'm going with some other kind," Anika said. "Did you notice how complex Reina's lyrics were? And her strange singing style?"

"And her strange accent," Ava said.

"According to Genesis, in the beginning, there was water and wordplay," Anika said as Ava nodded. "And in the end, the game will be the same. Music, voice, and poetry can combine to affect one's thoughts and emotions. A low form of magick. But ramped up as Reina had done, it becomes a greater form."

"They're right, Robert," Ava said. "There is a connection between art, magick, and the Flood. And us."

"Yeah…" Robert stared at his empty glass. "And our cute little artist used her song to break open a piece of space and time. For no other reason than she fancies herself an artist who doesn't act on reason. She can do it, so she does it."

Fallen angel territory, Ava thought. *Infinite Definite territory.*

"We don't know enough about the subject," Anika said. "There's nothing useful to you that we could find through our usual channels. Not in two weeks."

"That's why Anika and I both wanted to tell you this to your face, Rob, after you saw Reina's performance. You really need to go to XynKroma. As soon as possible." Ava perked up. "The answers you want, the answers we couldn't find, can be found there."

"We're sure of it," Anika said.

Ava was liking these two more and more. She'd remember them, try to keep them safe through the Flood.

Robert continued to stare at the glass, addressing it with several four-letter words. Ava recognized he belonged to a lower order of angels, but she didn't think a clean vocabulary should be so hard for him to maintain.

"Fine," he said eventually. "I'm out of choices. We all are." He scooted his chair back and stood up. "Let's go, Arkangel."

"Aren't you two going to eat anything?" Kurtis said.

"No time," Robert said. "We've put this off long enough. As you said, we need to take the next step ASAP."

Ava had been trying to get him to accompany her to the deepest dimension of Reality, emphasizing its importance and necessity, since the day they'd met. But it had taken a song-and-dance number to sway him. *Delightful.*

"It was nice meeting you two," she said as she stood up.

"Likewise," Anika said. "We hope we'll see you again."

It sounded innocent enough, a common parting phrase anyone would utter after a first meeting. But after she sat in the Mustang, Anika's words echoed in Ava's thoughts more like a warning. *Hope.*

"Where are we going?"

"The Burrow." Robert started the engine. "Vince works late."

"Uh-uh. No way. I'm not going anywhere near him."

"Don't be goofy. He supervises all Watcher trips to XynK-roma. He makes sure it's done safely. That we come out *sane.*"

"I said *no.*"

"First you wanted to go more than anything—now you have conditions?" Robert clicked his tongue. "Charming…"

She understood his frustration, but there was no way he'd understand how she felt about creepy, suspicious Vince. She wished Sam doubled as the Institution's psychological mapmaker, but there was only Vince.

It was her turn to stare at glass while muttering. She only saw the windshield, nothing on the other side, as she came to realize Robert was right. They were out of choices.

"Let's go back to your place," she said.

Chapter 7

Cyrus parked on the cul-de-sac's curb, at a safe distance away from the circle at the end.

The air wasn't chilly, but he shivered when he got out of the van. He always shivered when he approached one of the witch's houses. It never had anything to do with the weather.

Cyrus rarely made after-hour visits to any of her properties, but his business was urgent. He hadn't called ahead. He—or a friend, rather—had figured she'd be there. It was one of many properties she held in the mid-Atlantic region, but based on the date, the day of the week, the weather forecast, and the order of the solar system's planets, a numerological calculation had been used to narrow down just where she'd be this evening. Of course, Carmilla was the superstitious type.

Also a tad too predictable. It was the one of the witch's qualities that unnerved him the most. He believed and often cautioned she'd be wise to choose a much more secluded location than this one on Reston's Lake Anne. It was too risky, even for just an occasional home.

It wasn't ostentatious. Just a regular medium-size house for a middle-class family. In contrast to the condos and other tightly packed dwellings dotting the shores of the lake, this was one of the few truly singular houses. But it lacked what Cyrus would consider a comfortable zone of privacy.

Many of Carmilla's Northern Virginia houses were ensconced in neighborhoods brimming with white collars and soccer moms. A safe, comfortable environment for some perhaps, but Cyrus believed such neighborhoods were also rife with snoops and busybodies. Those were usually just the types of folks HSA officials loved most, so long as they kept their fat noses out of the Agency officials' business, not to mention that of their private business partners.

He'd no idea why Carmilla had purchased the Lake Anne property. The dwellings around Reston's Lake Thoreau were much nicer; the houses in the Hunter Mill Estates section were a better personality fit; and, best of all, there were all those stately manors in the Wyndham Hills section of town—nothing but millionaires allowed. Carmilla could've bought the whole neighborhood, but she'd need a rock-hard reason to do so. Nothing she did was just for show.

Cyrus just hoped she was keeping the redheaded girl someplace remote. Far, far away from wherever Stavan Darden might go.

He pounded on the front door and rang the bell. After two more rounds, he heard footsteps on the other side. Whoever it was, she was barefoot. It just had to be a "she"—and *she* wouldn't be so uncouth as to pad around this house wearing socks. Cyrus was very familiar with the type of women who hung around the witch. He wasn't familiar with the one who opened the door and glared at him.

Three-hundred-dollar hairstyle, exotically patterned tunic, denim leggings, and bare feet. The denim leggings were the only mild surprise. The witch's sentinels didn't lack for high fashion sense, or other extra senses.

The six-foot-five brunette didn't say anything. It was almost as if she wanted him to take in the full spectacle of her before she bothered or he dared.

Cyrus held up his HSA badge and identification. He'd no hope of intimidating her. He only wanted her to see the name before he asked, "Where's Carmilla?"

The amazon curled the fingers of her free hand. Cyrus heard the bones cracking as the fist tightened and the faint hum of electric static as the fingers slowly uncurled.

She wasn't intimidated. But neither was he. He wasn't dumb enough to come to this house unarmed. He could have his hand on the Sig Saur P229 pistol in half a second. He could take her out with it in less than two.

But it would be bad form to shoot a business partner's bodyguard on her very own doorstep.

"Stand down, Wendy."

Carmilla spoke to her acolyte from the top of the stairs.

"I'll take care of that one. Go finish what you were doing."

Wendy left the door open and retreated into the foyer. She turned toward the staircase, made an exceedingly formal bow toward Carmilla, then padded out of the large foyer into an adjoining room.

Cyrus shut the door behind him and gazed at the young woman making her way down the stairs. Bare feet were not her style. She wore glittering slippers and walked as if she were revealing a new and expensive evening gown to a rapt audience. Cyrus wasn't as enamored of her as most others might've been, but he did take immense interest in certain aspects of her appearance. As she moved with deliberation, his eyes moved from her jeweled ankle bracelets to the jewels on her ringed fingers, those lining her necklace, and those adorning the many loops in her multiply-pierced ears. Cyrus swore she slept in all those stones, maybe even bathed with them, and would definitely get one of her girls to break the fingers of anyone who tried to touch any one of them.

She was certainly something to behold. But one had to keep in mind—repeat it as a mantra if necessary—that nothing was ever just for show. *Beware of her snares.*

According to one of his most trusted informants, Carmilla had secretly referred to herself as "the girl of many charms" when she was passing through the awkward stage of adolescence. Whether a muttered joke or a whispered esteem booster for a girl shunned by many potential friends, the phrase had become a far more accurate description than it possibly could've been at the time. "The girl of the curious complexion" would've been just as good a designation. Cyrus had always figured her odd skin tone to be the result of an unwise combination of off-the-market pills and too many free sun rays; it certainly hadn't been inherited from her pasty parents.

"At the very least," he said as Carmilla's first slipper touched the foyer's floor, "your housewench could've offered to take my hat."

"You were not invited here." Her expression was placid as she sauntered toward him.

"How kind of you to say"—Cyrus hung his porkpie on the coatrack—"about the house my labor built. I do believe I have a standing invitation."

"Then I won't invite you to sit down." She turned a shoulder to him and headed for the foyer's right exit. "In the house my money paid for."

Her money. Sure. Cyrus followed her, taking in all that the money had bought. Only the crystal candy dishes made him smile. Overfull with speckled jellybeans that were sweeter than honey, stronger than LSD. As if she needed drugs to make anyone sick in her presence.

Carmilla had made a deal with her parents during her senior year in high school, just a little under two years ago: if she could somehow earn a million dollars before graduation, then she wouldn't have to go to college. She'd been just a few months shy of being old enough to legally play the Virginia lottery, and she'd steadfastly refused to get a job. Nevertheless—miracle of miracles—she'd managed to earn a cool million and a half before donning her cap and gown. Her parents had asked few questions and never received the true answer of how she'd won most of her money by gambling on highly illegal "animal" fights. She'd been honest enough with them, telling them just what they needed to hear. She'd exercised the same level of honesty with the government, paying the right amount of taxes but being less than forthright about the true source of the money. She somehow knew the perfect words to put on the IRS forms in order to keep the red flags flying low.

It wasn't long after she'd turned eighteen and moved away from home that Carmilla began to diversify into many other games of chance. Always careful enough to keep a low profile, she'd had across-the-board success; the animal fights, however, remained her true bread and butter. Her parents pretty much left her to her own devices, paying her little attention save for a brief phone call or text message on certain holidays. They were good people, just very busy. Pharmaceutical researchers. Old friends of his. Their only child, however, seemed to be born with her own unique traits, inherited from another world.

Much of Carmilla's earnings were invested in real estate, gems, and precious metals. Cyrus hadn't flexed a muscle to build or furnish a single one of her lavishly decorated houses, but he had played a significant part in helping the nineteen-year-old accumulate much of her wealth. He'd made sure no one looked too closely into how such a young girl had gotten so rich so fast. And he'd made doubly sure the settings and provisions for the Trinfecta-sponsored animal fights remained a deep, black secret. *Her* money, indeed.

"Uncle Sam has been generous. Uncle Cyrus even more so." He followed her into the kitchen. "But there is that invisible hand, my dear. This recession may just slap—"

"What do you want here, Cyrus? I'm busy." Carmilla opened the wine cooler next to the refrigerator and ran her index finger across the bottles.

"Busy doing what?" he asked. "Planning to get drunk?"

She selected a bottle and studied the label. "Just for that, maybe I won't offer you a glass."

"I don't want any." He didn't need anything softening his senses.

"Tea, then? Coffee? Candy? I certainly wouldn't want you to have me spirited away and locked up for being inhospitable. Not in the house your crooked labor built."

"Watch it, witch. Whatever I've done hasn't been nearly as shady as what you've been up to."

Carmilla stopped twisting the corkscrew and glared at him.

"Don't you dare call me a witch."

It was the first time since he'd stepped inside the house Cyrus saw her facial expression change. Ironically, the shift in her mood seemed to brighten her complexion.

He wasn't scared, at least he didn't think he was, but his "I'm sorry" was sincere.

He sincerely believed she was a witch, in every sense of the term. She sincerely considered herself to belong to a much higher order of beings. Today he'd humor her. He hadn't come to fight.

Carmilla turned her attention back to the bottle's cork and asked, "Are you sure you don't want any?"

He shook his head. She wasn't looking at him, but he knew she saw him. Regardless she took two long-stemmed glasses out of the cabinet. She wasn't going to take no for an answer.

"Try some with me," she said. "I haven't had this before."

"What is it?" Cyrus sat on a stool at the kitchen's bar.

"Chardonnay." She poured an equal amount into both glasses. "Sonoma County. Fifty-seven dollars a bottle."

"California? Don't you usually do France?"

"Let's just say I'm in a sunny mood."

Cyrus chuckled. "And a sixty-dollar bottle. What's the special occasion?"

Carmilla set a glass in front of him and looked him in his eyes. "I'm thirsty."

She moved her glass in circles on the counter. Cyrus looked from her hand to his wrist. The watch's minute hand made a full revolution, and she was still going.

"If you're so thirsty, my dear, why aren't you drinking?"

"I just took it out of the cooler. It's too cold. Chardonnay—all fine wines—can only truly be enjoyed at just the right temperature. This needs to warm up a little."

Cyrus looked at those greenish-orange fingers grasping the wineglass's stem. All those diamonds. *Ice.* She had the typical world-weary attitude of the rich, but Carmilla didn't have it all. And he just couldn't resist pushing her hot button. Especially after that "crooked" crack.

"And when are *you* going to warm up? All those rocks on your fingers, potential suitors might think you've been married twenty times over rather than shunning the institution every chance you get."

"Every chance?" she said. "Name one. A good one."

Good point. "Maybe if you made an effort to get out more, mingle with the fairer sex—"

"For what? I'm sick beyond sick of women hurrying to get married as if life is a sport and marriage is the finish line."

Her wineglass was racing now. Cyrus knew her button all right. To tap it was to push her to nuclear, forcing her toward what she most wanted and, in this world, could never have.

"Oh, really?" Cyrus said. "A sport?" *Rant on, witch.*

She snorted. "More like a grand game. One played according to the Diamond Rule: Dare All, Spare None. The winners get kids as trophies; the losers get the same, as a consolation prize. And the big joke? They don't even want them!" Her free arm was gesticulating wildly. "They want living proof of their success, but they don't really want *them*. But they make them, bake them, and spit them out—right out of the woman's guts—just because the couple thinks they should. The navel-gazing patriarchy thinks they should. It's the right thing to do. Makes them look normal to their peers. Children as trophies, made to sit in a corner, on a shelf, in a case, and be shown off to everyone once in a while, but usually, preferably, left to sit still, quietly, in the corner, in the dark, and gather dust."

Maybe he'd pushed the button a little too hard. It was like her words were on a drunken drive—never mind that she hadn't even taken her first sip of wine yet.

"Carmilla, my dear, that's quite a mouthful. I never suspected that you were so bitterly against love."

"I'm not against 'love,' you oaf. I'm against a fractured concept…A cardboard house and a broken picket fence whitewashed by a noncommunicating community that assumes to know what is *right* for one and all. And what the hell's left? There are piles and piles of broken children—pink and blue toys—mixed among the leaves and dog feces in many families' backyards."

"My dear, you have the makings of a great po—"

"Stop calling me your 'dear,' pervert. Save that shit for your little blonde trollop."

She picked up her glass and walked toward the kitchen table. With all the hot air she'd released, her Chardonnay was surely warm enough now. But still, no sipping.

Cyrus followed her, leaving his glass behind. Enough chatter. Time to bring her down and talk business.

"Carmilla, listen to me. I'm sure you've heard by now what's happened. You know why I came here."

"I know what happened." She set her glass on the table and took a seat. "But I don't know why you're here."

The witch playing dumb for once. *Funny.*

"Hernandez has apparently reverted back to her old ways," he said. "She broke some of our projects out of The SeptiGuarden."

"Ezra told me there'd been a breach." Carmilla seemed to be addressing her wine. She'd lifted her glass to just a few inches in front of her eyes, gazing as she spoke. "He didn't have time to give me details. Nor did I care to ask for any."

"There was a serious breach. It's obvious I can't turn to any of my usual channels for assistance in fixing this, so I came to you."

Carmilla lowered her glass and put her nose near its rim. She closed her eyes, then began mumbling as she opened them. "Mango…fig…Wonderful. The nose on this—"

"Carmilla."

"I heard you." She set her glass on the table and moved it in circles, swirling the liquid. "I just don't understand what's so serious." She began to raise her glass to her nose again.

"The HorrorShow."

Her glass stopped halfway. The easy smirk on Carmilla's face vanished. Cyrus didn't need any special abilities to read her mind. He knew she was remembering her last confrontation with the eight. Money and a mastery of witchlike crafts had made her feel invulnerable for some time now. That feeling was now being tested. She didn't need to say anything.

But Carmilla wasn't the type to keep anything bottled up for too long.

"I warned you about that damned prison," she said. "From the beginning. You and your fucking pet projects—"

"It is not a prison, and I don't need a lecture from you, girl. I need help."

She snorted a laugh and stood up. "Of course you do."

"I need a Gatherer."

"Of course you do." She turned toward the bay window. He could tell she was trying to erase her fear, make believe she hadn't heard a word he'd said. She took a sip of her Chardonnay and looked out toward the lake.

"Hmmm," she said a moment after swallowing. "Very well-balanced. Lemon…hazelnut…vanilla…"

No matter how mature and wizened she wanted to be, Cyrus knew she was like other girls her age. She had hopes and plans for the future. A future that wasn't set in stone. A future that could be snatched away, hidden, and dismembered, long before its arrival. She couldn't turn her back on reality.

But she tried. She walked as if in a daze toward the door leading to the balcony, murmuring about the wine's complexity, its hints of various flavors. She left the door open behind her.

Cyrus fought off the urge to slam it behind him, making a noise that would snap her attention back to where it should be. Carmilla may not have even noticed him as he stood next to the patio's table, staring at the back of her head, trying to read her body language while she looked out over the railing.

It was twilight. A sparse gathering of trees stood in the few feet of ground between the house and the lake. Carmilla could've been staring through the dusky air at the water three stories below or at the rows of lakeside condos lining the shore. If she'd the supernatural visual abilities of a Virus-carrier, she could've seen through the condos and trees on their right and spied on whatever activity was occurring at Lake Anne Plaza, just a brisk five-minute walk away. More likely, though, her sight was focused inward, reading the horrible thoughts about the near future.

"Flood's coming," she said after a few minutes. "Nothing anyone can do to stop it. The escape of those eight is just part of fate."

"Okay. Fine." He approached her. "Creation as we know it will cease to exist and be replaced by an anarchic, Godless mess. No laws of man, no laws of physics, no laws of sense. I know you don't care about that. And, yes, my dear, I know you've even been working on a plan, working on something to help you ride out the Flood of XynKroma, maybe even dry it up, somehow remake Creation in your image."

Carmilla reacted as if to a sudden breeze Cyrus didn't feel. He'd hit the target.

"But let me ask you this," he said. "Is your plan ready? Are you sure it will work? Are you ready to take that big of a gamble? Because these eight, they've learned things. They're not as they were the last time they went on a spree. That was a game of tag compared to what they can do now. Remember who had a hand in shaping their minds, conditioning them, before we could get them confined in the camp? And we were nowhere near making a breakthrough with them. Yes, they learned from us, but they didn't unlearn what they'd already known. And what Hernandez could teach them…Whatever kind of Dirty Light Magick they practice, they could open the floodgates at any moment. Heaven knows what Hernandez wants with them. I hope it's something penny-ante, like robbing banks. I hope she can keep them relatively restrained. But even if she tries, it won't last for long. And with every Virus-carrier in the world trying to make their way here, we need *those* eight under our control."

He stood close enough for her to feel the warmth of his breath on the back of her bare neck. She'd worn her hair short for as long as he'd known her. He could never see it, but he'd have sworn the hairstyle was for the sole purpose of letting some sort of invisible third eye watch her back. It was probably staring right at him. But he didn't flinch.

And Carmilla didn't turn. She only took another sip of her Chardonnay, took time to savor it, then shrugged.

"*Que sera, sera*," she said.

"Not unless you help me."

"Do you want them dead?"

"Of course not, girl. I wouldn't have come to you for that. I want them returned—unscathed—before they do something horrible. That's why I requested a Gatherer, not a Hunter."

"My Gatherers are too few and too far away. Even if I called out to them, not a one of them could get here in time. You're right about one thing. Whatever those eight—those *nine*—are going to do, they're going to do it soon. Hernandez wouldn't have risked such a prison break if she didn't need the extra allies now."

"But you have other acolytes," Cyrus said. "Other people in your employ. Couldn't you round them up and—"

"Everyone serves a very specific role. The Sprytes have their function. The Raynes have a separate function. Everyone has their slot. That's why my world turns so smoothly."

"So none of them can help?" Cyrus moved so he could see her two visible eyes. "I can't believe that."

"Against those eight?" She faced him and didn't blink. "Believe it. You know those eight came of age in a very special way. A very unique and chaotic way. And from what Ezra has told me about the methods used in your SeptiGuarden, the only way to stop them without killing them is via XynKroma."

"Fine," Cyrus said. "Just go there and—"

"I don't go to Xyn. And won't. Ever. One of my most trusted would have to make the journey. And even then it could take weeks to set up the perfect ritual to enable them to land just in the right spot, ready and effective enough to do what needs to be done. We just don't have the time."

"You have something that can buy time." He hesitated, almost afraid to say it. "Magick."

She looked at him as if he'd told an obscene joke.

"Carmilla, please." He was ready to beg. "Teach me something. Give me a crash course in just one of your charms. Something that can help me. Help *us*."

Her expression softened, but she continued to eye him strangely. She was waiting for the magic word.

"I'm willing to pay," he said. "You probably don't want money, but—"

"Recession, depression, whatever," she said. "Money is the real power in this world. That's one reason I won't be sorry to see it pass away. But, in the meantime, money will do."

Cyrus began to follow her back inside, but she held up her hand.

"Stay. I'll be back."

She had something up her sleeve. *Good.* And she was willing to share. For a price, yes, but when dealing with Carmilla, that was as good as charity.

He walked to the railing. Bursts of noise traveled over the waters to his ears. Sounded like some folks were having a real good time over at the Plaza. Too bad he couldn't see it. It'd be nice to have abilities that exceeded the talents of mortal men, but it just wasn't worth the trade-off. Anything he needed could be bought, one way or another.

Cyrus knew nothing about how magick worked; he only knew XynKroma was somehow a big part of it. He'd heard of "Light Magick" and "Dirty Light Magick," the former practiced by many Virus-carriers, the latter practiced almost exclusively by associates of The ID. Carmilla had her own unique brand of magick. Powerful stuff. She'd used it to earn herself a fortune, to keep herself immune to every known disease, and to keep a whole range of Virus-carriers subservient to her, totally obedient, even as she made them increasingly stronger and smarter, presumably just so they could serve her more effectively. He wondered which charm she'd sell him.

Her highly personal system of magick was a syncretistic one, made up of a number of linked "charms"—discrete processes of reading or influencing the natural order of things. Like yin and yang. On the *reading* side were the common arts of numerology, astrology, tarot, and so on. The *influencing* side—the black side—was the mystery. Darker arts perfected by Carmilla and taught only to her most trusted, most of whom it seemed happened to be female. Cyrus knew nothing about the black charms; he'd only heard whispers about them. But his agnostic self was ready and willing to take a leap into the baptismal fire just to learn a piece, a fragment that could help him—help *them*—in their time of need.

Carmilla was the right one to turn to. She was the only one he could turn to. The good witch of the East Coast. She'd see him out of this mess.

The door opened behind him. Cyrus turned to see Carmilla carrying two glasses of wine. Wendy was three steps behind her, carrying a wine bottle in an ice bucket. The silent sentinel had changed clothes.

"Here."

Carmilla extended the glass in her right hand to him. His eyes moved from the glass to her to Wendy and back to Carmilla.

"What the hell's this?"

"A decadent Chardonnay," she said. "I want you to try it."

She'd lost her damned mind. They'd just been discussing something of utmost importance, and she was already focused on wine again.

"I told you I didn't want any," he said.

"You're not going back to work at this hour?" Carmilla said.

"Of course not."

"Then take this."

"I don't want any damn wine. I thought you—"

"You're a guest in my home. This is my welcome." Even in the darkness, he could see something—a shadow—pass over her countenance as she spoke. "A down-home wine, from a Virginia vineyard. Drink it."

He felt a twinge of paranoia. She just might be trying to poison him. Rather than sell him a magickal secret, she simply and elegantly would take out the one who was her primary connection to the eight, and then take out the eight by paying some magick-wielding Hunter to do it.

No, that was silly. She'd no good cause to get rid of Cyrus. And Carmilla never did anything without good cause. Still…

"Let me have your glass," he said. "The glass in your left hand."

She cocked her head. "Why?"

"You don't have germs, do you?"

She glared at him for a moment but softened her expression to a broken smile as she extended her left hand. He took the glass with a smirk and a nod.

"You should really learn to appreciate good wine," she said as she swirled hers, looking him in his eyes. "It's one of the few true pleasures in this world. The true pleasures should be indulged fully before our time on the face of this planet is up and we fade away with the storm's winds, returning to the worms."

Cyrus listened, barely comprehending, as he returned her gaze, pupils meeting pupils, and swirled his wine.

"You know," she said, "we are just weak echoes, made flesh, from a Ghost's last shouted wish."

The staring unnerved him but not enough to look away. There was nothing else to look at. Their eyes were locked.

Carmilla stopped swirling. Cyrus stopped swirling.

She raised the rim of the glass to her nose. He raised his glass to his nose.

He didn't pick up the aromas she'd claimed to with her previous glass. It was hard to say exactly what he was picking up. But then he wasn't big on wine. He figured maybe he was smelling it wrong.

Carmilla lowered her glass, smiled, and took a sip. Cyrus did the same. She continued to stare at him as they both let the wine settle, coating their tongues and every part of their mouths. He tasted something. Many somethings. Fig. Green apple. Pear. He swallowed, tasting a hint of nutmeg, then smoke. Where did she say this wine was from?

"Well?" she asked.

"It…wasn't bad."

"What wasn't bad once will be even better the second time around."

She again swirled and sipped. Cyrus mimicked her. They continued the routine, over and over, never needing to move as Wendy took care to refill both of their glasses, again and again. Habitually. Ritually.

It was only after Carmilla stepped around him and walked to the railing that Cyrus realized what had taken place. *The witch.*

It would've been nice if she'd warned him, asked him for his permission to participate in whatever the hell she'd just done. He may've happily worked for the government, but that didn't mean he enjoyed being treated like a damned puppet.

He set his glass down on the table and threw an angry glance at Wendy before turning toward Carmilla.

"What was that?" he asked. "What did you just do with me?"

A moment of cool silence passed as Carmilla stared out at the black lake and finished her wine. She was in a trance.

Cyrus approached her cautiously as her free hand went to her necklace. She fondled its pendant—a diamond snowflake, big as a quarter, worth a billion times as much—while her lips moved.

"A world is at stake. A heavy widow, bothered. When the game is finished, the winners will win one another…" She seemed to be having a muted, cryptic conversation with the lake. "A November leaves. A December enters. A season splinters. And into lives, into hearts, a stake—"

Cyrus found a good, safe spot in which to stand. He could wait until she finished.

After six or seven minutes, Carmilla blinked wildly and staggered, grabbing for the rail with her free hand. Cyrus stood his ground. "I…have a very good idea of what Hernandez is up to," she said finally. "And have a very good idea how she thinks she's going to accomplish it. She's not finished gathering allies. There's one more."

Cyrus took a step toward her. "Who?"

"Never mind." She straightened herself. "Just know that I'm on top of it."

"Well, my dear, I'd appreciate a little hint about what the hell's going on, if you don't mind."

"All I can tell you is that I am going to do what you are unwilling and, quite frankly, unable to do. I am going to stop them cold."

"I want them unharmed, Carmilla."

She shook her head and began muttering in what sounded like a foreign language. Whatever it was, he could tell enough to know it was a string of curses, profanity directed at him.

"I'm serious," he said.

"Give me a fucking break."

She turned toward him. He turned away before she could establish another visual link, but she kept her eyes on him, and he felt the heat of her breath, smelled the fruit and alcohol, as she ranted on.

"If Hernandez gets what she wants, you can forget about your dream project. You can forget about everything. She is going to be stopped. *Dead.* She's too dangerous in any other condition. As for the others, you just better prepare to write them off. All eight of them. Acceptable losses. You of all people should understand that concept."

"I understand it," he said, "but I don't accept it. You, with all of your tricks, and charms, and whatever the hell else, you can't find another way to end this, end whatever they're planning before it starts, without anyone dying?"

"No."

Great. "Then how can you be so sure what you're thinking will work out as planned? Precisely how are you on top of the situation?"

"My arts are stronger than hers."

Whatever other witchy habits Carmilla might've followed, he figured she'd never be inclined to put questions to a magick mirror. She knew she was the fairest one of all, and the vainest.

"Also," she said, "I'm sending in one of The Big Three."

His anger changed into something else entirely.

Cyrus had worked with the Three on a few very special occasions. He'd never gotten along with any of them, but he'd fought hard to stay on their good side. Carmilla was just creepy; the Three were genuinely scary. Carmilla wasn't infected with the White Fire Virus. She was just a master craftswoman. The Three were master Diviners, expert manipulators of electromagnetic radiation, Light Magick practitioners of the highest order. They were the results of a Trinfecta experiment code-named "SunSafe," an experiment that had been mostly successful, save for a few unspecified complications. The Trinfecta researchers had decided to halt the experiment after the first phase and go down a different path with their test subjects, but Carmilla had swooped in, bought the Three, dubbed them her "Moon Keys," and began to conduct her own pharmaceutical experiments on them. The Three spent a lot of time out of the country, off the radar, in Third World shit holes, far beyond Cyrus's electronic reach, but he knew enough about how they usually operated. They were exactly what he didn't want to add to the equation.

"Just one?" He didn't bother to cover his sarcasm. "Are you sure that's going to be enough?"

"To lock down Hernandez, just one of my Keys will be."

"I'd offered to pay you to teach me one of your charms."

"You wanted a quick-trick course in the Charmic Arts. You got one. It's all out of your hands now."

"That wasn't what I meant."

"What you *meant* has always been the problem, Cyrus. What you *meant* for the oh-so-wonderful Doctor Linkins. What you *meant* for the eight. What you *meant* for the redheaded girl. You're a fucking klutz. Whatever you mean to happen happens some other way—always—and usually the worst way. You can't be trusted with a charm. I wouldn't even trust you to water one of my gardens. I'm handling this now. I'm handling *everything*. And you better hope to whatever god or dog you worship that I succeed."

"I'd better hope that you succeed? What have you succeeded in doing so far but using me and everyone else to enrich yourself, protect yourself, and surround yourself with a cult of freakishly long-legged skanks?"

Carmilla laughed. Not a girl's giggle or a witch's cackle or a drunkard's outburst, but a cheerfully authentic belly laugh. Not the reaction he'd expected his words to elicit.

"Very good question, my dear Cyrus. Care to answer it, Wanda?"

Cyrus turned around and stumbled, his feet seeming to move in three different directions at once as he discovered the tall women who'd been standing silently, impassively, between him and the door. Several pairs of heels on a wooden deck, and Cyrus hadn't heard a single footstep, or one heartbeat, or any breaths from the women who'd been standing five feet behind him for who knows how long. The closest one—Wanda, presumably—stood directly in front of Wendy, who was flanked by two other amazons. Behind those three stood four more. The fact they all seemed dressed for a night at the opera wasn't comforting; Cyrus knew what they were and what they could do. Time to call it a day.

"Ladies, my apologies." Cyrus held up his hands as if he were fending off a too-generous offer. "I'm just under a lot of stress today. If you'll allow me, I'll leave in peace."

He almost expected one of them to crack wise about him leaving in pieces, but the ladies said nothing. Cyrus looked to Carmilla.

"You win," he said. "Let's just end this. Do what you have to do."

"I wouldn't do anything else."

"Would you at least tell your sentinels to make way?"

She turned her back to him, making a to-the-wind wave with her free hand. The statuesque women parted to allow Cyrus free passage as he approached the door to the house.

"Oh, and don't forget," Carmilla said. "You owe me for the wine you gurgled down."

He ignored her. There was nothing more he could say. Carmilla's Moon Lackey, in one fell swoop, would lay waste to his detailed plans, his long-term goals. He'd be left playing with the mere wisps of fantasies. There was nothing else he could do at this point but go home and try to get some sleep, dreaming about what might've been for the next world, *his* world: Flood averted, but a planet cleansed of angels, saints, mages, and witches. A world ruled by one philosophy, delivered unto humankind by the Prophet Cyrus. Sweet, pleasant dreams.

Chapter 8

Eunice had wasted little time or expense. The lock she'd had fastened to Robert's apartment door—probably right before she knocked off for the evening—was state-of-the-art.

"I can get us in," Ava said. Robert shook his head.

The numerical combination he'd used to get into the building was the same for everyone; no way Eunice could've changed that. And there'd been no nighttime concierge to block his passage inside. But he recognized the insignia on the lock. He knew if he let Ava break the lock on his door, the private security firm who'd attached it would have some boys over there in minutes. Big boys. He didn't need any additional grief tonight.

He drove them to a motel on Glebe. He knew the manager, a silent type who was smart enough not to install any hidden cameras to record whatever guests did in their rooms. Robert did his usual check anyway.

Ava performed her own ritual of x-raying every surface and examining every corner, remarking on each object's lack of immaculateness as she went along. She had plenty to say about the bedsheets. Robert was more concerned about the lights and the window.

The bulbs in the room's two lamps were gradually dimming and brightening and dimming—all on their own. Ava's doing? A sign of nervousness she couldn't control? Hell, for all he knew, it could've been him. He wasn't looking forward to the journey ahead, and he shuddered to think what might happen at sunrise when the eastern-facing window let in an abundance of light through the cheap curtains, bathing their unconscious bodies. Even if they made it out of Xyn in one psychological piece, they might awake in agony, their bodies looking much like Agent Canton's.

"Aren't you going to take off your shirt?" Ava said.

She'd already taken off hers and tossed it onto the recliner. Robert stared without really meaning to. She was a C-cup. Thirty-four inches. Before tonight he would've sworn she was a B-cup. He'd had many opportunities to play tricks with his eyesight and tell for sure, but he considered himself a gentleman. Since contracting the Virus, he'd fought hard to remain one, especially in the presence of women.

It had been a hard lesson learned. The first class had started right after his father had walked in on him and Leigh. The friend his father had gone out to visit hadn't been home, so his father had come right back, only to catch his fifteen-year-old son half-naked on the couch with a white girl. Robert had had to sit there and listen to the "not while you're under my roof" speech—at close range and high volume—as Leigh, unacknowledged by his father's eyes or voice, gathered her things and fled from the house. It wasn't that his father had been a racist; he'd just been attuned to the attitudes prevalent in Wallace, Virginia, the area where they were trying to make a nice, quiet, respectable living. He'd been trying to protect his son—and himself—from any unnecessary grief, but there was only so much a protective father could do. Try putting up a roadblock on one route—*thou shalt not*—the passionately curious will always find other avenues to explore.

A little more than a year after his dad's unpleasant discovery, Leigh's physician father had made an unpleasant discovery of his own. He'd seen nothing; he'd merely heard of his daughter's secret relationship. He'd heard of Robert's strange behavior at school, and he knew very well what "that filthy little…" was carrying inside him. Never mind that Robert had only begun to exhibit symptoms long after the short-and-bittersweet physical relationship with Leigh had ended. Never mind that Leigh had never even exhibited the symptoms of a head cold. The girl's father felt duty-bound to act as protector. Clearly Robert hadn't suffered enough. No—his ex-girlfriend's father had felt duty-bound to sprinkle the boy's brain with buckshot.

How he'd managed to sneak the weapon into Richmond's secure HSA-run hospital, Robert would never know. But he had managed to get to Robert's room, where the physical confrontation began as father versus father, with Robert's shouts adding vocal coloring to the cacophony of the men's threats. Before they could come to actual blows, though, it was Robert who'd picked up the mantle of the protector by ripping off his gown, letting every available light ray dig in and play over all his bare skin as he took Leigh's father down to the floor, then deeper—into another dimension. Shortly after recovering consciousness in a Sterling, Virginia, forest a week later, Robert discovered his own father had seemingly vanished from the face of the earth.

Despite his flaws, Robert's father had taught him to respect women—*all* women—unless they proved to be a physical threat. That was Ava at times, even when her fists weren't balled and her forearms not entwined in vines of orange-and-yellow light. But from the beginning, Robert had tried his best not to see her as a member of the opposite sex, one to be romanced and conquered. Even if she did stir something within him, something other than feelings of mistrust, he'd tried his best to remain the gentleman. And Ava had been exercising the same level of restraint and modesty, until now.

She reached for his belt buckle.

"The hell're you doing?" Robert covered it and turned away.

"We've got to wear as little as possible if we're going to do this right," Ava said. "Whenever the Archangel ushered my soul to Xyn—"

"If you say one more thing about that damned Archangel…"

Robert trailed off into incoherent profanity as he took off his belt. He knew the position they'd have to assume during the process; he was worried Zel's specially made buckle might pinch her when pressed against her skin. Perfect gentleman.

"The pants stay on," he said.

"Robert, if we don't do this properly, there's no telling where we'll end up."

It was bad enough they had to go at all. XynKroma wasn't just a rotten slice of dimensional pie one might see in an old episode of *The Twilight Zone*. It wasn't another world, or an alternate reality. It was a plane of existence beyond conventional space and time, separate from but connected to the everyday world. Most with any knowledge of it called it the Ultimate Reality, the realm of the One that created everything in existence, seen and unseen—the dimension of God. But Robert agreed with Vince Ceniza, who'd once described it as the aftermath of mythological Heaven married to mythological Hell, the culmination of one real, tumultuous Honeymoon.

Neither Robert nor Ava nor anyone else—"angel" or not—could travel to the dimension with their corporeal bodies. Only the essence of a human's consciousness could make the journey. Upon arrival, this essence would take on a figurative body, a shape representing what many travelers to Xyn referred to as their "soul." In size, shape, color, and composition, this body was just a symbol of everything that made that individual unique as a person; in the dimension of Ultimate Reality, however, symbols translated into hard facts. The "soul" was the pure essence of a man or woman, and any benefit acquired or injury sustained while in Xyn would permanently affect the soul bearer's body and mind. XynKroma was no fantasyland.

"Don't worry," Robert said. "I've been there before. I know what I'm doing."

He unplugged both lamps and turned on one of the bathroom's lights. He then pulled the bathroom door so that only a needle-thin crack of light showed through. The environment for the beginning of the journey could be neither too bright nor too dark. The window filtered the streetlights outside so that a wan glow spread over two-thirds of the room. The setting was near perfect.

There were numerous ways of entering Xyn: various effective methods of meditation; the right combinations of certain drugs; and, oftentimes, a combination of meditation and drugs. Vince had taught Robert and other Watcher agents a few relatively "safe" methods for entering the realm of Heaven&Hell, whether alone or with a partner. Ava was correct in her belief that bare skin was a positive factor when Virus-carriers were involved. But too much skin-to-skin contact could lead to trouble.

She, in bra, panties, glasses, and nothing else, sat on the bed, watching him as he double-checked the window to ensure it was locked.

"I'm on top," she said as he triple-checked the door.

He crooked an eyebrow.

"Yes, I know you think you know what you're doing," Ava said. "But there's got to be a dominant one in this process. That's me."

Robert lowered his head, slowly shaking it before laughing to himself and saying, "Fine. Whatever makes you happy." He approached the bed.

Ava took off her glasses and laid them behind the alarm clock on the nightstand.

"Your eye patch?"

"Like the pants," he said. "It stays on."

"You sure?"

Unless she wanted her face burned off. "Yes."

Robert lay down on his back, straightening his arms at his sides. Ava straddled his hips. He tried to steady his breathing as she touched his forearms with her fingertips, dancing them up his arms, as she tilted her face closer to his.

In such close proximity, without her glasses, he got a good look at her eyes for the first time in a while. Her irises were doubly hued, tiny patches of mud brown and sapphire blue, bleeding into each other at their edges. Weirdly unnatural, but he knew this was just a prelude; there were far freakier sights awaiting him in Xyn.

"Don't be nervous," Ava said as she gripped his shoulders.

His shoulders plunged in temperature as he sucked in a shot of air through clenched teeth.

"I'm not nervous," he said. "Your hands are freezing."

She bent her head closer. Their noses were just inches away from touching, and her breath gave off vague hints of pickles. She hadn't brushed her teeth since their grab-and-run lunch at the mall. He wanted to gag.

"You need to be calm."

Easy for her to say. Maybe not *easy*, but certainly *easier*. She was possibly on the verge of recovering her lost memories, a prayed-for gift. Robert was on the verge of being confronted with memories he'd desperately wanted to lose, all those associated with his pregnant mother's murder—the details of her being ripped apart and his baby brother being ripped from her, spirited off by the murderous cousin and raised in mysterious circumstances… still alive, he'd heard, somewhere out there in the wide world.

In Xyn, with the soul exposed to so much of Reality, one could too easily learn facts best left unknown. Robert didn't want to deal with anything having to do with his mother's fate. He wasn't ready. He wasn't strong enough.

"In the Name of the Word," Ava said, "inholy Sun, the buried Mother—"

Robert squirmed. "What the hell are you doing?"

"Keep quiet, and stay *still*." She tightened her grip on his shoulders.

Robert clenched his teeth again and sucked in sharp breaths of air as what felt like frozen lightning shot through his shoulders, ran down his arms, and crawled over his chest. He felt a breath away from having a heart attack and being done with it all.

"You need to concentrate," Ava said. "Listen to the words."

"I was." His chattering teeth made him stutter. "And I didn't like them."

"No," Ava said. "You didn't understand them. You will, if you would just let me do this."

She restarted the mantra. Robert tried to concentrate. Her words sounded like terribly obscure poetry, a lot like some of the translated nineteenth-century French poetry he'd read during his two-week time out. Ava seemed to be rambling, and he was still trembling. He knew her words had a purpose, but it took a special temperament to withstand bad poetry under duress.

"*Stop* it," Ava said. "Stop pushing back. *Relax*."

He couldn't resist a full-body shudder. He and Ava were too close to each other, becoming more and more intimate. And he was getting colder. His body couldn't help but react with movement, otherwise it felt as if it were slipping into death…heart beating offbeat…brain throbbing…eyeballs vibrating…inner ears drumming in tune, off tune, with the heart—blood cells, brain cells, humming—blood vessels entangling, pulled taut, thrumming like guitar strings—nerves unraveling, traveling—

A ripple of anxiety rushed through his body.

This went beyond a mere feeling of fear, far beyond what one might feel while lost in the woods at midnight. The moment of frisson was a lightning-strike realization of his—*their*—his and

Ava's impending *nonexistence*. The subsequent rumbling thunder in the body was the understanding that the seeds of their own nonbeing—oblivion after death—had been planted in them since birth, or prior, maybe at the moment of conception, the spark of their very creation, the seeds growing in darkness inside them ever since, and now ready to flower.

She was in him now.

No time for Robert to get secure in the fact he was losing himself. No time for anything. No space, either. But some-one—something—somewhere—was speaking.

Paradise Frost…

All he saw was white. The white of—

Lost, pair of dice…

Snake eyes…

Robert heard a white noise, then he felt it. His body frizzed. Each cell stuttered. Every atom of him jittered at once, shaking themselves out of and into and out of existence, entering and exiting multiple planes of imperceptible dimensions, resulting in a transdimensional mist of himself, confused and interspersed with particles of his partner.

Robert felt the snowflakes before he saw them. Just a few at first. All symmetrical. All with black-dot centers. All designed intricately, if not intelligently, with multihued crystals. Their number soon grew and blew into a blizzard.

A blizzard in oblivion.

That was his thought, brought forth involuntarily. He was re-integrating. The white noise had given way to howling gusts, the kind heard during the fiercest rainstorms. But there was no rain here. There wasn't even snow. There were only explosions.

So much for reintegration.

Each varicolored crystal shattered simultaneously, releas-ing bursts of color and longer-lasting drops of liquefied crystal, spraying every which way until a gravitational force kicked in.

The drops shot like bullets in a single direction, in rows, in sheets, stopping finally when hitting a soft, leathery surface.

Like the surface of a tree's leaf in spring.

Reintegration again, proceeding much more rapidly this time. The drops absorbed into the leaves and traveled with increasing speed into the leaves' stems, through the branches, into the trunk, and down into the roots before seeping out into the surrounding soil, mixing with it. Breaking the surface of the soil, they slowly rose, metamorphosed: two humanoid figures, on their hands and knees, newly arrived in XynKroma. The souls of Robert Goldner and Ava Darden.

If Robert could have blinked, he would have. The lack of clothes and hair was a given, as was the fact her figure looked much like it did on Reality's surface, if maybe a few inches taller. It was the substance that gave him pause. *Honeymud.* The term sprang to mind as Robert stared at the brown-and-ivory composition of her body—her *soul*—a thin, translucent sheath holding it all together, giving it shape. Honeymud—the symbolic representation of the pure, undiluted essence of Ava's consciousness.

In XynKroma all sights and sounds were figurative, metaphorical. It was the only way a human mind could comprehend experiences in a realm beyond conventional space and time. Vince Ceniza had told him that Xyn was where the mind went when it traveled beyond the usual human senses, and even beyond itself. The way there was meditation; the destination was the Power within: Enlightenment…ideally. In its current state, Xyn wasn't bliss but chaos. A dimension full of polluted light. A visiting soul had to manipulate this dirty light, play with it in order to create symbolic shapes and sounds that would enable it to cope with the environment as best it could. But a soul's abilities and the range of use were limited. Too much conflicting energy from too many sources—streams and rivers of subconscious thoughts from all sentient beings—fed into the realm.

Xyn, like the Creator itself, could only be spoken of poetically; there was no specific or direct language one could use to describe it. Even direct thoughts about God, the Source of All, were impossible. Consequently, while Xyn was either a wild playground or tortuous prison for light-manipulating "angels," the Creator, the metaphorical Ground on which it all lay, was largely off-limits, impenetrable to the human mind if not completely impregnable to all the mysterious powers of the human "soul."

Robert didn't know what the color or substance of Ava's soul represented symbolically, but that was okay. He recognized her; there was a good measure of coherence. If *nothing* looked or sounded sensible, the end of their journey would've been the equivalent of a plane crash. Neither would ever be able to find his or her way *through* Xyn, let alone find his or her way out of it.

Presently they were in a forest. More good news. It was a familiar landscape, stable underneath. The fact they were in a setting familiar to them showed they had some measure of control, that during their journey they'd used their light-manipulating abilities to conjure and forge a setting in which they'd be comfortable upon their arrival. Or, more likely, Ava had. Robert surely hadn't exerted any of his will to create a forest for their reception. He found wooded areas anything but inviting.

"You okay?" he said.

Ava was checking herself over. Robert noticed she lingered on her right hand longer than any other part of her soul's figure.

"How do you feel?" he said.

She looked at his face, seeming to study it for a moment before swinging.

The right hook hurt far more than it should have. Robert didn't go down, but it took him a moment to recover. When he did, he looked at her again. Her fist appeared more like the hammer of Thor than a collection of fingers. Apparently she'd transformed it right before she struck him.

"I told you not to *fight* me!" she said. "I told you not to resist! The process is supposed to go a *heck* of a lot smoother than what we went through. You're darn lucky I was able to pull us back together into one piece!"

She was right. He had resisted, and it had affected their journey. And their destination. He saw now that the forest was teeming with small creatures, birdlike, squirrellike, and others that had no earthly comparisons. None of them were quite right.

One rodent that had been skittering nearby halted to stand upright, balancing only on its coiled tail, as it in turn studied the forest's two new foreigners. Auburn fur covered its back and legs, but its underbelly was gray-tinted glass. Robert could see through it dimly; he could just make out the complex arrangement of mechanical gears and fleshy organs. The rodent's tail, a seven-inch-long rope of metal, seemed the least complicated part of it.

While looking at the creature's six sets of razorlike claws, Robert caught a glimpse of his own hand—it was shiny. He took a closer look at the rest of his soul. It was as if his regular body had been wrapped in aluminum foil and had all the crinkles smoothed out. The tone was gunmetal, and the metallic skin acted as a tarnished mirror, giving off a dull reflection. Looking into the palm of his hand, he saw he had no opening for a mouth (but was able to speak), no ears or nose (but could hear and smell), and a baseball-size ruby embedded just below a bald scalp, representing and serving as his eye. A red eye. And yet he saw the phantasmal setting around him clearly, with not even a vague reddish tint.

The rodent creature drew his attention again when it dropped back down to all sixes and scurried on its way. Robert watched it hurry up the closest black tree and disappear. The left-behind claw marks secreted clear-colored nectar. When Robert moved closer to examine the slow-running streams, he found they'd already hardened to glass. All the other trees seemed to have scores of glass streaks on them, all difficult to see against their black background, all probably the result of climbing creatures.

He'd thought he and Ava had just created this environment. Why did it have markings suggesting it had been there for some time?

While considering that, he caught a glimpse of something—a hint of pink—through a slim gap in the dense cluster of trees. There appeared to be another broader clearing in the forest far beyond the space he and Ava were standing. Robert could hear faint rhythmic sounds coming from its direction. He tried telescoping his vision, but he got no better sense of what was there. Despite the slightly enhanced visual abilities he possessed in this dimension, the trees were confounding and misdirecting his sight.

He gave up and turned to Ava, who'd also been studying their surroundings.

"Any idea where we are?"

"Yes," she said. "No thanks to you, we're in the forest that hides and helps protect my temple-palace, the Forest of Correspondences…I think."

"Forest of…What do you mean you *think*?"

"It's where I was trying to guide us, but it didn't look like this before. There weren't all these…things. There were never any creatures here before, of any kind. They're probably all here thanks to you, too."

"You're welcome, Arkangel. Now, if you're through giving me kudos, how about you get us to your T.P.?"

Ava looked up. There was no sky. The trees were so tall and thick and visually confounding all one could see was an intricate weave of glistening black branches and rust-colored leaves. Ava continued to stare upward as she turned and moved to the side, trying to get a different perspective. Then her countenance changed. She looked as if she'd been shot. Two long, crooked spears jutted out and up from her shoulder blades.

Robert recoiled at their sudden appearance. Although he knew one should always be on guard in Xyn as if in a war zone, it wasn't easy to do in a realm where anything and everything could happen at any moment. But he saw to his relief there was little to worry about. The spears were of Ava's own conjuring, rods from which unfurled curtains of clothlike feathers. The Arkangel was simply displaying her wings.

"We're going to have to get up and out of here to get our bearings," she said. "Can you fly? Or do you need me to carry you?"

"Funny, Arkangel. Real fun—"

A rustling sound came from behind them. They both turned to see another creature, much bigger than any of the critters they'd seen so far, entering the clearing. Worse—it was a chimera, compositing multiple creatures that existed in Robert's and Ava's home dimension, the surface of Reality. The chimera's appearance mocked that realm. It even mocked the most popular fictional representation of Hell. It was Cerberus-like, but the largest and middle head was a reindeer's; the smaller heads on either side were a vulture's and something reptilian. The creature's body also resembled a reindeer's, but leaner, with thicker, stronger legs than any ever seen on Reality's surface. And the two tails weren't spitting snakes; they were live wires. The Cerberus had not come to bring glad tidings.

The creature paused when Robert met its gaze, but it was no deer in the headlights. It stayed put for only a moment before resuming its approach, its lazy trot picking up speed, quickening, and launching at a finger's snap into a headlong charge.

Robert had time to jump and roll out of its way. Ava had time to jump but not to hit the ground. She landed like a ball in glove in the reindeer head's antlers. She struggled but mostly stayed put as the creature ran on, maneuvering through the gaps in the trees and galloping on deeper into the forest.

Robert shot after them. He hadn't been to Xyn in quite some time; it would take him a while to become reaccustomed, but for any adept light manipulator, it never took too long. A Virus-carrier's abilities on Earth were greatly multiplied in the dimension of dirty light. He was already running faster than any creature on the surface of Reality, moving at least as fast as any man-made earthbound vehicle, but he was still barely able to keep pace. The Cerberus would slip into and stay in his sight for a few seconds before pulling ahead, forcing Robert to rely on sound alone until he caught another few seconds' glimpse of the creature. All the while, he didn't seem to be gaining on them.

He tried to figure shortcuts by measuring angles and distances while calculating his rate of speed versus the creature's. But his geometric genius failed him in this forest. The trees confounded his mathematical and visual abilities. At least he still had the physical.

Robert tried to accelerate. The Cerberus remained inevitably faster; this was its territory. Even for Ava, who'd undoubtedly visited Xyn far more times than Robert, the creature's nimbleness was proving to be too much. In the glimpses he caught of her, he could see the creature was moving at a pace and weaving in such a way as to make it impossible for Ava to put up a decent struggle or to even gather enough of a voice to scream.

She wasn't completely helpless, though. She'd chosen the composition of her soul wisely. The pliability of it and the toughness of its flexible shell were to her benefit. Ava lay cradled in the antlers, bunched up and definitely uncomfortable but not pierced or bleeding even a trickle of the honeymud inside her. Her wings were just as resilient, trailing over the back of the creature's sleek body, flowing like two large rags of sown feathers that wouldn't be shredded or sundered no matter how many times they plowed through low-hanging branches.

Ava wouldn't remain in such a helpless, unharmed state for long, however. The reindeer wasn't running aimlessly.

As Robert finally seemed to lessen the distance between them, he realized they were approaching the clearing he'd seen earlier. He'd initially guessed the clearing to be much nearer to their landing spot. He would've never guessed what was actually there.

Robert chased the Cerberus into a city, leaving the wooded area behind. A glance over his shoulder revealed it hadn't been a forest. In this grand metropolis, it was the equivalent of a park the size of a city block, and he immediately understood that the block possessed its own unique geometry, making it bigger on the inside than outside. A hyper-forest. Outside, it wasn't unlike many of the parks Robert had seen in Washington, DC. But this seemingly un-populated city was nothing like the nation's capital.

It had office buildings, odd monuments, courthouses, and other structures that may've been museums—everything that downtown DC had—but everything was twice as large. And the surfaces of these structures weren't brick, metal, or glass; they were pinkish gray, translucent, with branching purple veins pulsating audibly beneath their surfaces. Abandoned, neglected—these structures didn't lose pieces and crumble. Rather, they had cuts and punctures; they exhibited ruptured veins; they bled a sub-stance thicker than water but more viscous than syrup, redolent of fermented fruit juices: apples, blackberries, and grapes. Robert ran close enough to touch, but he didn't dare. He'd more senses than five while in the realm; he didn't need to touch to tell these buildings were organic. Living structures making up a city devoid of any living creatures on its streets—except for Robert, Ava, and the Cerberus.

The creature zipped and weaved through the streets like a drunken tour guide on a souped-up Segway, turning corner after corner before stopping on a dime, right at the edge of the grand pond, boasting an even grander statue at its center, standing firm on the water's rippling surface.

Ejected from her cradle, Ava flew in an arc, giving full voice to an energetic scream, before landing a few feet in front of the enormous statue's flickering base.

Robert expected to hear a splash, but there was only a loud crack. Ava had somehow managed to freeze the lake solid before impact. The will the Arkangel possessed, even in the most perilous situations, was impressive. But willpower wasn't everything. The statue stood on a hostile pedestal.

On Reality's surface, the Statue of Liberty stood on a pedestal that welcomed visitors, promising freedom and security. This twice-its-size statue had one hand covering her eyes, another covering her mouth, and stood on a cage housing a fierce blue flame that fought against the sheet of ice Ava had created to save herself.

The sounds of cracking ice multiplied. Ava still needed saving.

Robert had been no more than a few dozen feet behind the creature when it stopped, and he didn't slow his pace for even a second when he saw Ava go airborne. Nor did he take the time to formulate a detailed plan of rescue. He'd only a malformed notion of leaping like a winged frog from the pond's edge, touching down just once—lightly—near Ava, grabbing her, and leaping safely to the other side. A task easier attempted than carefully considered.

He left the ground. In an eye's blink, the Cerberus transmogrified and launched itself upward, catching Robert's foot in a talon and flinging him like a rag doll away from the pond and back into the city.

Robert slammed against a building's resilient surface, bounced off, and fell more than one hundred feet downward, hitting a much less forgiving pavement with his elbows and knees. He thanked fortune he'd the subconscious foresight to armor his soul during the journey to Xyn. When he looked up, he wished he'd had the foresight to do more. The beast stood at the end of a street the length of a football field, an uneven pathway of potholes, steaming manholes, puddles, and more incongruent features.

The Cerberus had transformed. The vulture's head was now dominant, centered and larger than the other two. Its body was as plumped, sculpted, and deformed as that of a steroid-abusing professional wrestler's. The fleet hooves had given way to vulture's talons, and the reindeer's antlers had shifted to the creature's shoulder blades, appearing now as skeletal wings. The repositioned antlers glowed white-hot as the creature's vulture eyes fixated on Robert's ruby-red one.

He wasn't really frightened, but Robert didn't move, unable to think as the creature's eyes seemed unable to blink. It would have to make the first move, forcing Robert to react. As if reading his mind, the Cerberus sprinted forward. Ungainly appearance aside, the creature was as swift as a wide receiver as it tramped through fetid puddles, deftly maneuvered around broken parking meters, jumped busted hydrants, and otherwise avoided all other obstacles on its uneven path. Through it all, its unblinking eyes were focused on one object.

Robert scrambled to his feet. He'd a flicker of an idea and just about as much time to act. He concentrated, focusing whatever will and soulful power he could access through his ruby eye. Some kind of light, some kind of *energy* within his soul, streamed into the gem, bounced off the various facets, amplifying as Robert held it in—until the Cerberus was a mere twenty-five feet away. Focused and released, the laser-light hit the creature dead in its muscle-bound chest.

The beam didn't even make the beast pause. Only the building's skin-wall stopped it, after the beast scooped Robert up in a hug and plowed into it.

The creature let Robert fall on his face and wasted no time pecking up and down his backside with its beak. He couldn't stop the rapid darts of pain, and he couldn't escape their source, caught between it and a building, wide and tall. He couldn't *think*. What the hell was wrong with him? He'd thought clearly enough in other situations of intense engagement. But this was different. This was Xyn. Hell…

After a dozen or so sharp stings, the Cerberus stopped pecking and wrapped its fore talons on Robert's shoulders, pinching as it lifted and again slammed him back-first against the building. The surface's too-thin skin had ripped during the first impact; the vessels underneath had been severed. Robert smelled an intense scent of black currant as a tarlike substance oozed into the puncture wounds on his back.

The creature let Robert fall again before stomping on his left arm. Pain rabbit-jumped throughout the upper half of his soul. Robert didn't scream. He had a fleeting thought of attempting to shoot between the creature's legs, but the creature would most likely block and grab him before he passed halfway through. Maybe even sit on him and rip his legs off. He'd hate to see how that injury translated once—*if*—he made it out of Xyn.

No more passiveness. Ava needed him. He had to get away from this thing, even if he had to rely totally on dangerous instinct.

The creature raised a hind talon to stomp on his other arm. Robert rolled out of the way, sprung to his feet, and shot his soul up into the sky like a rocket, all in one smooth motion. The fluid movement of shifting from one position to another was second nature to him, a useful skill acquired during his wrestling days and, thus, ably performed without having to pause and think about it ahead of time.

But no skill acquired or honed in high school or with the IAI would allow him to hold his own against this beast. He didn't even want to try. He'd nothing to prove here in Xyn. At the moment, he only had a soul to save.

Robert flew at a forty-five-degree angle out over the frozen pond and stopped to hover high above the surface in order to get his bearings. In so little time, so much had changed.

The ice was no longer ice, and the curious statue—while still the tallest feature—was no longer alone.

The pond had doubled in circumference, and the ice had become slush, a process undoubtedly helped by the three-dozen army-green statues that now stood on—*in*—the melting ice. Scattered randomly across the pond, positioned in various poses, each one looked like a discarded prototype of the Statue of Liberty, without the dress and without the comforting promise of freedom. Or maybe they were the sisters of the original statue shadowing Ava—a Statue of Tyranny, seeing nothing, hearing nothing. Like their older sister statue, the thirty-six others carried no frozen torches, but flames lived and leaped fiercely within the iron-bar-cage pedestals on which the statues stood. Some of the statues held whips, bows, or spears in their upraised hands; others raised pitchforks, spades, or a variety of other garden tools. Still others held weapons or tools for which Robert didn't know the names. The statues' other hands, closer to their bodies, displayed some sort of cryptic signal: the thumb and ring finger touched, forming a circle, while the other three fingers were outstretched.

A secret society of sister statues, all of them enemies to Ava's well-being.

The imprisoned flames caused the lake's transition from ice to a thick mixture of gray slush and black ash, an ugly composition acting like quicksand. Ava's soul slowly sank with the statues, unable to swim or fly free. She was already waist-deep in the muck, her arms waving, her wings flapping, neither of them of any use. Robert would just have to swoop in, snatch both arms, and pull her free.

A claw closed around his ankle and pulled him first.

Robert tumbled downward for a hundred feet before catching himself. The Cerberus had shifted again; its reptilian face was just inches in front of Robert's. The creature grabbed him by the neck and tossed him toward the ashy slush below.

Robert managed to stop his hurtle a second before impact. Whatever was the equivalent of adrenaline in this realm coursed through his soul like river rapids; a glimmer of a thought considered the organic building's tar that had entered and mixed with the composition of his soul—but just a glimmer. His partner was short on time. Fuck this creature in his way, and fuck whatever ended up happening to Robert's soul, dinged, dented, or damaged beyond repair. Nothing would stop him from rescuing Ava from an unimaginable fate.

He launched himself at light speed toward the beast. It didn't move.

The creature didn't even budge when Robert slammed into it.

Robert felt the brunt of it all, but he was amped up. He didn't hesitate to engage the three-headed beast in a midair wrestling match.

In its reptilian incarnation, the creature had a scaly but less bulky body, grand-spanning leathery wings, and nostrils emitting wisps of sandalwood. Robert knew he had no hope of subduing the creature, no chance of making it cry the equivalent of "uncle" in whatever language it used to communicate. Robert only wanted to break it. Break off an arm or a leg or whatever, and use it to beat the creature into a temporary stunned submission, forcing it to back off long enough for him to get to Ava.

Nothing worked. The beast was far too strong for him, far too big for him to get a firm grasp on anything, far too swift for him to even poke at an eye or plug a nostril. He only succeeded in enraging the Cerberus even more.

A claw throttled his neck, immobilizing him as the creature curled its lithe body into a crescent and dug its live-wire tails into two wounds in Robert's lower back.

He screamed as icy-hot currents washed through his soul: a flowing wave of near absolute zero, the ebb leaving billions of flaming pinpricks in its wake.

He was done. He knew it. The Cerberus knew it. With triumphal disgust, the creature flung him away.

Robert landed with the force of a man-size meteor midway between the grand pond and the living-dead city. The impact pushed no scream out of Robert. No sound at all. Upon impact, all he saw and heard and felt was *black*. A void. In his dimension, it would've been the equivalent of a brief blackout. In XynKroma, it was the equivalent of his soul kissing oblivion, making brief love with extinction.

Most lost battles in Xyn left visitors with psychological damage, physical handicaps, or severe personality changes. Robert had lost a couple of minor skirmishes there before. There was nothing minor about this.

The creature took its time descending, as if relishing what was coming next. Robert tried his best to pull himself up and out to a standing position; he only managed to get out and up to a slumped, sitting position on the edge of his crater. That was as good as it would get. He felt as if he were magnetized. He couldn't move, but he had a more intense awareness of his soul. He couldn't see the wounds on his back, but he felt as if they'd been adequately patched by the dirt of what he'd just emerged from. Some of the wounds on his shoulder, however, continued to leak—a rose-colored liquid and a fainter vapor, redolent of strawberries.

The creature landed. Its reptilian eyes glowed coral orange. The incense continued to waft from its nostril slits. Lightning-blue bolts shot through the veins of its brownish-gray wings. Whatever the beast was planning to do to Robert's damaged soul, it would undoubtedly be colorful as well as painful.

In his final moments, he had just two hopes: to see the colorful display of his soul's rendering before his consciousness dissolved into oblivion, and to have some benevolent force, from somewhere, sweep in and save Ava's soul before it was too late for her.

Fatigue set in. Dimly, he looked to and from each of the creature's heads as it approached and stopped ten steps in front of him. He almost wanted to laugh as the creature's left claw shape-shifted into a circular saw. He did laugh as the creature's right claw and arm lifted, the whole limb transmogrifying as it did into a three-barreled shotgun. Stupid bastard couldn't even make up its mind how to end it.

The Cerberus focused all six of its eyes on Robert's ruby-red one. There was no blinking—just several clicks.

The beast didn't move. Three dozen amber spears stuck through its body. The life flickered out of its eyes.

Robert could only look at the sight for so long. The sounds he heard above him were of greater interest.

He saw four new chimeras. Amalgams of insect, plant, and sea creatures. He'd known from the start the Cerberus had merely been toying around with him and Ava. These new arrivals meant business.

Chapter 9

By all rights, Ava should've been a broken-down wreck. Not just from her immersion in a freeze-burning lake of broken crystals and crushed ice, but mostly from all the energy she'd expended in signaling her temple-palace guardians to send a rescue party.

Instead, in the presence of the Widow-Queens, she'd felt a warm comfort, a sense of calming serenity, from the moment one of them plucked her from the middle of the lake to the moment she was set down safely on the bank.

The Widow-Queens were denizens of XynKroma, native to the dimension and loyal to Arkangels. She trusted no others in Xyn, not even the one she'd brought with her.

A short distance away, Robert was on his hands and knees, shifting his studious gaze from the unmoving heap of a beast that had attacked them to her and her servants. At this point, he couldn't possibly know what to make of the situation.

Ava at first hadn't known what to make of her rescuers. They'd arrived in a greatly altered form than when she'd last seen them.

But once they'd saved her and Robert, and she'd managed to regain her wits, their forms modified to an appearance more comprehensible if not entirely familiar. The four now stood nine feet tall, surrounding her, studying her. Ava gave them all a good look in turn.

The Widow-Queens' torsos were those of adult human women, but their lower halves appeared as if each was astride a giant mantis. It took a few moments for Ava to recognize they were all of one piece, like centaurs. She couldn't be blamed for the trick easily played on her vision. The Widow-Queens, under a transparent, paper-thin sheath that acted as their skin, were made up of just orange light and shifting shadows; the colors signified their caste. These four were soldiers. They were Ava's soldiers. The orange light and black shadows swirled almost perpetually, halting only every few minutes, giving the appearance of a constantly changing camouflage pattern.

Not only did their arms seem to double as some kind of combat tool but each of the Widow-Queens bore a crystalline longbow—clear in the middle, stained glass at either end, and strung by spyders' silk. The bows were a part of them, attached to their bodies at the back and positioned so the limbs appeared as crooked, stained-glass antennae. The abundant light in XynKroma provided all the raw material needed to fashion ammunition for the powerful weapons, though the Widow-Queens' appearance alone might be powerful enough deterrence from battle.

The Widow-Queens had nothing resembling hair, but they each had a mouth, a nose, and two eye sockets. Instead of eyes, thick pools of steam filled the sockets, reservoirs of gaseous tears from which wispy strands wafted for the length of an eyelash before evaporating. They still saw well enough, and the four were a beautiful sight for Ava's eyes. She longed to see the other 428 Widow-Queens who populated her temple-palace. The soldiers never strayed far from home; Ava reasoned the temple-palace must be near. Maybe Robert hadn't bungled them too far off course after all, if not for lack of trying.

He approached the gathering of five slowly, rubbing his arm. His stainless-steel-like armor—the symbolic result of him resisting her influence all the way to Xyn—was no longer so stainless. The red ruby in his forehead was glowing. Robert was no doubt studying the Widow-Queens, trying to assess how much danger he might be in, how scared he should be. If only he'd relaxed in the bedroom and let Ava take complete control over everything, they would not have had to endure the rough landings, the fight, or the near drowning. They would've landed right at the temple-palace, and, rather than fear or uncertainty, Robert would've felt an almost overwhelming sensation of being at *one* with All, empathetic with everything in existence. So close to the Source of Creation; that was how a *blessed* soul was supposed to feel in XynKroma.

Ava knew enough about her partner to know it wasn't her, and it wasn't the Widow-Queens, but something about being in this realm worried him, almost unbearably. What was it?

Two of the Widow-Queens kept their focus on Robert, while the other two addressed her.

"Arkangel Ava. Greetings."

"Widow-Queen Beryl. Widow-Queen Cheryl." Ava bowed her head in answer to their honorific gesture. She'd had a hard time recognizing the two who long ago had assisted in her inversion to the Arkangel rank, but the voices confirmed their identities. "Greetings to you."

"We were afraid you would forget us," Beryl said.

Ava shook her head. "Never."

"There is no such thing as *never*, Arkangel," Cheryl said. "We were badly damaged during the attack. And the aftershock did even further damage."

"Aftershock?"

"The Errorists' ambush of you on Reality's surface," Beryl said.

"*Excuse* me."

All turned toward Robert as the prisms on the Widow-Queens backs rapidly shifted colors, gathering light. They were ready for attack.

Ava held up her left hand.

"Stand down, everyone. He's…He's with me."

"And here mostly against my will." Robert stood about ten steps away, looking at them each in turn as he spoke. "So, if none of you mind it too much, I'd appreciate the courtesy of an explanation of what you all are talking about."

The Widow-Queens remained silent as they glared. Ava had been creeped out beyond measure when she'd first arrived in Xyn and gotten the same reception. It was one thing to be stared down by creatures with colorful, if angry, eyes. It was another thing entirely to be on the bad side of armed, statuesque creatures with steam streaming from their eye sockets, as if their entire brains were boiling over with hate.

If Robert was intimidated, he did an excellent job of hiding it. He assumed the same rough-and-ready stance Ava had seen him use on Reality's surface. He still seemed ready to fight, so soon after almost losing a big one, too soon before fully recovering. Ava had to put a stop to this before it started.

She concentrated. XynKroma's resources, its inhabitants, and its visitors were all essentially made up of the same polluted light—but some things were more pure than others. Angels had an advantage when visiting the realm; their light-manipulation abilities were most often enhanced, but the ratio of pure and impure between the manipulator and the object mattered. During Ava's inversion process, the Archangel Artemisia had taught Ava how to ensure her soul remained as pure as possible when entering and traveling through Xyn. It was essential that, at the very least, the Arkangel's soul remain more pure than the substance of her servants. She'd been moderately successful in altering their appearance to something more comprehensible to her senses; she hoped she could do a better job with their attitudes.

It was a subtle and difficult trick, one that had to be exercised with the utmost care. Use too little force, the servants would feel a mere prickling and merely become irritated at what was being done to them. Not good. Use too much force and the servants would become as puppets. Also not good. The servants would only tell the Arkangel what she wanted to hear and move only as and when the Arkangel directed. Very dangerous in precarious situations such as a large-scale battle, as Ava had found out the hard way. The trick was to provide intense hints, pushing the servants to act and speak freely in the service of the mistress's goals.

Ava had failed during the assault on her temple-palace. This time, however, she'd done it just right.

The Widow-Queens relaxed their weapons, clearing their prisms as they gave Robert a tense but respectful nod.

"Perhaps we should move on," Cheryl said. "Leave this place before another skent shows up."

"Skent?" Robert said.

"A creature that protects the territory in Xyn claimed for ownership by any one of a number living in another realm."

"This creature belongs to one from your realm," Beryl said.

"I don't under—" Robert began.

"Guard dogs," Ava said. "Protecting pieces of Xyn that have been claimed by angels. Corrupt ones."

"The Errorist to whom that skent belonged will feel its death," Beryl said, "and come here soon to investigate."

"So"—Ava turned toward the edge of the city—"we're nowhere near the temple-palace."

"No," Cheryl said. "Which is why we must make haste."

"No argument," Robert said. "And, by the way, thanks for the save."

Beryl and Cheryl turned their backs to him as they revealed and flexed their wings, both pairs of them. With such a gesture, it almost seemed as if they were mooning Robert. Ava shook her head; she could only do so much to alter their attitudes. Even when she wasn't trying, she knew the Widow-Queens fed off her psychic energies—her wishes, wants, dislikes, fears, and so on. And she, to a lesser extent, fed off them. It was a symbiotic relationship. Maybe that's why Robert had taken on the armor. He'd had an inkling of what he was thrusting himself into. In this feminine midst, he wanted neither to eat nor to be nibbled on.

"Do we have to carry your companion?"

"No," Ava said. "Appearances to the contrary, he is an angel. You do think you can keep up, right, Watcher?"

"Just lead the way. Arkangel."

One after the other, the Widow-Queens made a short hop into the air, hovered, then shot like arrows into the sky. Mimicking them to a degree, Ava spread her cloth-feathered wings and lifted herself a few feet off the ground before reconfiguring them and launching herself. Forgoing the use of wings, Robert shot his silver soul like a bullet through the air. He and Ava flew side by side in the middle of the diamond formation of the Widow-Queens.

They left the city behind and rapidly passed over terrains more or less familiar to those from Reality's surface—fields of chattering flowers, deserts where something imperceptible drew complex patterns in the sand, a grand canyon coated with snow—until, without warning, their surroundings shifted and they flew over a brown ocean under an olive-hued sky. The odor of fresh sewage almost overpowered Ava and Robert, causing them to dip and sway in their flight.

"Stay steady," one of the Widow-Queens said. "Your senses will adapt."

Ava trusted her servants. She trusted them to take her on the most direct route to the temple-palace. She didn't even ask questions as they approached and weaved through the gigantic Grecian columns, half a mile thick and stretching from beneath the ocean to somewhere above the sky. They were riddled with moving pictures of otherworldly creatures, incomprehensible symbols, and spigots emitting puffs of reddish-gray dust. The Widow-Queens did not take any care to evade the dust, so neither did Ava. There was, however, one thing that concerned her.

"Whatever happened to the Forest of Correspondences?" she asked. "It's what I was aiming for in our journey here."

"Gone," Beryl said, leaving it at that.

Robert picked up the incredulous line he'd begun in the other forest. "Forest of *Correspondences*? What—"

"I didn't come up with the name." In this time and place, Ava preferred to ask the questions.

"I was just going to say it seemed like a fitting name for something that would be here," Robert said. "As if conceived by the French symbolist poet Charles Baudelaire."

"Never heard of him," Ava said.

"About a hundred and fifty years before our time. He wrote a poem called 'Correspondences,' which talks about a forest of symbols. Pretty interesting artist. He thought nature was inherently corrupt. He called his first book *The Flowers of Evil.*"

Ava did find that interesting, as her forest was one composed of glass, foil, and mirrors. "Sounds like he didn't exactly fulfill the stereotype of the romantic Frenchman," she said.

"But it does sound exactly like the type of thought we have dedicated ourselves to combating," Cheryl said.

"Oh?" Robert said. "And what do you mean by that exactly?"

"Diseased thoughts," Beryl said. "The perverted thoughts of humankind. That is what is responsible for the state of Creation, and the condition of XynKroma. Look around. Look at the state of *your* realm. It is not the fault of the Creator. Not all of it."

The stench of sewage was no longer prevalent, nor did it matter as the Widow-Queen formation darted—taking Ava and Robert along—into a spigot emitting puffs of white vapor. They traveled through a short tunnel of sights and sounds before emerging into a grotesque landscape, where craters rimmed with ice and full of bubbling cherry tar marked the ground, while white roses masquerading as clouds filled the sky. The roses were beautiful and smelled sweet, wonderfully so, deceptively so, as the party discovered when they drew close to one and saw the giant black-and-green worms embedded between sheets of petals. They writhed and stretched out their heads, each one searching for another that had also peeked beyond the folds, writhing toward it until kissing, biting, then retracting deep into the rose, hidden from sight. Symbolic flowers of evil, indeed.

"We are almost there," Beryl said. "Into that crater ahead."

They dived into an empty, seemingly bottomless crater and emerged into the worst landscape yet, its horror compounded by the fact they had reached their destination.

The sky was blank as fresh snow. The ground seemed to follow some kind of indecipherable pattern…a dead angel's skin, alternating between pale patches, Caucasian and African flesh-colored spots, and blackberry bruises. Dried rivulets, and mini-volcanoes still spewing strawberry-jam-like pus…All of it was the aftermath of an inholy battle. The ground was scarred but not hardened; it could still bring forth life, even if the corpse of a felled and half-buried giant made it appear as a grave.

It had no head. Ava remembered the decapitation had been the killing blow. Since then the body had lain where it fell, rotting, remerging with the soil from which it had originally sprung while the Widow-Queens of the proper caste went to work on it. Even now, the red-and-black Widow-Queens hovered and crawled over the fallen enemy like ants going to work on a fallen human-size sugar fairy, masterfully and methodically examining and dissecting the creature.

Mutated mares accompanied her servants. Four legs, four diaphanous wings, two equine heads, and three tricolored horns on each—Ava had called them "lightmares" when she'd first seen them. When she'd seen them last, the mares had only two wings apiece. Then, as now, the wings were transparent and displayed fluorescent veins of flowing liquid light, but the mares' bodies no longer had their zebra stripes of yellow and blue-black; they were now the color of Georgia clay. Their horns were also no longer uniformly red, green, and blue, but a candy-cane twist of all three primary colors. They were still beautiful. But overshadowing them, the red-black Widow-Queens, and the giant corpse on which they all operated was an almost unspeakable sight.

Another headless giant. This one wasn't a corpse but a statue very similar to those populating the lake in which Ava had almost met her end. Those, she realized now, were simply the by-products of feverish wishes; this one was a big wish come partially true. At least three hundred feet in height, the statue with a woman's body knelt on its right knee toward the corpse. Its right arm was extended and upraised, its right palm upturned, and an imperfect diamond the size of its missing head hovered above it. The statue's left arm hung limply at its side, grasping a broken bow, strung by a rainbow of just four colors: red, orange, yellow, and green. The soil on which that statue knelt was marshy, but it produced vines—fertile vines that entwined it from foot to waist.

"What is all this?" Robert asked.

"That diamond," Ava said, "is my temple-palace."

The squadron of six flew straight toward it. After passing through the transporting sheets of mist all too familiar to Ava, they appeared in what she'd once called the "throne room," though presently there was no throne. As she'd expected, the room's walls were one big window. Golden hieroglyphic designs inlaid the crystal walls, like the golden anchor-cross embedded in her diamond pendant on Reality's surface. The designs didn't in any way hamper the view of the grand blank sky and all the devastation under it. Inside the throne room itself, a dozen Widow-Queens composed of yellow light and black shadows surrounded Ava and Robert and their escorts, each of them scurrying about the room to momentarily study one of the several dozen two-dimensional free-floating monitors giving view of various hot spots within XynKroma. Not a one of the Widow-Queens paid the least bit attention to the new arrivals.

It was just as well. The main attraction for Ava was in an upper corner: the primary caretaker of her temple-palace, the one Ava had come to see. Nurse Marion was splayed like a starfish, with several dozen crystalline wires snaking in and out of her light-and-shadow body, connecting her most intimately to the throne room and, by extension, the temple-palace itself, such as it was.

Ava tried to meet her gaze, but the Nurse's sockets were sealed shut. The Arkangel exerted her will, prying open the seals. Streams of vapor wafted from the slits to mix with the wider atmosphere as the Nurse saw and acknowledged the Arkangel, sending a shiver through the circuitry that connected her to the temple-palace, causing the entire structure to shiver as the monitor screens momentarily scrambled.

The Nurse had always been a curious one. Not considered a Widow-Queen while at the same time considered the supreme Widow-Queen, according to the convoluted ranking system of temple-palace hierarchies. Despite the absence of her sardonyx throne, Marion appeared much as Ava remembered: the shape of a human woman dressed in flowing waves of red, orange, and yellow light, her body composed of shifting swatches of white spots and black shadows.

"Well, Arkangel." Nurse Marion addressed her while remaining in her attached position. "What do you think?"

Ava was at a loss. What did she think about what? "All this destruction…"

"We have had to use bits and pieces of the Forest to rebuild the temple-palace."

"This?" Ava said. "*This* is reconstruction?"

"It is a start," Nurse Marion said. "Remember, *you* are the one who brought the Errorist, the corrupted angel born Marie-Lydia McGillis, here for reform. It is *your* fault we were attacked."

The Nurse had always been the one inhabitant of her temple-palace Ava had been most unsuccessful in influencing when it came to words or actions. Her tone could not be smoothed; her barely concealed anger could not be extinguished.

Ava remembered the attack. Her soul had brought Marie-Lydia's soul there for reform. Marie-Lydia's soul had fought her all the way from Reality's surface, to a far greater extent than Robert's had. Once they'd landed, the trouble multiplied. There had been no skent, just Gast giants, conjured by Marie-Lydia to help her soul battle Ava's and the Widow-Queens. Ava's side had eventually prevailed and, afterward, her soul—her essence of conscious-ness—returned to her flesh-and-blood body on Reality's surface; the Widow-Queens had tried to correct Marie-Lydia's soul while her body remained comatose. From there, things had just gotten worse, in both realms apparently.

"We won," Ava said.

"Barely," Nurse Marion said. "The soul was a strong-willed one. She was not just off the right path. On Reality's surface, you thought you were her mentor, but she had another. A hidden and more powerful one. Under the guidance of this dark one, the Er-rorist has now attained a higher order, and adopted a new name: Saint Alva, the Divine."

Ava stiffened. Robert may not have noticed her discomfort as he said, "What exactly are these *Errorists* you keep mentioning?"

The Nurse turned her eyeless gaze to Robert but said nothing.

"Uh…" Ava was unsure what to say. Telling Robert to keep his mouth shut in Marion's presence would've been futile. "He's with me."

"Is he?" the Nurse asked. What was that supposed to mean?

"When the skull of the Creator aches and cracks," Cheryl said, "when the *Ground of Being* quakes and erupts, you get Errors in the Creation process. Inevitably, you get Errorists, agents of chaos, those whose sole purpose and core goal is to derail the completion of Creation."

"The Infinite Definite," Robert said. "You're talking about—"

"The souls of corrupt angels."

"There was little we could do for the one born Marie-Lydia McGillis," Beryl said to Ava. "And we did not have much time to try."

"Other Errorists somehow learned of what we were attempting to do," Cheryl said. "Learned of whom we were trying to reform and decided to take her for themselves."

"Who?" Ava asked.

"In your dimension, they were known as Veronica Blake and Vanessa Blight."

"Blink and Blank," Robert said. "They were the ones holding Marie-Lydia's body on the surface."

"Clearly, you are easily fooled," Beryl said. "Willingly, even. Someone only wanted you to believe those two Errorists were the true villains."

"All right, then." Robert seemed to take the rudeness in stride. "Tell me what I should believe."

"The two Errorists were formidable. You beat them far more easily than should have been possible. Our Arkangel had a tougher time with them. And so did we."

"Initially, their souls attacked the temple-palace to capture the soul of Marie-Lydia McGillis for themselves, to be their toy. We launched everything we had at them and lost. They had giants on their side and beasts like we have never before encountered. They took the soul and they took several dozen of our Widow-Queen sisters and enslaved them, converted them into prison guards."

"So they imprisoned her soul here in Xyn," Ava said. "Who kept watch over her body on Reality's surface?"

"Her dark master."

"We do not know the name or location of this individual. Believe me, we have tried our best to uncover both. We were not even able to discover where the soul of the corrupted angel was imprisoned. But we do know how it was freed and reunited with her body."

"Her mentor adopted and seasoned another angel, turning him into a warrior-prince strong enough to enter XynKroma, overcome all obstacles, and free her soul, allowing her mind and body to reunite."

"They had to prevent you, Arkangel, from finding her before that could happen."

"Why?"

"They could not let you disrupt the wedding to come."

"The Dark One had gone through a great deal of trouble to find just the right angel to make a perfect union with her prize angel."

"Tell me who," Robert said. "Maybe I've come across him before."

"You have," said Beryl.

"Saint Violet Valentinus," said Cheryl.

"Saint Alva and Saint Violet Valentinus," Beryl said.

"The most powerful pair of corrupted angels now in existence," Cheryl said.

Valentinus. Ava looked at Robert.

"I've been hearing and seeing a little too much of that name lately," he said.

"There is much you do not know," the Nurse said to Ava. "A lot this metal midget does not need to know."

Ava interrupted Robert's response. "Nurse Marion, please, I need my memories back. I need to know everything."

"There is only so much I can give you. As the temple-palace goes, so goes your mind."

"I know," Ava mumbled as she cast her gaze around the broad window, viewing the misery beyond it. "But, please, fill me in on everything that happened since I brought Marie-Lydia's soul here and it was taken away."

"Very well. As your soul brought the girl's here to XynKroma, authorities back in your dimension took your bodies to a hospital. From there, Marie-Lydia's body disappeared from the world, only to end up in the operating theater of one Doctor Jim Linkins, a powerful Archangel, now known as Hell's Crow. He attained his powerful status after his soul clashed with that of Heaven's Raven-Dove here in XynKroma, a legendary battle."

"Heaven's Raven-Dove?" Ava said. "*My* Archangel? What has she to do with this?"

"She disrupted the doctor's operations before disappearing herself. The doctor had come into possession of the corrupted Marie-Lydia McGillis with the intent of corrupting her even further. He attempted to perform an elaborate ritual to turn the girl into the Cardinal Bride, an angel powerful beyond comprehension. But the girl's body was still comatose; her mind and soul here in Xyn, captured by the Errorists, hidden from us. The doctor could do little with Marie-Lydia McGillis before Heaven's Raven-Dove attacked him. The two of them disappeared, and the girl's true mentor, the Dark One who had corrupted her in the first place, recovered her body. In order to get her to wake up, she had to perform her own complicated wedding ritual.

"Alva and Valentinus, they are continuing the ritual, attempting to conceive—capturing a young soul lost in Xyn and re-creating it—so that the three of them, under the guidance of the Dark One, will control the end result of Creation after the Creator's demise. Their ritual is based on a story."

Robert mumbled, "Competing narratives…dueling tales…"

"You spoke of poets and philosophies of corruption." Nurse Marion directly addressed him for the first time.

"How do you know?" Robert said. "You weren't there."

"Anything a Widow-Queen hears, I hear," she said. "Now, if you will permit me, Arkangel, I would like to tell this Watcher another narrative—on the origin of *evil*. Or maybe it is more correct to say I will *remind* him of the origin."

Robert took a step backward. "What are you talk—"

"There is Fundamental Evil," Nurse Marion said. "And then there is the evil with which you are familiar. Some of your poets are correct. Both human nature and the natural world *have* been corrupted. However, the widespread and erroneous belief among the majority of human beings is that this corruption is all due to the actions of the legendary *Eve*.

"The dimension of XynKroma is not just a realm of polluted light. It is where the deepest thoughts of the most highly evolved sentient creatures—their subconscious hopes, wishes, fears, desires, resentments, and so on—mix and mingle with the gasping thoughts of the dying Creator. What happens in this dimension affects what all sentient creatures in existence see and experience. What sentient creatures see and experience affects what they think. And thoughts trickle here to XynKroma like melted snow traveling down a mountain to a river, to a sea. In other words, beliefs affect and can change Reality."

"I know all this," Robert said. "You can stop talking now."

"But most singular thoughts," Nurse Marion continued, ignoring him, "belonging to only one or a few creatures, matter little at this level. Ideally, the process would be mutually beneficial: the Creator's energies mixed with its creatures' energies to beautify, diversify, and, ultimately, finish Creation, bringing it to the condition of a timeless, limitless Paradise that has no use or need for a God. That idea was lost, however, when long ago—according to how time flows in your dimension—one pernicious idea took root and became so pervasive, believed by so many humans—among the most highly evolved of the Creator's creatures—that Creation's progress, the meaning of life, has become something far different than what it should be."

Robert shook his head and took two more steps backward. He'd no face to show expressions, but Ava could tell he was trying to shut ears he couldn't shut. What was going on with him?

"The pernicious idea of a bad woman named Eve," the Nurse said, "and her leading all of humankind into perdition."

"Yes!" Robert shouted. "And it's all crap! I never bought into any of it—"

"Too many humans did," Nurse Marion said. "And continue to. As I said, there is a Fundamental Evil and a Familiar Evil. Familiar Evil was invited into your world by the mental actions taken *against* Eve. This despicable stain on the symbolic first woman, acknowledged as the Mother of all humans and believed to be the ultimate cause of human suffering. These enemies of Eve, they are the reason there is evil in your world."

"But there was no real Eve," Robert said. "There was *no* real Eve." He seemed to be trying to convince himself more than anyone who heard him.

"Of course not." Ava tried to calm him. There was far too much tension in her temple-palace, and it was in bad enough shape already. "I mean, I used to believe Eve was a real person, before I was raised into angelhood. And I bought into the whole story of Eden. Even though I often taught about how the Christ had redeemed humankind, there was still this thought that Eve had really ruined everything, and nothing would really change until

Armageddon. And you, Robert, despite what you say, I know you were raised in a Christian church."

"How?"

"I *know*. And, whether you buy into the Adam, Eve, and Serpent story or not, at some point, maybe when you were really young, you probably believed it."

"When I was really young, I was smarter than you might think," Robert said. "I always knew it was bullshit, even when I was too young to say that word."

"And please do not say it here, either," Nurse Marion said. "The environment here is sensitive to words as well as thoughts. It is our duty to keep Arkangel Ava's temple-palace sacrosanct."

"Bullshit," Robert mumbled before muttering a few more words too low to pick up.

"Eve and the others in Eden are symbols," Ava said. "Eve was at first a symbol of harmony and completion, and then of evil and corruption. But it all goes deeper than that…Ruminating and dwelling on symbols can translate to harsh realities."

"In your dimension," Nurse Marion said, "Eve is rarely if ever directly referred to as 'evil.' Rather, evil is represented by the figure of a devil-creature who lives *underground*. And most of you are taught that Eve aided and abetted evil, ushering it into the world by allowing the devil, in the figure of a serpent, to enter her body—her *head*—through seven openings: her two ears with its delicious words, her mouth and nostrils with the fragrant fruit it offered, and her eyes with the mysterious beauty of the fruit and itself."

Ava said, "The legendary Eve and the mythical devil have become, in the minds of too many, if not synonymous, then married to one another, joined arm in arm if not at the hip."

"As a result of this ridiculous myth of Eden's destruction," Nurse Marion said, "the reputation of Eve was demonized. Humankind's thoughts of her cracked, shattered, and scattered her once pristine image. Thus, innumerable pieces settled into the Ground of XynKroma and eventually sank to become buried deep beneath."

"Metaphorically," Robert said.

"That is the only way we can speak here," Nurse Marion said, "when dealing with the abstractions such as evil and its end. The first human beings did not have this idea or create this myth. It began with the onset of modern humans, within a subset of a very particular group of humans, when they *stepped up* a level in consciousness. As time runs differently here in XynKroma, their decrepit and diseased thoughts of women and sex spread and settled in such a way so it seemed that the idea of the evil Eve had always been present rather than having been planted rather recently.

"Minds numerous enough, focused enough, and strong-willed enough to have serious effects here, and thus color what the rest of thinking beings experience. The *story* you were once told on Reality's surface, Watcher, is for all intents and purposes *true*. With Adam's blessing, partisans of Cain took and dismembered Eve's body for her alleged sins; Lilith, Adam's first and estranged wife, gathered the bits and pieces and planted them like seeds in another dimension. Remember that narrative…you Watcher dog of *Adam*?"

"We're leaving," Robert said. "*Now.*"

"Wait," Ava began, "I—"

The Nurse ignored her. "Alva and Valentinus are in the process of creating a more powerful narrative, a stronger story than that of Adam and Eve. The two only need a third *soul* for everything to fall into place. In order for creation to be completed in their image, they need the soul of your sibling."

"What?" Ava looked from the Nurse to Robert. Robert stumbled around like he was playing pin the tail on the donkey, undoubtedly looking for an exit.

"We are called Widow-Queens," the Nurse said, "because we are widows to the dead idea of how Creation was supposed to unfold, but we shall be the Queens of the surviving humans in the end." She was now intent on addressing Robert after being so intent on ignoring him. "We earn our future queenship as we conquer and unite sections of XynKroma. Our sacred role and duty is to cultivate the Ground of Being, specifically the sections containing Eve's seeds. On these sections, we raise our temple-palaces and surround them with farms, orchards, and gardens connected to Reality's surface. See, dog of Adam, Eve *will* triumph. *Our* efforts will succeed. *Our* narratives will reign. As you and your kind go extinct, we shall ensure the survival of the chosen children into finished Creation."

"Arkangel," Robert yelled. "If you care about this…thing, if you don't want to see me break it apart and tie it back together with those freakin' cords, get us out of here—*now*."

"I—" Ava was confused. She was well-versed in the Eve Under philosophy, had been taught it thoroughly when she was inverted. But why was Marion making it—somehow—about Robert? And his sibling? What was—

"Go," Nurse Marion said to Ava, "*with my blessing.*"

Ava heard the frizzing before she saw it, before she *felt* it. Her soul and Robert's both shifted to pure white; they briefly looked like a snowwoman and snowman before they began dissolving. Like baking soda mixed with vinegar, it was loud and pungent, not Ava's usual way of exiting XynKroma. But this was an unusual visit, and before her sense of presence faded away completely, Ava intuited an unusual message from the Nurse, poetically encrypted: *Misunderstandings stand over Love, buried…*

She got it, then went black.

Chapter 10

Cyrus considered himself a simple man. A simple man who once just happened to have a grand little plan. To achieve it, he'd made a nefarious pact. Not with one devil, or even two, but with a whole slew of the craftiest satans in existence. It had been a Faustian bargain like no other in history. But, despite the setbacks, despite the disappointments and lack of expected support, Cyrus still intended to get the best of them all in the end, ushering in a perfect world ruled by a perfect order. Flood or no damned Flood.

He stopped to stare at the screen of one of the laptops on the kitchen island. He watched as the scenes from live recordings flashed by, each scene lasting no more than three seconds. He waited until one cycle had been completed. All clear. None of the cameras in or around the building picked up anything out of the ordinary. He watched cycles complete on the other two laptops before continuing on to the refrigerator.

It took a couple of minutes, but he finally decided to stick with his physician's orders: a bottle of mountain springwater and a Tupperware container filled with fresh spinach, sliced carrots, and radishes. No meat till tomorrow. He'd promised he'd try the new diet, eating meat only on alternate days. He didn't mind his girth, but he'd made a promise to himself and others he'd start looking out for his heart. Promises, promises—all the baggage and mileage. Well, if nothing else, he was a man of his word.

He placed his dinner on the TV tray and finished off the shot of Hennessey XO he'd set there ten minutes ago. He'd put off meat, but he'd be damned if he'd end a day like this one without a little nip. In a way, it was also for his heart. Just a little something to keep him steady.

Then he heard a noise. From outside on the balcony. Sounded like rustling leaves. Sounded like, but couldn't be. His apartment was far too high for trees to leave anything on his patio.

He shut his eyes and put his right hand on his hip holster. Letting his ears act as his eyes, the sound waves making like light rays, Cyrus moved slowly toward the coffee table, picked up his 9mm Glock, then listened his way toward the balcony's glass door.

It was just after 9:30 P.M. The vertical blinds had been closed. But even if they'd been open and it had been noontime, his eyes would've been of little use, especially if the threat was something that could easily mask its presence by bending light around its body, appearing nonexistent. His ears were his best physical asset.

Though maybe not tonight. Cyrus had heard nothing beyond the initial rustling.

He stopped in front of the blinds and stilled his breathing, attempting to listen extra hard for anything awry. He opened his eyes and used the gun's barrel to part a section of the blinds. Nothing. He saw and sensed nothing.

He removed his right hand from his hip holster and brushed aside several blinds, giving himself a full view of the entire balcony. The lights in the room behind him were dim; the reflection on the door's glass was minimized. Cyrus saw clearly. And he still saw nothing. He still sensed no threat.

He trusted his senses enough to know he was alone. Alone with his nerves. They'd undoubtedly made him think he'd heard rustling in the first place. If that was the case, just how well could he trust his senses? He'd a right to be nervous, but he couldn't allow his own body to become an enemy, sending him false alarms. He had to be sure.

He unlocked the patio door's three locks, removed the wooden plank acting as a jamb, and slid it open, just wide enough for a man of his size to squeeze through, before closing it behind. Even the craftiest of the diseased bastards couldn't pass through glass.

He glanced to either side then tread carefully toward the railing. He peered over the edge, then smiled. Only a Hollywood ninja could scale up to this height without being detected by any of the sensors he'd ensured were installed in all the right places.

He lived on the top floor of one of the tallest condo buildings in Arlington. It'd been his home for three years. The building itself wasn't much older. Government employees and contractors had been given first dibs on the units in the building. Before committing to buy, Cyrus had made damn sure only those on his most-trusted list occupied the other units on his floor, as well as those directly below. Not that it mattered that much. The entire building was wired with all sorts of optical and audio devices, to which he'd complete and near-exclusive access. There was rarely any cause to worry about his privacy or his safety.

He took a long, deep breath of the young night's air and—much more quickly—exhaled, rudely reminded that even at this height he wasn't immune to the atmosphere's many pollutants. A momentary lapse in consciousness. He'd have to travel quite a ways from the area if he wanted to take in truly fresh air. Farther even than Spencer, Virginia.

He turned around to head back inside, still doubting his instincts, those tricky pricks that had urged him outside for no good reason. He then spotted something in the corner of the patio and cursed his carelessness.

It hadn't been leaves or a trespasser. It'd been the two sheets of computer paper he'd read, crumpled, and tossed aside earlier in the day. *Karma.* His fit of anger in the morning had come back to bite him in the evening. An unfair karma, actually, as it wasn't his fault.

The *Washington Times* editorial had sent him into a fury with its approving description of the latest campaign tactics being used against Senator Sinha. He was surprised the winds hadn't blown the wads over the edge, and he was happy they hadn't. Cyrus hated littering. If he had his way, it'd be punishable by a lofty fine and a mandatory week's stay in a cell. He'd have his way soon enough.

Changes were imminent. Changes working in the country's favor for once. Changes benefiting the passionate defenders of the country's security. He was pulling hard for the Indian American candidate and the administration he was sure to bring in. He'd a faint desire to see Sagan and her crew pushed out of the White House, literally, with brooms. The symbolism alone might help reinvigorate the American people, pushing *them* onto the proper path, a more *correct* way of seeing things.

It wasn't totally the administration's fault that American kids these days were more and more likely to belong to violent gangs or Trixster rings of young thieves and prostitutes rather than two-parent households. The downward spiraling economy and soft-core media had made being a thug, a crook, or a whore—or a combination of all three—more appealing to young polluted minds than being a good dutiful kid. He'd hoped Jenifer Sagan, as the nation's first Mommy in Chief, would've been more amenable to radical ideas on curbing bad juvenile behavior ranging from murder to sex trafficking. Maybe women just couldn't think straight once they'd gotten hold of too much power.

It had only been fifteen years since the First Lady had murdered the very popular President Anthony Sullivan after catching him entertaining his mistress in a bedroom a few blocks away from the White House. Her lawyers contended the gun had gone off by accident; she'd only intended to instill the fear of God. Cyrus believed the woman had been psychologically unsuited to be married to such a powerful man in the first place; she was bound to destroy him one way or another.

When Vice President Ken Gunderson had assumed power in the wake of the tragedy and, in an extraordinarily compressed amount of time, almost ruined the country with a series of well-meaning social programs, Cyrus had cheered. At the time, as a government defense contractor with many close friends at right-leaning Washington think tanks, he'd seen the writing on the wall. Gunderson's actions paved the way for Congress to shift to the right in the midterm election and the conservative Jenifer Sagan to win the Oval Office two years later. One nation-improving item that hadn't been on Gunderson's ambitious agenda was the establishment of the Heartland Security Agency. A scrappy conservative Congress had proposed the idea, and the fatigued soon-to-be ex-President Gunderson couldn't argue and didn't even raise a whimper against the concept of a government agency whose official vision would be "to preserve America's families, protect her children, and promote safe and happy communities," using whatever legal and rational (and fundable) means necessary.

Cyrus had been very fond of President Gunderson. The man knew how to keep a secret. Very *beautiful* secrets. And Cyrus honestly had nothing against President Sagan. To his perpetual delight, the repeal of the Second Amendment had not been reversed under her administration; she'd agreed that only *sanctioned* officers should be allowed to bear arms. Two years ago, however, there had been another shift in Congress. The will of the people, and all that shit. Since then, the President had been bending more and more on issues where she'd once stood firm. It was time for her to pack her bags and head for the sunset. It was time for a change.

As a well-connected, highly tuned federal agent, Cyrus had enough goods on enough people—particularly those in Sinha's camp—to persuade him and them to give Cyrus anything he asked for. Senator Sinha was smarter than his opponent (something the *Washington Times* editorial denied more than once), but the good Senator would also be so much easier to convince, to persuade, to bring around to his way of thinking. Cyrus didn't need magick to deal with his kind.

He picked up the garbage and went back inside, locking up behind him. After tossing the wads into the recycler and laying his Glock next to the laptop on the kitchen island, he again watched and waited for the screen to complete a cycle of scenes. Nothing to see there. Still, he needed another shot of cognac after what he'd just gone through.

He swallowed his third shot as he sat on the couch, behind and to the right of the TV tray. Perfect position. He wanted an unobstructed view of the seventy-six-inch high-def screen for to-night's edutainment.

Cyrus pushed a few buttons on the remote and began to watch the first film, number one in a series of eight. He'd recorded them off the Internet well over a year ago, shortly after they'd first began appearing on certain dark sites. He'd studied them at the time. To-night he was taking a necessary refresher course.

The film began with a voice-over, an introduction spoken by a twenty-two-year-old Infinite Definite affiliate who used the mon-iker "Saint Candice Flavius."

"The Kids of The ID welcome you to witness the latest and greatest of the fateful eight!"

It sounded like several female voices—high-pitched, smoky, and everything in between—were talking in unison, saying the same thing. In truth, it was only Candice. Real name: Natalie

Dorff. Shy, withdrawn tween turned humbly popular high school cheerleader turned roaring drunk sorority bimbo turned supernaturally talented mass murderess. Exactly how she'd contracted the sexually transmitted Virus had never been a mystery. Current whereabouts: unknown. Whereabouts eighteen months ago: Spencer, Virginia—the set location of most of the films Cyrus would force himself to endure.

The voice-over had been added to each of the eight films after they'd been recorded and before they'd been launched into cyberspace. The original introduction to each flick was a simple, wordless action: an innocent knock on a house's front door.

A few days before the first video was recorded, eight drug-addled, diseased, and otherwise troubled teenagers had run away from their homes. No big deal. All of them had run away from their dysfunctional homes before; most of them had done it fairly often. The parents had been used to the antics of their bad-egg children. They'd stopped caring. None of them had bothered to even look for their missing offspring, let alone call the police. The troublesome brats had always come back sooner or later, always of their own free will. And, sure enough, after the latest and last scrambling away, each troublemaking teen paid one last visit home. The heartbreaking (and skull-cracking) reunions were all captured on film.

There'd been no script, but the recorded performances followed a kind of pattern. All the home invasions had taken place during the breakfast hours. Each film opened with a scene of a kid ringing the doorbell or knocking on the front door of his or her own house. When the door opened, both Saint Candice Flavius and Saint William-Jack—Candice's twenty-three-year-old partner and former frat-boy boyfriend—shouted "Tricky treat!" as the hapless door opener was pushed down or struck in the face. While the kid and his seven new pals rushed into the house, Candice's voice-over always recited the same semi-poetic babble:

"Up-Dawn of the Loving Dead! Bringing rays of joy to disinfect the fear of inevitabilities! Like Love—"

"And Death!" William-Jack always interrupted to finish the phrase.

Cyrus had never understood what their words meant, but they'd probably made sense to the terrorist duo.

Under Saint Candice Flavius's and Saint William-Jack's firm direction, the eight teenagers had been conditioned, trained, and grouped together as a traveling troupe of sadists calling themselves the Kids of The ID or, alternatively, the HighSkule HorrorShow. For their first act, they'd planned to break free of the bonds that had kept them losers for the entirety of their short lives. Saints Candice Flavius and William-Jack both remained behind their cameras the entire time, filming, laughing hysterically, and providing running commentary while the eight teenage players shone, performing all the beatings, the stabbings, the hackings, the chokings, the murders, and the rapes.

Throughout each film, the two so-called saints shouted obscenities and slogans—"Kill all the parents!" and "Rape all the siblings!" were favorites—but the eight players never said a word. The eight only communicated by flashing hand signals at their fellow players, or by hissing at their victims if they begged too loudly for mercy.

After felling a victim, a player would sometimes use hand signals to ask nonengaged players for advice on a method of assault. The advisers would either flash a hand signal in response or toss the requester a prop. Hatchets, axes, knives, and machetes were brought into play when the use of fists, nails, feet, and teeth became too dull.

Each of the eight players had slightly different assault techniques and favorite moves, but they shared certain similarities as well. The White Fire Virus infected them all; all of them were freshmen in high school; and all of them performed barefoot—but they also had interesting costumes. Each of the four boys wore tattered, ripped blue jeans and an unbuttoned white baseball jersey emblazoned with the number eight, six, four, or two. Each of the four girls wore a ripped, torn, and very short black cheerleader skirt and a too-small, white T-shirt that featured the number one, three, five, or seven. Aside from the numbers, fresh and dried bloodstains served as the only other decoration on their clothing.

Notwithstanding all the blood, the numbers served as the best signifiers for identifying which player was which, because their faces kept changing, adopting grotesque expressions and bizarre appearances, trading colors, shades, and tones, all of it depending on how much light hit the skin and where the camera was situated. Cyrus had once read that a sudden and unexpected shift in what is believed to be reality is the essence of true horror. These films were proof positive of that theory.

After a player scored a kill, before moving on to another target, he would blow a kiss and bow to the dead body—or, if a she, would blow a kiss and curtsy. It was partly for the viewing pleasure of the audience and partly for the dying eyes of the victim. Perverse love at last sight.

Stomach-churning.

Cyrus had forgotten all about his dinner. The performances on the screen were as engrossing as they were repellant. He hardly even blinked during the scene in the fourth film where the lone survivor of a household, a fifteen-year-old girl who'd been stripped and beaten raw, was pierced with forks and cut with knives in the kitchen before being dragged into the backyard.

The other members of the girl's family were already dead, sprawling in the backyard's grass, their heads busted open, their eyes gouged out or scooped out with spoons. All of them but the film's star, the fourteen-year-old boy in the number four jersey, the one who'd been first among the male players to rape his sister.

The team of eight gathered in a loose circle around the fallen. As the still-living girl lay twisting, sobbing, far beyond the point of screaming or yelling for help, the eight coated the entire family with generous amounts of Pixie Dust, the multihued sandlike crystals that had once been used to fill the hourglass of a popular children's board game until the dust's harmful effects were discovered after one too many sessions of heated game play. Pixie Dust's crystals burned as they settled into open wounds or eyes; the pain lasted far longer than the sting of rubbing alcohol. The eight players, however, had something else in mind for the dust and their victims. They'd wanted to provide their future audience with a big, beautiful finish.

When the sunlight fell upon the crystals, millions of multihued fingers appeared in the air around the dusted victims. Curling, writhing, wriggling tubes of colored light—fingers without hands or arms—seemed to grab on to some crystal-sprinkled body part and slowly but surely lift it into the air, by a few inches or by a couple of feet, leaving severed chunks and entire bodies suspended. The dead levitated, as did the dying girl as she breathed her last. A sacrifice to the life-giving sun.

"This has been a rehearsal for the HighSkule HorrorShow!" William-Jack announced, reciting the words that signaled the end of every film. "A better class of zeroes!"

The screen faded to black as Candice spoke her joyful warning: "We're coming *live* to a set near you!"

Cyrus hit the Pause button on his remote. He'd made it halfway through the series, but he needed a respite. No normal man could sit still through eight straight showings of material like that, no matter how short the films were.

He stood up and went through his stretching exercises, trying to loosen up, improve circulation, get his head right.

Most observers would've considered the flicks nothing less than snuff films. A minority might even consider them extremely explicit documentaries. A twistedly brilliant film student could even have found the films to be fascinating for what they had to say about interrelatedness of sex and violence and the modern American family.

Cyrus only considered them research materials. That's all they were tonight, and that's what they had been intended to be two years ago, back when he and Dr. Jimmy Waldo Linkins had devised the entire scheme.

If those eight kids had been truly bad seeds—and they truly had been—then the parents had been diseased trees and the siblings rotten fruit. Cyrus had little sympathy for any of the fallen. They'd provided no benefit to society. Because of them—so abusive and neglectful—their kids had gone so far off the straight path, they'd forgotten any kind of moral, upstanding way even existed in this dark world.

Goddamned parents.

They butted heads often, but Cyrus and Carmilla also saw eye to eye on many points, one of the most important being that people who don't want children should be made incapable of producing them, for their own good and for the well-being of greater society.

The witch had proven to be a great—if irritating—business partner. She was even more valuable than the sum of her abundant jewels.

In spite of her misgivings about Dr. Linkins, she'd collaborated closely with Cyrus on Project Can&Will, the "art project" of enlisting Infinite Definite affiliates Candice Flavius and William-Jack to turn eight wayward teens into a talented team. Carmilla had provided the off-the-market drugs. Saints Candice Flavius and William-Jack had provided a variety of psychological and physical training, all over the span of one week. And after the families of the eight had reaped what they'd sown, Cyrus and his most trusted HSA Peacemakers had swooped in to round up the

HorrorShow before they could expand their tour too far beyond Spencer, Virginia.

Good, strong hands had gathered up the eight. Unfortunately, the eight's dim guiding lights had been a little confused about the details of the original agreement. Candice and William-Jack believed the eight would be theirs to keep as they traveled the country, committing spectacularly random acts of horrific violence forever. Yet Cyrus had always intended to use the eight as a black ops group that would go after the human sex-slave traffickers operating with impunity inside America's borders. When the saints woke up one day to find the eight long gone, they'd figured they'd been cheated. By the time the duo had gotten set to settle the score, Cyrus was long gone from Spencer, en route to The SeptiGuarden to make a special delivery to Dr. Linkins. So the two pissed off saints made their way to Carmilla's house, just as Cyrus had initially figured and hoped they would.

Carmilla hadn't expected Candice and William-Jack to show up out of nowhere. Cyrus hadn't expected there to be middle school kids on her property when they did. He'd later learned she'd been tutoring them in the practice of Charmic Arts. Once upon a time, Carmilla was somewhat generous about sharing her knowledge of the dark mystic arts. But during that same time, she wasn't yet expert enough in her own arts to defend herself against the most malicious Infinite Definite pair the HSA had ever classified. Lucky for the Girl of Many Charms, a certain protégé of hers happened onto the scene just in time to prevent the slaughter—if not the scarring—of innocent children. The charged-up redhead (who maybe or not coincidentally had also adopted the "saint" title for her own new name) made quick and spectacular work of Candice Flavius and William-Jack.

Both Candice and William-Jack were severely burned, and both were expected to expire in the HSA medical facility in which they'd been placed. But less than one month after their placement, they had both disappeared from the maximum security facility. Neither one had been seen or heard from since. Despite his connections, Cyrus had never been able to determine with certainty just what had happened, but he'd always figured the witch had had something to do with their disappearance, meaning it was probably permanent. And as for what became of Dr. Linkins…*Que sera, sera.*

Cyrus stopped stretching and walked toward the kitchen. Once again he stopped to check the laptop monitoring his building. This time he saw something.

A girl was in the hallway outside his condo, moving awkwardly but quickly in the direction of his front door. Although she only appeared on the screen for three seconds, Cyrus could tell the girl was highly agitated. She was carrying something in her right hand. Something Cyrus couldn't quite make out. This had better not be bad news.

He downed another shot of cognac and picked up his Glock. There was a furious pounding on the front door. He inhaled and moved forward.

Cyrus knew the girl—but what was up? Was she being followed? Had she stolen something? Of course she had. That's what the dirty little blonde was best at. That and one other thing. But she damn well better not've dragged trouble to his doorstep.

He checked the peephole and studied the yellow-blonde's face. Yes, she was definitely worried about something, but she didn't have the look of someone being chased or followed. It was more like the look of someone who'd just made an unexpected and unsettling discovery.

He undid the locks and cracked open the door.

"Password?"

"Let me the fuck in."

"Manners, girl," he said.

"*Please*, Uncle Cyrus."

Her voice had a whining element to it. Damned irritating. "Please, *what*?"

"I really *really* need to pee."

He shook his head as he pulled the door open wider. The girl squeezed in and made a mad dash for the restroom in the hallway. On the way, she laid what she'd been holding on the kitchen island.

He waited till the girl closed the bathroom door before he stepped outside his condo, into the hallway. He looked to either side before closing his eyes, stilling his breath.

No other heartbeats. No other breaths. No one there but him.

He stepped back inside and redid the locks. He thought briefly about setting the alarm—but no. The motion-sensing detector was only for when he was away or asleep. He didn't want to accidentally trip it and bring his shoot-first-and-ask-later boys there on a false note.

Cyrus walked into the kitchen, laid down his gun, and picked up what the girl had dropped. It was the size of a smartphone but as powerful as the strongest laptops used by military high officials. He'd given it to her in April, as a just-because gift. By July, she'd configured it to be one of the most sophisticated handheld identity-thieving devices on the planet. Powerful enough, say, for her to sit on the other side of a lake, reading a romance novel in a pontoon boat near the farther shore, while the device locked in and recorded all it needed to.

He looked at the screen, curious as always about what the girl was up to. Whatever it was, it made no sense. He only saw a stream of indecipherable symbols, and the screen's backlight seemed about to burn out. As he stared at it, the screen grew bright by degrees only to grow dimmer by the same number of degrees. The cycle repeated, and Cyrus saw a shift in the screen's symbols. He then realized there was nothing wrong with the backlight. The device was running a decrypting program of some sort, slowly translating the symbols to something sensible, something he was sure he'd want to know about.

He stood transfixed until he heard something moving a couple of feet in front of him. Cyrus jerked his head up, giving the girl the perfect opportunity to smack him across his left cheek. He'd be feeling the sting for the next fifteen minutes at least.

"I hope you washed your hands."

"Why the hell didn't you tell me about Ava?"

She was a foot shorter than him, but the girl's glare directly into his eyes almost had the desired effect. Almost. He'd nothing to apologize for. Not to her, anyway.

"Sally Ellin, of what concern can she possibly be to you?"

"She's going to kill me!"

Cyrus smiled as he put his hands on her shoulders and bent his head closer to hers.

"She is not going to do a thing to you."

"I want protection." Her voice was calmer now, but its tone was still uneven. "And I want to know why you didn't tell me, the second you found out, that that heifer is going to be armed, out roaming the streets like an escaped psychobitch."

"Calm down. Here." He kept his hands on her shoulders as he guided her toward the couch. "The Darden girl is under control. She's no threat to you. I've confirmed with the IAI, multiple times, that her memory bank still has insufficient funds."

She crossed her arms and pouted. "I'm a marked woman, and you're making dumb jokes."

"I'm serious." He uncrossed her arms and pulled her to sit down next to him. "That girl has bigger concerns than settling some petty grudge against you, assuming she even remembers you. And she has no reason to believe you're even in the area."

"Not yet, but—"

"But I'm keeping an eye out. I've made sure that a trusted watchdog will stick to her and alert me the second she strays. You just keep doing what I've told you to and there'll be no problem."

Sally Ellin didn't look convinced. She sulked, but didn't say anything more. Damn, when would she finally grow up?

Cyrus put his forefinger and thumb under her chin and lifted, raising her head until their eyes met.

"Are you with me," he said, "or are you with me?"

It was slow coming, but something approaching a smile appeared under the blonde's pert nose. Cyrus smiled in return.

"So what goodies do you have for me tonight?" he asked. "Or did you just stop by to smack me around?"

"You know I never come to you empty-handed." Her smile twisted into one suggesting so many pleasant possibilities.

"Thatta girl."

"But I can't give you what you want, Uncle."

She leaned forward and pushed him away, then hopped up and hurried for the kitchen.

For a moment, Cyrus sat still on the couch, staring after her, waiting for the punch line.

She wasn't going for the Glock—was she?

He scrambled to his feet, his hand on his hip holster; it held an ADS weapon, capable of firing a microwave beam, causing unimaginable pain at a finger's snap. His was a smaller, experimental version of the Active Denial System weapon commonly used to control riots. He'd been practically salivating for the opportunity to try it out against an Infinite Definite animal. If necessary, however, Sally Ellin would do for a first target.

But he relaxed. No need to use it just yet. She hadn't gone for the gun, just her RFID device.

Cyrus walked toward the kitchen. He needed another shot of cognac.

"I tried and tried and tried," Sally Ellin said. "But I just couldn't get into Carmilla's system. Whatever charms that dyke relies on, I know she also believes in technology."

"She's smart enough not to keep anything sensitive written down," Cyrus said as he picked up the bottle. "Electronically or any other way."

"I doubt that. And I doubt she's using her computer just to shop and play games."

Cyrus nodded, then swallowed.

"But which or whatever, it don't matter. What does is that she's nuzzled up to one or two lezzies that haven't gotten hip to the way of the world yet. The way of *my* world."

"Oh, really?" Cyrus smiled and slid his right arm around Sally Ellin's shoulders.

"Yes, Uncle." Her twisted smile reappeared. "That dirty witch may've refused you, but I never will."

Cyrus pulled her close and kissed her on her forehead. "Good girl."

"*Great* girl," she said. "Look." She thrust the device toward his face. "A detailed explanation on the hows and whats of Verbalism. Carmilla's own special brand of so-called Word Magick."

His eyes widened. Had Sally Ellin actually—*finally*—deciphered the code to one of Carmilla's charms?

"Fuck that bitch for trying to keep it from us," Sally Ellin said. "We're going to fuck her!"

"Whoa, whoa, whoa there." Cyrus repositioned himself behind her and massaged her shoulders. "Carmilla is not the enemy. She's difficult, but she's on our side. Ultimately, she's on our side. You need to make peace with her, be friends."

"You make friends with that freak."

He'd tried, but Cyrus knew no massage technique could ever soothe her when discussing the witch.

"I already went out of my way to make nice with the monkeys at school."

"Only two of them," Cyrus said.

"Make nice with two darkies, you gotta make nice with twenty," she said. "Their kind sticks together. Like brown rice. Makes me sick."

So many things about Sally Ellin made Cyrus sick. Were his words, the many, many things he'd told her, taught her, whispered into her ear over the past few years just lost on her? Maybe he should've skipped the pillow talk and just used pills. The girl was smart as a whip when it came to cracking technology, but nowhere near evolved enough to appreciate the benefits of looking and judging by what was under mere surface appearances.

"You should stick to the higher purpose, Sally child. When I tell you to do something, it's not to humiliate you or make you suffer. It's for a reason."

"As opposed to a rhyme, huh?"

Cyrus smiled and took his hands from her shoulders. "From whom did you pull that information?"

"Dimwitted Wendy Watson. Real name: Teresa Watson. One of Carmilla's fresh acolytes, studying the ways of her dark mistress."

And unable to simply hear and commit the lessons to memory, as Cyrus certainly knew Carmilla instructed all her initiates in the Charmic Arts to do.

"She typed up the lessons into notes?"

"Yep," Sally Ellin said. "In a precious little shorthand. Tried to encrypt, too, but—"

"Let's get that to the printer." Cyrus took the device from her and headed toward the living room.

"You know," Sally Ellin said as she followed, "she didn't exactly transcribe everything in plain English. I was lucky to decipher a description of the file in which she hid it."

"I'll go over it with a translator." Cyrus plugged the computer into the printer on the shelf next to the television.

Sally Ellin looked at the TV tray, then cocked her head toward the screen.

"Whatcha watchin'?"

Good Lord, he hated those little hick-girl affectations she used. They were few and far between these days, and he'd loved them when she'd been much younger, but now he wished she'd just pick an adult's age and act it consistently.

"Precious memories," Cyrus said as the first page printed. "Home movies from your hometown."

"Oh. The HorrorShow." She picked up the remote and pushed Play.

Cyrus started skimming the pages coming out of the printer. She was right about the lack of plain English. A mélange of letters, numbers, and music notes. There was nothing he could do with this information on his own.

When the twenty-second and final page printed, Sally Ellin pushed Stop on the remote. She apparently couldn't take any more. Cyrus knew she didn't have a weak stomach. She'd seen these films—all of them, all the way through—at least three times. Maybe his remark about memories had actually made her remember something else. Maybe she couldn't stop thinking about how the original plan called for nine players instead of eight, and how the redheaded ninth one might've turned out to be much better (and much worse) than the other eight combined. A precious thought indeed.

He didn't want her to dwell on it. It wasn't healthy.

"What time is your first class tomorrow?" he asked, taking his first forkful of salad from the Tupperware container.

"Uh, nine, I think."

"One of your computer science courses?"

"No. Political."

"Ah." Cyrus took a swig of water and checked his watch. Two minutes after ten. "Joke of a subject. Nothing you couldn't stand to miss."

"Guess not."

Sally Ellin switched the television off video mode and started clicking through the channels. She stopped on the local Fox station. The nightly news program had just started, leading off as usual with the most recent and most mysterious and most gratuitous murder in the DC metro area. At least a dozen more would be reported before the news hour ended. Ethnic gangs would be the suspects in all. For Cyrus, Infinite Definite associates or other Virus-carriers would be the actual culprits in most. Time keeps on slipping…

When they started talking about a massacre in West Virginia, he turned off the television. "You'll be staying the night."

No time for an answer, so he didn't pose it as a question. It was just a signal that she should get ready for bed, unless she had something else for him tonight.

"Guess so."

No. Nothing.

He removed the items from the TV tray and, before placing the food into the refrigerator, stopped to watch a cycle pass on all the kitchen island's laptops—the one tuned in on the building, the one linked to the drones over Arlington, the one linked to the drones over Washington. He then time-set the motion sensor detector for ten forty-five. Satisfied, he began to turn off the lights.

Sally Ellin was in the bathroom, getting ready. She'd be in there for ten minutes, at the very least, freshening up, deciding which of the silk negligees or other garments in the closet she'd want to wear tonight. Cyrus hoped she didn't take too long. He wanted to get it over with and then get some sleep. He needed to get up in time to place a phone call, invite himself to a meeting. He wished tomorrow would hurry up already.

Chapter 11

The Watcher had a secret. Of course that was it. That's why he'd resisted going to XynKroma with her. Ava wanted her memory back, but the Watcher wanted to keep a part of his memory suppressed. His consciously created armor in Xyn now made sense. It might've even worked if not for the damage wrought by the skent. Nurse Marion further needled and prodded his mind until the thoughts spilled out, filling Ava's mind as they exited the realm.

She now remembered. She now remembered so much. And she now knew so much of Robert. The dirty son of a—

Ava had to get away from him.

She stood next to the bed, watching him, careful with her blinks. She had awoken earlier than he, but not by much; otherwise she would've fled. Instead she hurried with her pants, just buttoning them as he stirred, grumbling and cursing. She acted nonchalant as she walked into the bathroom and closed the door. She put on the rest of her clothes and her watches, then exited, cleaning her glasses with toilet tissue.

"Time for lunch," she said.

"Adam…Eve…Cain…Abel…" He was still mumbling, perhaps on the verge of delirium. Even though she hadn't been in a while, Ava had enough practice in recovering from the soul-twisting journeys to and from Xyn, and the subsequent deep, dreamless sleeps on Reality's surface. She recovered as if waking from a catnap. Robert recovered as if waking from a trance. She didn't care to rush him.

"You don't mind," she said, "I'm going to step outside for some fresh air."

Robert continued to mumble as she closed the door behind her. Glasses still in hand, she looked toward the sun as her eyesight unfocused and she concentrated. She remembered so much now—including how to send signals on Reality's surface.

Message sent, she reentered the room to find Robert dressed and sitting on the edge of the bed, rubbing his arm. He glared at her when she closed the door but said nothing. He wasn't even muttering anymore.

"You hungry?" he said finally. He had the look of a man who knew his date was going to order lobster, steak, and a bottle of French wine, then conveniently go powder her nose when the check came.

"I could go for a ham sandwich," she said.

Robert stood and looked around the room. "Let's make sure we don't leave anything we don't want left." He continued to rub his arm as he walked around the room. Ava kept her eyes on him, this follower of Adam.

They returned the room's key to the motel manager and got into Robert's Mustang, neither of them saying a word to the other. When he pulled out of the lot, groggy as he seemed, Ava expected him to drive like a grandmother heading to the market on Sunday morning; instead, he drove like a Sunday school teacher whose alarm hadn't gone off. He drove like *her*.

Ava considered the situation mathematically. Their souls mixed in Xyn, and they'd kept a tiny fragment of each other. Not ideal, but she was okay with that. She wasn't okay with the fact that Robert was a *Watcher*, the type of angel whose sinfulness, according to apocryphal scriptures, somehow brought about the biblical Flood. What's more, he was a follower of a man who called himself "Adam," a man who claimed his number one goal was to find his own child or children, one or more of whom had a name rhyming with the letter *R*. However many there were, they didn't belong to him.

In addition to revealing to her that God was dying and the dimensions were collapsing, Heaven's Raven-Dove, the Archangel Artemisia, had told Ava during the inversion process that, when the end was near, a Most High "son of Adam" would appear to assume control over the hereafter. Marie-Lydia—*Alva* and Valentinus were trying to produce their own child to fill this role for their dark master. But Adam, using Robert, had his own plot.

She'd sensed it when she'd broken into his apartment two weeks ago and entered his mind as they'd talked, but now she remembered it clearly. The "son of Adam" that will arise would have the blood of Robert's mother running through his veins. The Archangel Artemisia had made that abundantly clear. Marie-Lydia—*Saint Alva* must have known, as well. Maybe that's why she was drawn to this area in the first place. But why had she adopted a new name, one so similar to Ava's?

Out of her passenger's side window, Ava saw half-built condominiums, rotting and vandalized. She saw lots overrun with garbage and weeds as tall as a small child. They even passed a wooded patch, by which Robert seemed to drive even faster; Ava still caught the graffiti on the trees, the hanging and fallen leaves that were neither brown nor of the autumnal rainbow, but instead orangish green, with a hint of something else. An alien tint. This is how the world ends.

When she saw a sign reading, "The Village at Shirlington," needles jabbed at her temples. She winced, then ran her eyes over the mash-up of buildings the sign had announced. Apartments, restaurants, a library, at least two theaters—the movie kind and the classier kind. This "village" had been kept up during the recession. "Probably somewhere in all that where we can get a decent sandwich," she said.

"Yeah," Robert said. "I'm looking for a parking spot."

"On the street?" Ava asked. "I saw a parking garage—"

"I'd rather park on the street," he said.

Odd quirk, Ava thought. She didn't see how it might've come about due to their recent trip; she did wonder where he'd park when he had to return to The Burrow. Whatever. It wasn't her problem. Neither was finding a spot on the street. While Robert slid coins into the meter, Ava again glanced at the sun. This time, she had a mild sensation it was communicating back to her.

At least something seemed to communicate with her. Robert said nothing, just rubbed his arm as they walked into the Village. He didn't even turn his head to consider any of the eateries they passed. Ava considered them all, especially one called Busboys and Poets. Pangs stabbed her temples again when she saw the name.

"Up ahead," Robert said as he lamely gestured with the arm he'd been rubbing. "There's a Subway sandwich shop around the corner."

Ava glanced back toward Busboys as they turned the corner. Something was calling her there. She had to break away. It was a strange feeling of relief to see the line in Subway was so long.

"Order me the Black Forest Ham. On wheat. I'm going to the ladies' room."

Robert said nothing as she walked away. She glanced back at him before stepping into the restroom. He wasn't looking at the menu. He wasn't looking at her. His mind was elsewhere. His eye was unfocused. *Perfect.*

Ava pushed the restroom door open but didn't go in. She instead bent the light around her body. When the door swung close again, she was invisible to all but those with the most special sight. The Watcher was one of those, but Ava strolled right by him as easily as she strolled by everyone else in the restaurant.

After she stepped onto the sidewalk, she didn't bother to look backward through the glass door. Robert was wherever, not focused on her or anything else nearby. Ava focused on keeping herself unseen as she made her way back to Busboys and Poets. After she turned the corner, someone spoke to her from behind.

"Arkangel."

It was a voice familiar and not so familiar. Ava tensed and turned, keeping her cloak of bent light pulled close to her body.

An amber-hued woman in knee-high black boots, short black leather skirt, and black leather halter top vest was looking straight at her. The stiletto boots raised the woman several inches past six feet. She tilted her head downward, gazing directly into Ava's eyes as she smiled, almost beaming.

"Greetings, Avangelika. I received your message." She seemed delighted to say it. Ava looked at the chestnut-brown hair that flowed down to her waist, and the studded crimson belt that wrapped it. She looked closer at the leather belt; barbed wire had been woven in. This seemed to be an angel who invited danger and was more than happy to strangle it when it came.

Ava waved away her invisible screen, but she was almost at a loss for words. "Greetings…uh…"

The woman cocked her heard and smirked, as if Ava were testing her. "I am Heaven's Hummingbird," she said after moment. "And I've come to help deliver you from the Watcher."

Ava narrowed her eyes. She'd sent out a call, not knowing who would come. Heaven's Raven-Dove, the Archangel Artemisia, had mentored her—was this a close ally of hers?

Ava stretched out her hand. The woman hesitated for a moment, appearing bemused, but only for a moment. She took Ava's hand, shook it, and pulled Ava closer, embracing her. *That* was familiar. It was the same way Ava used to embrace her fellow evangelicals, back in her past life, before and after every Bible study meeting, and whenever they met one another in the school halls or on the street.

"Blessings to you, Avangelika," Holly said. "Blessings to us."

The gesture was familiar. But that name again.

"Avangelika?"

"Yes," Holly said as they disengaged. "You."

Ava stared at her as her lips gradually parted. It seemed the Nurse had only gifted Ava with a partial memory restoration. That made sense, as the temple-palace had only partially been restored.

The woman regarded Ava's expression. "You don't recognize your own name? Or me?"

"You're an Archangel," Ava said.

"Of course," the woman said. "I am the Archangel Holly. Would you like to go for a ride?"

Chapter 12

God *damn* it all. Robert had tried. He'd tried his damnedest to forget it all—forget everything he'd learned during his month-long high school nightmare: the news he'd contracted the White Fire Virus, the disappearance of his father, the death of Davin, his first mind-and-soul-twisting excursions in Xyn, and his beyond-hellacious encounter with his cousin Artemisia.

At the tender age of five, his mother had called him a mistake. At the age of sixteen, Artemisia had accused him of being the Most High Son of Adam, a man who had Eden's rejected seeds buried under his skin, a man who was destined to tip the world into irreversible chaos. And at seventeen, in Xyn, he had learned he had a brother, one whose very soul was raised in Xyn, one who most likely would have something important to say about the final state of Creation. After all that, he'd promised himself he'd find his brother, in the flesh. That was the primary reason he'd become a Watcher in the first place. But there hadn't been any leads, not in three years. So in all that time, he had done what he could to help find other children until he had a clue, a hint of where his brother had ended up. The chairman gave him periodic updates. Each one was the same. Nothing new to report. The chairman…*Adam.*

The first time he'd gone to Xyn, he had been told that the Creator was going crazy; more recently, that God was dying. He initially didn't believe the hokum about his brother's soul living in Xyn while his body quietly aged on Reality's surface; he'd always doubted his brother was really the key to Creation's survival. But over the past few weeks, the barriers between realms had clearly been eroding. Xyn was seeping into the familiar world. And he'd been hearing more and more about his brother. From Vanessa Blight. From the Nurse of the Widow-Queens. But not from Adam. Never from Adam. Never from curious Adam, who'd lately had a very curious attitude.

Robert had some hard decisions to make, and he'd need to make them damn soon.

"Can I help you, sir?"

Robert blinked as the kid's pocked face came into focus. He'd moved up the line. It was their turn to order, but he wasn't hungry. He turned to Ava.

Where was she? He looked all around and, just at the onset of panic, remembered she'd said something about taking a tinkle. But he'd forgotten what she wanted. He ordered her a six-inch veggie sandwich on wheat with everything and moved down the line to pay. He swiped his debit card without thinking about it and took the sandwich toward the first empty seat.

His left arm was killing him. A tingling began in his left shoulder and traveled down through the nerve to the tip of his ring finger, then back. The bones were throbbing. The skin almost felt numb. In Xyn, the skent had stomped on the arm. And now… Dammit, where was Ava?

Robert stood up, involuntarily shifting his vision across the spectrum at he turned his head this way and that. *Screw it.* He walked to the ladies' restroom and peered through the door. There were comments, but he ignored them. The only voice he cared about right then was the one in his head telling him that Ava wasn't in the restaurant.

As soon as he'd woken up, as hungover as he'd felt, he'd sent a message to Adam via his watch, telling the chairman where he was, telling him what had happened, and promising to bring Ava back to The Burrow ASAP for a debriefing by Vince Ceniza. And now he was screwed. He bolted out of the restaurant, looking every which way, every possible way.

Where could she have possibly gone?

His car. If he were her, that's where he'd go. All the safeguards with which Zel had outfitted the vehicle would be nothing to her. She'd bypassed the toymaker's alarm system when she'd broken into his apartment two weeks ago, and that system was far more sophisticated that anything in his Stang. Ava was probably seconds away from hot-wiring the damn thing. Robert took off.

He knew the Village well and took a quicker route to the street than the one they'd taken to Subway. Despite having the queasy déjà vu of running through the undead city in Xyn, he ran as fast as he could, not even slowing when he turned a corner and saw his vehicle. Two people were leaning against it. Neither one was Ava. Neither one was familiar. Robert got ready to throw as he ran toward them, sizing them up.

Two girls. One white with spiked hair. The other Korean or Japanese with a mop top. Both seventeen or eighteen years old, and apparently ready for a day at the beach. The white girl wore a yellow bikini, the Asian girl a white one. And there were scars on their thighs, midsections, and forearms. No…not scars. Tattoos.

About thirty feet away, Robert slowed to a jog, then a walk. The tattoos were of mouths, all shapes and sizes, lips of various colors, tongues of various others. They were moving, *speaking*.

"What's the matter?" This came from the mouth of one of the girls, he thought. "You got a problem with the female body?"

Robert wasn't sure which one was speaking as the mouths on both of their faces were moving.

He focused on the tattoos. They now looked less and less like mouths to him, more and more like vaginas. He shook his head.

"Oh yeah," the Asian girl said. "You've got a problem."

Both girls stepped forward. Robert stopped walking. "Where's Ava?"

"Who?" they said simultaneously.

"You know who." He took a step forward. "I'm sure you do." It wasn't a coincidence that he'd just been verbally abused at Ava's temple-palace full of Widow-Queens only to now find himself confronting two weirder women near his car. There was no such thing as a coincidence anymore.

"Confidence is a hell of a drug," the white girl said.

"Too many men overdose," the Asian girl said.

Both of them walked toward him. Robert moved gingerly. He didn't consider himself a chauvinist, not in any way, shape, or form. But these girls, this *pair*, certainly had some sexual hang-ups. The Infinite Definite were all about neurosis and its associated shit. Ava had undoubtedly called this pair here to cover her escape. But to where? He'd have to get one of these two to tell him, if he could beat them without beating them senseless.

Robert ran toward the girl in yellow, planning all the while a thirteen-part sequence, a double takedown combination that would start with a shove of one and flow into a kick in the head of the other.

"Calystegia," the girl in yellow said. "Take 'im."

"Got 'im, Dandy," the girl in white said.

Calystegia rushed forward. Before Robert could even stop, let alone duck or dodge, the girl had locked her hands on his elbows, head-butted him, and tossed him backward onto the roof of his car.

Robert landed on his back, but most of the pain seemed to shoot in a lightning streak down his left arm.

He tried to sit up. He'd only managed to raise his head when a load landed on his hips. The girl in yellow—Dandy—straddled him, grinning like a jackal.

"More like a *lion*. Don't you think so, Watcher dog?"

Shit. She was reading his mind. Robert tried to push her off him and off the car. He succeeded in the first, only to have her knee him in the groin before pulling his momentarily limp body up, hoisting it in the air, and throwing it across the street into the field of untamed grasses.

He landed on his shoulder and hollered as he rolled to his back. A cloud of other sounds enveloped him: insects buzzing and teeth chattering, lips whispering and dice (or bones) shaking. Calystegia stood at his head, Dandy at his feet.

"Bindweed?" Dandy said. "If you don't mind?"

"Certainly not, Dandelion."

The tattoos on the white-bikinied girl seemed to open wide, sticking out long, tubular, multipronged tongues to flick and lash at Robert as the grasses underneath him lengthened and wrapped around his arms, legs, and neck. He struggled, but most of the movement was in his mind as his body was tied down.

"The thoughts of his heart was only evil continually," Dandelion said as she knelt, pinning Robert's head between her knees. She focused her eyes into his. His couldn't or wouldn't blink as it saw tiny white florets dropping from her pupils, swaying in their descent like feathers as they metamorphosed into something more impossible—tiny, white, winged fairies that flew like darts into Robert's pupil. As each one dived in, he felt a hunk of his flesh being grabbed, *clamped*, as the weeds under him lifted his body higher.

Robert felt like screaming but sucked it up and grunted while several sections of his body burned as if under a magnifying glass tilted toward the sun. Dandelion cupped her hands under his head and lifted, giving him a better view of his body, letting him see the strings and beams of green and honey-hued light spooling from his skin and through his clothes, attaching to all the leaves of grass and trees within a fifty-foot radius.

"You're not only on the wrong side of history," Bindweed said.

"You're on the wrong side of nature," Dandelion said.

Both girls left his view, but their laughter carried on in his ears for what seemed like eternity.

Chapter 13

The Archangel Holly drove a black 'vette. Ava wasn't sure what she was expecting, but this seemed to fit. More impressive than the car was the angel behind the wheel. The old Ava, the plain human version from two years back, would have praised God for the answered prayer. Now Ava simply passed a silent thank-you to her Widow-Queens for doing what she'd asked, completing the task so soon. Her command had been fulfilled. Being in the monitor room of her temple-palace, she couldn't help but think of Adam Smith and the videos she'd watched while in his office. After her return to Reality's surface, she had passed an unspoken command to her helpers to telepathically find, contact, and send her a fellow angel, one who'd helped her in her mission during the dark, forgotten days. This Holly, if not exactly a godsend, was at least the next best thing.

"Still don't you recognize me?" Holly must have felt Ava's eyes on her. Ava knew she should have—she felt the rumblings of recognition deep down—but she was drawing a blank.

"Honestly," Ava said, "not really."

"Don't worry. It'll come."

"Where are we going?"

"First thing," Holly said. "We need to put serious distance between you and the Watchers."

"Well, my car—*their* car—is at the Watcher Robert Goldner's place. There's some stuff I need to get out of the trunk."

"Guide me," Holly said.

Ava gave her directions, then said, "I'm glad you found me."

"I only wish I could've found you before Veronica Blake and Vanessa Blight," Holly said. "I heard they did quite a bit of damage, on every level. I honestly didn't expect you to know me, at least not everything about me."

She pulled into the parking lot in front of Robert's building. "Get what you need, and hurry."

Ava sprung out of the car. On the first trip, she took off her watches and tossed them in the glove compartment, then grabbed her clothes from the backseat and ran to put them in the trunk of the 'vette. On the second trip, she opened the trunk of the Miata and pulled out the crystalline bow she'd borrowed from Zel Bernard.

"Nice," Holly said as Ava got into the passenger's seat. "That will come in handy where we're going."

"Where *are* we going?"

Holly glanced at her, smirking. "To save the children, of course. One in particular."

"Who?"

"Seems there's a little conspiracy being hatched, in part by your Watcher friends. Did you ever wonder how you weren't able to beat the two Sprytes, but the Watchers easily did? How you weren't able to find the girl Marie-Lydia McGillis, but they easily did? And you never even got a chance to see her? The Watchers, the government…They call themselves saving children, but they are in *error*, far from the straight path, traveling one far more serpentine."

Ava considered it all.

Holly smirked again and shook her head. "I'm surprised you didn't know from the beginning. I would've thought in your previous life you would've become conversant in all of the relevant scriptures. Of course, they're not wholly true, but they contain truths. And there are tales about the Watchers."

Ava furrowed her brow and looked down toward her lap. Of course she knew of the Watchers. She knew they were bad, somehow connected to the coming Flood, but what she knew from the scriptures read long ago was still in bits and pieces.

"I would expect you to be telling me this," Holly said. "I should be listening to you tell me about the Book of Enoch and how it relates the truest tale of the Watchers. How these dirty angels engaged in illicit sexual acts and incurred the wrath of God, a God who responded with the Flood in the time of Noah. The same Noah who was instructed to build an ark to save himself, and his children, who would procreate and populate the new world. Prophecy, Arkangel. Signs for our times. And it is now time for you to come back home. Carry on with the Mission of saving the children."

Of course she was right. The blessed Archangel was right. Those at the Isaac-Abraham Institution *were* in error. How dare they tell her to hold back, to not act if she saw a child harmed or in trouble. This is why the Widow-Queens were so sketchy in Robert's presence; she'd brought another Errorist to them, just like she had with Marie-Lydia McGillis. They had learned their lesson from last time, and Ava was paying the price. Thank the Word she was at least wise enough in her mentally fractured state not to have the trip to Xyn supervised by that Vince Ceniza. Who knew how much worse the experience could've been. But no need or time to dwell on it. It was time to move forward.

∞   ∞   ∞

They parked two blocks away from the campus library. One block away, they turned themselves invisible. It was nothing to levitate their bodies, a step at a time, to the third-floor window. And all it took was two swift kicks of Holly's boot to shatter the glass. No one inside was near the window. If anyone heard and came running, they got to the scene long after Holly and Ava had left it.

Ava had wondered what type of child or children could be in danger inside a college library, but she trusted Holly's judgment. She'd believed Holly when she had said Ava would no longer be blind once she saw the target.

The two descended the stairs and rounded several bookshelves until they came to the computer area. Ava looked in the direction of Holly's pointing finger. She was no longer blind.

She saw Sally Ellin Chambers, her old high school nemesis, laughing it up with Kurtis and Anika, Robert's pals. She trembled with rage. Holly put a hand on her shoulder.

"We're in a library," she whispered. "We're here to read the blonde one."

The blonde one. The girl who went out of her way, out of the blue, to befriend Marie-Lydia back in school, just a week before Marie-Lydia snapped and tried to massacre the student body. It was no coincidence. No such thing.

She walked forward, dropping patches of invisibility with each step, appearing to the turning heads as a three-dimensional puzzle solving itself. The sickening trio in front of her turned and stood from their computer stations as Ava gradually revealed all of herself, everything but her head. She'd left her bow in the car. If she'd had it, she would've swung it like a sickle, taking off Sally Ellin's head. Instead, Ava squared up with her, almost nose to nose, as she unbent the light around her face.

"Judgment day, heifer."

Sally Ellin wailed like a banshee, pushing everyone within earshot to rush for the nearest exit. Everyone except Kurtis and Anika. Grinning like the father witnessing the return of the Prodigal Son, Holly revealed herself and pinned the two between her body and Ava's. Kurtis and Anika had plenty of room to make a dash for it, but they were friends of Robert's, *smart* friends. They knew they couldn't escape an angel.

Sally Ellin wasn't as smart. Out of breath from her scream, she tried to cut left and dash for the elevator. Ava grabbed her left arm and swung her against the computer table. Sally Ellin hit it, fell to her knees, and started screaming in short loud bursts. Ava stepped forward and grabbed her throat with her right hand, squeezing, lifting the girl off her feet. Sally Ellin stopped screaming, but she scrunched her eyes and tried clawing at Ava's forearm as the Arkangel used her free arm to fend off her attacks.

"You can close your eyes," Ava said, "but you can't close your ears." The muscles in her right arm stiffened and tingled; it was getting tired. Ava put her left hand on the girl's throat to help support the weight. She tensed the muscles in both arms as she concentrated, pulling all light from the fixtures and lamps to her face and forearms. Glowing strings, thicker veins, then plumper vines of yellow and orange strangled Ava's forearms as darkness overtook the room and her pupils dilated. *"Look...at...me..."* She connected with the pulses in the girls neck; Sally Ellin's lids pushed farther apart.

Ava gathered grains and drops of light from the computer screens into her eyes, filling them with pools of radiation before winking, unspooling thin threads of light through her pupils, through her glasses, into and through hapless Sally Ellin's blue irises. Threading and threading, the twisting light shot deep into the girl's mind, and the Arkangel used it to stitch patches of the girl's memory with her own desires.

Ava chanted words from something possibly memorized years ago, something that may have once been a perfectly innocuous poem before she reordered the words, remixed the verses, over and over again. Her own memory hadn't been perfectly recovered, but she remembered well a trick the Archangel Artemisia had taught her. Pushing a target's consciousness to the edge of XynKroma, without taking them or your own soul there, you could read whatever memories you chose, like flipping through the pages of an encyclopedia. Ava was nowhere near as gifted as her mentor, and she wasn't up to full mental strength, but she did what she could with Sally Ellin, searching for all memories of her with Marie-Lydia and any associated memories.

She saw faces, names, murders, a near massacre, and a molestation…a molestation of a teenage girl by a short, fat, slobbering federal agent.

"Ava? Ava, what are you doing? Stop, please…" She heard Anika's voice pleading with her. Even in her entranced state, Ava knew she already had all the useful info she was going to get. She released Sally Ellin and exhaled, relighting the room as a white cloud of condensed breath sprinkled with multicolored sparkles passed her lips. Sally Ellin collapsed. Anika knelt to care for her as Kurtis took a step toward Ava.

"What's going on?" he asked, as if she'd stoop to explain to the likes of him.

"What did you read?" Holly still had an odd grin on her face, or maybe Ava's normal sight hadn't recovered just yet.

"Everything…" Ava almost felt like collapsing. "Everything I need." The trick, not performed in so long, took more out of her than she'd expected. "I'll fill you in outside."

"Fine." Holly grabbed Kurtis and put her hands around his throat. "Let's snap their necks and be on our way."

Ava's knees wobbled. "There's no need…They're not…"

"They are in *error*, Arkangel," Holly said, tightening her grasp. "You've seen proof of that. Now, whose side are you on?"

Ava looked from the flushed face of Kurtis to Anika, whose pleading eyes met her weary ones. The girl didn't need to say a word. Last time they'd met, Anika had said she hoped to see Ava again. She couldn't have meant like this. But then Ava laid eyes on whom Anika was comforting. An enabler of evil. What was an angel to do?

Chapter 14

"…preserving our families, protecting children, promoting safe and happy communities. By doing this, we secure our heartland, and our future."

"Yes, Mister Shahrooz, thank you," Peter said. "We are well aware of the Agency's official Vision—"

"So you don't have to repeat it at every meeting," Howard said.

"And we are well aware," Peter said, "of what the HSA has been trying to accomplish, but—"

"*But*," Howard said, "the fact is the HSA's damned Rings of Light haven't done a damn thing to curb the region's gang problem."

Cyrus smiled. "Is there anything else you'd like to damn?"

"Yes," Howard said. "The money bleeding like a red sea from the taxpayers. The ones paying for these damned expensive Rings. The ones who've had more than enough of this damned recession."

"Well, pardon me, Mister Jameson," Cyrus said as he scratched his temple. "But have you paused to consider the price you'd be paying if a certain one-eyed agent of yours got a little too *free* with a gun a couple of weeks ago?"

"That wouldn't have happened," Sam said. "Robert Goldner is very responsible."

"Yes," Patricia said. "He's responsible for loosening the teeth of a teenage girl and knocking her unconscious, permanently impairing the vision of another girl…Oh, and traumatizing an innocent little boy. For life. We may have to take him away from his mother and put him in a special facility."

"That's what should've been done in the first place!" Sam said. "Someone should've done something as soon as his twelve-year-old mother got pregnant. No one that young is fit to raise a child."

"Yes," Howard said. "Those teenage girls our Watcher agent confronted were seventeen and eighteen years old and acted like perfect savages."

"Well, hell," Patricia said, "the Goldner kid almost matched them in savagery!"

"He's twenty," Zel said, apparently unheard as Patricia ranted on.

"Restraining a frightened, four-year-old boy's wrists with a leather belt and refusing to let him go until the police forced him to? While trying to get free, what if that scared little boy had bitten him?"

Silence overtook the room. The conference room was as bright as a theater a moment before the start of a film, but the discomfort and displeasure Patricia's comment had evoked were more than apparent. At least it was to those who hadn't cast their eyes downward, toward the marble conference table.

Cyrus's facial expression mirrored the others, but in truth he was loving this.

The biweekly briefing meetings between the Isaac-Abraham Institution and Heartland Security Agency representatives were anything but joyous occasions, due in no small part to the mix and dispositions of the individuals who most often attended them. That particular morning's IAI attendees included medical specialist Sam Goines, engineer Zel Bernard, and the Institution's government affairs liaisons, Howard Jameson and Peter Levy. The HSA was represented by Nicola Treinz from the Agency's science and technology component, Patricia Bix from the Office of Health Affairs, and—a last-minute invitee—Cyrus, from the Office of Operations Coordination.

The primary purposes of the meetings were to exchange ideas on curtailing juvenile delinquency and to provide updates in the mission of locating missing children. Today's meeting had been especially tense, set off when Cyrus confirmed the rumor that some higher-ups at the HSA had recently decided to expand the role of the Peacemakers, the Agency's specially trained and heavily armed field operatives. In addition to their plethora of other duties, and pending official approval, the Peacemakers would be responsible for locating and rescuing misplaced children. The most immediate and obvious consequences of their new role would be to make the IAI's Watcher agents redundant and to render most of their beyond-The-Burrow actions illegal.

"No sense in having a nonprofit's brash and viral young adults doing such an important task that taxpayer-funded and well-trained *real* adults could do much more effectively, and much more safely" was the implication. It was a peace-of-mind issue for some, but its announcement had shattered the small peace within the stuffy conference room. Cyrus gave it another whack of the hammer when he, on a whim, suggested the Rings of Light would be expanded, as well.

Sam and Howard had been agitated enough to point out that the government agency was just too fat and inefficient to handle all it was proposing; its size was actually a handicap. And, anyway, the Agency already had its hands full with its primary tasks of conducting surveillance for domestic threats to the nation, coordinating the appropriate response to such threats, and countering threats to domesticity by confronting, arresting, and prosecuting negligent parents, child molesters, members of violent youth gangs, and other hazards to ideal communities. A partnership between the Agency and the Institution could be possible—a continuation of the status quo—but not a subsumption.

Nicola had interrupted and tried to restore the peace in the room by reasoning how the adoption of the locate-and-rescue role would create jobs for people. "And raise taxes for many other people," Howard had said, "to pay the salaries of those few people. Just what the dying economy doesn't need." To which Nicola had countered that the HSA, in accordance with its Vision and mission statement, was more suited for the work; plus, its high-tech Rings of Light surveillance system, as it expanded and evolved, would probably—naturally—prevent more children from being lost or kidnapped in the future.

And the arguing had gone on.

As recently as five years ago, American citizens more often trusted the private sector rather than the government to do the right thing when it came to respecting people's privacy and liberties. Cognizant both of this view and of the state of the economy, the government had been content to let certain nonprofits and small businesses assist with the government's role of keeping the general peace. But times were changing. People were changing. And some, like the IAI's Watcher agents, were overstepping their bounds more and more. It was time for the feds to step in and step up.

Even discussing the transfer of the White Fire Virus was a topic that was disturbing enough on its own, but for Patricia to mention the transfer of the Virus to a young child had been enough to vacuum the air out of the room. Cyrus coughed, clearing his throat twice, before saying, "Maybe they—impetuous Goldner and the rambunctious girls—maybe they all just forgot the law was watching. We will do more PSAs in order to remind everyone about the cameras on the streets, parking lots, and public transportation…

and of course to explain the ways of a safe and loving nation to its insecure citizens."

"Forgot?" Howard said. "Those girls on the train brought their own camera! They wanted an audience!"

"Mister Shahrooz," Peter said, "you know as well as I that the terrorist associates of The Infinite Definite and others, like these girls, have taken more than a small liking to the cameras that comprise these so-called Rings. They use them as an excuse to show off, to create even more heinous acts of intimidation and terror."

"And somehow the recordings of the acts always end up on the Internet," Zel said. "*Glamorized.*"

The Institution's reps all took turns glancing or glaring at Cyrus. Understandable. When it came to the public surveillance system, they knew the buck stopped with him. He mostly didn't mind the unspoken accusations, but Zel's disturbed him. It was those cherry-tinted sunglasses of his and the seemingly hollow eyes behind them. *Freak.*

"Not all of them end up on the net," Nicola said.

"Too many of them do."

"Hackers," Cyrus said. "We've already directed resources towards a new task force to study and stop them. We consider it a form of cyberterrorism, you know."

"Yes," Nicola said. "And the FBI is assisting us with this initiative."

"In the meantime," Cyrus said, "everyone should consider these cameras a blessing. Progress on the road towards a pure security."

"Yes, after all, what are the alternatives?" Nicola said. "There just can't be—and we definitely don't *want*—a cop on every corner…any more than we'd want an angel in every kid's bedroom."

"What in the hell do you mean by that?" Sam said.

Nicola appeared confused by Sam's reaction, as did Patricia. Why wouldn't they? The two cows didn't have access to the same resources as Cyrus. They'd no idea about Chairman Adam Smith's ridiculous dictate that all Virus-carrying members of the IAI refer to themselves as "angels," all for the pillowy benefit of Ava Darden's fragile mind-state. Cyrus tried to maintain his poker face—but he almost lost it as Nicola stuttered to offer an apology for, she had to believe, no good reason.

"I guess," she said, "that was probably a poor choice of words. But you know what I meant."

Cyrus again cleared his throat and raised his voice, drowning out the beginning of Sam's even angrier response. "Gentlemen—and ladies—we're talking in a circle, so permit me to stab it in the middle. Virus-carriers from all over the world have suddenly seen Washington, DC, as their mecca. They've turned their eyes and unspoken hopes for whatever in this direction. They are running, walking, lurching, and purchasing tickets here. The HSA and other security agencies are doing everything we can to stop the migration. Until we do, we don't need your people out there *helping*. With the potential for increased numbers of Infinite Definite associates in the area, trigger fingers are itchier than usual."

Zel sighed heavily. "Point made, Mister Shahrooz. We'll discuss all of this with our chairman and the rest of the Board this afternoon."

Cyrus nodded his thanks.

"Moving along to the next item on the agenda," Patricia said. "We believe the CDC has made a breakthrough in developing new medications for the infected, with fewer side effects. Only catch is they may have to take them more often than some of the drugs currently on the market."

"More often?" Sam asked. "Three and four times a day isn't often enough?"

"If you'll excuse me," Cyrus said, rising from his seat, "I need to visit the little boy's room." He didn't give a shit if the animals had to take their medication twenty times a day. He'd said his piece; he could leave the meeting now and get on with his real reason for coming to The Burrow today. "Please go on. Don't mind my absence."

Now you see him; now you don't. Good magicians knew well how to play with the concepts of absence and presence in fresh and surprising ways. The great ones could shock the shit out of you. Abracadabra.

There was nothing surprising about the near absence of light increasing the presence of shadows in the serpentine hallways of The Burrow—Cyrus was a big boy; he'd stopped fearing the dark decades ago. Yet his hairs stood on end as he made his anything-but-straight way toward the restroom. The peopleless halls contained the presence of something else; he was sure. Something other than black illusions. Mouse-furry, static-frizzy—but silent, intangible. He felt it. Currents of some kind of dark energy. He wasn't quite ready to be shocked.

He barged through the bathroom door, almost sighing with relief. It was brighter there, at least, if not exactly a safe haven from all things dirty, dark, and disgusting. There were odors of stale piss, faint traces of cannabis, and hints of mildew. But there were no stains Cyrus could see, nothing smeared or scrawled on the stall walls, not even a stray paper towel littered the floor. Still, it was a facility used mainly by *them*. How clean could it really be? The wall-mounted air freshener spurting out a sweet and fine jasmine mist every fifteen seconds simply told flowery lies. His ears may've been his best physical asset, but his nose was second best. He'd never trust his eyes. Not in this world.

Cyrus let the hot water run for sixty seconds before putting his hands under the stream. He grinned when he did, recalling the look on Sam's face when Patricia had raised the issue of drugs. Samantha Goines, poor self-sacrificing doctor. Upper-middle-class background, Georgetown educated, but dedicated to helping the unfortunate, the wretched. And just as clueless as they were.

Drugs had been put in the nation's water supply since the turn of the century, primarily in major metropolitan areas, strictly for the high purpose of encouraging people to lower their defenses ever so slightly and become more suggestible, easier to convince of the propagated idea that there really were no supernaturally talented beings on the planet, only penny-ante magicians showing off and competing to become better and better at their craft. A vainglorious message massaged into the minds of the populace: there is nothing greater than mankind, and any signs to the contrary are dollar-store magic tricks.

So what if some construction workers on a street in Columbus, Ohio, imagined they saw a woman ascend to the roof of a ten-story building as if she were running up invisible stairs? How credible were the Minneapolis night-lifers who said they were robbed by a glowing-eyed man whose face kept changing? After a long day of hiking, did a group of doped-up campers in southern North Carolina really see three twelve-foot-tall men who each looked like their bodies were clothed with aurora borealis? None of it was as fantastic as it seemed. *Trust us.*

The plan and program had been initiated with the full knowledge and tacit approval of President Gunderson. One of his last great acts in office. Like the act of surreptitiously planting a tracking chip in every newborn likely to become an at-risk kid, the water treatment program had successfully continued for eight long and strong years without anyone in the know seeing the need to inform President Sagan. Still, after almost a decade, not all bought into the myth of competitive magicians. For a variety of reasons ranging from the biological to the just plain logical, not everyone in the population could be convinced. But more than enough believed to help maintain the grand illusion.

Silly Sam Goines of course knew real magick existed. She may've even have known of the treated water supply; despite the President's ignorance of it, it wasn't among the most beautiful secrets Cyrus and his compatriots had been keeping. But the doctor and others like her at the IAI and in the federal government would remain silly, clueless clowns in his view, until they got serious about studying magick and learning how it might be used for the betterment of mankind, mind, and Earth—pushing the species leaps and bounds beyond the current Darkening Age.

Cyrus's allies in the Trinfecta took magick seriously. So did the man whose office lay behind the gray panel at the end of the next curving hall. Cyrus left the restroom and, despite feeling as if his sense of balance was being siphoned away, made his way down the darkly energetic corridor without falling on his face. He pushed the waist-high blue button next to the panel.

"Cyrus Shahrooz. Heartland Security Agency."

After responding to the recorded voice's question, he looked into the scanner, waiting two full minutes for the device to match his voice pattern, his name, and the unique print of his irises. He didn't mind the wait one bit. Years ago, like every other first-time visitor to The Burrow, he'd had his identification information programmed into Zel's unique security system for purposes of future recognition, and for Adam's purpose of tracking everyone's movements throughout the structure. This was secure technology at its finest—at least by the standards of today's world.

The door slid open. Talk about another day's world.

Cyrus walked into what he imagined to be a replica of Sherlock Holmes's consulting room. Growing up, dreaming of becoming a law enforcement agent, he'd certainly seen his fair share of old movies and TV shows featuring the great detective to be immediately struck by the impression. There was the cluttered desk, the dusty bookshelf weighed down by thick hardcover tomes, the three-tiered shelf displaying a range of bottled chemicals, and the furniture, all of it antique, dating from the latter half of the nineteenth century. Stacks of paper and paraphernalia of all odd sorts were scattered about the room, on tables, shelves, the floor, and elsewhere. This really could've been the famous room at 221B Baker Street, picked up whole and plucked down into a twenty-first-century bunker, if not for some stark incongruities. Rather than a violin, there was a Minimoog synthesizer next to the far wall. Rather than windows, the room had just one large rectangle of black glass directly above the instrument, spanning almost wall to wall, allowing only a little space on the right side for the green door that provided entry into the adjoining room, where Vince Ceniza conducted the bulk of his research.

While Cyrus eyed that impenetrable black glass, the green door slid open and closed so quickly that Vince seemed to pass through it solidly, like an apparition. No telling what he'd been doing in the back room, but the look on Vince's face seemed to indicate it'd been wicked fun.

"Mister Shahrooz." Vince peeled off white latex gloves and tossed them into a waste receptacle. "This is an unexpected pleasure."

"Uh, please don't think me rude," Cyrus said as Vince approached with his unprotected hand outstretched, "but I just left the restroom, and I'm embarrassed to say I neglected to wash my hands."

Vince eyed him with mild suspicion. *So what?* A dirty look was far better than making skin contact and allowing the dirty freak to skim his consciousness like it was the front page of *USA Today.* Cyrus had memorized his file—he'd memorized all their files—and he was well aware of Vince Ceniza's talents. In the past, the so-called psychological mapmaker had occasionally been called in (off the record) to assist with the hands-on interrogations of particularly obstinate Infinite Definite detainees. Today, Cyrus needed him to use those skills for a different purpose.

He reached inside his sports coat and pulled out a folded stack of papers.

"What's this?" Vince asked.

"A puzzle." Cyrus handed the papers to him. "One that I really need to figure out."

Vince unfolded the stack and began reviewing. Cyrus watched his lips move as he focused his ears, listening hard for something intelligible. But the sounds were as Greek to him as the rows of randomness on the printout.

The mapmaker turned his back to him, continuing to read as he walked toward the shelf of bottles. Without lifting his eyes from the papers, he took a small tin from the second-tier shelf and walked toward the table cluttered with papers, books, and other scattered objects. One of those objects was a pipe, lying in the crease of an open book. Not exactly the calabash pipe seen in so many filmed depictions of Holmes, but it was curved, and presently Vince poured into it a small amount of the tin's powdery contents before lighting and placing it in his mouth, all without moving his eyes from the papers Cyrus had handed him.

After taking a few good puffs, Vince said, "Where did you get this?"

"Dangerous new gang of Virus-carriers is out there," Cyrus said. "A gang with a game plan. A gang whose members take notes. One of our Peacemaker agents found that on one of them."

Vince squinted at him. Those turquoise eyes…They weren't glowing, but there was something about them. It felt almost as if the pulsating dark energy he'd felt in the hallway was now in the room, flowing from Vince's eyes to his. Cyrus tried to maintain his poise. He tried not to stiffen, or shift his weight, or swallow, or hold his breath, or make any of the other telltale signs signaling he was uneasy or may not be telling the honest-to-goodness truth. Silence wasn't helping.

"Why?" he asked. "Do you know what it is?"

"Yes." Vince started walking toward him. "And I think maybe you do, too. Otherwise you wouldn't have brought it to me, of all people."

Cyrus took deep breaths through his nose. He could do this. He'd been trained as a special agent. He'd had a distinguished twenty-year career. He could keep his balance on the razor wire between truth-teller and liar without showing a single bead of sweat. Unfortunately, his deep breaths were not pushing fresh air into his lungs. With each inhale, he took in more and more of the pungent scent from the pipe. Definitely not tobacco.

"I believe…" Cyrus coughed. "It's notes for"—he coughed again—"uh, what I guess you would consider a magick spell. For real magick."

"Yes." Vince took a puff. "A very sophisticated kind of magick. Not the low-down dirty brand used by The Infinite Definite. There's intelligence behind this." He was now five paces in front of Cyrus, squinting, puffing. "Where did you get it?"

The man wasn't being accusatory exactly. Despite his own discomfort, Cyrus could hear it in his voice. There were traces of his favorite emotion in the undertone. In spite of the cool facade, Vince was worried, maybe even a bit scared about what he'd managed to decipher on the sheets. Cyrus stood a little straighter. The smoke and his watery eyes be damned—detecting fear in a potential adversary was nothing short of arousing.

"We took it off a woman," the big man said, "who belongs to a cult of Sprytes."

Vince turned away, staring off into nothing. No—not nothing. Vince was staring at that opaque black panel of glass. He took a puff from the pipe. "I've heard of them." The worry hadn't left his voice. The stinkweed, whatever it was, certainly wasn't relaxing him. "A few Sprytes jumped one of our Watcher agents a couple of weeks ago. Darryl Ridley. He's with your agency now."

"Yes." And a better man for having been put through the ritual for which Cyrus had paid handsomely. "He's told me all about his ordeal. And I've seen the footage his tormentors recorded. Now that we have this, we think we can get inside their heads a little bit.

Figure out how they operate and why. They're still a small group now, as far as we know. We don't need a more powerful Infinite Definite out there."

"Get inside their heads." Vince turned his gaze from the black panel back to Cyrus. "So you came to me."

"For a translation of that document. Understanding their magick is the first step toward defending against it."

"Or using it to a greater effect than they've thus far been able to."

The two men locked eyes. The silence was more discomforting than the smoke.

"You know the HSA's position," Cyrus said.

"But I don't know yours." Vince turned again toward the black glass panel, this time moving toward it. "Yet."

Cyrus almost wanted to laugh—something about that weed—but he kept his lips pressed together as he watched Vince tap the contents of his pipe out onto a metal plate on the table before laying the pipe next to it. The mapmaker then sat on the bench in front of the keyboard and propped the papers up like sheet music.

"Mister Ceniza, you've assisted the HSA and our contractors enough times to know—"

"But I've never worked closely with you, Mister Shahrooz." Vince plinked a few keys, seemingly at random.

"Until today." Cyrus moved closer, with more and more trepidation as he began to have an unpleasant déjà vu experience, recalling his conversation with Edward. "Please, just help me."

"Only if you let me keep a copy of this." Vince played a few more notes. "For insurance—you know?"

What the hell was he up to? "Fine. You can have that copy if you just tell me what it's saying."

"No great mystery here." Vince continued to tap at keys as he spoke. "But I'll do my best to put this in terms you can understand.

From a man of art and science to a man of bureaucracy…who hides and seeks societal order from the messy chaos of the masses."

Cyrus cocked his head. "Mister Ceniza, there is nothing wrong with standing for order."

"Unless you don't stand for justice and fairness, as well."

"Listen—"

"What I'm getting at, Mister Shahrooz, is that we human beings, those of us whose psyches have not been damaged beyond repair, we are predisposed to pick up signs of order in nature. We have the latent talent to detect patterns. And, based on another's actions, we have the ability to guess and sometimes be right about what another is thinking. Thin- or thick-skinned, hero or villain, we are pretty much all sensitive to the concept of *fairness*. These are some of the fundamental elements of *consciousness*."

Cyrus stepped forward, his lips parted, preparing words for a thought.

"Yes," Vince said. "And there are other elements not up for discussing this morning—my dear Watson." Vince tossed a smirking glance over his shoulder. Cyrus caught it. The creepy son of a bitch. He seemed to be reading and responding to more than one of Cyrus's unformed thoughts. The big man took a step backward.

"This universal sensitivity to fairness," Vince said, "pattern detecting…it's all part of a theory held by some who study the mind. It's entirely possible we may all be living under a grand illusion. But those of us who've a smidgen of faith in something beyond our own nose tips believe that consciousness is not a sad accident, something that happened by chance. Its emergence in humans—and possibly others—is a sign and part of the process of a Creation that is fast moving toward an omega point."

Cyrus resisted the urge to move forward again. "You mean Armageddon? An End of Times doomsday scenario, right?"

"Not necessarily. It all depends on one's perception. Reality is a funny, funny thing." Vince stopped tapping random keys and picked up the papers again, running his finger over a few lines before flipping a few sheets and doing the same on another page.

The mapmaker didn't speak as he went over the pages, but Cyrus heard something new in the room: a droning noise that sounded almost like a voice coming from somewhere nearby. Whatever it was, it seemed to get on his skin—literally—and crawl there. It was as if someone—*someones* hidden were watching him, talking about him…

Cyrus quickly scratched his elbow and neck and said, "What type of magick are we talking about here? What exactly are we dealing with?"

"A virulent form of what's known colloquially among students of magick as Verbalism. Word Magick. Somewhat dense poetry that is not only confounding to some senses—sight and hearing—but also effective in affecting one's experience of reality. There's a good reason, Mister Shahrooz, why the great narratives of Heaven, Hell, and the Supreme Being are written in verse. The works of Dante and Milton, the Bible and Qur'an, the Vedas…"

And it was just one of Carmilla's charms, one cog in the wheel of her entire magickal system.

"In truth, all language we apply to the Creator is inadequate," Vince said. "At this point in our evolution we are unable to perceive the Creator as it is or describe it as it truly is, so we use metaphors and similes. Poetry. Though some, through meditation or revelation, claim to have reached a good understanding of the Supreme Being, they always revert to poetry—or near-incoherent images, or sounds open to infinite interpretations—when trying to express what they claim to know."

"Incomprehensible art produced to express the experience of the inexpressible," Cyrus said. The HSA special agent who headed the task force on stamping out The ID often described the terrorists' productions with these very words. The special agent was talented at identifying personalities and patterns of activity. Too bad he'd no clue how to put an end to them, or how to use them for mankind's benefit. He showed some really pretty pictures during his need-to-know presentations though.

"That's about right." Vince began to tap on the keys again. "Understanding poetry of any merit requires a shift in consciousness. It can't be read like a magazine article, or listened to as if one were hearing a lecture. Not if one really wants to get into the *deep* of it. Great, and even good, poetry is concentrated language. You have to really concentrate your mind to read it properly.

"So few people really read poetry these days, and even fewer truly understand it, but most people recognize that there's something *primal* about it. That's why we always turn to it in the tumultuous situations of love or death—more often in times of tragedy than times of blissful contentedness. Whether understood or not, we all react to poetry. It affects us. And it's effective because it works on the fundamental level of our very being."

Speaking of fundamentals, there was something about the notes Vince was playing. Cyrus felt enough at ease to move three paces closer and peer over Vince's shoulder at the propped up pages. About seven feet away, he could see just fine, and he saw, among all the various symbols, no recognizable musical notes. He shook his head, wondering what Vince could've been seeing, then spoke under his breath. "Verbalism."

"Linguistic magick," Vince said, "is the more scientific term. It begins with the contemplation of various alphabets, then moves on to absorb numbers, and then musical notes. From there, shapes and symbols are drawn, words are written, sounds are made… Musical language is the end result. Poetry."

None of this was too surprising. He'd dealt with enough Virus-carrying adversaries to know that, out of all the arts, poetry was for some reason very near and dear to their rotten little hearts. But…"How can poetry be so powerful? What does it have to do with this omega point?"

"Practitioners hold to a mystical interpretation of the biblical creation story," Vince said. "When God gave the first Adam permission and power to name the animals, the deity in effect gave man the power to create his own world. But man also had limitations. Man was forbidden to use the true name of God—in speech or writing—lest the creature turn and take power over the Creator."

"And there are creatures now trying to do just that." The witch-bitch Carmilla.

"Always have been. Now we're at a very unique point in humankind's history." And now Vince was playing a melody, or trying to. There were more than a few sour notes. Stops and retries. "Chains binding chains branding brains…"

Vince went on to say something about gods and slaves, and the sanctioning of slavery in various holy books, and how freedom was scarcely counted among the meanings of life in systems of thought involving deities, but Cyrus could only pay partial attention. As he spoke, and played, Cyrus heard those other noises again, voices speaking under Vince's. It was like the muffled buzz of a television playing in the next room, behind a thin wall, but it was coming from the room in which they were standing. It was coming from Vince. Like a cologne of sound, doubling and redoubling. An audible fragrance of low, droning voices, growing in number, subtly modulating and shifting their tones, seeming to react to whatever Vince was saying, as a flowing fragrance might shift in reaction to the wind. God *damn* his ears—Cyrus couldn't shut them out. He could hear Vince clearly; these other sounds, however, gave him the impression of an angry echo of words that Vince wasn't speaking but, maybe, what he was really thinking.

And those thoughts, those voices, that *noise*, had wafted through his ears, gone on to crawl under his skin, subtly gaining in intensity.

Cyrus had to discharge these secrets, push them out. He had to get Vince talking about something besides this slave-and-master crap. But Vince changed course on his own accord, seeming to react to a mere unspoken desire.

"The serious practitioners of this magick call themselves HyperVersists or NextPoets. Creators of the Next Universe. Their grand metaphor of existence is that the Creator, formless and unimaginable, came into being at the same spark of a moment it began to produce a musical phrase, a line of poetry. Sung-spoken outside of our concepts of space and time, the rhythmical phrase is the instrument of an ever-diversifying Creation. The phrase is also the Creator's true name, *felt* by all if not exactly understood, and it's killing its owner as it plays out. While it plays, the Creator remains *crazy*, but once spoken, the Creator will cease to exist and Creation will reach a state of maximum organized complexity—the omega point. The End of History. As far as I know, no great thinker or talented poet has yet been able to adequately describe what this might be like."

"I'm sure some have their wishes and desires for it." Cyrus had to sit down, reflexively putting the heel of his left hand to his forehead. It was damp, but he wasn't hot. Uncomfortable, yes—but why was he sweating? He took a handkerchief out of a jacket pocket.

"Everyone has their own vision of Heaven," Vince said. "And some of these HyperVersists have dedicated their lives to doing what they can to put themselves at the center of this omega point, ruling whatever there is to be ruled."

"A mess," Cyrus said as he wiped his forehead. Hot, no. A little nauseous, yes.

"Thought you would think so." Vince was really into a groove now, playing tunes that were at once familiar and strange, discordant melodies. He switched and swept through styles like some kind of musical triathlete, playing dexterously with one hand when he needed the other to turn a page, not once taking his eyes off the symbols.

Cyrus heard Bach, broken. Jerry Lee Lewis, jazzed up. Chopin, chopped up. A mixed salad of piano music. And dressing it all was the invisible chorus, the fragrance of voices emanating from Vince. Millions of imperceptible, pin-size mouths aiding and competing with one another. If this continued for much longer, Cyrus was certain he'd vomit.

It was unlikely Vince would have been concerned or sympathetic, even if he had turned and noticed the queasy expression on his visitor's face. There was purpose to what the mapmaker was doing; it undoubtedly was part of the translation Cyrus had requested. So the big man had to suck it up, swallow it down, and let the freak continue. He kept an eye on the nearest trash can just in case.

"Some people," Vince said, "who think deeply about all things having to do with the brain and consciousness contend that there is no such thing as a mind an individual may call his or her own. Milton was only fractionally correct—the mind is *not* its own place, but it *can* make a Heaven of Hell, a Hell of Heaven. A 'mind' is actually part of a network."

Cyrus thought about it as he muttered it. "XynKroma."

"Yes. *Xyn*. A realm of polluted light ruled by a paradoxically silent magickal spirit. It's the cauldron for all effective magick. It being a realm of nearly pure light, those of us carriers who've managed to establish a détente between our own willpower and the will of the parasites infesting our skin and blood can gain access to and navigate the realm easier than most living beings. But, whether infected or not, humans have another way of accessing and manipulating Ultimate Reality. *Artistic* ways. The truly creative men and women, in history and today, have always peeled back layers of their own consciousness while in the state of creativity. They may not realize it, and even those who do may not be able to explain it, but the creative process requires one to tunnel deep inside oneself. Some delve deeper than others."

Vince continued to play as before, but the music had shifted. It was now more consistent, less discordant, and becoming increasingly complex, as if other instruments had come into play. The sick feeling in the pit of Cyrus's stomach floated away like a rain cloud bowing out for the sun. The noise under his skin seemed to lift away like a vapor through his pores. The sweat on his forehead and hands dried. Cyrus shook his head and blew his nose on his handkerchief before putting it away.

"I'm assuming what you're saying is not limited to artists?" he said. "We could also be talking about scientists, inventors."

"Yes. Anyone who doesn't accept the status quo and seeks to change it in some area. But there are nearly infinite layers of the conscious mind—and, as I said, some go deeper than others. My research and experience have led me to conclude that, among noninfected humans, there are certain creative types who manage to make quantumlike jumps and go deeper than almost any others. The musicians and the poets."

Vince's words made Cyrus consider Bob Dylan. Anyone who grew up on his music couldn't dispute there was something almost supernatural about his prodigious talent, not to mention the wide-ranging effect he'd had on Western culture. But Vince's playing sounded like something off a Queen record. Bombastic, intricate, and over-the-top, while at the same time subdued. Harmonious voices and instruments. Yet Vince maintained a normal tone of voice, and Cyrus could hear him clearly above everything else. How was he doing that? The big man stood up and moved closer to the music maker.

"The language of the Creator is music," Vince said. "And as any music lover knows, music is food to the imagination. At this phase in the process of Creation—in terms of planet Earth's human time—the crazy Creator's sung-spoken phrase is a very coarse, aharmonic music that can be felt and seen in a harsh world with plentiful signs of order—like, say, the cycle of the seasons—as well as signs of chaos—Mother Nature, red in tooth and claw."

"And human natures."

"A human nature just as bloodthirsty as jungle creatures preying on one another and equipped with the talent to tap into this music of Creation and translate it. HyperVersists believe, throughout history, art and nature have been the by-products of the Creator's poetic phrase. And art, particularly music and lyrics, may engage directly with the unconscious mind and bend the listeners' perception of reality. An ordinary song can do that. An extraordinary song can do that and more, going deeper, linking minds and changing reality for all listeners."

"Tapping into the mind of God?"

"Yes, in order to assist in the process of Creation. Or help disrupt it."

Goddamned poets. There really was a method to The ID's madness. There was a reason to the rhymes of Candice Flavius and William-Jack. When they spoke in verse, they weren't just mindlessly babbling. And their artistic inclinations weren't just quirks.

"The system began," Vince said, "as a mishmash of various nineteenth- and twentieth-century poetic theories and heterodox theologies, most of which were incomprehensible when first proposed by self-important poets, and many of which are still incomprehensible to the layperson. But the combination's result is an abstruse theory of poetry extended to all 'art,' which is defined broadly as 'indirect communication.' Music, above any other art form, and maybe alone, communicates 'soul' to 'soul.'"

"As any respectable bluesman would attest."

"Or any respectable Buddhist. Those who study and practice meditation—the breathing and chanting—are well aware of the effects and power over the mind and body that can result just from a pattern of controlled breathing. But real power, actual manipulation, requires musical *language*.

"Symbols and language play a huge role in how we perceive the world—human beings' Reality is constructed by communication. So again we come back to the primacy of language. Poetry. But what we read and write doesn't filter Reality for our comprehension. Rather, what we read, write, paint—the *creation* of art—what we think and say *creates* Reality—perpetually, constantly.

"The notes on these pages are essentially a restatement that there is a relationship between imagination and the world. Reality results from imagination perpetually shaping the world. The world, the entire *universe* is in flux. Nothing is static. The Creator is still speak-singing its name.

"As Creation progresses, consciousness evolves. Living beings weren't always conscious. The emergence of it is a step up, just like the ability to communicate. At this point in our and Creation's evolutionary paths, we can never grasp the whole. We can only grasp parts of a world, pieces tied to particular places, specific times, and other trappings. Nevertheless, the sixth sense we all have detects a greater coherence, underlying Unity. We have a dim idea of an overall Order. So those of us most in tune with things, most in touch with ourselves, we go on—looking, loving, living passionately, existing in a tension, dreaming of the ecstasy and the release."

"Ecstasy and release..." Cyrus shook his head. "Must have been some dirty-minded theologians that came up with all this."

"Theologians can make anything sound dirty, just as poets can render the simplicities of life nonsensical. But the 'living passionately' injunction actually has a noble, if a bit esoteric, meaning: one evolves spiritually from self-involvement to altruism, an achievement attained only by a deep search of self, an inward divination. Some of our kind have summed this up with the poetic term *inholiness*."

Cyrus chuckled. "Seems like I learn a new word every day."

"And a new trick every week."

Vince abruptly stopped playing. He'd reached the end of the last sheet of paper, and it appeared the concert was over. He turned to face Cyrus with an expression that was part grin, part snarl, all squint.

"What's the real reason you came to me with this, and not one of your cohorts at the Trinfecta?"

"Excuse me?"

Vince stood up and stepped forward. "You know them, and I'm sure you trust them far more than me. Ezra could've broken all of this down for you just as well as I. And without as much effort."

The squinty-eyed bastard. There was a reason the HSA enlisted Vince for interrogations. But there was also a reason Cyrus was in the position he was in today. Time for an expertly mixed lie.

Cyrus swallowed and narrowed his eyes. Squint to squint. "I wanted to warn the Institution—you in particular—that someone dangerous is in your midst. Someone who's probably been studying the HyperVersist script."

"Who?"

"The newcomer. Darden. Stavan 'Ava' Darden. I personally have reason to believe she has a connection to the Sprytes. I'm practically alone in this belief, and I'm one of the few trying to keep tabs on her."

Vince laughed. The millions of pin-size voices seemed to laugh with him. The music had stopped, but they were still in play—thankfully, though, they were no longer causing Cyrus's skin to tingle.

"I'm a member of that exclusive club, as well," Vince said. "I know for a certainty that girl has been up to no good. We have reason to believe she has her own contingent of vigilantes."

Cyrus nodded. Vince had surely seen the MC³-produced flicks of Ava that were on the web. Cyrus and Sally Ellin had made sure the films were widely distributed to all sorts of dark sites. "Sounds like we're fans of the same movies."

"I wouldn't say I'm a 'fan.'"

"Well, regardless, I believe Verbalism is part of Darden's modus operandi, whether or not she has a connection to the Sprytes. I could down two birds with one stone coming to you rather than my regular people. She's here. You can keep an eye on her."

"I can keep an eye on her when she's here. But, at the moment, she's not."

Damn. Hopefully, she was out in Cyrus's domain, encircled in the Rings of Light. He knew about Darden's poetic inclinations—"save the children," and all that. And he'd worried about Goldner's sudden affinity for the art form, something not mentioned in any file he'd read on him. His former partner, Darryl Ridley, was the poetry lover, a fact Cyrus now fully intended to exploit. But in the years they'd been teamed together as Watcher agents, from what Cyrus had seen and read, none of that love for poetry had rubbed off on Goldner. Not until very recently—*after* he'd partnered with Ava for an off-the-books mission. And now he and dangerous Darden were partners. Who knew what territories she might tempt him into?

"I need to know more," Cyrus said. "If I or any HSA agents should encounter the girl while she's on one of her crusades, I'd like to know all about this, as much as I can. So let's say I buy into the theory that Creation is unfinished, a process moving along toward an omega point as you described. *Why* does linguistic magick work?"

Vince looked up and away, considering something. He then nodded slowly and gestured for Cyrus to take a seat at the table. As Vince did the same, he grabbed a leather-bound book, second from the top of one of many stacks, and opened it.

"Are you a religious man?" Vince seemed to be reading, searching for something in the text, as he spoke.

"I would say so."

"Then you're intimately familiar with the Bible?" The book Vince was poring through wasn't the Good One, Cyrus could tell.

"The significant sections of it, yes."

"I'm sure the account of Creation's beginnings is on that list of significants?"

"It is."

"Then you know how the Book of Genesis begins, by describing a sort of pre-Creation, the Spirit of God moving on the face of the waters, until God said 'Let there be light' and began to bring all that's familiar to us into existence."

Cyrus had never actually read that section of the Bible so closely; his interest-starting point had always been the story of Moses and Exodus. But pre-Creation? He might have to peruse Genesis with this evening's nightcap.

"Now," Vince said, closing the book—titled *The Shekinah*. "To bring that metaphorical myth closer to Reality, think of those waters in Genesis as XynKroma. Then imagine XynKroma as a *sphere* of water. At the deepest, darkest level of those impenetrable waters—like a grain of sand at the center of the sphere—is God. And the moving Spirit of God on the *face* of the waters, together with God's magickal words, these are the elements stirring up the waters, causing storms consisting of liquid, wind, and light, the effects of which extend far beyond the space and time of sphere, bringing pieces and fragments of Reality into existence that are removed from the sphere's space-time.

"An immaterial action in one realm of space-time may have a very material effect in another."

Cyrus wasn't an artist or a scientist, but if there was one thing he didn't lack for, it was imagination. He actually felt, both on the surface and deep down, that he understood what Vince was saying. He thought of the butterfly effect: a butterfly beating its wings on one side of the world could eventually result in a hurricane on the other side. Vince was speaking of the butterfly effect multiplied.

"Keep that metaphysical picture in your mind," Vince said, "while considering biology and physics. Many recent studies have shown that the abilities of words and music are linked in the brain. There's a strong connection between the way we process language and structured music—that is, music distinguished from mere sounds and random noises. Poetry is *musical* language. Listening to it, speaking it, ruminating on it, and *understanding* it lights up and links several different sections of the brain."

Cyrus nodded with a wry smile. He was starting to get the picture of how Carmilla had come up with the name MC³ Productions. It was energy. Potent energy. Matter was essentially energy. $E = MC^2$.

"Now," Vince said, "while considering all that, place that sphere of stormy waters in the brain, in the center of *all* brains. That one sphere of its own unique space-time existing at the core of *every* sentient being's mind, simultaneously."

Quite a conceptual leap, but Cyrus just made it.

"The multisensory process of making musical language—'Let there be light'—when we focus and delve deep enough, a thread or two of our thoughts can connect and become intertwined with a filament of God's thoughts. God's spirited language—an oscillating stringworm of one of Creation's near infinite storms—can become united with ours, briefly, just long enough to have an effect on Reality. Spells that tell matter what to do.

"*That* is Word Magick, Mister Shahrooz. A magick based on the fundamental philosophy that everything that exists is nothing but patterns and processes. Everything is connected, and all processes interact with all other processes, with the processes separated by varying distances of spaces and times."

"Plural?"

"Yes. Both 'spaces' and 'times' have multiple meanings. You—and usually I—measure time linearly in seconds, minutes, and hours, all of them moving forward. But that is not the only definition of time. I won't bore you with a breakdown of the current theory of relativity, but just keep that bright and chaotic watery sphere in mind. Some refer to it as the collective *sunconscious.*"

Cyrus had heard of the term before. He'd also heard different metaphors describing it, some stronger than others.

Metaphors, similes—everything really did come back to poetry. Language shaped and colored human perceptions. He now understood that all too well. "Let there be..." The gasp of a mad, dying God. "A powerful magick." Carmilla was a heavier hitter than he'd thought.

"An understatement," Vince said. "Musical language working on the fundamental level, connecting the subconscious and Reality, all while the objects of the spells are mostly oblivious. Yes, it's heavy. But keep in mind, there are very few willing and talented enough to delve to their own depths, peel themselves to fully reveal their naked souls in order to create great art."

"That is very small comfort."

"Well, here's a bigger one: each form of magick has its own cost. With Verbalism, it's the prospect of the practitioner losing his or her own soul, or that psycho-spiritual essence we humans have defined as the 'soul.' Go too deep for too long, the practitioner risks having it disperse. The soul's irreparable disintegration. And the body... As it is below, so it is above. Whatever happens in Xyn has some effect on Reality's surface, most often minimal. Likewise, whatever happens to the soul has an effect on the body. Might make it tougher—might make it weaker. The effects could be internal or external, major or minor, at the molecular level or something far more obvious. But there is *always* an effect. It just depends on the experience."

Cyrus suspected the witch had lied to him. She most likely had been to XynKroma, long ago, at a very young age, involuntarily. She'd learned a little during her journey, but there had been an effect on her soul and body afterward. Hence her odd skin color. Still, she'd gotten wise, and she remained hungry for the power of Xyn again but repulsed by the thought of ever going back. So she'd trained others to go in her stead, trained them to travel as her emissaries so that she might benefit while they lost little bits and pieces of their own souls, becoming more and more dependent, more and more subservient to her. Long-legged sentinels who spoke very few words.

"Now, in a controlled environment," Vince said, "such as my workshop, I can send 'souls' to Xyn, minimizing the effects, rendering them mostly harmless. The smartest way to go is under the supervision of someone like myself."

"And the dumbest way," Cyrus muttered, "is under the supervision of someone like a witch."

"Pardon?"

"Nothing," Cyrus said. "I was just wondering, how can one protect himself against this form of magick, protect himself from being an unwitting victim of Verbalism?" He'd be damned if he allowed the witch to dupe and link up with him again.

"The easiest and best way to counter it," Vince said, "is to see and know what's being done, and to actively—*consciously*—push back. As I said, understanding poetry requires a shift in consciousness. That's pretty much all I can tell you."

Vince rose to gather the papers off the keyboard and handed them back to Cyrus. Cyrus stood, his brow furrowed.

"Aren't you going to make a copy?"

"I have." Vince smiled. "I have everything I need."

Cyrus looked from the smug expression on his face to the keyboard. That black window. Something behind it, something in the other room, had recorded what Vince had played. Vince's translation. Symbols into musical notes into—

His cell phone beeped. A text message. Cyrus was a little surprised he could get reception so far underground. Then he saw it was from Sally. *Shit.*

Vince said nothing more, but the frisson Cyrus felt as he rushed from the room told him the buzzing of millions of voices—the fragrance transferred from the mapmaker to him—hadn't left his skin.

To hell with it. Cyrus had an innocent young girl to save.

Chapter 15

The web had dissolved by the time Watcher Agents Seife and Mintner arrived. Chairman Adam had traced Robert's car and sent Unit X_5O when Robert hadn't returned to The Burrow within the promised time frame.

Robert lay in the weeds, breathing heavily, eye fluttering, until his fellow agents helped him to his feet. He wasn't fine to drive, but he insisted he was. The agents either believed him or didn't care to argue, leaving Robert to walk to his Stang as they continued on their own business.

He took the slow route back to The Burrow. He needed time to think. Fresh off house arrest, under the microscope to re-prove himself, and in fewer than forty-eight hours he'd failed at the one simple duty the chairman had given him. The Watcher agent had failed to be watchful. Or maybe Robert was failing himself, unaware all these years whether his labors for Adam weren't for the simple purposes that they'd seemed. Then again, maybe Ava's Nurse was just trying to mess with his head.

During the entire drive back and the too-brief elevator ride down, he went over and over what he would say to Adam. Mask or no mask, how could he face the man? By the time he stepped into the dark twisting corridor toward the chairman's office, he had nothing close to a good excuse for losing his partner, and the suspicions that he was being played—by Adam or someone else—just wouldn't go away. His head was swimming when he felt a tingling sensation on his right wrist. He put two fingers on the watch's face to intuit Adam's message. The chairman instructed him to see Zel; Adam was busy talking to Peter at the moment.

Robert pushed the blue button at the side of the toymaker's door and nearly held his breath during the two-minute open-sesame ritual. Zel was a close friend, but why was the chairman shunting Robert to him?

"Come in." Zel's workshop but Vince Ceniza's voice.

Both men sat on stools at a table more cluttered than any-thing in Vince's office. Plastic and metal objects of various sizes and geometric shapes, circuit boards ranging from the size of a palm to that of a thumbnail, thick books that could've belonged to a grad student in physics, and sheets of paper spread out like a winning hand of cards. Facing each other, the two men had ap-parently been engaged in a deep discussion before Robert entered.

"Rough night?" Zel gestured toward an empty stool at the table.

"Enlightening night." Robert waved off the offer to rest his legs. "Rough morning after."

"It's about to get worse," Vince said as he gathered the table's scattered sheets into a neat stack.

Robert nodded. "Adam's pissed I lost Ava."

"Sacred shitless would be a more apt description," Vince said. "Though you could probably never tell. Adam knows *to whom* you lost her. A notorious killer, an affiliate of The Infinite Defi-nite. She'd dropped off the grid a while ago. Now, as soon as she reappears, she makes a beeline for Ava—then both of them disappear." Vince put a finger on his temple. "It's not a coincidence."

"Yeah," Robert said. "No such thing. I got jumped by two of her ID buddies." It was only now that Robert realized the duo didn't kill him, as ID pairs would normally do. Why had they spared him? Who *wasn't* toying with him today?

Zel held up something that looked like a smartphone but that Robert knew was much more sophisticated than any such device on the market. "The tracking system I installed in the Miata tells me Ava has been inside it since ditching you, but it's still in front of your apartment building."

"She hasn't responded to my signals," Robert said.

"Her watches are also in the car," Vince said, "unattached to any beating pulse."

"So…" Robert looked from one to the other. "Are we sure she's not dead? *In* the car?"

"Adam's sure. He sent Unit $X_{12}O$—the nearest Watcher agents in the area—to verify."

"Yeah," Robert said. "I figured. I also figured her trigger's been pulled. She's following her programming. There was an incident at the mall yesterday—"

"We know," Zel said. "Adam showed us the Pentagon City security footage."

"She became a different person," Robert said. "Not quite Jekyll and Hyde, but like a very committed actor slipping and falling into a role. Determined, just like she was on the movies we saw yesterday." For the first time today, he had a good idea. "So maybe the map you made will give us a clue?"

Vince shook his head. "I thought of that and reviewed my copy when I found out what happened. No insight."

Robert's shoulders slumped. "So we're in the same position we were in with Darryl two weeks ago."

"The crystalline bow Ava used during your last outing is also missing," Zel said.

Robert nodded. "Okay, so maybe we're in a much worse position."

"Maybe you're right." Zel began fiddling with two earbuds. "We had a very unwelcome visitor in The Burrow this morning."

"A senior HSA agent dabbling in dangerous potent magick," Vince said. "An agent who is dead set on going after Ava."

"That's *good*, right?" Robert said.

Vince squinted at him. "If she hasn't already, I believe more than ever she is on the verge of coming fully out of her cocoon, now that she has the right kind of help."

Robert watched Zel's fingers work as he remembered Ava's increased strength during the mall incident. "What are we expecting?" he asked.

"What I read and heard today convinced me of what I already knew," Vince said. "For the past eighteen months, the Arkangel Ava and others have been involved in an elaborate magick ritual, attempting to create a temple to protect themselves against the end of the world, or a palace from which to rule the new one."

"Yeah," Robert said, "I know." He told them about his trip to Xyn, hardly pausing as he saw their facial expressions pass through concern and bewilderment before coming to rest at grim understanding.

"A temple-palace," Vince said. "And a garden, too."

"Crazy, right?"

"Not when you have the magickal skills to make it work."

Robert pulled up a stool. His legs were about to give up their confidence.

"Problem is," Vince said, "all magick has a cost. In this case, it's—" He glanced, almost with a plea, at Zel. "Well, it's serious."

Robert knew Zel didn't approve much of strong language, whether four-letter obscenities or that which evoked strong, repellant imagery. He seemed to have a softer nature that set him apart from Vince the poet, Sam the doctor, and most others in The Burrow. Some saw this as a character flaw, a weakness the rendered him barely fit to survive in the real world, Virus or no Virus. Robert saw it as a uniqueness to be embraced, which is how he and Zel had grown to be so close. But, still, he just had to ask Vince, "How serious?"

Vince looked once more at his colleague. Those eyes behind cherry-tinted shades betrayed no sympathy, so the psychological mapmaker spelled it plainly. "Sacrificial lambs. The young and the innocent on the altar."

"You mean"—Robert almost choked on the realization—"the children she's been saving?"

"We need to find her as soon as superhumanly possible," Zel said. "Without the HSA's help."

Using his new phone's Panic button was now out of the question. "So I guess Adam's on—"

"It's primarily on *you*," Vince said. "Map or no map, out of everyone here at The Burrow, you know her the best. And now that you've made a jaunt to Xyn together, intuition should help guide you."

"As long as she stays out of sight of the Rings of Light," Zel said, "as I'm sure she'll try now that she's wise to their near ubiquity, there's not much anyone else here can do now that she's unlinked from all toys designed to track."

No matter what he designed or created, no matter what its purpose, Zel insisted on referring to them as *toys*—as if everything and anyone associated with The Burrow were part of some big game. Well, maybe it all was. Hide-and-seek, tag, red rover… games children played for no prize. Play for too long, someone always ended up getting hurt. As some anonymous poet said: life is just a game of war, and we're all born defensive. "What am I supposed to do if—*when* I find her?"

Vince's eyes narrowed. "Neutralize her."

"Put these in your ears." Zel handed him the buds he'd been toying with. "Orange one in the left ear. Black one in the right. Can you still hear me?" Robert nodded. "Clearly? There's no ringing? No static?" Robert shook his head. Zel smiled. "Good. I didn't have a lot of time, but it seems I hit the mark."

"The Heartland Security scumbag that was here gave us a gift," Vince said. "An instruction manual for linguistic magick—HyperVersism—which it seems, based on your journey to Xyn, your partner was well versed in, if you'll excuse the pun." Today Robert would. "I was able to use some of the information I copied and translated to conjure up a little code. Zel programmed it into the buds. Put your finger to your ear—*not* now—but when the time is right, put your finger on your tragus—this part of the ear here… It'll push the button activating the device to shriek out a subaudible sentence, a poetic verse."

"Kind of like a dog whistle," Zel said, "for angels."

"The second you see Ava, don't hesitate. Push the button."

"The orange will take out every Virus-carrier in a half-mile radius, knocking them unconscious, protecting you alone."

"And the black?" Robert asked.

"A backup. It'll do the same as the orange, except it'll knock you out, as well."

"It'll also send us a signal that it's been activated so we can send the authorities to pick you up."

"And if that fails?"

"Give her a hug."

Shit—they're serious. A directive for one Virus-carrier to give another a "hug" was a euphemism for a suicide play. Take out both yourself and your enemy at once.

"Time's wasting," Vince said. "You better get back out there."

Zel nodded at him. A nonverbal "good luck." Vince just cocked his head and squinted, waiting for him to get out and on with it.

Robert left the workshop, trying his best to keep his finger away from his ear. (Try not to think of a pink elephant.) The new devices fit snugly and were comfortable enough, but they were new additions to his person and he was freshly aware of them. He just had to touch—

He put his index and middle fingers on his right-wristwatch, intuitively requesting an audience with Adam. He still needed to meet with him, face-to-"face." At the very least he wanted to apologize for losing Ava. He also wanted confirmation that he really was under orders to "hug" Ava if necessary. Part of him also wanted to see what type of vibe he'd get in Adam's physical presence—suspicion or fatherly comfort? Adam signaled back that he was far too busy to see Robert but, yes, Ava was now considered expendable. Adam and Peter had spoken with their contacts in law enforcement and, in light of current circumstances, the Watchers had temporary permission to act out in the field, on one mission only. Adam was now working on finding highly trained and available Watcher agents to send out in the field to assist him. In the meantime, if Ava had gone nuclear—Adam's term for irreversibly rogue—Robert's primary directive was to ensure whatever damage she could cause didn't spread.

Robert took the long elevator ride to the parking garage, wishing the entire time there was a faster way out of The Burrow. Too fast coming down, too slow going up—time never managed to keep the right pace for the race. The Burrow, of course, had emergency escape tunnels, but traveling the length of even the shortest one took three times as long as the elevator. Robert could only clench his teeth at the inconvenience of time lost, knowing deep down he desired nothing but time and space to think about what he needed to do next. When he reached fresh air at last, his cell phone rang.

Cyrus?

No. Kurtis.

His friend had undoubtedly used the callback function on his own cell since Robert hadn't even known let alone given out the number for the phone Cyrus had gifted him.

It was difficult to discern; it was barely coherent. But all Robert needed to hear was the word *Ava* before he sprinted for his Mustang.

His driving made hers seem tame.

Chapter 16

Cyrus had barely come to a stop at the curb before Sally Ellin ran up and clutched at the passenger's side door handle. She launched herself into the seat shoulder first and screamed "Go! *Go!*" before Cyrus could even ask what was wrong.

He pulled away from the campus shuttle stop slowly at first, giving his little girl a chance to close her door and buckle her seat belt.

"What the hell is going on?" Cyrus said.

Sally Ellin screeched, "Speed up! Those bitches are following me!"

Cyrus turned onto a traffic-free side road leading away from the school's buildings and pushed down on the gas. He began to ask who was following her—and how—when he saw something a few yards in front of him. It almost looked like an upright log, about ten feet high, with branches for legs and arms. The thing was dashing like an Olympic sprinter toward the van. Cyrus shook off his bewilderment and slammed on the brakes, realizing he was the victim of a Dirty Light Magick trick—but realizing it too late as the log launched itself sideways at his windshield.

The bulletproof glass wasn't meant for human bodies. It did a fine enough job, however, of repelling the woman who bounced off it and onto the ground.

"Step on the gas!" Sally Ellin said. "Step on the fuckin' gas and run that bitch over!"

Holly Hernandez was stunned. Eyes closed, light-tricks stopped, she looked like she was supposed to—like someone who'd just been hit by a speeding van. Cyrus wasn't sure what she was trying to accomplish by throwing herself at his windshield; she couldn't have believed it would shatter like in the movies. But whoever knew what an associate of The ID was thinking? This was perfect.

Cyrus put the van in Park, grabbed his ADS, and opened his door. He ignored Sally Ellin's hysterics as he stepped out. After getting the girl's distress call and before heading out, he'd strapped on his vest: bulletproof, fireproof, and a bunch of other shit. He carried two sets of cuffs, intending to use one for her wrists and the other for her ankles—after he took off those damned stiletto boots of hers. First step in securing her, however, lay in a secret pouch in his vest. Six syringes, any one of which would ensure she slept for at least twelve hours.

He kept his ADS pointed at the body as he stepped forward, reaching for his secret pouch with his free hand. He narrowed his eyes at her, looking for twitching eyelids and twitchy fingers. He tuned out Sally Ellin's wailing completely while listening for any irregular breathing. After five steps, he was convinced the woman was out cold. After one more step, he felt a block of ice hit him in the back of the head.

Cyrus grunted a curse as he stumbled forward and dropped his syringe. He spun around, his ADS weapon ready. He saw nothing. He only felt a baseball of ice slamming into his right temple, followed by a quick and cold blow to his left.

He cursed again. He couldn't see it, but he knew Holly's invisible partner was in front of him, slugging him. He raised the ADS waist-high and fired.

A leather strap wrapped around his neck and tightened. Something other than leather was there, something prickly. It ripped his skin as it rubbed, drawing rivulets of blood. Cyrus snatched it with his free hand and tried to pull it away.

"Hey there, fat boy," a voice behind him whispered. "Ready for your mind-fuck?"

Holly. She'd been playing possum. Now she was choking the life out of him.

Cyrus tried to turn, but she turned with him, staying right behind him. He could barely see, or breathe. He dropped his ADS and tried to use both hands to make space between the belt and his throat, slashing his fingertips, managing only to put a quarter of an inch or so between the barbs and him. He tried to wiggle and shift his hips, positioning himself so he could flip her over his back. But Holly kept her hips low; he couldn't even raise her off the ground. The woman was strong. Maybe even stronger than him. But not stronger than the knockout juice.

He took a hand away from his throat and fumbled with his hidden pocket, sliding out another syringe. He'd no time to be skillful as he jammed the needle into her leg, the only part of her he could reach. It hit just below the knee, snapping on the boot.

Holly laughed. "I will peel off your face and wear it as a bib while I feast on your girlfriend's entrails."

"Let him go, bitch!"

Cyrus heard Sally Ellin's voice coming from the direction of the van. He couldn't see her until Holly turned, putting his body between hers and the blonde girl pointing the Glock at them.

"Are you kidding me, hussy?" Holly said as Ava slid from a shroud of invisibility and kicked Sally Ellin in the head. The blonde girl dropped the gun and fell on her side. Ava kicked the gun far away from everyone, then kicked Sally Ellin in the face.

"Switch you, Arkangel." Holly jutted a knee into the small of Cyrus's back and, with a heave, turned the big man's world upside down. He landed on his stomach and face. He only managed to hoist himself up on his elbows and knees before a hand yanked his hair and another clutched his shoulder. Slight Ava, from behind, turned him over with little apparent effort before straddling him and wrapping her hands around his neck.

He wasn't dead. He had sufficient energy. But for the life of him, Cyrus just couldn't buck Ava off, nor could his fingers loosen hers.

"Look at me, pedophile."

He couldn't help but look into those sapphire-blue eyes of hers, kaleidoscoping, the blue draining out to green as blood vessels appeared in the whites of her eyes, vessels that burst to color the whites brown. Grass-green and muddy-brown eyes pierced his—blades of grass transformed rapidly into green grapnels, trying to snatch at something deep within him.

Cyrus felt no pain at his throat, no discomfort in his eyes, only simultaneous sensitivity in his teeth, as if biting into too-cold ice cream, and a brain freeze, as if sucking up a milkshake too quickly. He felt it as he saw the four-dimensional images gradually appearing and ripping in the space between his and Ava's face: a doctor…a doctor's office…a surgical procedure…aborted…mission…a garden…a field of lust and torture…

Ava released her grasp and fell back. At first she seemed merely exhausted from the memories she'd extracted and experienced. But she didn't move, lying as if catatonic. Maybe she'd experienced more than she wanted. Cyrus was also fatigued, but he was damned pissed, too.

He heaved himself up to his feet. Ava was in no shape to move anytime soon, so he turned toward the other one. Holly grinned back at him. One of her boots was planted on the pavement, the other on the right side of Sally Ellin's head. Cyrus took two steps toward her.

"You have no idea," Holly said, "no *idea* about the ways of the world, do you?" The boot on Sally Ellin's head traded its black hue for gunmetal and the stiletto heel looked more and more like a stiletto dagger. "You think, *you* among all of them think you have your finger on the pulse of what the endangered species is doing, thinking, *feeling*." Holly pushed her heel deeper into Sally Ellin's temple. It sunk in like a blunt stick steadily pushing into a water balloon. Sally Ellin's head oblonged slightly—like a cartoon character's—as she let out a piercing wail. "We think far more deeply." Holly stamped her foot down, collapsing Sally Ellin's skull into a salad of bone fragments, brain matter, and eyeballs.

A cry came from deep within Cyrus, so deep he didn't hear it. He felt it, as if his throat were a fire hose aimed at Holly, the incarnation of the devil. But no matter what epithets he screamed at her, she stood grinning, unwavering.

"You're not a man," she said. "Not the man you think you are." She plucked her heel out of the mess and took a step forward. "Let's see what you're really made out of."

Cyrus's unbridled anger had initially paralyzed him, but fear and awe kept him that way as he saw amber spikes jutting out of Holly's bare skin, growing longer as she moved closer. She appeared almost like a human porcupine, until he saw the violet-green heads emerging under the spikes. Birds' heads. *Humming*birds. Neck, shoulders, forearms, thighs—they appeared on every exposed area of her skin.

The sight alone unnerved, but the incessant buzzing went further.

Cyrus couldn't prevent what seemed like a blizzard of recent memories from swirling around inside his head. The walk through The Burrow. The dark energy. The tiny, tinny voices he'd heard in Vince's office.

Holly moved closer, walking like a supermodel on a catwalk as Cyrus felt his skin, his muscles, even his bones—acutely—turning into stone. He couldn't blink. He couldn't shut out the sound of "life's a bitch, and then you die," accompanied by a chorus of 144,000 hummingbirds darting out of the woman's skin and straight for him, pile driving, chiseling his stout, stocky body into an entirely new shape as he screamed his lungs bloody, his voice becoming just another part of the concert killing him, drilling into his skin and senses.

Experiencing a furious mixture of sounds and sensations, Cyrus couldn't help but *feel* sights from the now, the near, and the far future—all of it seemingly in one second—before blacking out.

Chapter 17

Robert saw the battle while he was still two blocks away. About one hundred kids had gathered in a Whole Foods parking lot. What had started off, he guessed, as a lot of verbal taunting had degenerated into dance battles, like something out of an edgy Hollywood musical fusing breakdancing and ballroom dancing. As he passed, the scene became one of ballet crossed with full-contact football. His gut told him the scene would degenerate even further once they were out of his view. But the "proper" authorities would have to handle this one. He hadn't the time.

He'd been able to calm Kurtis down long enough to get a location. Wilson Boulevard in Arlington. He parked two blocks away from the exact address, in the least seedy of the back lots he could find. He'd learned to never park too close to a target site, even if just meeting friends. If followed, either to or from the vehicle, he wanted plenty of opportunities to spot the spy and take a detour if necessary.

He performed his usual inconspicuous surveillance as he walked briskly—manipulating the light and shadow near his face to make himself appear forty years older, more sad than determined, and down on his luck (just the type of faces most passersby go out of their way to ignore) as he scanned the faces and sized up the expressions of the people nearing him, as well as those who kept their distance. He shot glances through car and store windows, up toward the roofs of shorter buildings, and took a couple of extra seconds to adjust his sight when it fell on a bush or tree branches. An enemy could be anywhere and anyone, and could appear in any guise at any time. Hell, a group of kids could run up on him and start rapping, challenging him to a battle.

But there was no danger he could see or sense, not even when he jaywalked through evening rush hour traffic, heading toward what appeared to be not the coffeehouse Kurtis had mentioned but, judging from what he saw in the barred display windows, an unkempt pawnshop that specialized in tribal artifacts from other lands. And that's exactly what it was, from 9:00 A.M. to 4:00 P.M. Beginning at 6:00 P.M., however, it became The Bungled Jungle, one of the "black markets for dangerous poetry"—or so explained the man who greeted Robert after he knocked and was buzzed into the shop despite the Go Away, We're Closed sign.

He didn't give a damn about the "uniquely Northern Virginian form of poetry more mind-altering than haiku"; he just wanted to know where his friends were. When the man finally shut up for three seconds, he responded to Robert's question by leading him to a narrow stairway hidden behind a towering display of tribal masks from around the world. Robert walked down three flights and was greeted by a stout, gruff man acting as checker, bouncer, and entrance fee collector. He opted to keep his windbreaker and wondered why a coffee shop would need a bouncer as he handed him a five and passed through a doorway of hanging multicolored stringed beads.

He'd been wise to keep his windbreaker, reinforced as it was by Zel for such environments. For an establishment located a story or two underground, it was surprisingly well lit. Feeling the layers of skin on his face, neck, and hands gradually acquiring the texture of sandpaper—each grain of sand a parasite grubbing, each unitary layer of skin rubbing against one another, creating a teeth-clenching friction—he knew his next wise move would be to get a bottle of water and take a battery of pills as soon as possible. But first problem first. He scanned the room for Kurtis and Anika.

The bungled jungle, indeed.

Nothing Robert had seen upstairs had given a clue to the type of coffee-barflies he'd be mixing with. Everyone he saw looked as if they were on break from their jobs as live exhibits at the newest, hippest, postmodern art museum. Every outfit was a composite of articles of clothing incongruent with all the other articles: girls wearing blue ballerina tutus, army boots, and sombreros; guys wearing football shoulder pads, pirate boots, and dark-pink berets.

An artsy vibe, helped in no small part by the atmosphere. Incense burdened the air with at least four competing fragrances—peppermint, rose, lavender, and something that gave the impression of a peach orchard. Despite it all, there was very little smoke. It would've been easier to search a dimmer room, but he finally saw his friends half-hidden behind a plant that seemed straight out of a 1950s B movie about earthlings invading Mars. Not exactly in the middle of the floor, but it offered a nice vantage point to keep an eye on any and all who might attempt to hide in any of the room's multiple corners. His friends knew him well. He joined them.

Whatever he'd been through over the past twenty-four hours, Kurtis and Anika looked as if they'd been through worse within the past twenty-four minutes. Peaked, ragged—they hardly looked themselves at all. And yet it was Anika who said it first: "You look like fossilized shit. Shall I order more coffee?"

A true friend. Judging by the looks of their mugs, and a quick x-ray of the pot at the table's center, it seemed they were ready for a refill regardless.

"Help yourself," Robert said. The adrenaline that had coursed through him during the drive over had been replaced with the adrenaline produced due to being in an unfamiliar place, sitting in a circle of freaky and unknown faces. He was plenty alert without caffeine. "I'll do fine with some water."

"I'll be right back." Anika grabbed the pot and headed for the bar. She stopped halfway to chat with a taller woman who looked much too comfortable in these surroundings, as if she ran the place. She was familiar, though he couldn't quite place the face. It seemed Anika knew her well; Robert had never seen her hug anyone like *that* except Kurtis. As the two women engaged in a discussion that became more and more animated, the taller one shot a glance at Robert just as he realized that Kurtis had been speaking at him all the while.

"The rabbit hole's being turned inside out, man."

"What?" He pushed his full attention to Kurtis. "What happened?"

Kurtis went through it all.

"You're sure you're all right?"

"We're alive."

"You should've called me sooner," Robert said. "Had me come there. I could've had Adam alert any agents in the area to—"

"We had to get out of there, man. Far away."

Robert nodded. "Any idea where they were off to?"

"No." Anika retook her seat, fresh pot in one hand and bottle of water in the other. "But one of them is more than happy to kill anyone along the way."

Robert took his plastic pill bottle out of his inner jacket pocket. "Holly, the Archangel." Neither Zel nor Vince had given him much background, only said she was an affiliate of The ID. Did Adam know more? He'd certainly known more about Veronica Blake and Vanessa Blight than he'd been willing to divulge until the last minute. How much did the chairman know that Robert needed to?

"Any idea who this woman is?"

"No," Kurtis said. "We never saw her likeness in all the footage we reviewed of Ava. Never read any mention of her."

"Forget Ava," Robert said. "What about researching everything having to do with this fucking Archangel cult?"

"Already done," Anika said. "And we couldn't find any mention or reference to this Holly person. After we called you, we came here with our laptops, and, well, here we are."

Yes, here they were. "Why did you come *here*?" Robert asked.

"It's safe," Kurtis said. "Plenty of light. But we know where the switches are."

Robert wasn't sure he liked the look in his friend's eyes. Gave him too much of the impression of us versus them. Us versus *your kind.*

"It's one of the places we come to relax," Anika said. "Get our minds off things. Plus, we know the owner. Coffee's on the house."

"So I have to pay for the water?"

Robert's attempt to soften Kurtis's expression with watered-down humor failed.

"Half price."

And Robert's expression went to depths surpassing his friend's when he turned toward the tall woman, who'd had her own joke. He now had her name. "VaShawna."

She'd approached the table without him noticing before she spoke. *Nice trick.* He gave her plenty of attention now.

The woman cocked her head as one side of her mouth curved upward into a smile, or a grimace. It was hard to tell which from the angle Robert viewed it. But there was nothing wrong with his memory.

"Were we ever introduced?" she asked.

"No," Robert said. "But last time I saw you, you were a new employee—a bartender—at a dawnclub where a friend works. Were you fired already?"

"Sonya," VaShawna said, as if reading his mind. "Right. I work with her in Shirlington. I moonlight there, so to speak, but just to help keep this place—*my* place—afloat. Economy's rough, you know. Most folks trying to make it have to wear more than one hat."

Robert saw the diamond studs and the jeweled rings on the thumbs, middle, and pinkie fingers of both hands. They fit with the high-fashion-designed dashiki dress she was wearing, but overall she clashed with everyone else in the joint. Out of place in her own place. "Economy doesn't seem all that rough for some folks," he said. "Might be a struggle, but maybe some of us could give up some of our more extravagant habits to make it through."

"Said the man who wears two uniquely exquisite watches." VaShawna smirked at Robert's frown. "Never seen anything like those before. Where do you shop?"

"Online. I just do random Google searches till I find what I want."

"And at what online watch shop did you find those?"

"I forget. My memory's not so stellar when it comes to things that don't really matter, like material items."

"Not a materialist, huh? Smart, in this day and age, passing the way it is. By the way, we have a concoction that maybe could fix that mental problem of yours."

"I'll stick with water, thank you."

"Tell you what, since you paid cover, and you're a friend of friends, I'll only charge you a dollar for the bottle. A quarter of its price. Enjoy it in good health."

Robert stared at the backside of the woman as she walked toward the bar. It was only after she'd entered the door behind it that he said, "You should be more careful about whom you pal around with."

"We'll make a note of that, pal," Kurtis said. The look, that mildly accusatory look, still hadn't left his eyes. Robert wasn't quite sure what to make of it. Thank fortune something else began to tug at everyone's attention.

A saxophonist blew his horn, walking slowly from the bar toward the stage. The notes seemed disjointed. Robert figured maybe that was on purpose, to get everyone's attention as the evening's entertainment was about to begin.

The performance area's wooden platform stood no more than two feet off the ground and gave the impression of being very unstable. Robert heard creaks as the horn player walked on it; he even heard creaks after the man had taken his place in the back corner of the stage and was moving only his fingers and neck.

The man stopped playing and gave a modest bow to modest applause as the lights dimmed and a teenager wearing frayed Hawaiian shorts, an open plaid shirt, and a tie-dyed bandanna over his nose and mouth trotted onto the stage. Before stepping up to the microphone, he went over to the saxophonist and pointed to something written on the paper in his hand, apparently giving the musician instructions on how to play during his impending recital. He then walked back to the microphone and glanced once more at the sheet of paper before crumpling it into a ball. He closed his eyes and tossed the wad out into the crowd, hitting someone two tables behind Robert's. As the man shouted threatening expletives in response, the teenager opened his eyes wide and, at the top of his lungs, shouted something that may've been in a foreign language Robert didn't recognize. After regaining his breath, the kid delivered his verses, in English and at a slightly more subdued decibel level. Whatever he'd shouted must've been the poem's title; beyond the title, the piece wasn't half-bad. Amid the wild hoots and applause, Robert also picked up some muted boos, and a couple more expletives from the man who'd been hit by the paper, but the catcallers were clearly in the minority.

So this was the type of place VaShawna ran when she wasn't moonlighting. It still didn't make much sense to Robert. He had nothing to fall back on but his admittedly limited knowledge, but nothing about her—nothing that was obvious and nothing that his skills as a Watcher agent had permitted him to surmise—fit in with the surroundings. It was like she'd been cast in a role only because she was blackmailing the moneymen behind the play. Robert wanted to toss his dollar on the table for the water, get out, and get on with wandering the streets for Ava, but something—some alchemistry of the atmosphere—kept him leaden in his seat.

The next poet performer was a mohawked woman wearing lacy, fingerless gloves and some kind of miniskirt apparently inspired by an old *Jetsons* cartoon. After giving instructions to the horn player on how to blow, she introduced herself by managing a twisting backflip that landed her right behind, if not almost on top of, the microphone. She then launched into a poem and other physical movements that defied sense, but once she'd finished, Robert offered a long round of applause. Anyone who could perform acrobatics on such a rickety stage while wearing such a getup and without breaking either her neck or the flow of a four-minute string of rhymes and alliterative puns about labium deserved kudos.

And he was able to appreciate, if not exactly like, all the performers who followed, all of them taking their turns at screeching, shouting, mumbling, humming, singing, whining, chanting, blowing, and beatboxing into the microphone and meeting various mixtures of heckles, cheers, and indifference as a response. One performer even attempted to throw cherry-and-liqueur-filled chocolates into the audience in an attempt to win over applause and cheers while he alternated between song and hard-left socialist rhetoric. Many audience members laughed and howled with glee as they gathered the foil-wrapped candy and tried their best to fastball those pieces back at the performer's mouth.

Robert chuckled all the while. He couldn't help himself. He was having a wonderful time, for the first time in…he couldn't remember when, but he felt comfortable. He was entertained. He felt *good*.

His tablemates didn't appear nearly as happy. They drank coffee like it was sugar water, wrung their hands, and mumbled as they busied themselves on their laptops. Robert hadn't been too concerned with what they were doing, though he'd faintly hoped they were looking for…whatever he'd set out to look for that evening. They'd grab his attention when necessary. He was more interested in the fact that, as time passed, the poetry he heard from the increasingly eccentric performers became more and more intricate, nothing like the half-hashed crap of the earliest performers. Ninety minutes after the first young poet had left the stage, the performers' words were now on the level of a Hopkins, or an Eliot, or a Melvin Tolson, while their body movements and stunts were something learned from the best schools of mimes and contortionists (if such institutions existed), all of it appropriately accompanied somehow by the versatile horn player.

Robert's one-liter bottle of water had been empty for almost an hour. He was ready for another drink. He glanced at Anika then Kurtis, momentarily considering asking them to use their connection to get him a discounted bottle of water. He then chuckled at his own cheapness.

"What's so funny?" Anika asked, appearing annoyed to have to take her eyes off her screen.

"Uh, nothing. Just enjoying myself."

Anika muttered something and looked back at her laptop, tapping furiously at her keyboard. Hell, they chose this place—claimed they were regulars—but they hadn't clapped, cheered, booed, or hissed at anything. Even if they'd seen this all as a sad parade of bad poets, they should've had some reaction to it all. Everything about them this evening was a little off, but Robert figured he'd never seen them in the aftermath of a traumatic experience before. Maybe this was their way of coping with almost being killed by an "angel." One of *his* kind. He excused himself.

He laid his four bucks on the bar and took a swig. He then sat on a stool and turned his attention back to the stage. He felt better spending a few minutes away from his friends. He was clearly no comfort to them. And they were ruining his wonderful time.

Another flamboyant poet took the stage. "The main event," Robert heard someone near him say. A guffawing, dangerously overweight man clad in a red frock decorated with silver and golden symbols and stitched white lines making strange patterns. Santa Claus crossed with Merlin.

The living cartoon patted his belly like a drum as the saxophonist provided backup, multilayering the music. The poet gave a blues musician's holler, then moved his left hand to drum the top of his head while his right remained on beat on his midsection. Without warning, he bellowed in the voice of Howlin' Wolf, "This is 'Born Again'!"—and began to recite poetry in voice like no other.

The man slapped words together so fast, not only could Robert's eye see nothing other than a blur where his lips were, but the words weren't absorbed and didn't begin to form themselves into symmetrical patterns in his consciousness until what seemed like two full minutes after he'd already spoken them. It was unreal. It was as if the poet was trying to push poetry beyond poetry—break the limits of the art form by using all the art form's devices to the extreme. Musical voice, rhyme, alliteration, assonance—he pulled every poetic trick there was out of the hat, faster than multiplying rabbits. *Art for art's sake*, Robert found himself thinking, *can sometimes lead to a kiss—or more—with* infinity.

And then it happened. It happened as fast as the poet's lips moved, as fast as the words machine-gunned outward. His right hand reached into the inner breast pocket of his frock and pulled out a serrated knife.

Before anyone could even gasp, the poet had plunged the six-inch blade into his chest twice. The first exhalations of shock came to Robert's ears after the twentieth stab, the last one before the man collapsed on his back.

At first most seemed too confused to scream. Even Robert had no reaction as he watched the blood and other objects fountain up and out from the many wounds: glittering blood more blue than red, spurting, accompanied by eruptions of what appeared to be pea-size gemstones. Robert telescoped his vision to confirm they were what they appeared; they were even translucent, with unrecognizable insects trapped inside. They shot up and downward in arcs, pelting the stage with the shower of blood drops, their force combined with the weight of their source finally making the stressed stage give way around the body. The screams were torrential.

As others jumped out of their chairs, Robert sat still, silent, staring at the fallen man. Even as the horn player gesticulated wildly toward the bar, toward VaShawna, standing no more than three feet behind Robert, he sat transfixed on the convulsing body rapidly devolving into a corpse. One minute watching an artist attempting to burst the seams of poetry and then...What the hell had happened? What the hell *was* happening?

No. It had nothing to do with Hell. Everything to do with XynKroma. And Archangels.

Someone tugged at his arm. A firm grip. A stronger tug. Robert was yanked off the stool and into a room behind the bar before he could protest.

"We've called an ambulance," VaShawna said. "The police will be here with them."

Robert looked at her as if she were on the other side of a frosted window rather than just two feet in front of him.

"What—what's going on?" he asked. "Why did you pull me back here? Where's Kurtis and—"

"Do you really want to be out there when the police get here?" VaShawna asked. "Do you really want to be interviewed as a witness, your name associated with a tragedy…Agent Goldner?"

Robert had no words, only a flurry of thoughts. Had Sonya told this woman who he was, what he really did? Or had his old friends betrayed him to a possible enemy?

"Don't worry," she said. "I'm on your side."

"Oh really?" He remembered the vibe he'd gotten from her the first time they'd met, the looks she'd given him. He wasn't a mind reader, but he placed faith in intuition, just as Vince had instructed. VaShawna was no ally.

"There're more than two dimensions to this world," she said. "You of all people should know that, Rob. Everything is not either X or Y. And if you're going after Ava and Holly, you need help."

Shit. That was what he was supposed to be doing. How had he allowed himself to stay here, in one place, for so long?

"I called someone who could help. I didn't expect this—this accident to happen. Something bad happens everything other night, but usually not like this."

"What *were* you expecting then?" Robert asked.

"Me."

Robert turned toward the man who'd spoken. He sounded like a man, but he looked like a teenager. He gave the impression of

The ID. Robert's iris switched to a hue of cherry red as he reached for his belt buckle, one of Zel's toys.

"No need for all that," the kid said. "The chickie didn't lie. We're both friends of the big man." With a smirk, he looked Robert up and down. "Heard you had a little Archangel trouble. I've got a little solution."

Chapter 18

Shoeless and shirtless, the kid couldn't have been more than two months over sixteen. He had stringy blond hair that touched his shoulders but probably hadn't touched shampoo in weeks. His jeans looked as if they'd gone a few rounds with a lawn mower, his trench coat as if he'd worn it out during an acid rain storm. Countless scars crosshatched his torso like games of tic-tac-toe gone horribly wrong.

Robert kept his hand on his belt buckle. His eye remained red as he looked the kid over—the painted toenails, the scarred skin, the barbed wire cuffing his neck like a dog's collar—before settling on the kid's face, toking on a stick that delivered far more than a mere nicotine fix.

"I'm Stewart Danger."

His breath smelled like a gas station bathroom. *Charming fellow.*

"Don't worry," Stewart said. "It's just my stage name."

Robert sneered at his extended hand.

Stewart withdrew the offer. "Perhaps you'd like to see my card instead?" He reached into an inner coat pocket and pulled out what appeared to be six silver credit cards. He spread them out in a fan as if he was about to ask Robert to pick one, any one, and have him guess the unseen number. Instead, Stewart picked a card with his left hand, showed both silvery-white sides to Robert, then swiped the razor-thin edge across his abdomen. A red line appeared instantly. Stewart rubbed one of the flat sides of the card across it, smearing blood on his skin and the card. He then turned the bloody side of the card up and held it out to Robert.

"If you think I'm touching—"

Stewart shook his head as he angled the card to catch one of the brighter lights shining from the ceiling. Photons hit and mixed with the substance of the blood. Robert saw stains on the card moving, seeming to shimmer, as a pinkish vapor arose and became more bilious before resolving itself into a three-dimensional image of Cyrus. The hologram was the size of a fist and extremely detailed.

Stewart was a Virus-carrier. No surprise there. Also no surprise he could construct holograms. Most skilled Virus-carriers could under certain circumstances, though not usually in such a dramatic fashion. Robert was about to say as much when the hologram moved, then spoke.

"Robert Goldner, this is Stewart Danger. An ally. Trust him. The situation has grown to include something more threatening than just Stavan Darden."

It was Cyrus's voice. Spot-on. And the hologram wasn't flickering or translucent. It appeared solid, like a flesh-and-blood miniaturized version of the big man was hovering there in midair.

As if any more proof were required of his skill, Stewart grabbed and flung the hologram against the nearest wall. The little big man exploded in a burst of blood, bones, and fleshy parts, seeming real enough to make Robert recoil and shout, "Shit!" before all the pieces dissolved in the air, mixing back into the light from which they were conjured.

"Dammit," VaShawna said, "take that foolishness outside—*now!* I've already got enough trouble to deal with tonight."

"C'mon, Patches." Stewart turned and gestured for Robert to follow. "Let's head out of this bedlam."

Out of the jungle, maybe, but Robert knew there was no escaping bedlam at this point. They left through an emergency exit. The cops and medics were already on their way, so it hardly mattered they'd set off an alarm.

"How'd you get here?" Stewart asked. "Cab?"

"Drove," Robert said.

"Good, let's go."

Robert was hesitant. He wasn't sure what to make of this character. But if he was going to get on with his mission, he didn't see any better options than to take up with him. As they walked, though, he couldn't help but pay more attention to Stewart's appearance than to their surroundings.

"Are you HSA?"

"Nah. Independent contractor."

"How do you know Cyrus?"

"Classified."

Something about the kid seemed really off, aside from his appearance and his unique manner of manipulating light. How could someone like Cyrus ever associate with someone like this guy? How could this guy ever be enlisted to help secure the heartland?

Robert made a move toward the cell in his pocket. If he just made a quick call to Cyrus…

No, he couldn't. He wasn't supposed to get the HSA involved in his search for Ava. That injunction probably stood for HSA contractors as well. He was stuck with this one, but maybe fortune would shine on him and he'd find Ava and alert Adam before anything horrible happened.

"This is your car?" Stewart asked.

"Yeah."

"What a shitbucket."

"No one's asking you to ride in it."

"Well since we can't fly, I don't think I have a choice."

"You can catch a cab. Or better yet, get your own damn car and—"

"Oh, stop pissin' your panties."

Robert rolled his eye. Did he *really* need to work with this cretin?

"You said you had a solution to the Archangel problem," Robert said. "I'm listening."

"Get in and drive," Stewart said. "Head toward Herndon."

∞ ∞ ∞

"I'm a Diviner. That's how I know."

Per Stewart's instructions, Robert had driven them to a high school parking lot and parked directly under a lamppost. This time of the evening, the lot was mostly abandoned, except for the occasional security patrols and cars maybe belonging to janitorial staff and a few dedicated teachers. Stewart bent a dome of light, encompassing them and the car so no one outside it could see them. It worked like a charm.

During the drive over, Stewart had told him all he knew—or all he was willing to divulge—about the so-called Archangel Holly Hernandez. She had attended school here, many years ago and under a different name. But her presence could still be felt, as could the presence of anyone who'd ever walked these grounds. The presences of those who'd visited more recently and those who'd visited most often were felt more strongly, but since she had taken the eighth letter as her signifier, her *high* school in *Herndon* seemed the best place to begin establishing the chain from her past to her current whereabouts.

"Here is the first link." Stewart held up a tooth, root included. "Hers."

"Where did you—"

"Don't worry about it. Just know it's necessary for what we're trying to do."

Much of what Stewart had said was magickal mumbo jumbo to Robert, but he had to ask him how he knew this method would work.

"I have direct access to the lowest levels of Xyn," he said. "The *source* of all magick. No need to put myself under and actually visit that realm of symbolism—just need to put a few distantly related elements in the right place and connections are made plain to me."

"Huh. Speaking of connections," Robert said, "you and I are in Herndon looking for Ava, when just two weeks ago she and I were here looking for—"

"I know all about it," Stewart said. "That's another reason I wanted us to come to Herndon. I hardly have any links for Ava, nothing but a couple of words that I can connect to her."

Robert considered Stewart's system. "She was in my car earlier."

"Good. She leave anything behind in there? Jewelry? Strands of hair? Tampon?"

Robert sighed and shook his head.

"How exactly did you two manage to find your old partner anyway?"

"Ava's intuition," Robert said. "I was driving around to spots marked on a map."

Stewart cocked his head. "Map?"

Robert hesitated, not sure how safe or wise it was to tell outsiders about IAI business. But he was trying to avert a crisis. He pulled out the map and explained it while unfolding it across the Mustang's hood.

A deviant grin spread across the Diviner's face. "Absolutely beautiful. I'd love to meet the son of a bitch who drafted this."

He retrieved several silver cards from a pocket in his trench coat and laid them on the map as if preparing to do a tarot reading. Maybe, in a sense, that was just what he was preparing. He laid nine cards down strategically before using the razor edge of a tenth to slice his fingertip. He placed the card in the center of the other nine, then touched each with his bloody finger. The tenth card also got an additional decoration—Holly's extracted tooth.

"You used Ava's intuition last time," Stewart said. "Now we'll use yours. Since you two willingly went to Xyn together, you now have a bond, an unbreakable psychic link. It's deep down, but you can tap into it and find her. Stand here and stare at the tooth. Just focus on it. When you feel ready, tell me what comes to you."

"What?"

"In exacting detail," Stewart said. "And no matter what happens, when you start, don't stop talking and don't stop focusing on the tooth until I tell you to."

It seemed a little silly, but Robert recognized Stewart as a kid of weird wonders. Recalling the miniature Cyrus made him shudder; no telling what would happen this time. Hopefully it wouldn't be a waste.

Robert stood squarely in front of the car and stared at the tooth; its dried blood touched the fresh blood on Stewart's card. For what seemed like five minutes, nothing happened. Then the lamplight above them flickered. It stopped, then began again. As instructed, he didn't avert his gaze as dots on the map became tiny letters and numbers, amassing into ten clusters, dust storms… two-dimensional images inflating into three-dimensional images of bushes burning with fiery words on each leaf, glowing graffiti on each branch, all of it connecting to make one big four-dimensional plant.

Robert spoke the words on the leaves and branches aloud, not exactly understanding what he was saying. It was a kind of poetry. A musical language. A mathematical language.

"Yes…*Yes!*" Stewart slapped him on the back, shutting Robert up and annoying the shit out of him. "That's the shape of the God-head, Goldy! A shape of the shapeless Godhead. The Tree of Love and Death. I figured right. You've got an artistic gift!"

Robert was about to say it was more mathematical than artistic, but he heard voices across the lot. The flickering light above must've drawn the attention of security guards. Either that or Stewart had inadvertently dropped the cloak. Whichever, they had to move.

"Get in."

"Next stop," Stewart said, "Lake Anna in Spotsylvania."

Chapter 19

"You've done well, Avangelika."

Ava's eyelids fluttered. She could tell where she was before she could see clearly, before her thoughts could get arranged with the here and now. She was strapped in, sitting in the passenger's seat of the Archangel's black 'vette. It wasn't moving.

"Let's go." Holly opened the driver's door and got out of the car. Ava gazed through the windshield. It was night. Late in the night. It had been evening when she'd passed out. Since then, Holly had apparently driven them to the edge of a lake. Ava didn't want to get out of the car.

"C'mon." Holly opened her door and put her hand on Ava's right shoulder. Ava felt and heard a humming sensation spread toward her neck and chest. The Archangel had apparently decided on other methods of encouragement besides words. "I can't do this alone."

They weren't alone. Holly's slow-crawling shock wasn't the only thing Ava felt. She grabbed her crystalline bow from the backseat and walked a few steps away from the car, looking around, moving her vision through every range she knew. It was no use. The full moon above was no use. Ava couldn't see the others she knew were there, near the lake's shore.

"What are we doing?"

"Just what you intuited," Holly said. "I saw and decoded the information you pulled when reading the child molester. You pulled information on a doctor, one who'd been working with the government agent to abduct and enslave the young and impressionable. The route to their rotten fruits is here. And you…Well, I need you to see the portal to the veiled territory."

"Me?"

"Of course," Holly said. "It's your territory."

Ava furrowed her brow.

"You don't remember?"

Ava slowly shook her head.

"Every correct angel has a hot spot," Holly said. "A sacred place on Reality's surface that connects to the sacred spot in Xyn-Kroma. You are most powerful there, as well as here, the area that conceals the portal to your hot spot."

Ava turned around, her heart rate speeding as she took in her surroundings. She knew exactly where she was. Lake Anna, in Spotsylvania, Virginia. She looked at the water, under the moonlight. Capillary waves appeared on the lake's surface, as if the water had been teased by a light breeze. Ava felt no breeze, only dread. She couldn't fight off the memory of that bright June day, fourteen years ago.

There was no ice, and it hadn't rained for days. Somehow, though, her mother had lost control of the vehicle. Ava was barely four years old at the time, and her memory of that day would probably remain forever patchy, stained…just like the knees of her mother's jeans. She could vividly remember the grass stains she'd seen up close as she had hugged her mother's leg, both of them bawling. It had taken three men to bring her mother to her feet, the same three strangers who'd jumped in and rescued Ava from the submerged car. Ava's mother had already jumped clear, before the car hit the water. Ava remembered that much. But she could never recall for sure: Hadn't there been another in the car? A third presence that became the second presence once the mother abandoned the vehicle?

Once rescued and deemed okay, Ava had seen her mother off a short distance from the edge of the lake, rolling on the ground in hysterics, screaming loudly and shouting incomprehensible phrases. Ava heard only two words plainly. *Save* and *Children*.

She now moved a few steps closer to the water. This place was somehow connected to what the doctor and the government agent were doing? Ava recalled her temple-palace's Nurse speaking of a doctor and what he'd planned for Marie-Lydia. Everything was starting to fit—but movement off to the side distracted her. Moving darkness. That was all she could see.

She asked Holly, "Are there others here?"

The Archangel grinned that odd grin of hers. "Other angels, yes. I sent out a signal for them to meet us here."

Ava moved away from the water, closer to her. "Why can't I see them?"

"They're of a higher order," Holly said, as if it was common sense. "What you *can* see is the portal we're looking for. Concentrate, Arkangel. Save the children."

Save the Children...

Yes. This is where she'd brought the children she'd rescued in her crusading days, before the IAI had found her. She walked, looking this way and that, trying to let intuition guide her as she manipulated her vision. Getting nowhere after ten minutes, she took off her glasses. Another five passed before she saw it: a circle with a ten-foot circumference, rimmed with a pinkish hue and filled with a kaleidoscope's shapes and colors of forest green, mud brown, and navy blue.

The pale-red tint that normally imbued everything she saw, the defect in her vision that Zel Bernard's glasses were made to correct, was really intended to help her find her way, hers and the children she'd been saving.

"Here." She waved her bow-wielding arm for Holly and the others to follow as she stepped through the portal and into the middle of a vineyard.

She then froze. No movement, no words, and hardly a single conscious thought. She was too stricken to even turn her head, but the movement was unnecessary for her to see, on the rolling hills spread out before her, row after row of hanging children.

They were of varying ages and ethnicities, lined up, tied to the trellises by the vines twisting around their necks, wrists, and ankles. No grapes were on the vines, just baubles appearing like pearls; the leaves and vines themselves were colored orangish green, with a hint of something else—an alien tint. Spyders fluttered about, crawling on the vines, the leaves, and the children, spinning their electrically charged filaments of amber-hued silk. The children were breathing in an exceedingly slow rhythm. Alive—thank the Word—but in suspended animation.

Holly came through the portal. While whoever or whatever came after her scattered, the Archangel put her hand on Ava's shoulder and ran another current, not to rouse this time, but seemingly to encourage Ava to remain still while quickening her mind and loosening her lips.

"Some piece of work, isn't it?" Holly said. "Overall, you've done something really amazing here. But you did one thing I'm not a big fan of. You captured and entangled my other half. My *partner*. Hell's Crow. Mind pointing me in his direction?"

Ava had no idea what she was saying, other than this—*all* of this—was her doing. It didn't seem right.

"Never mind," Holly said. "I think I see where you've strung him up. You don't mind waiting here, do you?"

Holly pinched her shoulder, then disappeared from sight.

Ava wished she could somehow blink and wipe herself out of existence.

Chapter 20

Robert's foot was lead on the pedal most of the way, but every now and then he eased up. Not because he saw a cop car; he curiously hadn't seen a single one during the entire drive. He only slowed down when he saw the night's sky ruffling like curtains in a strong breeze, parting briefly to expose subhuman giants working on gargantuan factory equipment, machines that were equal parts metal, bone, glass, and mammalian organs. At the third such revelation, he asked Stewart if he was seeing it, too. The Diviner chuckled.

"I've been seeing it for weeks, chief. 'bout time you did."

Robert now saw his surroundings more clearly than he'd ever wanted. It was no longer just litter, pollution, and random violence on the streets. The factory giants were the most shocking revelation, but they weren't the only one. Robert also saw the weeds and tendrils of other dimensions growing out of patches of air to either hang and drift unsupported or to connect with the flora or debris of the familiar.

"We're running out of time," he mumbled, partly to his riding companion and partly to himself, hoping it would somehow make him drive faster. "People have to be freaking out at this."

"Not yet," Stewart said. "They're probably feeling the effects, the creepin' suspicion that the space-times, they are a'changin', but they can't see what we're seeing. Normally, you wouldn't even be seein' it. We had to vitamin-up your water back at the club."

Robert almost swerved into the other lane. "What? *Why?*"

"You need to more clearly see and understand what's happening around you. The spiked water and the immersive experience of poetry, well, I figured it would make you easier to manage."

He didn't care for the insinuation of a master-slave relationship, but Robert let it slide as he recalled his experience in the club. The weird behavior of Kurtis and Anika, his growing enjoyment of the weird proceedings, the suicide that may or may not have been orchestrated for who could guess what reason…Who in the club *hadn't* been on drugs? "None of that was necessary."

Stewart chuckled again. "Man, what you don't know, you don't know."

"I know that man probably died for nothing."

"Chief, human life may be cheap, but no matter how they go out, folks' lives won't be in vain. Not if we have anything to say about it."

Robert glanced at the kid, considering his affiliations. "I'm not yet positive we're on the same team."

"And that's your problem, thinking of life as a game. Sport and play. You'd be better off thinking of it as a work of art in progress. Just like God…Shit, we wanna blame The ID for a lot of this, but most of the noninfected and so-called sane are just as culpable in what's happenin' now. Their perception of God prevents them from lookin' too deep within themselves and too far beyond themselves. They could've brought order to their own lives and those of others by trying to bring order to their soul, their *real* soul. Instead we get The ID, bringin' chaos to all of us. Some artists got it right…It's all about diggin' deep to expose yourself to the world. The question isn't whether one has a *right* to share their vision with the world, but whether one has a *duty* to."

"Everyone?" Robert said. "Or just the chosen few?"

"Take a look around you, chief. What do you think?"

Robert saw the sky's curtains flutter again. He didn't have an answer.

"Crazy as it sounds," Stewart said, "at this point, only the High Perversists can save us."

∞   ∞   ∞

The lake was like a giant witch's cauldron. The sights Robert saw in the sky during the drive were nothing compared to the grotesqueries he saw while looking in the water.

Stewart, meanwhile, was unfazed by anything he was seeing. After examining, then vandalizing, the Corvette they found, he just went on and on about the wonders and necessity of drugs during the end-times, pausing every now and then to exhort Robert to use his now drug-fueled sight to locate some kind of portal.

Robert scanned the area while trying to block out the kid's babble.

"…exposure to art and drugs to shift human beings' perspectives, chief. Mix in a little illness and drugs to fight it, enhances the whole thing, ying and yang…Folks go deeper, get closer to God, play on the ground of Memory…memories make us who we are, make the dead live forever…"

Robert couldn't block Stewart out completely as, while searching, he also remembered all that he'd suppressed: Humanity's problem—*his* problem—children becoming adults before their time, without values, without meaningful rites of passage. Participating in a bisexual orgy in high school was his rite of passage.

He was remembering too much, too clearly. Anger and anxiety, whirlpooling; frustration rising up…

He shook his head and blinked. The portal was a few feet away. "Over here."

As Stewart trotted over, Robert tried to refocus on the task at hand, but the memories were haunting and taunting him. Why now? Why couldn't he banish the vivid recollections of high school, the unpleasantness of his peers when he'd first started exhibiting symptoms of the Virus? Why was he only now dwelling on the fact that Kurtis and Anika had been absent from school during the week he'd experienced his worst episodes?

He approached the portal in an almost dreamlike state, wondering why he was now so focused on the memory—with twenty-twenty hindsight—of him in high school becoming an adult, or something more, before his and humankind's time.

He had no answers. Not for himself, and not for what he presently saw spread out before him. Rolling rows and rows and rows…

Before, he'd heard it all in the abstract. Impotent poetry. But now, witnessing the hung children, the countless sacrifices, Robert had his first all-sensory experience of God dying in the flesh.

Almost absentmindedly, he took out his smartphone and pushed the red button.

Chapter 21

Cyrus didn't wonder why no one had seen, raised an alarm, or come to his aid. He just didn't care. He'd been there for hours; how many he didn't know. The agent in him was buried too deep within to worry about such things.

The man, the loving being in him, was satisfied to be alone on the stained side street, deep into the night, cradling his lover's corpse.

He'd never stopped crying. Since he'd seen her killed, the emotion had never left him. Nor had the sound. The sounds.

Mourning—*truly* mourning, as if one's entire world had been lost—required a shift in consciousness. Cyrus's thoughts were moving so far beyond him, he felt he couldn't understand his own world, couldn't understand the meaning of death or the purpose of life, couldn't understand *anything*. He couldn't feel anything, but his thoughts…*Imagine the Earth was God's skull, space Her vacuous thoughts*…Cyrus's thoughts reached out and felt. They touched upon smartphones and laptops, cameras and surveillance drones, even certain *toys* specially commissioned by a once-and-future giant—anything within a five…twenty…eighty…320-mile radius that was ultimately connected to a system.

He hacked. He hacked like Sally Ellin used to, like a supernatural organic computer. Then he tracked. He was now one with the grid, and he had an urge to create, to innovate, to *mate*—to connect with like minds, those who viewed *life* itself as the Kingdom of Heaven, those who believed humans had reached the end of physical development but were psychically on the verge of release, a grand orgasm, culminating in either a grand eternal life or a pathetic little death.

He was losing his soul—uncertain and uncaring whether he ever really had one—as he saw patterns, equations involving dark energy, dark matter, consciousness, and *musick*.

As if gasping on his last spiritual breaths, he focused on a sign, a signal, a symbol of impending redemption: a vineyard tucked away in sleepy Spotsylvania, Virginia.

Chapter 22

Robert got in Ava's face, almost nose to nose, spitting on her lips.

"What the *hell* is this?"

The same sight that had chilled her apparently got his blood boiling. Ava envied him; that was the correct reaction. But, he, the Watcher, hadn't done this. She, the Arkangel, had.

"Speak to me, goddammit!"

The guy who'd come through the portal with Robert tugged on his elbow.

"Forget her, chief. She's nothin' now. The one we want is over there. C'mon!"

Robert gave her one last look—full of confused hatred—before turning to run after his new partner.

Hell. Goddamned. Ava thought of Robert's profane words and the look in his eye. He may've been right about her all along. In this dying world, on the cusp of a finished Creation, what was right or wrong? Who had the Truth?

She wriggled the fingers clasping the crystalline bow, the one Zel Bernard had originally made for Darryl Ridley. *Truth versus appearances.* Her feet were planted firmly on the surface of Reality. All this around her certainly didn't seem right, but what did she really know?

She moved forward down the nearest row, looking at the children suspended on either side. She made a point to look each one in the face. Sure, their eyes were closed, but she needed to screw her courage back into its place. She needed to face what she'd done. She studied faces and read the nameplates that some-one—her?—had affixed on the trellis near each captive's head.

Something was happening in another part of the vineyard. She heard Robert's voice and that of his friend's. And Holly's. Definitely not a friend. How could Ava be so easily duped?

She came to the end of the row and gazed at the red barn a few yards in front of her. It stood three stories high and had black windows lining the uppermost level. Robert and the others were on the other side of the building. Ava paid them no mind as her eyes traveled to the roof of the barn, up to the Y-shaped pole on the top. A man was tied to it. Dark-skinned, unconscious. On his outstretched arms sat winged chimeras—big black birds, with fish-scaled bodies and tiny silver antlers on their heads. Pole-pets—six on each arm, squeezing their talons, leaning this way and that to peck on the neck, chest, or head, any skin into which they could dig, like impatient vultures on a living-dead carcass.

Hell's Crow, Ava presumed.

She gripped her bow tightly. She didn't know the guy, but if Holly wanted him by her side, Ava wanted him dead—*fully* dead. She concentrated, took a breath, and then climbed the air like stairs toward the roof. She got no higher than the level of the second story before bodies crashed through the barn's windows. One of them tackled her on its descent.

It had moved too quickly for Ava to defend herself. She only managed to twist her body so nothing would break when she hit the ground. Upon impact, her tackler immediately let her go and got to his feet, backing up to join his seven friends standing in a semicircle between Ava and the barn.

She now clearly saw the ones she couldn't see on the other side of the portal. All of them older teenagers or young adults, cut up badly by the broken glass but apparently feeling no pain. She scooted backward while they laughed at her.

There were four girls and four boys, the former dressed in bikinis, the latter in nothing but bikini trunks. Aside from the cuts, each of their bodies featured three-dimensional tattoos—blooming flowers or moving lips. The markings shifted into another dimension when they began to speak.

"Up-Dawn of the Loving Dead!"

"Welcome to the FlowerShow!"

"Introducing the new Kids of The ID!"

"The latest and greatest of the fateful eight!"

"Bringing rays of joy to disinfect the fear of inevitabilities!"

There were a countless number of voices, all of them speaking over one another. The only thing Ava understood was "The ID." She got to her feet.

The eight stepped forward in unison. Ava held her ground as she lifted her bow and looked at the full moon. It was bright, but she would've preferred sunlight or any other strong source for what she was about to attempt. She sucked as much light into her eyes as she could manage in the few seconds she had. Then, holding the bow horizontally in front of her, grasping it at both ends, she released all she'd taken in. Using geometrical talents acquired from Robert during the journey to Xyn, she was able to filter a single but strong stream of radiation into the bow at just the right angle so it shot out eight thinner, stronger streams that hit each of her targets square in their chests.

The eight stopped in their tracks. They turned to look at one another, then laughed as their tattoos shouted a barrage of insults, threats, and profanities. Ava adjusted her vision, looking closer for a sign of any damage she might've inflicted. She only saw the damage they'd already inflicted on themselves; she even saw tiny glass shards still stuck in some of the wounds. Nothing seemed to faze them. The eight turned to look at her again, each trying to make eye contact as they continued forward in unison.

Ava backed up several steps, back into a row between trellises. No way she would let any of them make eye contact—but what was she to do? She looked to either side of her, again seeing the sleeping kids' faces, their names, their helpless bodies. She had a responsibility to fix this, redeem herself.

She raised her bow, gathered as much light as she could, and shot it, as concentrated as she could make it, directly at the eye of a guy in white trunks.

His head knocked back as if he'd been shot by a bullet. But he didn't stumble. He didn't stop. He and the others kept walking, like the undead, into the vineyard.

Ava raised her bow, preparing another shot, then hesitated, not knowing who or what to hit. She only knew it would inevitably be a weak shot. Damn this darkness.

The eight stopped their approach once they were fully in the vineyard, surrounded by the hanging children. They arranged themselves into two lines, boy standing next to girl, as they reached behind their backs, retrieving vials tucked in the backs of their trunks. Each poured the vials' contents into his or her hand, then tossed their handfuls into the air. Multihued dust showered the eight as they finally spoke using the mouths on their faces.

"Bindweed."

"Dandelion."

"Stitchwort."

"Buttercup."

"Foxglove."

Each of them spoke the name of a weed flower as they arranged themselves into a cheerleaders' pyramid. But the formation was only temporary. Each of their tattoos and fresh wounds spun out strings of multihued light, tying the eight to one another as they grew larger in height, their bodies contorting in ways no human body should be able to.

Ava backpedaled as the monstrosity grew bigger, stretched, and attached to the vines, the children, and the spyders within its reach, subsuming them, making them all a part of its growing patchwork self.

Only seconds passed before she felt she couldn't go any farther. She stopped running, fell to her knees, and shuddered while tears streamed down her cheeks. It was all out of control. All she'd done, all she'd thought she'd been doing since the Archangel Artemisia inverted her, had come to this.

A creature of young humans, plants, and radiation stood several yards away, towering over her. It had stopped growing and started attacking, projecting around itself loud images of sadistic brutality and screaming scenes of gruesome violence. All the images and scenes involved the children who'd been hanging on the trellises but now were a part of the beast. The creature was projecting memories or nightmares or fantasies of the minds making up its being.

Ava didn't miss the resemblance. It was one of the methods Marie-Lydia had used when trying to take out their classmates. Then it had been on a much smaller scale, and then as now the projected holograms seemed exceedingly real…so real the actors and actresses in these scenes began to strike out, attacking the kids nearby who remained hanging on the vines, unable to defend themselves from being cut, kicked, stabbed, or bitten.

This torture-garden, this *hot spot* of Ava's, was an extradimensional one, much like the scene on the plaza a few days ago. Lake Anne Plaza.

She wiped her cheeks dry as she got to her feet. The memory of the plaza and subsequent journey to XynKroma stirred a memory of something else—parting advice from the Nurse. A magick rallying cry. Ava sprinted away from the creature, running up stairs of air as she did. She had to get out of the thing's shadow. She had to get a better view of the moon.

At about the right height and distance, she stopped and turned, holding her bow in front of her, gazing through it at the bright moon as she shouted-sang out, "Misunderstandings stand over love, buried," and the remaining lines of the verse.

While she sang, Ava saw between dimensions and unlocked portals, the same way she had unlocked doors and broken through security systems on Reality's surface. As her body descended like a feather back to the ground, pockets of air ripped open around her, letting infantries of Widow-Queens fly through. Paying her no heed, they swarmed like locusts and descended on the creature, fighting the holograms and the self-proclaimed Kids of The ID while also trying to cut the innocent kids loose. The warriors needed no instruction.

Ava kept her distance and observed. Not much she could do to aid in the fight. She could only try to ensure her allies kept the thing contained and that no more innocents were harmed. One Widow-Queen held back from the battle and approached her.

"Arkangel."

"Beryl," Ava responded. "I really screwed things up, didn't I?"

"By letting the Errorists onto sacred ground, yes."

"And this?" Ava gestured around. "Kidnapping children? *Crucifying* them?"

"You were doing as instructed. Saving them."

"Instructed by *whom*?"

"The Archangel Artemisia. This ground *is* connected to the ground on which your temple-palace rests. By her instruction, you and others have been bringing lost children here, and we in XynKroma have been harvesting their souls. Assuming we had completed reconstruction before the Flood, these children would have survived to enjoy Paradise, living in the finished state of Creation as unblemished immortals."

Ava's knees wobbled as if bags of sand were being heaped on her shoulders. She didn't know how she remained on her feet, but she couldn't prevent another stream of tears. She *had* been doing right, all along—until tonight. Tonight it had all gone to hell. "What now?"

For a moment, Beryl said nothing, gazing without eyes into Ava's. Then, "We do not know. The End is almost here."

Beryl hopped off to join her sisters, who had all but finished the creature. All the innocent children had been cut free, and only three of the Errorists remained standing, losing against a small army of Widow-Queens that shot them with arrows and bound them in lassoes of light. In a matter of minutes, the three were ravaged and beaten into unconscious submission. Without a word, without even a salute, the Widow-Queens faded out, returning to XynKroma.

Ava was left alone to view the devastation. She was left without hope, made all the more clear when she gazed upward at the full moon and saw it transmogrify into a crystalline skull.

She limply raised her left hand and fingered the pendant around her neck before yanking it off, then tossing it as far away as she could before her body collapsed.

Chapter 23

"I just don't understand this." Robert ran two steps behind Stewart, who seemed far more focused on a target than their surroundings.

"This?" he said. "It's magick, chief. All magick has a cost."

The otherworldly vines weren't just tying the kids; each vine had numerous filaments spaced a quarter-inch apart that dug into their skin like a pliable needle. Robert remembered his last conversation with Zel and Vince. The things Ava could do that other Virus-carriers couldn't, it was sourced in magick—and its cost was human sacrifice. *Child* sacrifice. Ava hadn't been saving the children from their parents or preserving their own freedom. She'd been making them slaves and stealing their souls…assuming this vineyard was truly hers. Robert wasn't so sure. He and Ava were specially linked now, and when he'd looked into her eyes a few moments ago, he could tell that this was not all her doing. She wasn't the architect of this project.

They rounded a bend to see someone climbing the side of the barn with her bare hands. The Archangel Holly, Robert presumed.

Stewart didn't bother to ask or even stop running before whipping a silver card out of his pocket and flick-flinging it. The razor-edged card sailed for several dozen feet before making contact, nicking the woman's left arm just below the elbow. The woman shrieked as she lost her grip and fell to the ground; she landed on her feet and spun around to glare at Robert and Stewart, both of whom stopped to stare her down.

There were still a few dozen feet of space between them. Neither Stewart nor the woman seemed anxious to close the distance.

"What are we up against?" Robert asked, placing one hand on his belt buckle.

"Nothin' too special," Stewart said as he reached in his pocket. "Me and my crew just took down a giant in South America. Happy Hooker Holly here won't be a problem."

"Yes, I heard about that, Diviner." Holly took a step forward. "It was impressive." The vague outline of a rhombus half the size of her body shimmered into view behind her head. "*Very* impressive…" The foggy rhombus solidified into a sharper shape, shiny as steel, unfolding, resolving itself into two large wings that had knives for feathers. Holly took another step forward. "Until I heard the giant wasn't armed." Amber snakes wriggled from beneath her halter top, easing around its edges; one of them bit at the zipper of her vest and pulled, opening it, allowing the snakes to stretch further. For a moment, the woman appeared as a mutated medusa.

Stewart cocked his head and snorted at the sight. Robert telescoped his vision and saw the six writhing things weren't snakes, but arms, and the "snakeheads" were hands, each one reaching to pluck a feather-knife and—before he could blink—fling it in their direction.

Robert pushed Stewart aside before ducking and rolling out of the way. The knives sailed past them. Robert turned and saw that two of the knives had found their targets hanging on the vines behind. A boy's neck and a girl's abdomen.

"*Fuck!*" he shouted.

"Aw, what's the matter, Watcher?" Holly said. "These are all *bad* widdle boys and girls. And we know how you feel about rotten-to-the-core brats." Her snakelike arms waved at him, all of them seeming to make obscene gestures.

"How the fuck is she doing this?" Robert got up to a knee.

"I keep tellin' you, dammit." Stewart hopped to his feet. "*Magick.*" He had cards lodged between all his fingers. "She sung open space and time to arm herself. Obviously the pick-me-up we gave you ain't doin' much good if you can't even hear her humming."

As Holly's hands reached to launch another salvo, the Diviner slashed his stomach with the cards and then tossed them. Robert was stunned motionless seeing all six cards sail clean and slice off the hands off the Archangel's conjured arms.

Holly didn't shriek that time. She only smiled as she let the handless arms retract beneath her skin. "That's the best you got, Diviner?"

Stewart spit on his hands and rubbed his stomach as he muttered something Robert couldn't understand. Despite the distance, Holly seemed to get it as the expression on her face soured a split second before tentacles shot out of the cards Stewart had thrown and wrapped themselves around Holly's legs, arms, waist, and neck. The Diviner rushed forward, taking more cards out of his pocket. Robert got to his feet and hustled toward the children who'd been stabbed.

No slow breathing like the others. They were dead. Worse, while checking them over, he saw two other kids who'd been hit by Holly's knives.

Robert turned toward the murderer in time to see her wings cut her free as she swung fists at Stewart. Stewart ducked, only to be kicked in the chin with a stiletto boot.

"To hell with this shit." Robert ran toward them, removing his belt buckle and transforming it into a spiked, metallic circle. He flung it, aiming for Holly's midsection.

The Archangel saw and dodged the spinning circle at the last second, letting the toy lodge into the side of the barn. Robert didn't care that it had missed. He'd just wanted to distract, getting close enough before pushing the bud in his left ear. It wasn't necessary; the orange device was designed to take out every Virus-carrier in a half-mile radius. But after Robert removed his finger, Stewart was the only one not moving. Holly kicked him twice more anyway before smirking at Robert.

"Go back home, Watcher. You're out of time, and you're wasting mine."

She turned her back to him and began climbing the barn again. The stainless steel wings were apparently just weapons. The Archangel couldn't fly. *Thank fortune.*

Robert kept his eye on her as he knelt next to Stewart. The kid was breathing but definitely out. He thought Stewart Danger might've been made of tougher stuff than Holly Hernandez. He then realized the pseudonymous Diviner had a very similar name to Stavan Darden. Some bit of linguistic magick intended to help him hone in on Ava? Was Zel's device designed to work only on her and those approximating her?

It didn't matter now. Now, it was just him and the Archangel, and he wasn't about to climb after her. He instead focused on those wings, those wings made up of oh-so-many shiny blades—like mirrors. It was like she *wanted* him to take her down. As his eye gathered all available light from a twelve-foot radius, his intuition drew a line from his eye to a reflecting feather, bounced it off to another blade, bounced it off to another, and on and on. In two seconds, he had the pattern, squinted, and released in a thin stream of what his eye had gathered and the parasites within had gobbled and regurgitated. Following the pattern, the stream gained strength with each bounce until it stung Holly right below the skull. She screamed as she fell, this time landing not on her feet, but on her back, never gathering the will during her descent to wish away her sharp wings. Several of the knives slashed and at least three stabbed her when she hit the ground.

She was slow in turning. Robert raised a finger to his right ear but hesitated. What if the black bud caused him to pass out but not her? He couldn't let her get away. He couldn't let her do whatever she was trying to do. He gazed toward the barn's roof and saw someone tied to a pole—a black man, being feasted on by chimeras from Xyn.

Robert lowered his head in time to see and feel the impact of Holly barreling into his stomach, shoulder first. The tackle knocked the wind out of him, but not instinct. He grabbed the woman and wrestled her until he was on top, her wrists pinned down by his hands. He straddled her, trying to keep his balance and figure out his next move. Holly foamed and shouted.

"Take off that fucking eye patch! Let's see what you're hiding!"

Her vest was still unzipped. Blood was smeared across her breasts and stomach. She must've felt the wounds on her back with her hands, found more blood than she'd expected, and tried to wipe it off. The surprise wasn't the blood; it was watching her chest and abdomen undulate. He now heard the humming Stewart had mentioned.

"While you're fucking with me," Holly said, "the FlowerShow is tearing your girl Ava apart! Her and a lot of those other brats strung up on the other side of the barn! You don't want to go save her?"

Robert tightened his grip and focused, ready to blast a beam of radiation into her right eye, blinding her if not knocking her unconscious. But out of the corner of his own eye, he saw beaks pecking out of her skin as if it were a brittle amber eggshell and birds' heads popping up, caked in visceral goo.

He fell backward at the sight and sound as the slimy hummingbirds darted out and swarmed him. Holly scrambled away while Robert swatted the birds away from his face, the largest area of exposed skin. But they weren't going for his face. The birds focused on his left arm, the one the Cerberus—the skent in Xyn—had stomped on.

Reinforced windbreaker be damned; the birds pecked through his sleeve and his skin as if both were tissue paper. His arm fell numb. The left side of his body soon followed. In seconds, he felt as if his entire body were paralyzed. But the hummingbirds didn't let up, never mind that he couldn't get up. He slumped, stung and drunken off the otherworldly nectar injected into his skin, dazed and pondering magickal holograms versus reality while he watched Holly scrambling up the side of the barn, rushing toward the man tied on what may've been a lightning rod, and freeing him as the pole-pets on his arms ascended into the air like drunken and disfigured doves. He watched the two embrace, kiss for forever, then walk hand in hand toward the edge of the roof to peer down at Robert and the rows of hung children behind him.

This is how his story would end, in failure. In disgrace. He didn't want to think about it. Just let it end, already. But there was the incessant humming throughout his body…the insistent, wordless song. He remembered, he was *forced* to remember how, on the eve of his seventeenth birthday, when the first symptoms of the Virus had incapacitated him, he'd sung a song of himself, transforming himself, trying to fight back. He couldn't help but remember his father, his mother, his lost sibling, his *bloodline* and its relation to the fate of Creation…

At no time had he ever truly felt like a hero, but he'd always felt—he *knew*—he had a place in this world and the next. He couldn't allow himself to die so easily.

Robert relaxed, accepting the humming running up and down the nerves in his body as something better and stronger than blood, as he concentrated, giving the song verses stolen from *The Blackbook of Autumn Numbers*:

One last bruised look,
perusing a human autumn,
reading deep upon a rusty rhyme
when numbered lives fell
to realize God isn't one,
neither is man
nor woman,
nor me, slumbering my way across
his
or her
or whose story?

He raised his arm, converting the birds with his words and their song. Focusing on the Archangel, Robert pointed his finger, and the birds flew like screaming, flaming darts. The multitude stabbed and burned, erasing Holly's face and pulverizing much of her skull before she could react. Her body slumped and rolled off the roof. Robert didn't see it hit the ground. His attention was on the man's inhuman wail as he too stepped off the roof.

The man didn't fall. He floated as his body transmogrified into a creature half man and half big black bird. Robert focused and pointed his arm, ready to blast the bastard with the next fatal trick up his sleeve. But the man-creature didn't give him the satisfaction. It swooped slantwise into the vineyard and snatched a child with its talon. At the same moment, the sky ripped open and a skeletal hand of lightning snatched the bird and its prey, pulling them up and out of sight in a blink.

Robert never had a chance to take the creature down. He could only search for a sign of it, his eye roaming and stopping on the full moon as he watched it wash itself over in wine red before cracking, going black for several seconds, then reappearing in the shape of a skull. A diamond skull. A skull that accepted the sun's rays and reflected a very different type of light onto the planet.

He kept staring as he slowly got to his feet. He—*everyone* was now in a different world. Just like that. An unnatural lightning strike and a cracked moon. As if to mark the strange occasion, he absentmindedly entered into a conversation with himself.

What is *evil*? Distance from God.

What is *God*? The Creator.

How does one *connect*? One must tell one's own story, in a unique way. One must make one's own life *matter*. $E = MC^3$.

Sirens in the distance shut down the introspection. Whatever veil had once been over this section of Spotsylvania had been lifted. Authorities were on their way. Authorities of the old world.

He looked at Holly's body. It wasn't going anywhere. He looked to where Stewart had fallen. The kid wasn't there.

Robert retrieved his modified buckle and trotted away from the scene, surveying the rest of the destruction, wondering how he could ever explain any of this to anyone. The police, the HSA, Cyrus…Adam.

He saw Ava on her knees, heaving, muttering something over and over. He got within a dozen or so feet before he could decipher it through her sobbing. He stopped walking when she raised her head, looked him in his eye, and shouted, "*Kill* me!"

The passion in her voice struck straight at his heart, shivering his very soul. But in response, he only shook his head, regarding her face's tortured expression. She was already dying inside and, from what he understood, probably didn't deserve to. He knew enough to know that she hadn't planted the seeds of what was around them. It was beyond her, beyond Holly, even beyond that thing that had disappeared into the sky.

Ava hid her face in her hands, choking with grief. Robert knelt beside her, slipped his arm over her shoulder, and pulled her close. She didn't resist.

"It's all right," he said. "We…we haven't lost. Not yet."

Ava removed her hands from her face. "You have no idea."

The sirens sang louder. Robert turned his head and telescoped his vision. There were at least two dozen vehicles making their way down a long dirt road, one that many years ago had served as the only entrance to the winery.

"I do have one idea," Robert said. "We need to make ourselves scarce. We can't be seen here, by anyone."

Ava said nothing. She'd stopped sobbing, but the tears still flowed, slower now, as she tried to control her breathing. "You go. I deserve whatever's coming to me."

He didn't have time to argue. And he knew there was no way he could carry her away without her consent. Instead he leaned in and kissed her on the cheek. "Whatever happens, wherever you find yourself, if you get into trouble, reach out to me, and I'll find you. No matter what." It came out sappy, but he meant every damn word of it. They were linked now. Not partners. Not friends. Something much stronger.

He kissed her again before getting to his feet. He saw Ava's bow off to the side. No need for it to fall into the wrong hands. He grabbed it and bent the light around his body as he ran in the direction of the rising sun.

Chapter 24

The elevator door slid open to reveal a dim hallway. Cyrus limped out first, leaning heavily on his new cane. Ava followed, shoved by Émilie.

"Welcome to the menagerie, bitch."

Émilie's words sounded like a discordant melody to Cyrus and felt like a flutter of pinches on his skin. Aside from the fact she was a Diviner, there was nothing else really special about her. Cyrus's reaction was simply how he received speech now, like a song assaulting him. That was discomfiting enough. He was also still recovering from the beating Ava and Holly had given him. It was impossible to stand or walk without an aid.

At least, presently, he only had to listen to one angry woman. Ava had said nothing when the junior HSA agent had turned her over to Cyrus and two of his most trusted underlings. The Arkangel also had said nothing when they'd injected the medicine to ensure she was unable and unwilling to use her abilities while they'd cuffed and blindfolded her. Even when they had taken the blindfold off in the elevator, she'd been silent.

And silent she remained, walking between Cyrus and Émilie down a curving hall in which scales similar to those of a striped bass covered the walls and floors and ceiling. A jade-tinged light seemed to hover, following them as they walked, illuminating a five-foot radius around them as they made their way to the portal: a large rhombus that appeared to be a door but was actually just opaque air. They passed through, entering a room the size of a coliseum.

With its multihued chessboard floor and undulating Creole marble ceiling, the room would've been distracting enough without the large geometric shapes planted in a scattered fashion around the room. Knowing some squares were dangerous to set foot on, but not which ones, Cyrus let Émilie take the lead.

"You are responsible for the death of a good woman," Cyrus said to Ava. "Blind justice says you deserve the same. But I can see more clearly than that. Your place is here, in The SeptiGuarden."

He was playing it cool for someone who'd spent the past twenty-four hours viewing and listening to reports detailing the aftereffects of the moon's transformation, a transformation brought about by the transformed doctor who was once an ally. At some point, the silent young woman walking in front of him had somehow beaten and subdued the wickedly dangerous doctor. He *had* to play cool while figuring out how she'd done it. He couldn't allow himself to be distracted by the reports of agitated oceans, fantastic structures and landscapes overtaking the planet, worldwide riots, mass suicides, and uncounted millions of people going absolutely insane. One nuke had—accidentally or not—already gone off in Pakistan. Much worse was on the horizon, but playing cool wasn't too hard for one missing most of his very soul.

At last count, The SeptiGuarden held almost one thousand of the nine-by-nine-by-nine transparent cubes, each one encasing a teardrop-shaped structure made up of various types of glass. Each drop held one prisoner outfitted in a skintight black garment covering him or her from head to toe. The prisoners could see and breathe, but they couldn't manipulate light or speak. On a strict schedule, and only after inhaling a sufficient amount of airborne chemicals, small groups of prisoners were released and escorted for a bathroom break and a brief reeducation session before being placed back in the cell to sway trancelike to faint music only the imprisoned were intended to hear and feel. Today Cyrus felt and heard it, as well.

The trio stopped in front of an empty cell.

"Welcome home," Émilie said.

Ava turned to look Cyrus in his eyes.

"I may deserve this," she said. "And I may accept it. But I want you to know, I know what you really are. What you've done, and what you'll do. You deserve worse. And my allies, those still out there fighting, will ensure that you get it."

Her words felt like sackcloth. But Cyrus gritted his teeth, pushed it off, and smirked at her. "Your allies will be mine. Or they will die, Miss Darden."

"We'll see, World-Ender."

Cyrus flinched at the term but kept smiling at her.

Émilie unlocked the cube and gestured. "In."

After she got in, Ava would be subjected to sights and sounds (and gases) that would appropriately prepare her for the undressing and refitting in her special black outfit.

She looked at the Diviner, then at the cell. Cyrus wondered if she would try to summon whatever willpower she had left to resist. But she seemed to be on empty. She took one step inside.

"Wait a minute."

Cyrus heard the honey-throated voice. It felt like silk wrapping his skin. A wave of frisson almost made him swoon.

"Before you begin deconstructing that one, I'd like a few words, if you don't mind."

Cyrus smiled as the young man approached, walking on air just a few inches above the ground. The lavender hints in his once vanilla-hued skin had become more prominent since he'd last seen him. He now appeared like a man from another planet, one populated by tall, violet men.

"Mister Ridley," Cyrus grinned, "Welcome."

"Mister Shahrooz. Émilie." Darryl nodded to both. "I and my compatriots have determined that Miss Darden here still poses an especial threat to the natural progressing order."

"Yeah," Émilie said. "That's why she's here. We need to get her in the cell and get on with it. The natural progressing order isn't progressing so well, in case you haven't noticed."

Darryl narrowed his eyes at Émilie. "You need to give me some time with her. Mister Shahrooz, under whatever authority I have as chief of the Dark Artzmen, I am requesting you allow me to interrogate this one. Alone. I'll only need twelve hours or so. Twenty-four at the most."

Cyrus trusted him implicitly, but Darryl's request was an odd one at this point in the game. "Why?"

"Because…" Darryl's eyes darted from Émilie to Ava, then back to Cyrus. "Before she becomes what you will make of her, my wife would like to speak to her."

That was it. Marie-Lydia McGillis wanted to speak to Ava, her onetime best friend, on Marie-Lydia and Darryl's turf in Xyn-Kroma. Cyrus had no idea whether this was a good idea or a terrible one. Émilie was certainly vocal in her opinion. But choosing between the personalities, and the voices, Cyrus made a quick decision.

"You have six hours," Cyrus said. "Beyond that, what we pumped into her will wear off, and she may be able to fight you off."

Darryl smiled. "Doubt it. But to allay any fears—yours especially, Émilie—I shall conduct my business inside the cell."

Émilie said something in French that Cyrus easily translated but only made Darryl look at her strangely. Nevertheless, Émilie went along, securing both the Dark Artzman and the Arkangel in the cell.

Cyrus turned away, leaving the rest of the procedure in Émilie's hands. He wandered about the expansive room, not much caring if he stepped on a dangerous square or not, lost in thought on something the Arkangel had said. *World-Ender.* That had a certain ring to it. It seemed to fit. He thought so more and more as he felt varicolored sounds about his skin, like flies composed of light, swarming a fresh carcass—the carcass of a Lord who wasn't quite dead.

He couldn't continue on in this condition, not for much longer. He needed some stability. He stopped a few feet away from a metal wall and stared into its imperfect mirror.

The SeptiGuarden had been designed to let nothing escape. The freaks who had designed it knew all about containment, all about secrecy, and all about the greater good. He wondered if he could get them to design him a special kind of containment suit.

Postscript

Robert had removed his watches. He'd thought about tossing them in the lake but opted instead to leave them buried near the shore. The unreal scenes and shadows he'd seen in and above the waters hadn't deterred him. He just wanted the devices in the vicinity in case he could readily think of a new use for them.

As far as he could tell, no one from The Burrow had been sent after him. Between Adam, Vince, and Zel, the three of them had undoubtedly homed in on his general location before he went AWOL. Hell, Adam had promised to do so before Robert had last left The Burrow. But it had been more than twenty-four hours, so there were only two possibilities: Robert was too far away from The Burrow for them to track, or he was no longer of any use to anyone there.

The latter possibility was the stronger, its plausibility enhanced by the hunch he'd had to return to the vineyard. The other night, he'd thought he had glimpsed something, but he couldn't check during the heat of the fight, and he didn't think about it again until he was safe off the premises. Now that the ground was clear, he could come back to assuage his fear. Or to stir it up.

Heartland Security personnel had swept the vineyard in record time. They'd freed the children and relocated them for whatever processing they normally did before trying to connect them with their families. The place still looked like a war zone. The Garden of Gethsemane after the arrest…if Jesus had put up one hell of a fight beforehand.

The HSA had also left its indelible mark on the scene. Robert spotted two cameras as he walked. There were probably more he couldn't see, even if he manipulated his vision, but he didn't bother to blur his face or camouflage himself from whoever or whatever might have been watching him; he was sure they had bigger things to worry about. He just kept walking in as straight a line as possible toward where it had occurred.

The nameplates were gone, of course. The HSA undoubtedly needed to keep those with the kids in order to help reconnect them with their families. But the plates weren't the only signifiers.

Ava had only been part of this. It wasn't a one-angel operation, and recordkeeping was clearly important. She'd been duty-bound to catalogue angels and children. Once a child was "saved," a place-holder was marked next to his or her body. Ava and her allies had probably tunneled into the kids' minds to discover their names and record them. The names were then etched into the wooden post closest to where the body had been hung. The metallic plates were probably created and affixed later.

Robert stopped in front of the post where it had happened, where that *thing* had grabbed the child before bolting skyward with him. He gazed at the name. Even reading it with his own eye, he didn't want to believe.

Charles/Charlotte Goldner.

The Heartland Security cameras had no doubt recorded his every step and transmitted the images to their satellites. Robert didn't give a damn about them. He tilted his head upward and gazed at Earth's newest, biggest satellite, still visible, sparkling in the daylight.

Two weeks ago he wouldn't have thought such a thing in the realm of possibility, but possibilities were gossamer now. He knew with surety in his heart that his mother's other child was up there, possibly gazing back down while being ritualized for immortality, transformed into transhumanity.

"Robert."

He froze, as if a hand of ice had clutched his heart. He didn't need to see her to recognize the voice, even after all these years. But he gathered his resolve and turned around anyway.

The imposing, black-coffee-skinned woman wore a milk-white tank top and shorts and—discounting the dozen or so tattoos—not much else. The body art of bizarre creatures covered her arms, legs, and neck. Her face was unblemished but decorated with a diamond nose-ring and four varieties of piercings in both ears.

Robert took a step backward. Almost a foot taller than him, she stared down, unblinking, into his eye. She was armed with an elaborate diamond ring on her right hand, balled into a fist. She held Ava's pendant in the left.

"Artemisia," he breathed as his iris flushed black-cherry red.

She smiled, flashing those stained-glass shards, those flesh-ripping teeth, the same that had come very close to ripping out his throat three years ago. "Long time no see, cousin. I think it's time we did a little catching up."

∞

About the Series

Eve of Light is a Dark Metaphysical Fantasy series chronicling the surreal events leading up to the Apocalypse—the Death of God. The setting is a contemporary, alternate Earth on the verge of a cataclysm that will warp space, time, and minds. The main narrative of those plotting and battling to save humanity is told in the *Eve of Light* series of novels. The short stories and novellas are simply flashes on the fringe—episodes told from the perspective of everyday men and women living in a world turned weird.

The Core Novels
BloodLight: The Apocalypse of Robert Goldner
Broken Angels *(Eve of Light • Book I)*
Divinities, Entangled *(Eve of Light • Book II)*

Stories on the Fringe
FoolKillers
The Lark
Heaven's Gun
Knotty & Ice
Rogue Beauty
Deviant-Hunter's Sabbath

About the Author

Harambee K. Grey-Sun writes under the broad umbrella of speculative fiction. He integrates elements of fantasy, horror, noir, black humor, and science fiction into his work and spins dark, surreal, mysterious, grotesque, at times challenging, and often blasphemous tales. Many of his stories can be categorized into one or more of the following subgenres: speculative thriller, urban fantasy, metaphysical fantasy, superhero, occult/supernatural, slipstream, and–*of course*–weird fiction. His Dark Metaphysical Fantasy series *Eve of Light* examines the dark nature of God and what it really means to be human. Find out more at the **Hyper-Verse Blog**: www.harambeegreysun.com

And SIGN UP for the **HyperVerse Blog Newsletter** to be among the first to learn about new releases, discounts, freebies, and other special deals: http://eepurl.com/_tzUv

www.ingramcontent.com/pod-product-compliance
Lightning Source LLC
Chambersburg PA
CBHW060950120726